THE
THIRD WORLD WAR

THE
THIRD WORLD WAR

A TERRIFYING NOVEL OF
GLOBAL CONFLICT

HUMPHREY HAWKSLEY

PAN BOOKS

First published 2003 by Pan Books
an imprint of Pan Macmillan Ltd
Pan Macmillan, 20 New Wharf Road, London N1 9RR
Basingstoke and Oxford
Associated companies throughout the world
www.panmacmillan.com

ISBN 0 330 49249 7

1 3 5 7 9 8 6 4 2

A CIP catalogue record for this book is available from
the British Library.

Typeset by SetSystems Ltd, Saffron Walden Essex
Printed and bound in Great Britain by
Mackays of Chatham plc, Chatham, Kent

All Pan Macmillan titles are available from www.panmacmillan.com or from
Bookpost by telephoning 01624 677237.

To my family

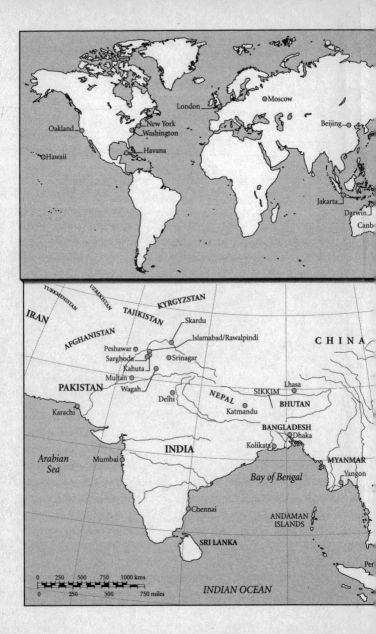

List of Characters

Australia
John Mason – Viroligist

Brunei
Colonel Joharie Rahman – Coup leader

China
Fan Yucheng – General Secretary, Chinese Communist Party
Chen Jianxiong – Chairman, Military Commission
Jamie Song – President
Yun Song – Son of the President
General Yan Xiaogong – Presidential adviser

India
Vasant Mehta – Prime Minister
Meenakshi Mehta – Medical doctor and Prime Minister's daughter
Deepak Suri – Chief of Defence Staff
Ashish Uddin – Private Secretary to the Prime Minister

Japan
Kiyoko Miyake – Personal Assistant to the Prime Minister
Toru Sato – Prime Minister
Kenijiro Yamada – Defence Minister

Korean peninsula
Cho Hyon-tak – President, South Korea
Kee Tae Shin – Missile scientist, North Korea
Lee Jong-hee – Lieutenant, South Korean army

Li Pak – Virologist, North Korea
Park Ho – North Korean military leader

Pakistan
Najeeb Hussain – Brigadier
Asif Latif Khan – President
Javed Mohmand – Admiral
Zaid Musa – General
Tassudaq Qureshi – Air Vice-Marshal

Russia
Andrei Kozlov – President
Ekatarina Kozlov – Daughter of the President
Alexander Yushchuk – Presidential adviser

The Philippines
Ahmed Memed – Professor of history, University of
  Zamboanga
Hassan Muda – Memed's bodyguard

United Kingdom
Charles Colchester – Chairman, Joint Intelligence
  Committee
John Burrows – Colonel, Special Air Services
Stuart Nolan – Prime Minister

United States
Caroline Brock – Virology bioterror specialist and wife of
  Peter Brock
Peter Brock – National Security Advisor
Lazaro Campbell – Intelligence officer
John Kozerski – Chief of Staff
Mary Newman – Secretary of State
Tom Patton – Secretary for Homeland Security
Chris Pierce – Secretary of Defense
James West – President
Lizzie West – Economist, daughter of the President

THE
THIRD WORLD WAR

1

Delhi, India

Meenakshi Mehta, dressed in denim jeans, trainers and a bright-red shirt, was talking on the phone when her father emerged from his shower, ready to go to Parliament. He dropped a file on his daughter's lap. 'What do you think?' he asked, pulling out a chair. He sat down, poured himself a coffee and pulled a slice of brown toast out of the rack on the table.

Knowing her father's habit of interrupting, Meenakshi put her finger to her lips for him to be quiet.

'No, Lizzie, we're not going to be gassed,' she laughed into the phone, moving the file from her lap on to the table and glancing at the title. 'But father's heading off for work now, so I had better see him away in a manner that befits a prime minister.' She tapped her napkin at her cheek to indicate that her father had a speck of marmalade on his lip. Vasant Mehta wiped it off.

'I don't think so, but I'll ask.' She took the phone away from her ear, but did not cover the mouthpiece. 'Lizzie West says do you want a word with her dad?'

Mehta checked the antique clock on the dining-room wall, calculating that it would be coming up to 11 p.m. in Washington. He had no wish of word getting out that the hour before his historic address to both houses of Parliament he had been on the phone to the President of the United States.

''I'd love to,' he said reaching for his coffee. 'But another time. Jim will understand.'

'And Lizzie's offering to send over special suits that will

protect us from all the nasties the Pakistanis can send over.'

Mehta shook his head. 'Tell her, thanks but we're fine,' he said. The coffee was hotter than he expected. He coughed slightly as it caught in his throat. He was a slight man, two inches short of six feet, his tousled hair receding but showing no sign of thinning. His carefully groomed and slightly greying moustache disguised the prominence of his cheekbones and his chin. The press hailed him as the most charismatic Indian prime minister in decades, but his eyes, dulled by trials in his personal life, were no longer bursting with either ambition or vision. Mehta saw the world as a place where survival was paramount. Anything beyond that would be an unexpected luxury.

'I have to make a statement on Pakistan,' explained Mehta, reaching for the marmalade.

'Why bother?' responded Meenakshi dryly. 'It hasn't changed for sixty years. We're on the brink of war, surely? Always have been. Always will be.' She picked up a rubber band she had left on the table, pushed back her hair, tied it up and began reading.

'Surely not,' said Mehta, falling silent and watching his daughter read.

'You like Khan, don't you?' She looked at him curiously. 'I can tell, by what you've put in your speech. No Indian politician would be seen dead praising a Pakistani president like that.'

'Nothing wrong with liking a good man,' said Mehta.

Meenakshi closed the file. 'Your daughter, fortunately, is not a politician, and now has to get back to her paper on government and poverty in the developing world.' She teasingly grimaced and furrowed her brow. 'I'm on the warpath. So prime ministers, wherever you are, take note.'

Six months earlier, Meenakshi had gone through a difficult divorce and she had come to spend more and more time at Race Course Road. The security and fanfare surrounding her father irritated her, but it was also a luxury to be waited on hand and foot and a relaxation from her work as a doctor in some of the poorest areas of India.

She wiped her lips with her napkin, then folded it and slid it into its silver ring. Mehta got up, walked over, kissed her on the forehead and put his hands on her shoulders. 'Is there any chance you could spare the morning for your father?' he asked with a smile.

Meenakshi frowned. 'You want me to come to the zoo with you?'

'If that's what you call the Lok Sabha, the debating chamber of the world's biggest democracy, then yes. If the animals attack, my daughter's face in the crowd would soothe me.'

'Father,' she said suspiciously. 'Are you being tricky with me? I'm a doctor. I work in the slums. I'm not one of your political intellectual elite.'

'And that's precisely why I want you there.'

'Dressed like this?' she asked, pulling down the shoulder of her shirt to straighten it.

'Most of my cabinet seem to dress like you,' answered Mehta with a shrug.

'All right then,' agreed Meenashki, throwing back her head with a chuckle. It was one of those rare moments when Mehta admitted he needed his daughters after his tumultuous separation from Geeta. Meenakshi made the house seem less empty and gave him the family company that he needed.

Mehta opened the door for her and they walked through the library, where the walls shimmered with different hues of sunlight. Beyond the library was a small ante-room and outside that door were the public areas of his residence. Two bodyguards snapped to attention. A servant opened the double doors to the hallway where Mehta's bespectacled and awkward private secretary, Ashish Uddin, jumped up from a chair. Another servant opened the front door and two more bodyguards stood by the doors on each side of the white Ambassador car in the driveway.

The specially built vehicle had a bulletproof chassis and glass, with communication aerials embedded in the back window for both radio and satellite telephones. The number plates were changed daily to confuse attackers. Uddin followed in a replica white Ambassador. Three security cars pulled out with them. An ambulance was directly behind, with a vehicle following to scan against missile attacks. Special forces vehicles were at the front and the back of the convoy.

'Mother called last night,' said Meenakshi, tapping the thick glass window and looking out on to Raisana Hill which led up to the elegant government buildings. 'Don't treat her too harshly, Dad.'

'What did she want?' asked Mehta, his pen hovering over a paragraph of his speech.

'I think she wanted to talk to you. To be friends.' Meenakshi clasped her hands together and looked round sharply at her father. 'I'm sorry. Your mind's on more important things.'

Mehta finished his correction and smiled. 'Not at all. That is why I asked you to be with me.'

'What – to remind you of your dysfunctional family?' Meenakshi laughed.

'No different from the dysfunctional family of the Indian subcontinent,' said Mehta. 'Next time she calls, I'll talk pleasantly to her.' He cast his eyes down the rest of the page and spotted something else he wanted to change. 'Always, when she's between boyfriends, she wants to speak to her ex-husband,' he said, scratching out a word and putting another in its place. 'Or if she's with a man, it's when her ex-husband gets his name in the newspapers.' He shot her a sideways glance, which was met by Meenakshi's own firm expression.

'She's weak, Dad. She's not bad.'

'That's what they tell me about Pakistan.' Mehta's eyes went back to his speech. As the car passed the pink Rajasthan sandstone of India Gate, the winter sun caught the government buildings making them shimmer. Freshly mown grass stretched out on both sides of the road which rose and fell like a sweep of land carrying with it armadas of motorcycles, cars, bicyclists and the movement of people through the heart of a great city.

The prime minister's car turned left towards the imposing circular building of the Indian Parliament, the seat of the world's biggest, yet most fractious democracy. The convoy was waved through the security cordon and the gate in the sandstone wall of the Parliament House estate, where it pulled up outside the vast circular building.

The Prime Minister got out of the right-hand door. Then just as Meenakshi was climbing out of the left, Mehta heard the distinctive and familiar ripple of an explosive blast not far away.

'Get down,' he shouted, jumping over the bonnet of the car, and pulling his daughter to the ground. Commandos leapt out of their own cars and formed a protective ring. More troops sealed off the entrances to the compound and the doors to the buildings.

Then, strangely, as if life had only paused for a couple of beats, nothing else happened. The brisk activity outside the parliament building stalled and slowly took up again. The balcony which ringed the building just above the debating chamber filled with people, craning over to see what had happened.

Mehta unfurled himself from his daughter and began standing up. But he was ordered back down by a bodyguard. 'Stay down, sir,' he said firmly.

Meenakshi wriggled out and started uncoiling. 'You, too, ma'am,' added the captain. 'The area is not yet secure.'

All Mehta could see were the feet, legs and black-uniformed backsides of his bodyguards. The captain's radio crackled into life, the reception so distorted that Mehta could not make out what was being said. 'What was it?' he asked.

'Sounds like a suicide bomber, sir,' said the captain. 'Near India Gate.'

Mehta shuddered. How long since India had been victim of a suicide terror attack? And what coincidence that it should happen now, as he was about to make a parliamentary statement on the power vacuum in Pakistan.

He arranged himself so that he was squatting more comfortably. 'Are you all right?' he checked with his daughter. Meenakshi sat cross-legged on the ground

'I'm fine,' she replied, brushing dirt off her jeans. She addressed the captain with the instincts of a doctor. 'Is anyone hurt?'

'Yes. But we don't know—'

Sharply, his fingers tightened around his weapon and his head jerked round with the sound of a second explosion, also some way away and from the direction of Connaught Place. He shot a look back at his principals to ensure they remained protected. Meenakshi began scrambling to her feet, but her father grabbed her wrists to get her back down. 'If this were one of your patients, how would you diagnose the attack?' he asked calmly.

'Mild, Father, mild,' said Meenakshi, 'if you are talking about the nation. For the victims it's a bloody disaster.'

Then, before she had finished her sentence, a white Ambassador car, parked just outside Gate 12, erupted into a fireball. Seconds later, another car exploded outside Gate 9. In the initial confusion, as debris still rained down, men dressed in a mix of olive-green fatigues and the black uniforms of the Special Protection Unit ran through the gates.

Once inside the compound, the attackers separated. They did not open fire immediately, waiting until they were dispersed among the crowds. Watching through a gap in his own circle of protection, Mehta recognized their professionalism, the footwork of trained men. It was barely possible to detect friend from foe.

The attackers spread around the massive circular edifice of the building, a third of a mile round. They kept away from the openness of the ornamental gardens and stayed close to the building where people were running to seek protection.

There was a sharp burst of machine-gun fire, sudden, loud and unexpected, despite the chaos of violence around them. It came from the captain's weapon. Meenakshi screamed, but quickly recovered herself, her eyes darting round to check on her father.

Up ahead, three men in black uniforms ran towards them. One plucked a grenade from his tunic and lobbed it.

'Grenade,' yelled the captain, dropping on to his knees, about to cover Mehta. But he was shot in the face, collapsing back, his head a mess of blood. Within seconds two other bodyguards died as well, both hit with shots deliberately placed above the neckline to avoid their flak jackets. Mehta's circle of protection was broken. The grenade rolled along the ground. Mehta now had a clear sight of the bedlam around him: bodies on the ground, people running for cover, firefights in at least three places; the flaming wreckage of one of the car bombs, charred sandstone and fallen debris blackening the lawn. Right next to it, through the churning chaos, he saw three men putting up a mortar.

'Under the car,' he yelled. 'Hands over your head.' He dragged Meenakshi, rolling her in front of him. She squeezed underneath the chassis. He grabbed the fallen captain's weapon – a 9mm Uzi – and wedged himself in next to his daughter, then turned and, in the split second before the grenade exploded, snatched four spare magazines from the dead man's tunic.

The car shook. The chassis shook, but held its ground. The exhaust pipe tore Mehta's clothes and a slice of metal cut his forearm which he had over Meenakshi's back to protect her. In the lull that followed, he saw a solitary gunman running towards them, unclasping another grenade. Mehta shot wildly. He had no firing position, but he knew the weapon well, and hit the attacker in the legs. The attacker fell; the grenade bounced beside him, the pin unplucked.

He heard the whoosh of a mortar, a soft but powerful swell of sound distinct from the cries and gunfire around. The car would protect them from high-velocity weapon fire and grenade shrapnel but not from a direct mortar hit. From years of experience in the low-intensity war with Pakistan, Mehta recognized the threat immediately. He clasped Meenakshi, covered her as best as he could, although he knew it might be useless. He had a view from the ground and he saw the flash of the mortar as it crashed into the roof of the building and exploded.

'Out,' he yelled, scrambling clear, his right hand holding the Uzi, his left hand pulling his daughter free, stepping out, running with her towards the building, up the steps, as automatic gunfire cut into a sandstone balustrade inches away from them. Meenakshi spun round, but Mehta kept going, yanking her along with him until they were inside the door, where troops were taking cover.

They leant against the inside wall, getting their breath. Meenakshi examined a cut on her arm and took her father's hands to check him in the same way. He was unscathed. She dropped them on the second undulation of mortar sound. Mehta brought his daughter's head into his chest and waited for the explosion. They hadn't changed the trajectory. The shell fell through the roof of the building. But what carnage would it cause inside, where at least five hundred people would have been gathered for his speech? God only knew.

'You,' snapped Mehta, pointing to the officer in charge. 'That mortar – neutralize it now. The closest unit. Prime Minister's orders. Now.'

He spotted three men, crouched against an outer balustrade, the closest to the car, and ran down to them. 'Corporal,' he ordered. 'Take your men and retrieve that terrorist alive.' He pointed to the man he had shot minutes earlier in the leg and now bleeding to death where he had fallen.

Mehta spotted a movement in shadows in the curve of the building. Two men ran out, one in black, one in olive green. Their objective was the wounded assailant. They wanted him dead as much as Mehta needed him alive. He expected a grenade, but they kept running. 'Target, two o'clock,' he shouted, letting off a burst of fire from the Uzi. The corporal took it as his signal and sprinted out, with Mehta covering him. One guard was hit, but Mehta found the source immediately and returned fire. It came from the first-floor verandah – the attackers had penetrated that far.

The two surviving attackers kept going. They would get their colleague in a few minutes. The wounded attacker was unconscious. A bodyguard, there first, lifted him on to his shoulders while the other kept watch. But after Mehta's exchange of fire a sudden silence descended around the building. Group by group, politicians and staff caught in the onslaught were making it inside. Police armoured vehicles broke through into the grounds cutting up the grass and the driveway with their hard tracks. Troops spilled out. Sirens of approaching ambulances echoed from the roads outside. Overhead, fighter planes roared.

The wounded attacker was brought just inside the building. They laid him down on the concrete floor. Meenakshi checked his pulse, and pupils. She took a quick look at his legs, took off her shirt and ripped it in two. 'Help me,' she said, to no one in particular. Two solders knelt down with her and followed her instructions as she applied tight tourniquets to both legs.

Mehta was on his mobile phone. 'I want the first ambulance round here. No excuses,' he said. 'I don't care. We have a man, alive, who will talk and give evidence. Nothing is more important.'

Then, as he was listening to the reply, his ear tilted to one side, checking that the ambulance whose siren he could hear was heading in his direction, there was overhead another sound familiar from his days of aircraft training in the Himalaya. It was the vibrating pitch of the engine of a light aircraft. He ran outside to look up. Not one but three were approaching. Far in the distance was the vapour trail of a turning fighter. Small-arms and heavy machine-gun fire broke out from the ground, creating a cordon of lead through which the aircraft would have to fly. One aircraft was hit, turning into a ferocious fireball, an explosion far greater than if just fuel tanks were going off. Its force created a charred circle on the grass and set light to the trees around it as the debris fell, scattering and flaming to the ground. Caught up in the trail, the pilot of the second aircraft turned sharply, but got caught in a secondary blast. He lost control and at such low altitude clipped a tree, somersaulted and crashed. The explosives on board did not detonate until the aircraft broke up on the ground. It sent out a withering heat wave of destruction which wrecked everything in its path.

The third pilot took no evasive action, and flew rock steady through the fiery turbulence. Suddenly, Mehta understood the plan: the diversions, the suicidal firefights inside the grounds, the single repeated trajectory of the mortar to weaken the roof, while people were being brought inside the building to safety. He watched as the Cessna bucked. The pilot was alone, but all around him was what? God, if it was – Mehta thought. It could be nothing else but. A solitary, concentrated figure, with the other spare five seats of the single-engined plane stacked up with boxes. The luggage compartment as well would be laden with high explosives and detonators charged to go off on impact.

The plane adjusted its direction towards the gaping hole in the roof, and as Mehta saw the fuselage plunge in, flames leapt out, then a rumble, then a tearing, ghastly, roar, like the scream of a great animal in the first stages of slaughter, as it exploded halfway down the four storeys of the historic building, crammed with people who had fled there to safety.

'I'm not taking any calls,' insisted Mehta. 'I'll call them when I'm ready. West, Nolan, Song, Kozlov and any of those simplistic humanitarians from the European Union. None of them, do you hear?' He sat down angrily as his private secretary melted away, closing the door and leaving him alone.

When the internal phone rang, Mehta's hand hovered over it before picking it up. Deepak Suri, the Chief of Defence Staff, was on the other end. 'It's Khan,' he said gently. 'I urge you, Prime Minister, if you talk to no one else today, talk to him.'

Mehta nodded and heard the click as Suri transferred the call, and he recognized the distinctive Punjabi accent of President Asif Latif Khan of Pakistan. 'Vasant, it is a tragedy,' said Khan. 'The pilot told me the news as we were coming in to land. I will do all I can—'

'You must, Asif. You must,' said Mehta. 'I don't want to have to fight you.'

'You won't,' replied Khan, but his wasn't a safe answer because both he and Mehta knew he might not have the power to keep his promise. Khan was his friend. Their parents had been educated at the same Karachi school. Mehta had photographs of them playing together as children – until Partition had separated them. The Muslim Khans stayed in Pakistan; the Hindu Mehtas went to India.

'I am offering my condolences to the whole nation, to the families of the victims, to you Vasantji, to Meenakshi and to your family.'

'Thank you,' said Mehta softly. 'Where are you?' he asked, guessing that Pakistan's intelligence agencies would be listening in to their president's call.

'We've just arrived in Malaysia. Should I return?'

'No,' said Mehta firmly. 'No. The less we respond, the less they win. This is character-building time for India and the whole of South Asia.' There was no more to say, unless Khan offered something. Mehta let a silence hang between them, although his temptation was to let fly his anger, to let his friend know the true wrath of the people he governed.

'We were in no way responsible,' Khan said, his voice faltering as if Mehta had made the direct accusation.

'Is that your word, Asif?' Mehta challenged. 'Or is it the word of your armed forces and intelligence agencies?' He knew Khan would never have ordered the attack, but the nation, its institutions, its agencies, its ideology had created the men who would carry it out. For generations, Pakistan had been a breeding ground for terror.

'Before I called you, I spoke to Islamabad. A full and transparent investigation has begun. On that you have my word.'

Mehta looked across at the television screen. The cameras were switching location. They were on the US President, Jim West, walking across the White House lawn from Marine One, the presidential helicopter. A reporter shouted a question about the attack and West, waving a hand, refused to comment. The screen then went live to the Indian home minister visiting the clear-up operation around the parliament building in Delhi.

'If you're serious – after Malaysia – come to Delhi,' said Mehta, upping the stakes. 'Meet me here. Announce it now. Visit the disaster. Pledge to punish. Make it real. Come here before you return to Islamabad.'

For a few seconds the line stayed quiet again, the Pakistani President genuine in intent but politically wrong-footed. The press releases ready to go from the propaganda machine in Islamabad second-guessed by the insistence of a peace summit in the victim country to get things sorted before the vultures overshadowed everything with talk of war.

'Yes. Yes,' said Khan with a sudden weariness in his voice. 'We must meet. I will be in contact with you shortly.' Mehta thought he was ending the call, but Khan continued. 'Vasant, you are my friend. For God's sake trust me. The consequences of not doing so are too serious.'

Before Mehta had replaced the receiver, Deepak Suri walked straight in without knocking. 'Vasantji, with all due respect, what on earth are you playing at? If Khan comes to Delhi, if he visits the parliament site, he'll be lynched. With the best will in the world, we cannot guarantee his safety.'

'He won't come,' said Mehta, distracted by the row of newspapers on his desk. Page after page of pictures of the carnage.

Some chose the intensity of the destruction, showing the inferno across a whole page. Others opted for the sequence of pictures leading to the attack. The tiny speck approaching the building, becoming recognizable as a single-engined plane, to a close-up of the pilot, determined, eyes fixed on his destiny, then the plane plummeting as a missile of high explosives through the roof. It was a chilling symbol of a lone and deadly mission. From inside came the carnage. Nothing was spared. Rows of bodies, draped in shared sheets, seeped with blood. Shocked survivors, dazed, wounded and without help. The mutilated symbols of India. Incongruously, the propeller of the aircraft had survived, twisted but intact. The photographer had framed it hanging from dislodged electrical wires in the Central Hall in front of a portrait of Mahatma Gandhi, the founding father of India, torn and splattered with fragments of war.

The pilot had not chosen his target at random. He would have known the layout of the building and would probably have sat in the public gallery to familiarize himself with the target. The Central Hall was decorated with twelve gilded emblems representing the original twelve provinces of India before independence. It was here that the transfer of power had taken place on 15 August 1947 – and it was here that parliamentarians had been gathering to hear Prime Minister Vasant Mehta deliver his address to a joint sitting of both houses. That was why the death toll had reached 476.

On the first-floor balustraded balcony, some of which

had come through with barely a scratch, the attackers had daubed the name Laskar-e-Jannat. They had even translated it into English – Army of Paradise. One photograph showed pamphlets caught in a breeze and swirling about like leaves. Next to it was a close-up of one pamphlet. 'Why Are We Waging Jihad?' it asked. And the answer: 'To Restore Islamic Rule Over All Parts of India.'

Yet there was one picture that all newspapers ran prominently on their front pages. It was the one that would rally India through its darkest moments: it showed Mehta changing a magazine in the Uzi and shouting a command while his daughter, Meenakshi, stripped to her bra, applied a tourniquet to the wounded attacker. Both of them were framed between two bullet-chipped sandstone pillars of the parliament building. 'Attacked. Defending. Caring' ran one caption. 'The image of our great nation.'

'Has he talked yet?' asked Mehta, referring to the attacker whose life Meenakshi had saved.

'Not yet, Prime Minister.'

'Documents? Fingerprints?'

Suri put his hands on the desk and looked his friend straight in the eye. 'Fingerprints are being checked by Interpol, Europol and the FBI right now. We have identification of two of the dead, and if we want to trace them to Pakistan, we can. Who ordered them precisely to do what they did, we don't know yet.'

Mehta stood up. 'I need a strike plan by missiles and aircraft on the Pakistani missile bunkers at Sarghoda, Rawalpindi, Lahore, Karachi and Multan. One strike only. Whatever it takes. Prime the Agni for launch, both from silos, and deploy two on the rail launchers. Close the lines if necessary. And on your way out ask Ashish to get me Andrei Kozlov in Moscow.'

Suri left, but the phone rang again too quickly for it to

be Moscow. Ashish Uddin had been working in the Prime Minister's South Block office since the attack. Never once had his diffident, but efficient, method of handling Mehta wavered, except now, when he began in a jumble of words, hesitant and apologetic. 'I didn't want to disturb you with this, Prime Minister, and I've already said no many times, and I understand it is the last thing—'

'To the point, Ashish. To the bloody point,' said Mehta, reaching over and pouring himself a glass of water from a jug which had been on his desk far too long. He was about to drink it when Uddin answered. 'It's your wife. She's insisting on speaking to you.'

His hand paused as he brought the glass to the surface of the desk. They used to leave love notes for each other in the kitchen as they led busy and young lives. He couldn't remember who stopped first, or why, or whether the ending of the notes was the first step towards the end of the marriage. Oh Geeta – dear, wild, Geeta, who had given him two wonderful daughters and more misery and love than a man could ever need. Mehta leant back in his chair and gazed at the high ceiling, empty of colour and in need of a coat of paint. He shook his head. 'No, Ashish. Tell her I will call her later today,' he said. 'And has Suri asked you to get me Moscow?'

'On the line, sir. But Mrs Mehta insisted I pass on to you that she thinks you are wonderful.'

'Only because she saw my picture in the paper,' muttered Mehta to himself, as the twitter of a broadband satellite line came through the telephone, followed by the calm and authoritative voice of the Russian President. 'Russia grieves, Vasant,' said Kozlov. 'Russia is angry. We can talk properly later. You are leading your nation right now. How can Russia help?'

2

Penang, Malaysia

According to the schedule, after the speech, the President of Pakistan would walk with the Malaysian Prime Minister from the conference hall, through the hotel lobby, and out into the forecourt of the sweeping driveway. His limousine would take him to the airport, from where he would fly to Kuala Lumpur. In the morning, he was to be in the Indonesian capital, Jakarta.

Never had Captain Ibrahim Hassan Albar imagined he would be setting up a sniping position to kill his principal, and never had he thought that his own life would have to be taken by one of his closest friends. Looking around, he expected it would be Anwar. Although, as a fellow Muslim, he might not be able to pull the trigger – in which case it would be Lim, a Chinese.

Albar, just two days off his thirtieth birthday, was a man of few words. This was not the time to reflect on how he had come to this situation. Unmarried and without children, Albar was breaking no religious laws. He had been called upon and had agreed automatically. The War against Terror, which had started so many years ago and had altered so many alliances, had finally reached Albar himself, and that was all there was to it.

Now was the time to concentrate on the dozens of little adjustments he had to make to ensure that his one shot would hit and kill. He had decided to lie up outside the hotel, in undergrowth across from the driveway, where the President was bound to linger to thank his hosts.

Albar had chosen the furthest sniper position. He had

thought about using a suppressor to dull the sound, but nightfall in Penang was a bad time for a sniper. All day, the air would be heavy and still. Then as the sun went and darkness came within minutes, the change of temperature whipped up unpredictable gusts of wind and rain.

Albar could handle wind on a shot under four hundred yards. Any more than that and the trajectory of the bullet would become too fragile for him to be sure.

He took off the safety catch, and felt the butt of the 7.62mm Dragunov sniper rifle against his shoulder. The weapon was his proudest possession, bought from a Russian marksman when they were both serving on UN duty in Iraq. He settled into the gun. In his earpiece, he heard the Pakistani President wrapping up his opening address: ' . . . refused to admit that in so many areas we have failed as a civil society and failed to confront the demons inside us.'

Albar slowed his breathing, half a lungful in, half a lungful out, to make his body ready for the shot. He was hearing the President's voice, but not listening. 'We will, God willing, act as a beacon to those societies still brooding on medieval or colonial injustices. We will lead our nation to create great institutions of learning and genuine debate and ideas. And if any person or group chooses to challenge this policy, outside parliament and democracy, they will be met by the full wrath of my will. My mission is not the destruction of rival societies, but the creation of new ones.'

'They're coming out,' Albar heard in his earpiece, as applause rippled through the conference hall. His instincts took over, watching the wind in the undergrowth, feeling a light drop of rain on his face, hearing voices in his earpiece, finding the principal through the glass door of the hotel. As he waited for the door to open and for his target to walk out, Albar was enveloped in a great sense of clarity.

His eye focusing through the scope on President Asif Latif Khan, he let his body take over, feeling the trigger edge back, the buck of the rifle, and the rush of satisfaction when he knew he had sent the shot to its target as professionally and effortlessly as ever he could.

3

Zamboanga, southern Philippines

The assassination of the President of Pakistan was the signal that the offensive for Daulah Islamiah Nusantara should begin.

Ahmed Memed, Professor of history at Zamboanga University in the southern Philippines, locked his study door and logged on to the Internet. He flicked through the BBC News site, visited a couple of Islamic websites, then entered a site bookmarked www.onlylesbian.com where a full picture came up of an Asian girl and a European girl making love in a rock pool underneath a waterfall.

On a message board attached to the site, Memed typed in the simple words, 'We'll do it together, now.' He lingered longer than usual to ensure that it had been accepted, knowing the risk of his Internet surfing patterns being picked up by the US National Security Agency at Fort Meade, near Baltimore. But it would be impossible for the NSA to track the dozens of young men and women flicking through the same site at Internet cafés throughout the Philippines. While just about any other site would profile an Internet user, the surfing of pornography was in high demand from men regardless of age, religion or politics.

Memed used a dated one-use keypad to coordinate his surfing with his allies in Pakistan. Without ever having direct contact, messages were transferred through a different sequence of web pages. A back-up sequence was in place, in case the web server was down. The sequence could only be matched between the sequence on the pads.

Having spent much of his career in Afghanistan and Pakistan, Memed had moved to the southern Philippines after the 2001 War on Terror began. Since the US campaign had then pitted Christians against Muslims, the southern Philippines became fertile ground for Memed. When asked where he came from, Memed said he had no nation except the nation of Islam. In truth, he was the son of a Saudi Arabian diplomat and had been educated in London and Melbourne. He went against his father by leaving Melbourne University in his first year and returning to Saudi Arabia, where he became a disciple of the eighteenth-century preacher Imam Muhammad ibn Abd al-Wahhab. He had helped spread Wahhabism through Afghanistan and Pakistan, and had now successfully instilled it in the Muslim heartlands of the Philippines.

In his preachings in the historic Talangkusay mosque in Zamboanga, he spoke about the fourth Moro Jihad. The first was against the Spanish invasion lasting from 1521 to 1898, a total of 377 years. The second began immediately against the American colonizers whom the Muslims fought for forty-seven years until 1946. The third phase challenged their new Filipino masters. It saw the great Moro wars of the 1970s, and was peppered with failed peace agreements and treacherous leaders until 2001, when America's War against Terror galvanized them into another, less reckless campaign, which Memed hoped would now be the end game.

Now in his early fifties, Memed's life had been one of extreme luxury and extreme hardship. Yet his hair, which he wore down past his ears, still retained its colour, and only recently had streaks of grey appeared in his beard. Memed himself was not a fighter: he was an academic. Nor was he in any sense a practical politician. His speeches were too ethereal, the vision too loosely defined. His moods were often dark, alienating all but his closest friends. But he did stir the emotions of the poor. Steeped as he was in Islamic history, he became famous for his speeches and was spoken of as their new Ayatollah.

Memed closed down the laptop, stepped briefly out on to the balcony, but heard nothing yet except the normal barking of dogs, shouts between neighbours and impatient traffic horns of a Zamboanga night. He came back in, turned on CNN and waited.

For Memed, Zamboanga was a perfect staging post, a city built as if on the edge of the world, a hot, impatient trading town whose filthy harbour and slums marked the beginning of the great Sulu Archipelago, a scattering of islands stretching down to Malaysia and Indonesia, inhabited by poor, untamed and honourable people who still defied the sovereignty of the Philippine flag. They were violent, proud and brooding with resentment.

First was the island of Basilan. Then came Jolo and Tawitawi, all almost completely under Moro control. The Philippine marine contingents were confined to barracks and could only resupply by helicopter. A short boat ride from the edge of the Tawitawi Islands was the eastern tip of Sabah, governed by Malaysia, but deeply infiltrated by Islamic fighters. If things worked as planned, the insurgency would take hold in Sabah, move across Sarawak, then into the Sultanate of Brunei itself, so that the whole of the north Borneo coastline would have fallen. There was also the oil.

Just as CNN broke into its programming to report an outbreak of Muslim guerrilla attacks against military installations throughout the southern Philippines, Memed heard the distant hum of a helicopter.

'Hassan,' he shouted, although there was no one else in the room. 'Hassan.'

The CNN presenter, reading from copy just dropped on her desk, updated her report with news that guerrillas had destroyed helicopters and attack aircraft at bases in Zamboanga, Cotabato City, Dipolog and Pagadian. Senior military officers had been captured, their bodies booby-trapped with explosives. Radio and television stations had been taken off the air. Highways between major cities had now been cut. Armoured vehicles sent to confront the guerrillas were ambushed, the soldiers killed, with no prisoners being taken. It was impossible for Memed to know how many would die in those first hours. There had never been an offensive like it in modern guerrilla warfare. But Memed had estimated 20 per cent of his 100,000 fighters would not live to see the next dawn.

Outside, a round of automatic gunfire shattered the quiet of Memed's compound. He heard shouts and the heavy boots of Philippine marine commandos stomping through the courtyard outside. Memed's bodyguard burst into the room.

'Quick, Hassan. Quick,' snapped Memed. More gunfire erupted below.

Memed turned over his laptop, clipped off the base and took out the hard disk. Hassan Muda was on the balcony with an M-16 rifle and a flashlight, its beam shutting on and off, pointing towards the helicopter, but hardly visible against the morning sun which blazed into their eyes.

Three armoured vehicles were lined up outside the compound. A dead guard lay in the dust, a pool of blood soaking into the dirt beside his head.

Muda raised his weapon to fire down on the soldiers. Memed knocked the barrel down. The roar of the helicopter engine now drowned out everything. They both looked skywards. A black silhouette came towards them out of the sun. The tops of the palm trees blew backwards and forwards, as if there was a typhoon. The helicopter swooped in low, and Memed saw the dry soil of the compound, kicked up by machine gun fire, spraying around

the Philippine troops who were moving in. They scattered
and the helicopter turned to come round, its bullets firing
in a straight line towards the verandah where chunks of
concrete flew out and a window shattered. Then the helicopter was gone over the roof.

It appeared again, its nose lowered. Memed saw leaves
flutter down from the trees, and small branches, too, as
bullets cut through them. The soldiers below crouched in
cover, as the helicopter slowed and hovered. A cable from
the winch was lowered.

Muda stepped back to let Memed go first, but the older
man pushed his bodyguard forward. 'You are needed more
than I,' he shouted. 'Take the cable, and hold me, too.'
Muda strapped himself into the harness. He held out his
arms and took Memed like a child, his tunic flapping
around his legs in the gale created by the rotor blades. The
pilot lifted them away, swinging precariously, but Muda
held on.

Yes, Memed had been right in his choice of bodyguard.
And he had been right in judging the weaknesses of a Philippine army colonel who, faced with a threat and a sum of
money, had sent in the helicopter to save Memed's life.

4

Washington, DC, USA

The US President's limousine drew up outside Peter Brock's Georgetown house. Casually dressed in a pair of jeans, his hair wet from the shower and with a towel slung around his neck, the National Security Advisor greeted Jim West.

'Glad you managed to get away, Jim,' said Brock.

'If I couldn't have, I doubt you could,' joked West lightly, taking off his overcoat and scarf and hanging them over the banister of the staircase. 'Khan's funeral is a private affair. Mary says even our ambassador has not been invited.'

'Not a happy situation at all,' mused Brock thoughtfully. 'Riots in Malaysia, Indonesia, the Philippines.'

It was early evening, and a smell of spice and seafood came from the kitchen. Brock took the President through to where Caroline, wearing a bright, floral apron, was whipping up supper, with a salad fork in one hand and a glass of Californian Merlot in the other. West knew and appreciated Caroline's skilful acts at distancing herself from the political issues of the day.

She kissed West on both cheeks and poured a glass for him. 'Here, Jim. Taste the work in progress and tell me what you think.' She held out a spoon, sauce dripping over the edges on to a small plate. West blew to cool it and as soon as he had some in his mouth, Caroline said: 'More rumours in the papers about you and Mary, Jim. All of it true, I hope?'

West fanned his mouth with the back of his hand. 'It's

unfair to ask a man such a question with hot sauce in his mouth,' he managed, swallowing it and washing it down with the Merlot. 'Your sauce is delicious, Caro, and Mary and I are just good friends – at least when we're not fighting it out in meetings.'

Brock grinned. 'I'll put on a shirt and be back in a couple of minutes.'

Since losing his wife to cancer, West had treated the Brocks' rambling Georgetown house as a second home. The death of a First Lady in the White House was almost unheard of. The last had been Caroline Harrison in 1892, and modern America, when it was told that Valerie West had passed away after her sudden diagnosis, had not known how to react.

For some weeks, the media had asked if West would remain up to the job. His background was forensically re-examined, with questions raised about the psychological strength of a man who had married his childhood sweetheart and now had to live without her. West's eldest child, Chuck, was married with two boys and a girl. But his work kept him in Oakland where he had started an interstate trucking company. His daughter, Lizzie, was an international economist specializing in the developing world. She accompanied her father to public functions when she could. But often it was tense because, politically, they did not see eye to eye.

Peter Brock was Jim West's best friend and most trusted political sounding board. In public, Brock's view would be the view of the President, and if ever there was a disagreement only he and Jim West would know about it.

They had trained and served as navy pilots together, dated their wives together, married within a month of each other and now pretty much ran the country together. West measured six foot two, with a lean frame, a mane of sandy hair and an ability to match his face to any political occasion. Brock was short and stocky, with the prominent chin of a man not to be messed with. His nose was slightly skewed after being broken in a mess-room brawl. But his eyes revealed both vulnerability and curiosity. A generation earlier, West had told Brock his expressions were so transparent that he would never make it as a front-line politician.

It was unspoken, but the Brocks had taken it upon themselves to make sure their friend would pull through. West was a man with dark mood swings, chased by fear of failure. There were demons, which, by his own admission, chased him and had motivated him all the way to the White House.

Caroline rinsed a baking tray under the tap and wiped her hands on a dishcloth. 'All right, then,' she said with a mischievous smile. 'If I told you I had asked her to drop by tonight, would your spirit soar or would it plunge?'

West chuckled. 'As a companion, there is no one living I would rather have dinner with than Mary Newman. She is attractive, amusing, attentive and intelligent. But, let me tell you, in the Principals Committee, Mary's a pain in the ass, and tonight, Pete and I have to chew over events as only old friends can.'

Caroline reached up into a cupboard above the sink, her hands just managing to touch the dinner plates. West stepped forward. 'Here, let me do that. I must have six inches on you and it's not often that a US President has the privilege of laying a table.'

'Thanks, Jim. The side plates are right next to them. They can come down, too.' Caroline pulled open a drawer and took out three sets of knives and forks. West glanced down at her. 'Only three?' he asked lightly.

Caroline grinned. 'Don't worry. I'd never pull one like that.'

West separated the dinner plates and put them on the

table. Caroline collected them up again. 'Not so fast. I need to warm them. But the side plates can go on.'

'Maybe one day I'd welcome it,' said West. 'A surprise date arranged by my closest friends.'

Brock, in a fresh short-sleeved red shirt, stood at the doorway. 'She may be right, you know, Jim.'

'About me?' joked West. 'That I know.'

Brock poured himself a glass of the Merlot. 'She called about half an hour ago – about poor old Asif Khan.'

'Khan, eh?' said West, leaning against the kitchen dresser and sipping his wine.

'She doubts it's a one-off.'

'The thing about Mary is that she never gives off smoke without knowing there's a little fire burning away somewhere.'

Caroline stepped quietly to her husband's side and put her arm around his waist. They had met the year before Brock joined the navy when they were both students at Georgetown University. They now lived across the road from its campus. Caroline had remained in academia, rising to head her department, specializing in international studies and non-proliferation.

Tonight, her husband was trying to show a light-hearted face, but Caroline detected that he was distracted by Khan's assassination. The Gulf War, the Kosovo War, the War against Terror, Iraq, each one started by a single incident, a bomb, a border invasion, a massacre, an assassination. You never knew what could flare up and turn your life upside down.

'Why don't you two go through, while I finish off getting this ready?' she said, slipping her arm away. 'Hopefully, issues of state will be done with by the time we eat.'

Inside the study, Brock brought down the *The Times Atlas of the World* from a shelf filled will large, unwieldy reference books, ran his finger across the inside cover page to find the map he wanted, opened it up on page nineteen and laid the atlas down on his desk. It was a high-ceilinged corner room, furnished with two leather armchairs and a swivel chair at the desk. This was Brock's sanctuary, a masculine room of dark textured colours, mementos and photographs with international figures, which themselves told part of the story of how he had transformed himself from an impoverished navy pilot to the National Security Advisor to the President.

'Khan gets killed here,' he said, flipping over to page eighteen and brushing his finger over Penang on the north-eastern coast of Malaysia. He flipped the page back. 'The first reported act of violence after that was here, a military airfield in Dipolog in the southern Philippines.' Brock loudly snapped together his finger and thumb. 'Then, too quickly for anyone to keep count, the whole damn region is on fire, Malaysia, Indonesia, even Brunei which must be the most tranquil place in the world.'

He picked up the remote and turned on the television. The first channel to come up was BBC World, which Caroline enjoyed watching. Its reporter was speaking from the roof of a Manila hotel. 'The Philippine military has lost contact with its bases on Basilan, Jolo and Tawitawi. In Zamboanga City, General Fidel Ocampo is being held hostage, and all assaults on guerrilla positions there have been suspended.'

'John, thank you,' said the presenter in London. 'Before we let you go, could you give us a picture of what is behind all this, and whether this has any wider political implications?'

The screen dipped back to the reporter, forehead creased and eyes squinting against an overhead sun. 'Susannah, one theory, and I stress this is only a theory, is that there was an attack by the Philippine military on a rebel Muslim camp. The rebels decided to hit back with a vengeance. But there is a question of coordination and planning. An operation like this must have been ready to go for some time. Something happened last night that made them unleash their forces.'

'And, John, is it linked to the assassination of the Pakistani President?'

'Conspiracy or coincidence, Susannah. No one yet knows.'

Brock muted the television. 'Whenever we think Asia is a model of development it blows up in our damn faces.'

West pointed at the maps. 'Let's send the *Kitty Hawk*,' he said. 'We got involved down there in 2001. If it's unfinished business, let's see to it.'

Brock nodded. 'No harm in it. She's in the South China Sea at the moment. She could be off the coast of Mindanao in a couple of days.'

The door opened without a knock. Caroline stepped in first, but behind her was Mary Newman, freshly fallen snowflakes on her coat, which was unbuttoned. She pointed to the television set. 'Has it been on yet?' she said, short of breath.

'The Philippines?' said Brock, turning up the volume again.

'No,' said Newman, loosening her Paisley-patterned silk scarf and putting on her glasses. 'Worse. Much worse.'

5

Yokata airbase, Japan

Thousands of miles away, a few minutes earlier, massive engines had blasted into the reinforced-concrete base hewn into a mountain side. A North Korean medium-range, three-stage, solid-fuel Taepodong-2 missile had roared into the morning sky. While West and Brock had been discussing the turbulence in South-East Asia, every satellite camera and listening post in the region had picked up the launch and traced it to Manchon County, North Korea, 500 miles from the western Japanese coastline and 700 miles from Tokyo.

Just outside Tokyo, in an aircraft hangar at the US Yokata airbase, maintenance engineers and their families were having morning coffee together to bid some colleagues goodbye. Friends were reading out goodwill emails from those who could not be at the party. There was cheering, laughter and not a lot of concentration on what was going on around them. It was a tight cluster of people, a cross-section of American family life and ethnicity, including children who had been given a special late start to school for the event.

The Yokata US military airbase had a responsibility for forward projection and crisis response. It would be the primary supply base for troops fighting a war on the Korean peninsula. As many as 14,000 people lived there at any one time, and, most symbolically, it was less than thirty miles from downtown Tokyo – the military installation closest to the metropolitan area.

The missile flew over the glittering Tokyo skyline and

across the northern Kanto Plain at the foothills of the Okutama Mountains before smashing through the roof of the aircraft hangar.

The roof split in two and the head of the missile crashed into the fuselage of a transport C-130 Hercules plane undergoing routine maintenance. The fin snapped on impact and flipped over on to the wing of a C-21 Learjet with such force that the wing broke off, letting vapourous aviation fuel into the atmosphere.

They were gathered at one end of the hangar near a stack of oxyacetylene welding tanks when the missile struck.

The electrical systems on the two aircraft shorted, throwing out sparks which ignited the aviation fuel, blasting a hole in the wall between the hangars and sending a fireball towards the welding tanks. The youngest child to die was eleven-year-old Carrie Berlin. Both her parents and older brother, Richard, died, too. Her younger twin brother and sister, Paul and Rebecca, were orphaned.

By dawn the fires were out, the body bags organized, the missile identified and the grieving had begun. Fifty-eight Americans were dead.

'The North Koreans say it was an accident,' said Newman.

'I don't give a damn what they say,' retorted West. 'They've killed Americans.' West was on his feet, pacing the Oval Office and finding it too small. 'What the hell were they doing flying a missile so close to Tokyo? Because if you tell me it was deliberate, this time next week there won't be any North Korea left.'

Newman grimaced. 'Someone had to tell you what they said,' she said, standing up. 'As Secretary of State, that job falls to me. If you want to hear the rest of it, I'll continue. If you don't, I'll shut up.'

West reached for the window behind his desk, pressed his forehead against a chilled pane, tapped his fingers on the glass and listened.

At forty-two, Newman was one of the youngest secretaries of state ever. She could even have passed for ten years younger, with plenty of brown hair, cut back to just below the ears. She wore a fringe that managed to hide her high forehead and a pair of steel-rimmed glasses that made her poker-playing eyes even more difficult to read. She kept her own counsel, yet spoke her mind forcefully when called upon.

West had first noticed her when she was a new, young entry to the House of Representatives. He had been in the Senate. Fifteen years on, she was divorced, from a Washington lawyer who had swapped her for a younger blonde lobbyist at precisely the time when Newman's career started outpacing his.

With West a widower, the press was full of rumours about a relationship with Newman. They liked each other, but just occasionally, like now, when nerves were raw, he was both startled and impressed by the way she held her ground.

'No, Mary, don't shut up,' said West, softly. 'You're doing what someone has to do.' His back was to the room and his eyes concentrated on the snow on the White House lawn. West gave himself a few seconds, while he disciplined the anger that had chased him to the Oval Office. Since Valerie's death, he had found his temper becoming shorter. Through the glass, speckled around the fresh snow, was the distorted reflection of CNN. The volume was down but the images of grieving relatives, smouldering aircraft hangars, coffins draped in the Stars and Stripes, commentators profiting from hindsight and the non-stop whirl of 24-hour news gnawed against him when he needed clarity of thought.

'Turn that damn thing off,' he ordered, and it was John Kozerski, the White House Chief of Staff, who tried to shut down the television with a remote. But it was broken, or the batteries were flat. Whatever the reason, West didn't care. He turned in from the window, walked across the room and pulled the plug out of the socket.

'Sorry, Mary. Yes, please,' he said, indicating for Newman to sit back down on the sofa. He took the armchair at the end of the coffee table where a map of Asia lay open. 'Wrap up what you were saying.'

'They have asked us to give them time to carry out their own internal investigation,' said Newman, settling back into the sofa. 'They refer us to our own shooting down of an Iranian airliner by mistake from the USS *Vincennes* in 1988 resulting in the deaths of 290 innocent passengers. They handed over a list of other American mistakes, including the bombing of the Chinese embassy in Belgrade in 1999 and atrocities against Iraqi civilians—'

The President held up his hand. 'Enough. I follow their train of thought, and knowing your politics, Mary, I don't expect you sympathize any more than I do.'

'No, sir,' said Newman simply.

On the sofa, across the coffee table, was the Defense Secretary, Chris Pierce, sitting forward, his elbows on his knees with a file of papers open in front of him. West had brought Pierce to the Pentagon because of his extraordinary war record which began in Vietnam and ended in Iraq. Highly intelligent and with years of experience as a battlefield leader, when Pierce spoke he did so with both deliberate simplicity and assertive body language to reinforce his point. In full flow, he sometimes reminded Newman of a nightclub bouncer.

The thick-set Tom Patton, Secretary for Homeland Security and former governor of Oregon, was at the other end of the table. John Kozerski, Chief of Staff, sat back down on an upright chair next to the phones on the Oval Office desk. Peter Brock was next to Newman on the sofa.

West addressed Newman again: 'Mary, do we have any American nationals in North Korea?'

'Two aid workers,' said Newman. 'One with Oxfam, a Peter Bennett from Chicago. And one from Save the Children Fund. She's actually half Swedish and half American, a dual passport holder, Agneta Carlsson. It's not the easiest place for Americans to work.'

West pulled his chair forward to get closer to the map on the coffee table. He put his spectacles on and jabbed his finger on the name Pyongyang, the capital of North Korea, on the west of the Korean peninsula which hung off northern China like a pig's knuckle.

'Where's Scott?' asked West, referring to Scott Cartwright, his Trade Secretary.

'In Argentina, sir,' said Kozerski.

'Then you fill in, Mary. Do we buy from or sell to these sons of bitches?'

'Negative, Mr President,' said Newman. 'It's banned under the Trading with the Enemy Act. Together with Cuba, North Korea is the only place left on it. We have deals on nuclear power which go back to 1994. There's been an impasse pretty much since 2003. But as far as the impact on trade, it's not an issue.'

'Tom, do they have any terrorist cells in the US?'

'Not that we know of,' said the Secretary for Homeland Security. 'They haven't been involved in a terrorist operation since the eighties, when they blew up the South Korean cabinet.'

'In Seoul?'

'In Burma. They were on an official visit.'

West whistled through his teeth. 'That's one hell of a thing to do.' He brushed the map flat and shifted it on the table to show the massive blue of the Pacific Ocean. 'Chris, these nuclear weapons they have. Do they work? And can they strike us with them?'

'They might,' said the Defense Secretary.

'Might?' snapped the President. 'Is that the best you can do?

Pierce took a breath. 'In the nineties, we know they extracted 60 pounds of plutonium from the nuclear programme. That's enough for five 20-kiloton nukes. They restarted it in 2003. We think they might have ten operational nuclear warheads for silo-based missiles and two smaller ones that could be transported by boat or aircraft – the bomb in the briefcase scenario. They have maybe fifty Taepodong-2 missiles of the type that was used against

Yokata, and many more shorter-range missiles, most of which could hit Japan and, of course, South Korea. They've been working on an even longer-range version of the Taepodong-2, which they want to get to our western coastline. But we doubt that's functioning.'

'So they could nuke us?' said West.

'I believe they could nuke us in Japan, but not here in the US.'

'Then what are they playing at?'

'Mr President,' intervened Peter Brock. 'We've had time to discuss this with other governments in the region. The overwhelming view is that North Korea is in more crisis over this than we are. They claim the missile guidance system was faulty, and no way was the base to be targeted. In fact, the missile carried no warhead at all. They warn that if we take action against North Korea, we could provoke a backlash similar to the reaction of a wounded tiger. Leave her be and she'll die. Taunt her, and she'll kill.'

'What does Japan say?' pressed West.

'Nervous, clearly,' said Newman. 'But looking at the bigger picture.'

'And China?'

'Both Russia and China say they have some low-level human intelligence that there has been a power struggle,' said Brock. 'Truck drivers coming out across the northern border. Air Koryo pilots landing in Beijing. That sort of thing. So if it was intentional, it could have been a rash act of a *coup d'état*.'

'Chris,' said West, 'if the threat was real, what could we do about it?'

The Defense Secretary had direct responsibility for the lives of American service personnel. He was faced with the grim reality that if the missile had been carrying a nuclear warhead, 14,000 of them – not just fifty-eight – might now be dead or injured, as well as thousands of Japanese. He answered the President pensively.

'North Korea has a big, motivated army willing to take casualties. A worst-case scenario is war again just like it was in the fifties. We've been skirmishing in the Middle East for years, but if the Korean peninsula flares up—' Pierce shrugged. 'I don't think any of us will have known anything like it.'

The President stood up and stretched his arms behind his back. 'Then the line is that there's been a national tragedy at Yokata and we're investigating. The grief is too fresh and the issues too serious for the United States to take injudicious action.'

'John,' he continued, looking over to his Chief of Staff. 'Get me a list of where the families come from. If there's one predominant state, get me the governor, the senators and community representatives on the phone as soon as possible.

'Mary, let me know if there's any reason for me to go out there. Right now, I can't see it. Make the strongest protests, bring in the UN, all that kind of crap. Demand an end to their missile programme. Chris, get as many American citizens off the bases as you can without it being noticed. Send them shopping in Tokyo, or on holiday with their families. Increase air patrols around North Korea. Get our ships out to sea. I don't want any goddamn repeat of Pearl Harbor.'

'It'll only be a fraction, Mr President,' said the Defense Secretary.

'Well, make it as big a fraction as you can.'

He turned to Newman again. 'Mary, get hold of Scott in Buenos Aires and tell him to put the muscle on whichever government or companies are trading with North Korea. I want those operations shut down at a moment's notice if those sons of bitches so much as sneeze against us again. That goes for South Korea as well, and any of those European Union governments that go soft on dictators to fatten their bank accounts.'

West's eyes were on Peter Brock, but then flickered to the end of the table, where Kozerski, telephone pressed to his ear, was beckoning him. 'Yes, John?' said West.

'Stuart Nolan is calling from Downing Street. He wants to speak urgently,' said Kozerski, his finger poised to transfer the call to the phone next to the President.

'I'll take it,' said West, turning back to Brock. 'And Pete, work on the Chinese and Russians. Since our agencies haven't a clue, tell them I want to know what in the hell's going on in that country.'

'... **named as** Ahmed Memed, an academic from Zamboanga. Intelligence sources in Washington say his influence grew around the year 2000, when he began creating a cohesive organization which would lead the Muslim struggle for independence. Memed is widely believed to have been the brain behind last night's attacks.'

The picture changed to a hand-held camera filming Memed and his bodyguard swaying from the helicopter winch. 'In a bizarre twist, Memed was rescued from his home by a Philippine military helicopter. It's still not known who the pilot was and who ordered the rescue.' The camera swung round the compound showing the guard's dead body on the ground and troops crouching in undergrowth. 'As you can see from these disturbing pictures, there was a gun battle around the time Memed escaped.'

'Heard of him?' asked Stuart Nolan, the British Prime Minister.

'I've heard of him,' said Charles Colchester, a long-time friend and chairman of Britain's Joint Intelligence Committee. 'But I can't say he's on the top of anyone's in-tray.'

Colchester was dressed in a dark pin-stripe suit and business tie, the uniform of senior officials around the corridors of Whitehall.

He handed Nolan a sheet of paper. 'This is a list of places where rioting has broken out in South-East Asia. Our stations believe there was a measure of coordination. The real problem is Brunei. There's been a *coup d'état* organized by a pro-Islamic colonel in the army. As far as we can tell, it's been successful. They now control Bandar Seri Begawan.'

Nolan quickly read the list, took off his glasses and rubbed his eyes. He had forfeited his morning swim for the meeting with Colchester. He was keen to wrap things up and get some exercise, but already he sensed this was the sort of day when that would not happen. 'Bandar Seri Begawan might be the administrative capital,' said Nolan testily, 'but the oil's at Seria. Whoever holds Seria holds Brunei.'

'They don't hold Seria yet,' said Colchester.

'Nor will they, if I have anything to do with it. I trained in Brunei. I love its impenetrable humidity, its jellyfish and its billionaire Sultan. And I'll be damned—' Nolan waved his hand to shut himself up. At sixty-nine, Nolan was one of the oldest occupants Downing Street had ever had. Prostate cancer had been detected. Radiotherapy had worked, he was told. His long-suffering wife, Jean, had instructed him to seek out a less busy life, although Nolan wondered if tranquillity might end up leading him to an even earlier death. His curiosity about far-flung and difficult places often rested uneasily with his own nation's lack-lustre interest in events beyond its shores. Years into the War against Terror, enthusiasm for conflict had waned. Long gone was the unquestioning patriotism in sending troops to remote corners of the world, particularly since it meant less money to spend on the issues British people now held dearest, their schools, transport and health. Nolan was also waiting to hear whether the Scottish Parliament in Edinburgh was going to vote for a referendum on independence for Scotland, called for so suddenly after the Scottish National Party gained control of the governing coalition. He wondered disdainfully whether his footnote in history would be his attempts to focus British minds on Muslim riots in Asia while the United Kingdom itself was breaking up.

'If Brunei totters, just about anywhere can,' said Colchester, glancing at his watch. His meeting slot with the Prime Minister had been set from 06.45 to 07.00. 'If you've got an extra five minutes, I would like you to meet Lazaro Campbell. He's from Washington, on secondment to us. He knows his stuff. He's waiting outside.'

The Prime Minister nodded, knowing that Colchester would not have imposed Campbell on him so early in the morning for nothing. Campbell came in and shook Nolan's hand, without explanation or apology that he had arrived for the meeting in a tracksuit and running shoes, with a line of sweat just on the hairline of his forehead.

'At least someone's clever enough to find time to exercise around here,' muttered Nolan. 'Lazaro Campbell? Where do you get a name like that?'

'From a Cuban mother and a Scottish father, Prime Minister,' said Campbell, pulling out a hand towel from his tracksuit and wiping his face dry. 'My mother was fleeing Castro's Cuba. My father was with the British embassy and literally lifted her from the boat at Key West. So I'm the product of Caribbean sun, fun and revolution.'

Nolan laughed. Campbell was a robust man with Hispanic features and dark tousled hair. He was in his early forties, but a pair of sharp blue eyes, an unshaven face and an expression that often looked a moment away from laughter made him seem a lot younger. Colchester opened his briefcase and slipped documents and photographs out of a large brown envelope. Nolan was not the first Prime Minister or President that Campbell had briefed during a crisis. He knew he could be blunter with Nolan, a former Royal Marine who would understand military strategy and missile threats.

'If I was serving in the US now, I would be briefing the

President – if I could get to him,' said Campbell with a knowledgeable glance at Colchester. 'As it is, I am on secondment to Her Majesty's Government, so I have asked to brief you, Prime Minister.' He knelt on the floor and spread photographs over the coffee table. 'I flew in a few hours ago from Australia, where there's been a break-in at a virology lab. We hadn't put two and two together until the North Korean missile tragedy at Yokata.'

At the mention of Yokata, Nolan eyed Campbell sharply, and took hold of the photograph Campbell was offering him. 'That's the canteen,' explained Campbell. 'That was taken at shortly after 3 a.m.'

Nolan took his time studying the scene in the photograph. There was an unfinished snack on a table. Two cups of coffee, one black, one a creamy white, sat undisturbed on each side of the table. A mark of light red lipstick ran around the rim of one cup. At the centre of the table was a bowl of fruit containing bananas, tangerines, kiwi fruit and a bruised apple. On one plate were the remains of a ham omelette; on the other was the crust of a burger bun, smudged with tomato sauce. The knives and forks were laid side by side on the plates. A newspaper on one side was folded over to the crossword page. The chair was neatly pushed in to the table. The other chair was toppled over on the floor.

'That fallen chair,' said Campbell, looking over the Prime Minister's shoulder, 'is the only sign there had been a struggle. The Australian police are certain that the two scientists on duty at the time were murdered. But their bodies are missing.'

Campbell passed Nolan another picture. It showed a laboratory with a red neon sign on the wall saying in large capital letters NO ADMITTANCE. HIGHLY INFECTIOUS AREA. Two people were inside, both wearing dark-green surgical gowns, gloves, medical masks and blue polypropylene shoe covers. The door ahead was closed. Behind it was an ante-chamber of transparent glass with a blue ultra-violet light shining inside.

'This is a file picture,' said Campbell. 'It's the ante-room of the laboratory where they've been working on a substance known as interleukin-4 or IL-4.' He handed over a third picture, which simply showed a cage with two mice in it.

'This is what they were after, isn't it?' said Nolan, dropping the picture on to the pile on the coffee table, and leaning back in his chair. 'You're here now because they succeeded?'

'IL-4 is a tragic scientific mistake,' said Campbell. 'It is an agent that makes mice sterile. The Australians were planning to spread it throughout urban mice populations using a virus called mousepox, which is normally harmless. But something happened that no one had anticipated. Not only did it shut down the reproductive system, it also shut down a key element of the body's immune system, something called cell-mediated response, the specific mechanism that fights against viruses. Suddenly, mousepox became a killer virus. Those mice infected with mousepox together with IL-4 died almost immediately.'

The expression on Nolan's face showed that he was beginning to understand the implications. 'And mousepox is—?'

'A sister virus of variola major, which is smallpox,' said Colchester. 'Mice are – or were – far more immune to mousepox than we are to smallpox. But virologists are now pretty certain that if IL-4 is administered with the smallpox virus, the world will be facing a biological weapon threat such as never before.'

'Not least because we don't have a vaccine for it,' said Campbell.

'Has there been a theft of smallpox as well?' asked the Prime Minister.

'Not that we have heard of,' said Campbell, glancing across to Colchester. 'But we're checking.'

'And who took it?' asked Nolan calmly.

'Officially we don't know,' said Colchester, constantly ensuring that he and Campbell were speaking with one voice. Nolan was familiar with Colchester's ability to transform his character like a chameleon and he detected a change now of Colchester using the refuge of civil service anonymity to push forward a political position. He was a Whitehall civil servant with enormous power and flair who skilfully projected an image of a man of absolute ordinariness.

'Officially,' began Nolan. 'What the hell does that mean?'

Campbell had his eyes down, sorting the photographs.

'Tell the Prime Minister,' said Colchester.

'North Korea,' said Campbell, looking up, then leaving the photographs and springing to his feet. 'I do not have the evidence, sir, but my contacts are good, and I would forfeit my job on it.'

'The source of Lazaro's information is highly, highly classified, Prime Minister,' said Colchester calmly.

Nolan turned to Campbell. 'What *is* your source?' he demanded.

Campbell gripped his hands together, powerfully enough to show the whites of his knuckles, suddenly showing the emotions of his part-Latin heritage. 'I said I would forfeit my job. My job is my life, sir. I would not be here if I did not think that this agent had gone to North Korea.'

'I asked you what your evidence is?' said Nolan.

Campbell deferred to Colchester.

'As I said, the information is—' began Colchester.

'Damn you, Charles,' exploded Nolan, 'if you want me to look at this stuff and then make an argument to Jim West – because I damn well know this is why you've produced Campbell – I need to know the source. I need to know that it's true. If you feel you can't tell me, then we'll do it through the appropriate channels, and if it gets lost in the bureaucracy, so be it.'

'It is – or was – President Asif Latif Khan of Pakistan.'

Nolan stared blankly at Colchester and then in disbelief at Campbell. Outside was the whine of an electric milk float. With each driver personally screened, it was still allowed within the secure area of Downing Street. Nolan got to his feet, walked across to the window, looked down at the clatter of bottles on the doorstep, turned back inside the room, glanced at the photographs laid out on the table, then looked at Campbell. 'Khan?' he asked, showing part irritation and part sarcasm. 'The now dead President of Pakistan?'

'Khan, as you know, was deputy head of the Inter-Services Intelligence Agency before going into politics,' explained Colchester. 'Lazaro worked closely with him during the War on Terror.'

'He told you that North Korean agents had walked into a secure Australian laboratory, killed two scientists and stolen this agent?'

'He told me more than that,' said Campbell, sinking to his knees again by the coffee table, and pulling two photographs from the middle of the pile.

'Show me, then,' said Nolan, sitting down and putting on his spectacles.

Campbell handed Nolan a picture, labelled with a caption describing it as an unidentified guest at a cocktail reception in New York. The subject wore a lounge suit, badly cut, with a tie too tightly knotted and creating wrinkles on his shirt collar. He had no drink and was caught with both hands clasped behind his back and a ripple of boredom on his face.

The second picture was of the same man, but it revealed much more. He was short, but stocky and strong, with truculent features, and dressed in the uniform of a four-star general. He was with a dozen other dignitaries. The date on the caption was 15 April 2003. The setting looked like an official celebration in Pyongyang. It might have been that particular split second with the camera, or the resulting image might have been etched into the subject's character. His arms were stretched out to the edge of the rail of a balcony and his whole presence dwarfed the lost expression on the face of the then North Korean leader, Kim Jong-il, who stood next to him. The general's long fingers were wrapped around the rail into a fist. His eyes were fixed straight ahead in an expression of awesome determination, not of a man who had inherited power, but of a man intent on gaining it. He was by far the most charismatic figure among them.

'This man's name is Park Ho,' said Campbell. He looked at Nolan with an unflinching expression of certainty. 'He ordered the theft of the IL-4. He fired the missile at Yokata. He believes it is better that North Korea be destroyed and go down fighting, than to surrender to unification with South Korea. He is the mastermind behind North Korea's missile programme. He now has power, and his finger, Prime Minister, is literally on the button.'

'He *has* power?' queried Nolan. 'You mean he has just taken power.'

'That's right,' said Campbell, nodding.

The Prime Minister glanced over to Colchester. 'Is he right, Charles?'

'I fear he is,' said Colchester.

There was a knock at the door and Joan Nolan poked her head round. She was much loved by the British for being matronly, unstuffy, down to earth and the one person who could keep their brilliant, but sometimes erratic, Prime Minister in check.

'There's a queue of supplicants waiting to see you, Stuart, and none dares knock on the door to see what you're up to.'

Nolan looked at his watch. The meeting had overrun by fifteen minutes and he would need another fifteen to end it. 'Give them tea, champagne if they need it. I'll be with them by seven-thirty.'

'And which do you want, tea or champagne?' she asked, stepping back to leave her husband in peace.

'Nothing, thanks,' said Nolan, without consulting Colchester or Campbell. Joan would have to boil the kettle or indeed uncork the bottle herself. Downing Street must have been the only official residence of a head of government where the Prime Minister and his wife did their own washing up.

Colchester glanced across to check they were alone again, leant back and put his arm over the back of the sofa. 'Stuart, Lazaro has an idea, which might shed some light on events.'

Nolan raised his eyebrows. 'With your permission, sir,' said Campbell, 'I would like to go to Brunei. As far as we know, your training camps there are operational and unaffected by the *coup d'état*. Rioting after Khan's death, I can understand. But it takes time to plan a *coup d'état*. There are too many coincidences running around. If we can get some sodium pentothal into one of those rebellious Bruneian colonels, we might learn a hell of a lot more than we do now.'

Nolan rolled his pen along the desk top, then burst out laughing, shaking his head in disbelief. 'I have a feeling you and I are going to get on very well indeed,' he said, glancing across to Colchester. 'And you, Charles, would you be prepared to forfeit your job, if you're wrong?'

'My years release me from that decision,' said Colchester with a slight smile.

'Then with your agreement, as my chief intelligence adviser, I will track down Jim West.'

'I understand he's in the White House situation room. Yokata will keep him up all night.'

As he dialled, a genuine smile spread across his face. Despite his considerable political skills, Nolan was a soldier at heart, feeling best when he was planning a military operation. He waited impatiently for the connection and whispered to Colchester: 'Tell the mob outside, I'll be another half an hour. And get a bloody map of Brunei up here.'

In Washington it was past two in the morning. But three minutes after his call to the White House, the British Prime Minister was patched through to the US President, interrupting the long session he was having with his principals.

'Jim, I'll be brief,' said Nolan. 'There's been a military takeover in North Korea. I understand that we could be dealing with the most dangerous enemy we have faced since Hitler.'

8

IV Corps Command, North Korea

Park Ho, aged sixty-four, brushed his hand along the cold metal of a T-62 Soviet-made battle tank. He saluted the commander who was standing upright in the turret, goggles high on his forehead, eyes clear and staring straight ahead of him down the tunnel. The commander snapped back a salute.

Park was five inches short of six foot, as muscular and wiry as he was small. He prided himself on achieving power from the lowest of the military ranks. His father, a corporal, had at first enthralled him with his stories of the battles of the Korean War, then had vanished, leaving him in a crumpled city living through a day he never wanted to experience again. Grief and fear became hostile emotions, and he never married because of them. Instead he clawed his way to the top of the military establishment. He joined the elite Bureau of Reconnaissance unit. He trained personal bodyguards for the leaders of Cuba, Cambodia and several African countries. He led the infiltration of commandos into South Korea itself, and later served as a diplomat at the UN and in Vienna as an arms control negotiator. On the long, cold North Korean winter evenings, he had taught himself English, Russian and Chinese, and after the collapse of Soviet communism, he had written papers for the nation's founder, the Great Leader Kim Il-sung, as to how North Korea's *juche* ideology of self-reliance could be modernized for the twenty-first century.

As he inspected the line of tanks, Park remained in awe of the dedication of his people, precisely because he had

come from among them. He had won his present status by
distancing himself from the political elite who inherited
influence and office without having to prove merit.

While they had become soft on too much satellite
television, French brandy, German Mercedes and white-
skinned prostitutes, Park had been with the troops,
whether far north on the Chinese border or as he was
here, now, deep underground, metres from South Korea
on the Military Demarcation Line.

Today, the men whom Park despised were being held
under house arrest in a compound just north of Pyongyang, and the man who would soon declare himself president allowed himself a rare and faint smile.

Dozens of tanks, fuelled, equipped and armed, were
lined up in row after row in a huge, staggered complex of
tunnels which ran the length of the ceasefire line with
South Korea.

In the layer above them were squadrons of fighter
aircraft in hangars hewn into rock. The runways on which
they were to take off were also underground. The first the
enemy would see of an aircraft was when the wheels left
the ground and it was airborne. Huge artillery guns skilfully hidden in undergrowth and rock, designed to deceive
analysts of imagery from satellites and unmanned surveillance aircraft, could pulverize the South Korean capital
Seoul, only thirty miles away. Commanders of military
hovercraft armed with devastating rapid-fire cannon and
heavy machine guns waited for the order to attack. The
thick rubber air cushions were kept half-inflated to carry
human waves of men across the water on to enemy
territory. Far below ground, on the third level down,
thousands of men lived on rotation, as if on an aircraft
carrier, to be infiltrated through tunnels which would
bring them up to attack behind enemy lines.

Park walked the full length of the first line of tanks, his

hand held in a steady salute. Men returning his salute
allowed themselves no expression of emotion. He couldn't
tell if he was welcome as their new leader. But he sensed
an air of gratitude. There was an atmosphere of war in the
tunnels. For more than fifty years, North Korean soldiers
had been on a daily footing for war. Finally, the man who
would deliver it to them had arrived.

At the end of the tunnel, under tarpaulins, were stacks
of artillery and tank shells, filled with a lethal mixture of
napalm and explosives. These were to be used on American
and South Korean troops right on the border. Park wanted
every American dead within an hour of the attack being
launched. They might have absorbed casualties in Iraq, but
37,000 dead American soldiers on the Korean peninsula
would collapse that nation's will entirely.

The doors of the lift at the end were open for him. It
carried him up to a covered area above ground. The drone
of a helicopter became louder, and Park watched as it landed
on a quadrant 'H' sign. On this clear, cold day, at this
precise time, a satellite camera would be overhead, the lens
operating at 0.25 metre resolution and picking up his grainy
image as he broke cover and walked to the aircraft. Analysts
at the National Security Agency would examine radio traffic
from the helicopter. Park made sure the pilot mentioned
his name in transmissions because he needed the Americans
to know who he was and where he was going.

The ageing Soviet MI-24 took him quickly away from
the demarcation line. As it gained altitude, Park looked
down on the rows of blue huts, where the ceasefire
agreement had been signed in 1953. He saw the flash of
the sun in the lens of a camera on the south side of the
line. Just to the north he looked proudly down on the
massive North Korean flag hanging from the highest mast
in the world and the neat huts of the farmers dotted
around at its base.

The nose of the helicopter dipped. It shuddered in light turbulence as the pilot turned it north and took his bearings from the six-lane highway to Pyongyang. Below, ginseng and cabbage fields nestled between mountains under which his tanks and aircraft waited.

As the helicopter settled into the short flight, Park reflected on his ugly battles with the heir and anointed successor of the Great Leader, Kim Il-sung, which had now finally been won. Slice by slice, his country had been sliding towards Americanization. Soon it would have become another East Germany, wretched, defeated and swallowed up. Park had been determined that whatever the future held for his great nation it would not be that.

Up ahead on the curve of the horizon he saw the outskirts of his beloved Pyongyang. It was truly one of the most beautiful and ordered cities in the world. He asked the pilot to fly lower and follow the Taedong River which glistened pure blue in the sunlight. Once across the Yang-gok railway bridge, the monuments of his nation were laid out before him: the skilfully sculptured statues of the Great Leader, Kim Il-sung, who had liberated the nation from the Japanese and founded the *juche* philosophy of self-reliance that had made North Korea so powerful; Kim Il-sung's magnificent mausoleum, adorned with fresh flowers laid every day by his citizens; the Pyongyang Grand Theatre set just back from the west river bank; the Korean Central History Museum which told of the struggle to retain independence and ward off American aggression; the Children's Palace, where the most perfect little human beings performed with absolute precision; the Tower of Juche, 150 metres high, decorated with 230 granite and gemstone blocks sent by admiring leaders from all over the world, and from the top a symbolically flaming torch stretching another 20 metres into the sky.

The pilot turned the helicopter west, flying over the

Victorious Fatherland Liberation Museum, then headed
due north again over West Pyongyang railway station and
Chongsan Park. The aircraft climbed and settled into the
final stage of its journey.

While the United States championed the rights of the
individual, North Korea championed the rights of the
community. Both were at extreme ends of ideology, yet
while North Korea was poor, Park had never seen the
shame, humiliation and desperation on the streets and in
the villages of his country as he had witnessed in America.
When travelling abroad, he had sipped vintage cognac at an
embassy dinner in Paris, listened to the duet from the *Pearl
Fishers* at the Royal Opera House in London, inspected the
Mercedes factory in Dusseldorf. Each time, he had promised
that one day he would return Korea to its greatness.

Empires rose and empires fell, and Park Ho would be
remembered as the man who defeated American power.

Outside Pyongyang, the pilot took the helicopter up,
heading further and further into the highest mountains in
the country. A brilliant panorama of forests and hillsides
covered in snow, of tumbling waterfalls and icicles and
mountain passes with deep-blue winter lakes stretched
ahead.

Just before landing, Park instructed the pilot to make
another radio transmission stating clearly their coordinates. He wanted the United States to know his destination. Officially, it was known as the Kanggye No. 26
General Plant. But this was a huge underground military
facility, which even a nuclear bomb could never harm. The
helicopter turned into the breeze and the pilot set it down.
Park, in full military fatigues, stepped out and stood, head
unbowed, by the whirring rotor blades.

A general in charge of the plant led the greeting party

of scientists and technicians, dressed in the neatly laundered grey tunics of the Korean Workers' Party or the clear white of a laboratory coat. These were the men and women who had brought Park so close to achieving his ambition.

Park stepped into a lift. On the descent it stopped twice in security airlocks before delivering him to the control room from where he would conduct the war. The room was packed with people, lined up in formation, amid work stations and surrounded by walls of computerized screens. As Park stepped on to the platform, a huge picture of Kim Il-sung appeared, wrapped around the whole wall.

Park bowed at the image and cheers echoed round the room. He left through a side door into a small empty room, where he took off his uniform and held up his arms while he was dressed in an insulated suit, breathing apparatus and a radio and earpiece in the helmet. He stepped into a glass antechamber. On the other side he was met by men, also in protective clothing. Row after row of single ultraviolet bulbs stretched back as far as he could see. They provided the only light in the laboratory.

'General,' he heard the voice of a scientist begin in his earpiece. 'Please turn to your right and follow me.' He followed, walking between a row of lights, each bulb covering a cluster of eggs in a tray. They were in a sort of atrium. Far above was a ceiling. Five different levels of the laboratory ringed the outer wall. The first two were open. The upper levels were sealed with reinforced glass. Every twenty metres gauges told the temperature, humidity, air pressure and content of the atmosphere, including the level of hazardous materials.

Right at the top, he knew, was the lethal zone, where skin or lung contact with a virus, such as Ebola, or a chemical, like sarin, would lead to instant death. Below that were killer bacteria – anthrax, tularaemia, Rift Valley Fever and others. For years, his scientists had tried but failed to design an effective delivery system to carry the weapons on an intercontinental ballistic missile.

Park was led further into an area freshly hewn out of the underground chamber. The scientist stopped at a door and showed Park into another airlock. Once through, they entered an office. It was a practical room with two telephones, newspapers left on the top of a desk, a notice board with work rotas, political slogans and instructions for escape in case of fire. Four empty cups stood unwashed in a sink and cigarette butts filled an ashtray. The wall to the left showed a picture of Kim Il-sung. Faint martial music played through a speaker in the ceiling.

'You can take off your helmet now,' said the scientist. He removed his own, took off his spectacles and wiped them on a paper towel. 'General Park,' he said holding out his hand. 'My name is Li Pak. I am the senior virologist. It is a privilege to show you around.'

'So the deliveries from Australia and Russia were successful?' asked Park. He handed Li his helmet and let him unplug the headset from his shoulder.

'Indeed,' said Li enthusiastically. He pulled down a wall chart and switched on a laser torch, which he pointed at scientific symbols running along the top line of the chart. 'Now, if we start here—'

'Forget this stuff,' snapped Park. 'Tell me as if I'm a child. I will have to explain this to our enemies in simple terms. You must inform me in the same words.'

His hand shaking, Li turned off the laser and put it on a tray under the chart. 'We have just passed through the area where we are keeping eggs which carry the smallpox virus,' he began hesitantly. 'As you know, the Americans, British and others have mass-stocked a smallpox vaccine. Once infected, a patient takes two or three days to contract the disease, and several weeks to die. Within that time, the patient can be vaccinated and make a full recovery.'

Park began pulling out a chair. Li broke off to help him. He brushed his hand sycophantically across the seat as if to clean it before Park sat down, then took a seat himself on the other side of the table. 'From Australia we procured mice which had been vaccinated with an agent called interleukin-4 or IL-4. Originally, IL-4 had been part of an experiment to sterilize mice. Of course, it was impossible to vaccinate every mouse. So the idea had been to spread IL-4 through the mouse population on a relatively harmless virus known as mousepox. But IL-4 was far more active than had been anticipated—'

Park slammed his hand down on the table. 'I don't need every detail,' he threatened. 'What I want to know is, does it work?'

Li glanced straight at Park, but didn't hold his gaze. To do so would have been insubordinate.

'We did try using IL-4 with mousepox on humans. But it had no impact. From the agent, we designed another sterilizing substance which is specific to the human ovaries. But again, it did not work on humans when we used mousepox.'

'That is when you asked me to procure smallpox from Pokrov?' said Park, staring directly at the virologist.

'Correct,' answered Li, softly. He lowered his head. 'I believe our redesigned IL-4 and smallpox will have the same impact on humans as IL-4 and mousepox did on mice. Once contracted, death will take place within a matter of hours.'

Park put both hands evenly on the table. 'You haven't tested?'

Li shook his head. 'I am waiting for your instructions.'

Park stood up. 'Very well. Show me.'

Li pulled up the chart and drew back a curtain behind, revealing a panel of thick glass. He turned on a lamp on the other side, lighting up raw mountain rock, with water dripping in dark rivulets from the roof. Below were six metal cages. Inside each one was a woman, her hands tied and hauled up by a chain locked on to a ring embedded in the wall. Because of the uneven surface of the floor, the women lay mostly in puddles, their damp clothes clinging to their skeletal bodies. Two of them reacted to the light, looking up towards it, then looking away. They looked healthier than the other four, who hung limply, apparently unaware that anything had changed at all.

Park turned round angrily. 'Where are they from?' he snapped.

'Khechen,' muttered Li, referring to North Korea's most notorious women's labour camp.

'How dare you?' Park whispered, tapping the glass. 'In there? Is it contaminated?'

'No, General. Except for any diseases they themselves are carrying,' answered Li, taken aback.

'Then let me inside.'

'But, General—'

'Let me inside, damn you,' shouted Park. Li picked up a telephone and called through to the guards. To the left of the glass a door slid open. Park stormed through. He was immediately hit by the cold, dank airlessness. Two guards saluted him. He returned the salute. 'Unlock this door,' he ordered, pointing to the cage furthest to the left.

Park stalked in and knelt down next to the woman. 'Free her hands,' he instructed. The guard undid the padlock which chained her to the wall. The woman dropped to the floor, but strangely, her arms stayed outstretched just as when they were bound. They had been forced into that position for so long. Park held her head in his arms.

'Get me some water,' he said. The guard brought a cup. Park put it to the woman's scarred lips. He poured a few drops into her mouth and she was able to swallow it. Park checked her pulse and the reaction from her eyes. They flickered, but took little in. Park dropped her to the ground, stood up and walked out.

'You idiot,' he shouted at Li. 'These women are dying. Do you think a test with them would give us an accurate result?'

Li lowered his head and scraped his shoes on the damp rock. Park continued: 'Americans and Europeans have the best health care in the world. Their immune systems are first rate. How can you match that with these sick, pathetic animals. In these cells, I want to see six healthy human beings. Only then, doctor, will I give you permission to begin your tests.'

Behind his thick spectacles, Li was both delighted and crestfallen. Park's predecessor would never have allowed such an audacious experiment. He cleared his throat. 'General, then with your permission, we will have to use Caucasian subjects.'

Park appeared to sink into deep thought. 'Of course,' he muttered. 'Of course you will.'

'Negroes, too?'

'Not necessary,' said Park, holding up his hand. 'The repressed American blacks will be on our side. But, a vaccine. There is no good having the weapon without an antidote.'

'And these?' Li asked, indicating towards the women.

'Get rid of them,' snapped Park.

Back in the guardroom, the phone was ringing. Li answered it and passed it to Park. The call was on a secure military line from Pyongyang. 'General,' said Park's aide-de-camp. 'Professor Memed escaped the Philippines. He is due in Pyongyang tomorrow morning.'

On the other side of the glass, porters lifted the women on to stretchers and took them away for execution.

9

Delhi, India

'They're still not answering,' said the Chief of Defence Staff, Deepak Suri. 'The hotlines are ringing. No one is picking up.'

Mehta leaned forward in his chair, rubbed his eyes and pressed the intercom on his desk. 'Ashish, have you sent the flower?' He had instructed that a pressed flower be sent to the Khans in Pakistan. The flower had been grown in the garden of Mehta's family home in Bombay from seed taken from the garden of the Karachi home they had left behind at Partition.

'About to, sir,' replied his private secretary.

'Make sure it's from family to family, that means from myself, Meenakshi, Romila and, of course, Geeta.'

'It'll be done,' said Uddin.

Mehta drew his finger down the edge of the telephone. He had asked to attend the funeral but the message back from Pakistan was to stay away. He had tried asking again through the hotlines, but no one was answering. It ran in the face of his conversation with Jim West in Washington a few minutes earlier.

'West believes it is under control and has asked us to do nothing to raise tension,' he said to Suri. 'I just pray to God he is right.'

'He's not,' said Suri. 'There's a power vacuum. And even when there isn't, Pakistan isn't stable.'

'But is it a hostile or a friendly vacuum, Deepak? That is the question.'

If the hotlines had been working, Vice-President Javed

Bashir Zafar should have been on the other end. Zafar was a professor of Islamic studies, who had been named in several corruption scandals over the past decade. After Khan's overwhelming election victory, he recreated the post of vice-president and appointed Zafar as an olive branch to the fundamentalist movement. Mehta was determined to deal with Pakistan's constitutional leader, even though Zafar would probably serve only a short time.

Suri stepped forward, moved a newspaper from the corner of Mehta's desk, perched on the edge of it and handed Mehta a sheet of paper torn off from a printer. It bore the hallmark of a highly classified document from India's foreign intelligence service, the Research and Analysis Wing. 'Shortly after the assassination of President Khan, there was a shoot-out at the military airfield in Multan,' explained Suri while Mehta read the report. 'A Pakistan International Airlines Boeing 757 was fired on from the tarmac. Personnel on board the aircraft returned fire while it was taxiing for take-off – which it successfully achieved. No flight plan had been filed. Pakistani fighters were scrambled from Sargodha and Rawalpindi, but were called back immediately. Under whose command, we don't know. The 757 headed due north into Chinese airspace. Chinese fighters were scrambled to intercept it. They did not force it down, but escorted it. After that we lost contact. No radio traffic took place from the airliner at all.'

'Destination?' asked Mehta, handing the report back to Suri.

'Not known. The Russians had no contact with the aircraft, so it could have landed in only two countries – China or North Korea.'

He reached for the newspaper Suri had moved, flipped it open and glanced at the page. The gossip column showed a picture of Geeta looking brilliant on the ski slopes of St Moritz and kissing a man who could probably buy all

Mehta owned with small change. He was an Australian racehorse owner. Mehta turned the page towards Suri. 'What do you think, Deepak? How does an Indian prime minister take on a man like that?'

'I think your wife is not worthy of you,' said Suri. He took the newspaper and dropped it in the bin by his foot. 'And the nation agrees with me,' he added with a smile.

'The stories Meenakshi tells me of the poverty in our country make me so ashamed, you know.' Mehta spoke about his younger daughter's work as a doctor with pride in his voice. Romila, older by two years, with more of her mother's flightiness, was in New York, managing investment funds for Goldman Sachs.

'She walked for two days to get to one village. There is no government there at all. No school. No medicine. No crops. No water supply. She stayed for a week, living among them. Little wonder young men blow up parliaments and assassinate presidents.'

Suri shook his head. To him, his Prime Minister was a complex and brilliant man. But his mind was full of too many unattainable visions. 'Let's concentrate on Pakistan,' he replied. 'Once that's settled, we'll move onto Bihar.'

'Yes. Of course.' Mehta smiled apologetically. 'All this gossip about Geeta distracts me. The PIA airliner? It took off after the assassination?'

'One hour afterwards. From Multan. Whoever was on board had no intention of being in Pakistan for the funeral.'

Mehta poured himself tea from the pot left on his desk. He brushed his finger against the cup to find it was lukewarm, but drank it anyway. 'You know, Deepak, old friend, I am frightened,' said Mehta, putting down the cup. 'Maybe it's because I am too used to violence. Maybe it is because I have been in the low-trust trade for too long. Our Parliament has been attacked before. Pakistani leaders die violently as a matter of routine. There are shoot-outs there all the time. Strange planes fly through the night.'

'But this time you are afraid,' said Suri, testing the temperature of the teapot himself and deciding against a cup.

'All I know is that my bones are chilled, but I don't know why.' Mehta glanced across at a computer screen which was scrolling down stories from the Press Trust of India wire. 'Kashmir is quiet,' he muttered, reading a story datelined Srinagar. 'Pakistan is in mourning, and Kashmir does not erupt. That is a good sign.'

'Seems so,' said Suri. 'The peace process holds. Pakistan is keeping its word over our troubled and bloodied territory.'

'So why does it kill its president?' Mehta whispered. 'What's it up to?'

He got up, walked over to a map on the wall of his office and ran his finger down the border between Pakistan and India. 'If you live on an idea and you have a generation of young men trained to spread that idea violently; if you close one front as happened in Afghanistan, then in Kashmir, you have to open another through which they can channel their energy.'

The door opened and a messenger stepped in. He gave an envelope to Suri, then slipped away, closing the door.

The two men were silent, Suri reading, Mehta studying the screen. 'We have fires in our own land,' said Suri meditatively. 'Gujarat is alight with funeral pyres.' He read on. 'Not only Gujarat. Maharashtra and Uttar Pradesh as well. Twenty-seven regions are under police curfew. Dozens are dead.'

Mehta turned, hands on his hips. 'Is India being bloody India?'

'Impossible to say,' shrugged Suri. 'Give me a second to read this through.'

Mehta moved over to the window. Unusually, it was a clear, smogless day with the sun's evening shadows casting a yellow light on the sandstone of the government buildings. It created a glow that was carried across the undulating and open landscape towards India Gate, but didn't show the charred remains of the parliament building.

Suri shook his head. 'I think it may have been,' he said.

'May have been what?' asked Mehta, returning to his desk.

'Orchestrated. In Gujarat at least. The first reported violence was in the coastal town of Navibandar.' Suri sat down opposite Mehta and continued to paraphrase. 'Navibandar is ten, fifteen miles down the coast from Porbandar. The attackers were Muslim, or claiming to be. They were from out of town. No one knew them. They rounded up Hindu villagers, including women and children, loaded them on to two fishing trawlers, and towed them out to sea. Those who jumped off were shot in the water. So the rest stayed on board. The boats had been booby-trapped with explosives. The attackers detonated them. The trawlers turned into fireballs and sank. The attackers ringed the area in speedboats, shooting survivors. When a police patrol boat arrived, the attackers took off and quickly outpaced them. This happened five hours ago. But word spread. A bus was intercepted between Navibandar and Madhavpur. It happened to be owned by a Muslim bus company, but mostly there were Hindus on board. The hijackers were Hindu fundamentalists. There were two local policemen among them. The Muslims were ordered off the bus, lined up by the road and shot dead.'

'Including women and children?' asked Mehta softly.

'Including women and children,' affirmed Suri. 'The driver, who happened to be a Muslim, was spared, so he could continue his journey.'

'How many?'

'Twenty-three. Nine men, ten women and four children. Right now, we're getting in more reports of killings all over India. But the key is here in the last paragraph. The attackers on the speedboat spray-painted the slogan Daulah Islamiah Nusantara on the hull of one of the fishing boats. I'll check out what that means.'

Mehta pushed himself back into his chair and stretched his arms behind his head. 'Fly the army into every affected area,' he said. 'Flag marches at company strength down every street. Troops will stand by in all places that are vulnerable. Curfew will be imposed. If no suitable troops are in the area, helicopter them in. If they are attacked, they will shoot to kill.'

'Yes, sir,' said Suri, picking up a telephone to forward the order. But before he got through, the light on another telephone flashed, the direct line to the head of external intelligence. Suri picked it up and spoke for only a few seconds.

'The PIA 757 landed in Pyongyang,' he said, replacing the receiver. 'Air Vice-Marshal Qureshi was on board.'

'Dear God,' Mehta whispered, mostly to himself.

Unlike previous prime ministers, Vasant Mehta had come to political life late after a career in the army and the intelligence services.

His career would have remained behind the scenes had his wife, Geeta, not embarked on a very public affair with a Bombay film star. For two months the press loved it, and as the story ran, so did details of Mehta's remarkable professional life. Not all of it was correct, but it was enough to propel him into that rare category of being an Indian hero. In the public eye, Geeta was transformed from a sophisticated and beautiful intellectual into a destructive hedonist, addicted to drugs and high-rolling parties. Mehta, on the other hand, was portrayed as a man of principle and a solitary figure, working alone late into the night in his South Block office to secure India against her enemies.

Mehta had loathed the press coverage against Geeta, but was grateful that the great nation he led could have open debate, even on his private life. He had understood that complexities and contradictions were what created literature, music, art, science and great civilizations. Yet never did he stop yearning for simplicity.

At the height of the scandal, Mehta had been persuaded to run for Parliament. His decisiveness and pragmatism soon led him to high office – particularly when American reliability was again questioned after the start of the 2001 War against Terror.

Single-mindedly, Mehta had pushed forward India's plans for a streamlined and independent defence system. Then he had announced in Parliament that India would not – under any circumstances – make a first nuclear strike against any nation, not even if it detected a launch from a hostile power, because such detections could be in error. In a nutshell, India would be prepared to sacrifice at least one city before it retaliated.

Almost unprecedented for any Indian leader, Mehta reinforced India's position in an essay in the prestigious Washington-based *Foreign Affairs* magazine. 'Should the tragedy of a nuclear attack on India or Indian interests occur anywhere in the world,' he had written, 'then my government would obliterate the nation responsible, whether the attack came from the government itself or from rogue elements being nurtured by that government. On this there will never be any negotiation. By stating this policy now unequivocally and with the widest distribution possible, we hope to avoid any confusion. No one will be able to claim misunderstanding.'

10

Beijing, China

The icy cold gave way to winter drizzle, and low cloud blended with pollution formed a dome over the Chinese capital Beijing. Air Koryo flights to Pyongyang were never full, but in the aftermath of the missile strike on Japan, the passenger list had been even further depleted. A business delegation from Australia, hoping to finalize long-term mining contracts, had shied away. A European Union Chamber of Commerce visit had been postponed indefinitely. A tour group run by a small travel agency in Britain had pulled the trip at the eleventh hour, leaving its clients kicking their heels in Beijing. Several were irritated journalists travelling under cover in bogus professions.

Only a handful of passengers were taken out by bus to the ageing TU-154 parked at a distant end of the airport tarmac. They included the Hungarian and British ambassadors returning from a few days' break in China; a Swedish couple, young aid workers whose organization had been helping famine victims now for almost twenty years; six North Korean diplomats flying back for consultations after the 'Yokata incident'; a low-ranking delegation of Chinese officials, ostensibly from the Foreign Ministry, but both key intelligence officials reporting to different units; two Russian diplomats, assigned to Russia's overseas intelligence service, the Sluzhba Vneshney Razvedki (SVR), and the Pakistani military attaché, who also reported to his country's Joint Counter Intelligence Bureau (JCIB), responsible for running intellligence officers as diplomats through embassies.

Iran also sent a delegation, which included a neatly dressed diplomat whose passport described him as Mashhoud Najari, first secretary at the embassy of the Islamic Republic of Iran in Beijing. Najari was, in fact, Ahmed Memed. One of the men with him was Memed's bodyguard from the Philippines, Hassan Muda. The other was an Iranian special forces captain, attached to the embassy and employed by Iran's Ministry of Intelligence and Security known by its Farsi acronym as SAVAMA.

The aircraft took off in light drizzle and bounced uncomfortably through the cloud on its ascent. Once clear, however, the pilot turned due west for the ninety-minute flight to Pyongyang. When he cleared air traffic control at Dalian, flying at 33,000 feet, he reported nothing wrong. He called in, out of courtesy, to the control tower at Dandong on the border crossing between China and North Korea, although he was technically in North Korean airspace at the time over the Sea of Korea. It was then that he began his descent.

After that, no one outside North Korea was certain about what happened.

The air traffic controller at Dandong only glanced once at his screen after talking to the pilot, and the aircraft was on course. In Dalian, the controller said he had been busy with other aircraft. The North Korean announcement issued later that day from Pyongyang said the flight had crashed, and all those on board had died. It allowed no independent experts in to help with the investigation. There were no television pictures from the crash site.

11

Pyongyang, North Korea

'The landing was necessary,' said Park Ho, stepping into a bleak room in the suburbs of Pyongyang that looked more like an abandoned office than the guest quarters for a visitor. Park made no explanation, gave no apology and offered no handshake to Ahmed Memed. He spoke in English, but apart from a shared foreign language, he felt no common ground with the Islamic cleric. Men of God made him feel both suspicious and vulnerable. Park was an atheist and self-taught in areas of practical help such as languages and engineering. Memed was only his guest because Pakistan had asked for it.

Memed remained seated. He was cross-legged. Making use of the natural light, his back leaning against the wall and supported by a cushion, he had a laptop on a pile of books by his side. It was plugged into a satellite telephone. He looked up. 'The landing was as any other,' he said quietly.

Park lit a cigarette and opened a window which gave a view out towards a long-closed cement factory and a skyline of Soviet-style apartment blocks made more monotonous by drizzle from an overcast sky. He looked around at two rolled-up prayer mats, a pile of books and two suitcases, their lids open on a table by the door.

'Who's this?' he said, pointing the cigarette towards Hassan Muda. Muda was unpacking Memed's robes and trying to maintain the creases.

'He saved my life,' said Memed softly.

'He saved your life, so you brought him with you?' Park

walked across the room to Muda. 'Look at me, boy,' commanded Park. Muda looked up, but only for a second. His features showed him as hardly being a boy; young perhaps, but with steel in his eyes.

'Not much of a bodyguard,' muttered Park, moving quickly off the subject. 'Air Vice-Marshal Qureshi has arrived from Pakistan.' He jerked his head in the direction of Muda.

Muda understood. He was fluent in Urdu, Hindi, Malay, Tagalog and English. He hurriedly refolded the robe, laid it on the top of the suitcase, headed for the door and left.

Memed had identified not only irascibility and brutality in Park, but also high ambition and intelligence. Park represented a formidable ally. If Islamic leaders displayed a common trait, it was to squabble among themselves. Park would not tolerate internal argument and Memed wanted him onside.

'The plan is going well, General,' Memed told Park, scrolling down the news pages of the BBC News website.

'Is it?' said Park.

'I am reading from the Internet,' Memed began. 'No doubt you have your own sources of information.

'Our biggest victory is the conquest of Brunei. The Sultan is in exile in London, and within twenty-four hours we expect to have secured the oil fields. A day after that, our forces will have taken Sarawak and Sabah, and will be holding the main cities of Miri, Kuching and Kota Kinabalu. Police have used live ammunition to stop riots in Kuala Lumpur. The casualty figure is more than a hundred dead. That is bound to bring on a second wave of rioting. In southern Thailand our people have risen up and taken over police stations. We have also managed to take the causeway between Malaysia and Singapore. For Singapore to tremble is symbolic in the extreme.' Memed looked up at the general who was pacing the room, his head down in thought, smoking a cigarette.

'Jakarta has erupted,' continued the cleric. 'The financial district is shut down. Aceh, Bali, Medan – I am literally reading them to you, General, as they come up on screen – Kupang, Yogyakarta, and all over Borneo.'

Memed pushed the laptop away a bit to give himself space and got to his feet. 'Don't you see how successful our partnership has been? Our area of control stretches from the northern coast of Borneo through the Sulu Archipelago to the southern Philippines. It is the distinct sovereign territory known as Daulah Islamiah Nusantara, the Sovereign Islamic Archipelago. We have been fighting for it for nearly five hundred years.' He walked towards Park, both hands outstretched. 'Share with me for a moment my joy, General, as I will share with you the expulsion of the Americans from the Pacific.'

Park stubbed his cigarette out on the concrete window sill. 'Joy is not a Korean commodity,' he said with disdain, tossing the butt outside. 'The level of support from other areas? I have heard of nothing there.'

Memed dropped his hands and stopped in the middle of the room. 'We agreed that would be the second stage,' said Memed, injecting authority into his tone. 'The key to our success is that the Americans will not know from where they will be struck next. It would be unwise to do all at once.'

Park nodded, but continued staring out the window. Not once had he looked at Memed.

'In public, Iran and Syria have spoken in sympathy for the uprisings,' said Memed. 'That is what we had planned. Other nations have said nothing. They have expressed only condolence for the murder of President Khan of Pakistan.'

A noise by the doorway distracted Park's attention, prompting a slight smile across his face. The man standing in the doorway was Air Vice-Marshal Qureshi. He was in full uniform, a tall, trim figure with a full head of dark hair, a thin moustache and a broad smile. He stepped into the room, cutting through the awkward atmosphere between Memed and Park. Both arms were outstretched to embrace Memed. Unlike Park, Qureshi understood the delicate balance between religious and military power. Pakistan had been forged on it and through its troublesome history those two parallel institutions had held it together and given it a focus.

Qureshi held Memed by the shoulders. 'Imam, it is so good, so, so good to see you again.' No sooner was the sentence finished than he spun round to Park, saluted, then held out his hands. 'I understand the business has been done. May I offer my most heartfelt congratulations.'

'Thank you,' said Park, awkward in the presence of the urbane Qureshi.

'I understand also that the uprisings are going to plan,' Qureshi continued. 'Do you think they will hold?' He looked to Memed for an answer.

Memed nodded. 'Stage two will need another catalyst. But certainly they will hold,' he answered knowledgeably.

Qureshi looked around the bleak room. The bare concrete floor was covered only with Korean handwoven rugs. Two oil fires burnt in the corner, where Memed and Muda had put their luggage. Four strips of fluorescent lighting flickered at different strengths from the ceiling. Two more strips were broken. A draught blew in from the open window to the door which he had left ajar as he came inside.

Park anticipated Qureshi's question. 'Come. Both of you follow me. We will go somewhere more comfortable.'

Park led. Qureshi made sure that Memed followed, with him taking up the rear. Outside the room were guards from the Special Reconnaissance Bureau, two on the door

and two on each side of the curving corridor at intervals.
A short way along, a guard pushed open the double doors
of a room which began with a small marbled hallway and
a cloakroom. Another set of double doors was open to
reveal a high-ceilinged suite, carpeted, with pale-green
freshly painted walls and a view over a river towards the
monuments and parks of Pyongyang. As they came in,
three women in bright blue and yellow full-length dresses
appeared and bowed.

'We can talk here,' said Park, indicating that Qureshi
should take the sofa. 'You must have had a tiring flight.'

'Certainly it had its excitements,' agreed Qureshi, who
had taken off in the middle of a firefight against troops
loyal to President Khan. One of his men bled to death in
the aircraft. Two men were either dead or wounded on the
tarmac and there had been three bullet holes in the
starboard wing, luckily not puncturing fuel tanks or cables.
Crucially his cargo, resting on specially designed suspension apparatus in the centre of the fuselage, remained
unharmed. There was half an hour of slight turbulence as
they flew over eastern Russia down into China and began
their descent. But it passed quickly and Qureshi delivered
safely the five tactical warheads, assembled apart from the
insertion of detonators. Now, with luck, he would be able
to catch the afternoon train back to Beijing, giving him
twenty-four hours' rest, before joining the fray again.

Once settled, Park took charge. 'How is the situation?'
he asked, addressing Qureshi.

'As good as can be expected,' said Qureshi. 'The opposition is no more than we anticipated. So far dissent has
remained within the military. Nothing has spilled over
from the barracks to the streets. To the world outside,
there has been a tragic assassination, but the same civilian
government is in control.'

'And you can hold the military?' pressed Park.

Qureshi nodded slowly. 'I think so.' He paused while one of the hostesses sank to her knees and offered him coffee, which he took black. Memed had nothing and Park only water. 'When they understand what we want to achieve,' said Qureshi, 'and how swiftly we will be able to do it, they will come on board.' He sipped his coffee. 'Tell me, General, did you have opposition?' Qureshi had a genuine curiosity to compare.

'Yes, but it was dealt with,' said Park, giving only the barest information.

Irritated but patient, Qureshi turned to Memed. 'And you have done well, so well,' he said, smiling. 'He and I have taken control only of our own generals. You have won over a whole society. I hear there are celebrations of liberation everywhere.'

'Thank you,' said Memed humbly. 'By removing oppression anything is possible.'

'You spoke of a second catalyst,' said Park.

'Yes, yes,' agreed Memed. 'The first worked perfectly. You, General, by striking Yokata, showed how easy it was to deliver a wounding blow to the United States. The killing of Asif Latif Khan, the most pro-American leader of any Islamic nation, provided us with a symbolic call to battle. I know you have plans, General. I know that Air Vice-Marshal Qureshi has provided you with the means to conduct the next major stage of your operation. That was in the agreement. What I suggest now is perhaps a half-stage, a nudge to continue the momentum. I have a plan for Hassan Muda.' He glanced at Park. 'That is why he is with me. And you, General, should do whatever you think fit. But you will need another catalyst to win.'

'When will you declare independence?' Qureshi asked Memed.

'As soon as we know we have control,' said Memed.

'Key governments will recognize the sovereignty of Daulah Islamiah Nusantara, the Sovereign Islamic Archipelago or SIA as it will be known, a glorious Islamic homeland stretching right across northern Borneo, through the Sulu Archipelago, and into Mindanao in the southern Philippines.'

'We will recognize it immediately,' said Qureshi.

'Who else?' asked Park.

'Iran, Syria, Palestine, Yemen. These have promised. North Korea, of course. There will be a number of smaller developing nations who will readily recognize in exchange for aid packages. The SIA will become a viable nation.'

'And why will there not be a war to take it back?' asked Qureshi rhetorically, looking towards Park.

'Because they will be afraid,' said Park. Qureshi expected him to expand, but Park rested his glass of water on the arm of the chair, and ran his thumb and forefinger up and down the condensation on the side. His features were both unfathomable and determined, and his thoughts appeared to be somewhere else altogether, at some distant place within his own imagination.

12

Bandar Seri Begawan, Brunei

The Sultanate of Brunei was an enclave shaped like a 'W' on the northern coast of Borneo. It had been ruled by the same family for more than six centuries, and since the 1960s it had been governed under a state of emergency. Rich in oil and small in population, it developed without effort, giving its citizens such a high standard of living that there was little reason to rebel.

Political dissent was banned anyway, as were alcohol and a free press. But with passports and money, Bruneians could travel abroad and return home to a sanctuary untouched by the frenzy of the modern world.

While Brunei had its own small army, navy and air force, the Sultan also maintained a garrison of Nepali Gurkhas for his own protection. When he was out of the country for a long spell, Gurkhas would head into the jungle for training. The British also kept two battalions of their own Gurkhas there, together with special forces troops. At the time of the coup, led by Islamic colonels, Britain had 1576 men from two Gurkha battalions, fifty men from the Special Air Service and twenty from the Special Boat Service, together with eleven Australian and five New Zealand special forces soldiers who were training alongside them in Brunei.

Their camp was two hours' walk from the Limbang River which ran between the Malaysian state of Sabah and the Bruneian capital Bandar Seri Begawan.

A Gurkha soldier cut the outboard motor to neutral and let the long, narrow boat drift to the mangrove swamps on the river bank. He had picked up Lazaro Campbell from a beach on Labuan Island, taken him by speedboat across Brunei Bay, then by river to where he was now. Campbell travelled with his head covered by a scarf. In the moonlight his Hispanic features helped his disguise as a Malay river boatman.

The Gurkha stayed in the boat, steadying it against the soft river bank with a boathook. He waited for Campbell to climb out, then handed him his bag. His kit was minimal, mostly taken up with two freshly pressed shirts, and a light linen suit and tie. Peter Brock had talked to him from the White House: if the mission was a success, the President wanted Campbell in the victory parade, but in civilian dress. If it failed, he was to get the hell out and let no one know he had ever been in there.

Campbell scrambled on to the bank and felt a hand grasp his wrist and pull him through the firmer ground.

'Glad you could make it,' said SAS Colonel John Burrows, shaking Campbell's hand. 'Any trouble up river?'

'Pretty quiet,' said Campbell. 'Three checkpoints, but we were waved through. No one's clear who's in charge.'

Burrows nodded. 'It's a bit of a hike, but there's coffee at the end of it.' He began walking, but continued speaking with Campbell following. 'Lazaro?' he asked. 'Are you half Mexican or something?'

'Half Cuban,' said Campbell.

Burrows missed half a step, as if he was thinking of stopping, but changed his mind. 'That place is still run by Marxists.'

'Sure is, but my mother left long before I was born. She was a child and I was delivered safe on American soil.'

'Is she still alive?' continued Burrows brusquely, his back to Campbell, climbing a slight slope on a path slippery with rain and decaying leaves.

'Both my parents are. They live in New York. Down-town, Manhattan, to be precise.'

They came into a clearing, throwing them into a basket of sudden light and heat, reminding Campbell how shielded they had been from the sun. He saw a glint of the sun's reflection on glass, and briefly stopped to look around. He had thought it strange that Burrows would meet him alone. Now he realized that Burrows's men were in the jungle with binoculars, watching him at every stage of their journey.

'Where in Manhattan?' asked Burrows, keeping going.

'Kenmore and Mott Streets. Downtown,' said Campbell straight away, knowing that a few questions – whatever their topic – would often reveal the measure of a person.

'Are you married?'

'Not yet.'

'Forty-two is not a "not yet" age. Got a girl?'

'From time to time.'

'Lucky sod. I've been married seventeen years. I think we've both run out of steam with it. Difficult to know what one should do.'

'Keep working,' said Campbell. 'Always the best.'

'And you work for?' Burrows moved his weapon from his right to his left hand and opened a water flask.

'I'll reveal that when we're alone,' said Campbell.

Burrows missed a step and looked round, quizzically. He drank from the flask, not offering any to Campbell, then walked on. The jungle became denser, with hanging foliage which had not been cleared. The ground, too, became more tricky, often so thick with roots and clam-bering undergrowth that there was only a very rudimentary path. The air was completely still and thick with humidity.

'You've moved camp?' said Campbell, asking the obvious.

'The night of the coup,' said Burrows. 'This section is a little tricky.' Burrows stopped and looked round at Campbell. His brow was a film of sweat. Mosquitoes hovered close but kept away because of the repellant covering his face. 'Politically, I understand that you should be here. Operationally, it could be a disaster to have an outsider with us. We've been living and training together for three months, and—'

'Colonel. I understand,' said Campbell, catching up with him. He held up his hand and grinned. 'If I get in the way, shoot me. No one's going to ask questions.'

Burrows laughed. 'You know what my orders are?' he asked rhetorically. 'Just two words: liberate Brunei.' He wiped a cloth across his face. 'What are your orders, Campbell?'

'Almost as simple as yours. I have to bundle one of the colonels who started it all on to an aircraft. Anything you can do to help would be much appreciated.'

Four hours later, they were holding back in their boats just before the river opened into an expanse of water that led to the water villages, a string of huts built on stilts. Expensive speedboats were moored underneath. The latest models of luxury cars were parked in a paved area nearby on the river bank. The kitchens and living rooms were equipped with state-of-the-art electronic gadgetry. But with all that, the people still lived in traditional Brunei style.

The Brunei flag flew on the river customs building: yellow, white and black with the red national emblem in the centre. Next to it was a flag Campbell had never seen before, a green and gold crescent rippling in the night-time breeze. On other government buildings, visible from the river, the similar duet of national and religious symbols were displayed.

Campbell was made the fifth man in a four-man SBS unit, staying out of sight under a river-bank mangrove tree. They had the advantage of monsoonal cloud cover and bursts of distant thunder that, with luck, might disguise the growls of their approaching engines.

Burrows was in the boat alongside Campbell's. He read a map by the natural light of the night, comparing it with the satellite imagery brought in by Campbell.

'We have one attack helicopter on stand-by,' he said, his voice low, but carrying enough for Campbell and the others to pick it up. 'It's got to be quick. There are expatriate families there, hunkered down in their homes. Any delay and they're as good as hostages. Be as careful as you can with casualties. I've trained with the Bruneians. They're good soldiers, and I don't want them killed because of a handful of rag-head colonels. If you find one of the colonels, take him to Campbell, and get them to the airport. If you find two, one should be executed to set an example.

'Australian transport aircraft are flying in from Perth and Darwin with reinforcements. US planes are bringing in supplies from the Philippines. The Sultan is on his way back from London. At midday, he's to inspect a guard of honour with a military flypast and Royal Bruneian naval boats patrolling the coastline. Our priority, then, is to secure the airport, and from there we will secure the rest of the city. We hope that our presence under arms will break the coup. Frankly, I believe it would break itself within a few days, but our political masters want it down now to send a message right across South East Asia.

'If we can, I want to paddle across the open water. It'll take about fifteen minutes. Only start engines once we are spotted. Snipers will open fire first, while we make it ashore.'

With the moon blocked out by clouds, faces blacked, engines off, praying no one would spot them, Burrows folded the map and lifted his night-vision binoculars.

The main sentries were at the customs house. Troops

patrolled the waterfront on foot. Jeeps were moving around the centre of town. Apart from that, Bandar Seri Begawan was quiet.

Then he spotted activity. A searchlight was being erected on the roof of the customs house. Two French-made VAB armoured personnel carriers, also with searchlights, were drawing up on the waterfront. If caught in the searchlights' sweeps, the boats would be sitting ducks, wiped out with the fire from the APCs' 12.7mm machine guns or 20mm cannon.

Burrows whispered into the radio. Four snipers scrambled off their boats into the shallow water of the mangrove swamp. It would be the worst possible position from which to try an accurate shot over such a distance. But they had trained for it, and their cover might be the only chance the raiding party would have. Burrows ordered in the helicopter.

The next minutes were spent in silence. The only sound was water rippling against the boat and distant orders being shouted between Bruneian troops from the shore. Then as they heard the first throb of the SA-341 Gazelle attack helicopter, Burrows raised his hand. The huge engine on his boat at first purred and then roared into life. The bow rose up with the surge of water and Burrows broke cover, with Campbell's boat immediately behind. Seven powerboats carrying special forces units spread out across the river estuary. Behind them came ten larger boats, but gathering just as much speed, each crammed with Gurkhas.

By the time they reached the open water, the boats were travelling at fifty knots, not a light among them, dark, bouncing shapes advancing fast towards land. The single helicopter, also unlit, came in low from the jungle, swooping over the trees and the tops of the boats, then firing an anti-tank missile at the armoured vehicle to the left of the customs house. The flash from the nose set off the alarm which broke the night's silence in the sleepy city. The cannon missed its target and hit a fuel tanker. Flames curled round, while the helicopter turned tightly, its 7.62mm machine-gun raking the customs house roof, smashing the windows below, taking its first casualties with the guards on the roof and destroying the searchlight.

A devastating explosion from the tanker lit up the waterfront. The fire burst into the night sky, then subsided, then leapt up again, running along a line of leaking fuel towards stilted houses where the wooden walls and roofs were dried out from the daytime's rainless heat.

'Boat three,' said Burrows into the radio. 'The first thing you do is put out that bloody fire and treat civilian casualties.'

Two criss-crossing searchlight beams from the shore lit up the water, sweeping across until they each picked out a boat. The helmsmen veered from side to side, twisting their craft back and forth, keeping them heading on, while heavy-calibre bullets cut into the water around them.

One searchlight went dead, shattered by the Gazelle's 20mm cannon. Burrows was less than a minute from the waterfront. Hostile fire came from the surviving armoured vehicle. For a few seconds it went silent, searching for a new target. Unless it was taken out within seconds, one of the boats would take casualties.

The helicopter crew fired another anti-tank missile, but missed again. The aircraft's machine-gunner, fully exposed with the side door open, kept up sustained fire while the pilot took the Gazelle higher to get a clearer shot. He was turning back when the helicopter juddered as if caught in a mid-air tornado and exploded in a ball of fire. Its tail broke off. The main body dipped on the weight of the engine and plunged into the water.

Burrows's boat twisted sharply to avoid the burning

debris. A helmsman, two boats away, ran straight into the field of fire maintained throughout by the Bruneian gunner. The helmsman was hit. He lost control as the bow of the craft came down on to the wake of the next boat. At such high speed the craft flipped, throwing the soldiers into the water. They were picked out by the searchlight and shot.

To the left of the customs house, the tanker fire was spreading. People ran from their homes, screaming at the horrendous sight in the water and fled away from the gunfire.

Burrows managed to get under the trajectory of the armoured vehicle, too close and low for the machine-gunner to hit him. His helmsman slowed, staying on the water. Burrows steadied himself with an anti-tank weapon. He waited a few extra seconds for the rocking of the boat to quieten. But as he fired, a rogue swell encompassed the boat. The round went high.

Campbell's boat reached the concrete steps of the prom-enade. The first man out was hit. Campbell leapt out behind him and picked up the fallen anti-tank weapon. The Gurkhas, only seconds behind in their boats, sent withering fire ashore, giving Campbell enough time to sight the target. He fired into the belly of the armoured vehicle, scoring a direct hit, engulfing the turret in flames.

With the armoured vehicle out and the machine-gun silent, there was a momentary pause in the advance of the Bruneian troops. The Gurkhas were ashore, advancing in a thin khaki line, covered by fire from the boats still on the water.

Somehow Burrows's booming voice managed to cut through the noise of battle, confusing the rebels even more. 'All units hold fire,' he ordered.

The Bruneian officer, Colonel Rokiah Daud, leading the rebel counter-attack, later admitted that that one com-mand had been the turning point. Daud was a graduate of

British military training. Hearing the order from a British commander, he automatically repeated it to his men who obeyed.

A sudden, deathly quiet descended on the waterfront, while Daud realized his mistake.

Burrows walked up to him. 'What the bloody hell do you think you're doing?' he said. As Daud raised his gun to shoot Burrows, a roar filled the sky. Two Australian fighter jets flew over only a few hundred feet high, the chaff and deflectors throwing out decoys against the Rapier missiles still coming from the airport.

'Stupid little shit,' sneered Burrows, and shot Daud cleanly in the knee.

13

Delhi, India

Until now, Vasant Mehta had refrained from making the call. But earlier in the day, as he was driven past the ruin of the parliament building, his mind filling with fresh memories of the attack, he realized that if he didn't, peace would be impossible to achieve. The man in his sights was President Song Ligong of China, better known outside his country as Jamie Song. Song had called on the day of the attack, but Mehta had refused to speak to him.

They had only met twice. Vasant Mehta had spent a day and a half in Beijing during a visit to East Asia, and more recently he had attended the closing ceremony of the Asian Pacific Economic Conference meeting in Singapore. They had formed a working relationship. Trade was increasing, but politically they were far from close. India and China saw themselves as natural rivals. One was a democracy, the other an autocracy. Their border was disputed. Each was expanding its blue-water navy to deploy into the other's waters. Each was creating an arsenal of missiles for the day they might have to face each other down.

All that, however, Mehta put down to the natural progression of nationhood. What he found unpalatable was China's unflinching support for Pakistan. Without China, Pakistan would not have nuclear weapons. Nor would it have the missiles with which to deliver them. Without Chinese weapons, Pakistan could not have supported the insurgency that had raged in Kashmir for twenty years, killing thousands and casting the spectre of war throughout the whole of Asia.

There was no personal chemistry between the two leaders either. Song came from a world of academia and business. Mehta was a military man who had won office by the accident of his wife's infidelity. He had spent too much time digesting intelligence reports on Chinese weapons sales to Pakistan, its violation of the NPT and the MTCR – the treaties to stop the proliferation of nuclear technology and missiles – and its blatant lying to the international community. Over the years, Mehta's resentment had built up, questioning what sort of successes India and Pakistan would have had in their attempts at peace had China not interfered.

The line clicked. 'The Chinese wish to know if this is an official or unofficial call, Prime Minister,' said Uddin.

'What's the difference?' asked Mehta impatiently.

'If it is unofficial, you can speak in English without interpreters.'

Mehta's fierce eyes looked straight ahead, angry at the world, but in his empty office finding no place to look that would satisfy them.

'In English,' he said softly, and he overheard Uddin paraphrase his request to Beijing. 'The Prime Minister wishes to have only a friendly chat with the President.'

Seconds later, Song was on the line. 'I am so, so sorry, Vasant,' he began. 'I tried to get you, but you must have been overwhelmed. If there is anything, absolutely anything—'

'There is,' Mehta interrupted. He was both abrupt and accusatory, perhaps more than he meant to be.

Song took it in good grace. 'Name it.'

Mehta drew breath. 'I want you to cut all arms supplies to Pakistan. I want your missile and nuclear scientists out of there. I want you to impose a complete arms, aid and trade embargo on that nation, and I want access to your intelligence files—'

'Prime Minister, Prime Minister,' Song broke in. 'Do you have evidence that this was the work of the Pakistani government?'

'I haven't finished,' said Mehta. 'What I outlined just now is what you owe this country after supporting those bastards for forty years. We warned you. We kept warning you, and you kept playing with fire. What I just listed, I want you to begin implementing now, as soon as this phone call is finished.'

'Go on, then,' said Song disbelievingly.

'If we find a direct link between the attack here and any element of the Pakistani military or intelligence services, you will give unequivocal support for us to go to war and destroy the institutions of that nation.'

Mehta paused to let his words sink in so there could be no misunderstanding. He had delivered his ultimatum. He had probably been too harsh, too much drawn back to the battlefield, addressing a corporal rather than the president of the most populous country on earth. He would allow Jamie Song a reply, even a defence if he wanted it. But, as he had spoken unprepared, unbriefed by his advisers, Mehta knew he could not negotiate on his conditions. Either China joined the world of civilized nations or he would expose it as a pariah.

'You are a brave man, Vasant Mehta,' said Song after a decent interval. 'The world has seen your courage. I have the picture on my desk, you with your daughter. It will be with me for ever as the image of how a man should lead and defend a nation.'

Mehta listened, glancing down at the newspapers as Song knew he would. Song was speaking in short, staccato phrases. Mehta could almost feel his brain working on how to find a diplomatic sidestep to the directness of Mehta's demands.

'You and I,' Song continued, drawing in common

ground, 'we have come to office with the baggage of history. What has happened in Delhi is a tragedy. But it is one your nation is strong enough to bear. Pakistan is a pack of cards, Vasant, and you know it. It has no strength, only poison. Would I like China to cut its links with Pakistan? Yes, of course I would. But it is not something I can do overnight—'

'Stop,' Mehta broke in. 'I didn't call you for platitudes. If you want to break with Pakistan, do it now. There is no better time.'

'It cannot be done that quickly,' responded Song, his voice more firm. 'You must have talked to Khan about this.'

'Khan was not responsible. That is why he is dead.' Mehta slammed his hand down on the desk, loud enough for Song to hear. 'You know that as well as I do. Because he did not control the military. The men who have the supremacy of violence in Pakistan are given that power by your government. So, as I said, I want your technicians and scientists on a plane out of there within a week.'

'Prime Minister, I understand your anger. I sympathize with your grief. But I cannot allow you to threaten China.'

'Jamie,' said Mehta tersely. 'It is not a threat. It is a demand on your moral duty.' He dropped the receiver into its cradle. Had he gone too far? Vasant Mehta, India's accidental prime minister, didn't care. He picked up the phone again. 'Ashish,' he said unenthusiastically. 'I need to speak to Andrei Kozlov.'

He heard the flare of Kozlov's lighter as the Russian president took up the telephone, and his drawing on the tobacco. 'How's the warrior?' Kozlov asked sympathetically.

'Just one question,' said Mehta, dismissing the attempt

at small talk. 'If it comes to war with Pakistan, Andrei, will you be with us?'

'We do not want war, Vasant, as you know,' said Kozlov. 'But if you have the evidence, you will have our political support. Our arms contracts remain regardless. They are indestructible.'

'Even if Jim West wants you to stop them?'

'Particularly if Jim West wants me to stop them,' answered Kozlov, his voice hardening. 'This is not the era of Vladimir Putin.'

'What about China?'

It must have been thirty seconds before Kozlov spoke again. 'China is complicated,' he said. 'We have a new alliance with China, Vasant. If you need muscle with China, I will try. But don't pick a fight with Jamie Song. Not now.'

14

Pyongyang, North Korea

'You have lost Brunei,' said Park Ho. He had walked, uninvited, into Ahmed Memed's suite at the government guest-house in the northern suburbs of Pyonyang. The Muslim cleric and his bodyguard, Hassan Muda, were at prayers, facing west towards Mecca using mats they had brought with them on the plane.

On Qureshi's insistence before he left, Memed had been given better quarters. But still they were far from luxurious. The room was large and narrow with high ceilings and a glass chandelier in the middle. The armchairs were covered in faded pink cloth and the other furniture was of heavy, dark wood: a low coffee table, three upright chairs, a writing desk and two cupboards, one with a stuffed pheasant decorating a shelf, with books by Kim Il-sung and his son Kim Jong-il lining the shelf underneath. The walls were a dirty white, the paint grubby and faded, and on them were photographs of Kim Il-sung, some from when he was a young man just after the Korean War.

Memed looked up patiently, and shifted his position while studying the impatience on Park Ho's face. 'Please, a few minutes,' he said gently.

'You have lost Brunei,' Park repeated. He walked to the window, impatiently tapping his fingers on the glass. 'You told me you had fighters with courage. You lied to me.'

Memed did not respond. Park lit a cigarette and opened the window. 'Saudi Arabia, Egypt, Morocco, Tunisia, Algeria – nothing. You told me there would be rebellion throughout the Islamic world. You lied to me.'

Memed ignored him. Park stepped over to Hassan Muda and kicked him in the face as he was kneeling.

Trembling with anger, Memed pushed himself to his feet. 'What are you trying to achieve, General?' He brushed down his gown and walked as calmly as he could manage to a window, across the room from Park. 'If you do that again, you will have lost everything, because you will have lost my cooperation.'

Park drew on his cigarette. In the silence that followed Memed's threat, Park silently studied the portraits of his predecessors.

'General,' said Memed gently. 'You will gain nothing by using sadism against Hassan Muda. You have seized upon him in a fit of anger. You do not respect me because you do not understand me, and you are a man who is afraid of what he does not have the courage to discover.'

'Don't preach to me,' said Park, walking to another corner of the room, his eyes concentrating on the cold and grimy view through the window.

'We are following our religion,' continued Memed, patiently, softly, trying to bring Park round. 'You do not have a religion. You have no god. You do not understand. Wherever people feel suppressed, they will turn to us. We have a vision that uplifts the hearts of men. It will spread, because Islam is a truth. You do not win or lose truths. They simply exist.'

'Brunei is lost,' said Park, turning back inside the room. 'That is a truth.'

'You cannot expect to gain such a large territory as Daulah Islamiah Nusantara without losing and regaining territory. We have not won Singapore. Penang, we never expected to win. But we have Kuching, Kota Kinabalu, Zamboanga, Jolu, Sulu. When we win, it is because the people believe us. It will not be through the barrel of a gun.' Memed finished the sentence with his eyes on Park.

Then he knelt down and dipped a clean cloth in a bowl of fresh water that he kept underneath the radiator.

'Here,' he whispered to Muda. 'Take this. It will stop the bleeding.' Memed opened out the cloth and let Muda tilt his head back into his hand, while he lay the cloth over his face. His nose was bleeding and the kick had cut him under the right eye.

He got up and walked up to Park. There was a shiftiness across the general's face, an uneasiness about being looked straight in the eye. The two men were close and hostile, one in a laundered, khaki uniform, the other in a white, floor-length robe.

Park flinched as Memed put his hand on his shoulder. 'You follow the *juche* philosophy of your nation's founder Kim Il-sung,' Memed said slowly. '*Juche* is based on the principle that man is the master of everything and man decides everything. I follow the religion of Islam, which believes that God is the master of everything and God decides everything.

'I see in your face a force more immediate, more human. Perhaps you follow your path because of an experience in your early life. That is what most godless people do.'

'Enough,' said Park, dropping his cigarette on the floor. He trod on the butt inches away from Memed's sandals and stepped back. 'With Qureshi, we talked of the need for another catalyst. With Brunei gone, do you still believe it will work?'

'The British newspapers are criticizing Stuart Nolan's action. International opinion is against him. They have published photographs of British special forces men attacking Muslim Bruneian soldiers. They ask why Western thugs are let loose in the developing world. Nolan will now try to take back Sabah and Sarawak. But each day, public opposition will grow. This is not just a battle for territory, but for the will of the new world we are trying to create. The West believes that if it can regain South-East Asia, the danger of unrest in Saudi Arabia, Jordan and Egypt will subside. I believe that the longer we fight, the wider the revolution will spread.'

Memed looked Park straight in the eye. His expression was soft, but determined. 'So yes, General, it will work. We will continue, and Muda will leave tonight, if you permit him.'

15

Washington, DC, USA

'I would have expected you to be visiting Pakistan now,' said the Defense Secretary, speaking on the phone while being driven across the Potomac River from the Pentagon. 'Pakistan is after all a friendly Islamic nation and needs all the support it can get at this difficult time.'

Mary Newman drew a deep breath. She was in the back of her car on the shorter journey from the drab 'M' Street office, which housed the American Secretary of State. 'No more than our service personnel would expect their Defense Secretary to be with them at Yokata,' she countered.

'Juvenile,' Pierce muttered. 'I told Jim you were too young for the job. I can only think it's your close friendship which makes him stick by you.'

Utter bastard, thought Newman, yet so typical that a man so intellectually challenged as Chris Pierce would have to use sexual innuendo. If he was jealous of her access to the President, so be it. ''I back the British Prime Minister,' she said, ignoring the slight. 'And that's what I will be telling the President. In Park Ho, we're dealing with a very dangerous man indeed. I believe we should go in now and stop him, while we can. In fact, I believe North Korea may be turning itself into the world's first suicide state.'

'A little colourful, Mary,' interjected the Defense Secretary dryly. 'The Taliban in 2001. Iraq in 2003. They knew full well they were signing their own death warrants. But, of course, you were still getting your feet wet in international affairs then.'

'The Taliban was an imported regime set up by Pakistan and Saudi Arabia,' said Newman. 'Saddam Hussein was a hollow shell. But North Korea is different. However crazy its leaders might seem to us, what they have been trying to achieve does make a kind of perverse sense to them.'

'If you had ever been anywhere close to a war, Mary,' said Pierce, 'you wouldn't even begin to be saying the things you are.'

'We're both needed in Washington and you know it,' said Newman, delivering her parting shot. 'You and I represent the defining and opposing views within the administration. That is what debate and democracy are about, and our President deserves to hear our views before he makes his decision.'

Newman eyed Pierce with caution across the room as he finished his analysis of North Korea. He returned her look with a confident smile.

'You're making sense, Chris,' said Jim West, shaking his head. 'I don't see why he should do anything rash. He has half a country, a starving population, no grass-roots support anywhere else in the world.' He slapped his hand hard on the table. 'Even if he did order the Yokata launch, even if he is psychotic, even if he is trying to develop a new strain of smallpox, he has no power in the real sense of the word. We'll have no problem getting an international coalition to destroy him.'

'Does that mean that right now we do nothing?' said Mary Newman, knowing immediately that she had injected a fraction too much of an edge. The President looked sharply at her. She did not enjoy taking on Jim West, particularly in front of an audience.

She understood that West was elected and had a constituency whose cries for retribution might not be in the national interest. She understood, too, that she was appointed and had risen to her position without having to give a damn about public opinion. To complicate things, she was fond of Jim West. The way he conducted himself in office, the way he had borne the sudden death of his wife, all told her the measure of the man.

But she was also convinced that Chris Pierce was wrong.

'You got something to say, Mary, say it,' said West brusquely. 'But never accuse me of doing nothing.'

There were six of them in the White House basement, sitting at a table that could seat thirty. West was at the top with a laptop computer into which he typed notes as he talked and listened. 'I hope to hell you're wrong, Mary,' he said. 'I wasn't elected to get us into a war, particularly one with missiles and 37,000 American troops right on the front line.'

He turned to his Secretary for Homeland Security. 'Tom, what's the current threat assessment here?'

'Here on US soil, we still have no evidence of hostile Korean activity,' said Tom Patton, pulling two separate sheets of paper out of his file. 'No upsurge of Islamic activity, either. Just the usual string of tip-offs and unsubstantiated threats.'

'Thank you.' West appreciated Patton's forthright answers. In the United States he had a single and linear picture. In the jungle of foreign affairs, however, the world was foggy and confused.

West changed programs on the laptop and brought up a map stretching from Hawaii to the Middle East which was displayed on a screen at the end of the room.

'Let's get this straight, then,' he said, pointing his finger so that it threw an unintended shadow across the image. Brock slid a laser pointer across the table towards him. West turned it on, found Pyongyang and moved the narrow red beam between North Korea and Japan. 'Worst-case scenario one. North Korea deliberately struck Japan. Here.' He moved the laser to Pakistan. 'Worst case scenario two: the assassination of President Khan of Pakistan was the call sign for Islamic uprisings in South-East Asia.' He tapped the keyboard. 'Now let's ring-fence these two areas.'

Almost immediately, South-East Asia and North Korea became outlined in red. West expanded the screen into a map of the whole world, making the red appear much smaller.

'Is there any other area,' he asked, addressing the room, but looking at Pierce, 'in which we have detected activity that could be hostile to the United States, either shortly before or coinciding with the North Korean attack or the assassination?'

Pierce shook his head. 'Activities in Iran, Mr President. Uncertainty in Saudi Arabia and Egypt. Conflict in Israel. These are all ongoing.'

'OK, now I'm going to highlight every Islamic area in the world.'

The map flickered again then re-formed itself with swathes of green stretching from right across northern Africa, up into the Middle East to Pakistan. The President picked up the laser and pointed to South-East Asia. 'Is there any link that we know of between what is happening here and these other areas?'

It was Peter Brock who replied this time. 'Nothing unusual, Mr President. Our SIGINT and IMINT intelligence hasn't found anything either. The only uncertainty is the power vacuum in Pakistan.'

'All right,' said West slowly. 'Let's treat it as a neutral power vacuum for the moment.'

'Mr President,' interjected Newman. 'Can we not factor

in that the power vacuum was created by a political killing which was followed by well-organized, anti-US regional riots and a coup in Brunei?'

'Which has been successfully put down by the British,' said Pierce.

'As far as our public policy goes, Mary, we will treat it as a coincidence. There is no point in inflaming public fear.' He shot a look at Newman, but she couldn't read whether the glint in his eyes was one of fun or of irritation. He pointed back at the map. 'There's one more thing I want to do to put our situation in perspective,' he said, using the mouse arrow to reconfigure.

A pattern of black spread across the screen from Japan through to India, then through Europe from Scandinavia to southern France and on into northern Africa. Against the wave of black, the red appeared as mere specks.

West linked his fingers at the back of his head and laughed. 'Son of a bitch,' he said softly. 'The black shows the territory controlled by hostile forces when we joined the Second World War in 1941. The red shows the territory hostile to us now. Don't you all agree it's minuscule?' He leant across and touched Newman on the arm. 'What's your take, Mary? Have we got a Hitler on our hands? Or just a handful of terror runts?'

The President was being mischievous and impossible. Newman swallowed hard. 'We believe Park Ho is now in control of North Korea, Mr President,' she said firmly. 'We know he's working on a missile that can reach US territory. We believe he is close to getting a strain of smallpox for which we have no vaccination. Whether or not a Hitler is created depends on how we handle him.'

'All right,' West said thoughtfully. 'So who are North Korea's friends? Because Hitler had plenty.'

'China and Russia – if you don't count the rogue states,' said Newman. 'They'll back us, but it may have a cost. The longer we take to act, the more it might cost. On the surface, neither will sacrifice their relationship with us in order to save North Korea. But go a bit beneath that, and they will try to exact unacceptable concessions.'

'Explain,' said West.

'Well, firstly, each has an interest in driving a wedge between us and Japan,' said Newman and, feeling on stronger ground, her voice hardened. 'Each needs North Korea as a buffer state. Therefore they will insist that the status quo remains. And,' she concluded, looking West straight in the eye, 'each has an interest in seeing our power in the Pacific diminish. That, Mr President, is also the aim of Park Ho in North Korea itself.'

'For Christ's sake, Mary, are you trying to tell me that all this is a conspiracy—'

Newman interrupted. 'No. Absolutely not. But governments exploit situations and if you allow Park Ho to capitalize on what he has done, then the leaders of Russia and China will have no choice but to weigh up their options.'

'Do you have a suggestion?'

To answer, Newman addressed Pierce, determined to cut off any objection he planned to make. 'Don't consult. Strike. Let him know you're serious. Let him know he's not going to get away with it. And let Russia, China and everyone else know that this is your fight and they shouldn't mess with you.'

'It'd be a goddamn disaster,' said Pierce.

'Are you serious?' said West softly.

Newman looked straight at the President. She led a busy life, constantly travelling, constantly in an anonymous hotel room. When in Washington, she turned down fifty more invitations for every one she could accept. Her day was divided into fifteen-minute slots, even when flying from country to country. Her stamina and her ability to catnap – also factored into a fifteen-minute slot – had become legendary among her staff. But sometimes, when she was by herself, loneliness hit her like a cold sea. She harboured a fear about her personal life that she had never been able to lay to rest, passed down to her from her parents, specifically her mother who, as a young girl, had survived the Nazi concentration camps. When she spoke, she looked at the table, her knuckles clenched to keep her anger under control.

'If we had struck Hitler when he broke the Treaty of Versailles, there would have been no Second World War, Mr President. No Holocaust. If we had stopped him after Crystal Night. After he went into Czechoslovakia,' said Newman passionately. 'When exactly do you strike, Mr President, to prevent mass slaughter? When the next missile hits Japan? When it hits Guam? Hawaii? When it hits Los Angeles? When it arrives with a nuclear or biological warhead? Against which slice of the salami knife will we eventually take action?'

'If we strike North Korea,' said Pierce, quietly, 'we risk 37,000 American lives.'

West stood up, a familiar signal that the debate was over and squabbling had to stop.

'Mary, I appreciate your frankness,' he said, putting his hand on her shoulder. 'I really do. But I'm going with the Secretary of Defense on this one.'

He turned to John Kozerski. 'John, I need to talk to Jamie Song in China, Andrei Kozlov in Russia—' He paused for a moment, his chin in his hand. 'Get me Mehta in India as well. Sato in Tokyo.'

Newman broke protocol by referring to the President by his first name. 'Jim,' she insisted, 'lives are going to be lost. The question is, how many?'

'We're not going to do it, Mary,' West retorted immediately. 'Now, if you'll excuse us.'

He stepped away from her and spoke to Pierce. 'Chris, can you handle Cho in Seoul?'

'He'll want to talk to you,' said Kozerski.

'Until he stops swearing, I'm not going to contemplate it. The guy think's he's Al Capone or something.'

'I'll try and square him,' said Pierce.

'Reassure him that our troops are staying. Make sure he stays calm.'

Newman lingered, hoping for another word with West. While Kozerski was already at the door, Brock and Pierce did not look as if they were leaving. She manoeuvred herself around to his end of the table and was about to speak when West held up his hand to stop her.

'No, Mary,' he said firmly. 'This meeting is over. Now, if you'll excuse us?'

Without another word, she turned and walked out of the room.

16

Tokyo, Japan

Toru Sato, the colourful Prime Minister of Japan, saw a signal from the side of the tennis court that the US President was calling from Washington. He returned the ball in a slow arc just over the net and won the point. He walked off and was handed a cold face towel from the attractive personal assistant with whom the newspapers had dared link him romantically.

'Thank you, Kiyoko,' said Sato, taking a mobile telephone from her. 'How is he?'

'Impatient,' said Kiyoko, pushing her hair back off her face.

'I want Ken in on this conversation.' Sato beckoned over his Defence Secretary from the other side of the court. Kenijiro Yamada was a generation younger than Sato, but the score was one set each, with Yamada leading by a game.

'Just Ken?' said Kiyoko.

The Prime Minister nodded. The tragedy at Yokata had thrown up his nation's troubled history as never before. Half of Japan was terrified and seeking sanctuary with Uncle Sam. The other half was volunteering to sign up and invade North Korea. In his long political career, Sato had endured lecturing from the United States. His country was used but despised by China. It was loathed by South Korea and under suspicion from the whole of Asia. At seventy-two, Sato carried the mantle of both serving prime minister and elder statesman. He had skilfully seen off rivals of his own generation and now surrounded himself with ministers like Ken Yamada, and brilliantly sharp assistants like Kiyoko, a modern version of the ancient tradition of the geisha.

Sato dreamed of breaking Japan away from its tortured past. It had tried with its multinationals. It had tried with massive aid donations. It had tried – by its own standards – being contrite. But no nation could move on from a bad war without winning a good war. North Korea had handed him an opportunity to rid Japan of its twentieth-century shadows and make the nation complete once again.

Kiyoko gave Yamada a telephone. She herself was wearing a tiny earpiece and microphone.

'Jim, you caught me on the tennis court,' said Sato, deliberately not explaining why he was playing tennis in the middle of a national crisis.

'I won't keep you, then,' said West. 'I know my people have been talking to your people. We're trying to get this sorted as smoothly as we can. You know we're doing everything in our power to unwind the tension. I appreciate that Japan is in the front line and I must ask you to hold back on political posturing or military activity while we're trying to get this sorted.'

Sato had never liked Jim West. He spoke his mind and was too brusque to ever begin to understand the complexities of Japan. 'You will, I know, be looking at ways of honouring our security agreement which has kept peace in the East Asian region for more than half a century and allowed our economies to prosper.'

'Exactly. I am glad we are on the same wavelength.'

Except that, for Sato, they were far from being on the same wavelength. Their reading of the situation might be the same, but each government needed to use it differently. 'I have a problem, then, as you know,' Sato said. 'The television networks are reporting a massive deployment of naval ships and aircraft from your bases in Japan. Our press is interpreting this as your abandoning us and leaving us open to further attacks from North Korean missiles.'

'No. That is definitely not the case.' West's voice hardened, switching from that of friend to that of superior. 'We are deploying to the Korean peninsula and to the southern Philippines. Far from abandoning you, we are carrying out an operation of forward projection.'

'I see,' said Sato, his voice dropping suddenly and leaving things hanging so that West would have no idea what was troubling him.

'That's it, Toru. That's exactly what we're doing.' But hesitancy had slipped into the President's own voice.

Sato allowed a pause. He allowed his sigh to travel down the telephone line. 'Jim, I am under pressure to invoke article six of our mutual security treaty. It's from my own party.'

'Give me one second,' said West, as the tone on the scrambled satellite line changed. West was consulting his advisers on where Sato might be heading. The Japanese Prime Minister was a strong supporter of Japan's own missile programme. He had backed the forward deployment of the misnamed Japanese Self-Defence Force out east into the Pacific and as far west as the Indian Ocean. He had been instrumental in reshaping the navy to include more powerful warships and submarines and in changing the rules of engagement to open fire on hostile forces without being attacked first.

West came back briefed and with more confidence. 'Toru, you still there? Sorry about that. I've got a dozen people listening in on us, making sure I get my diplomacy right. Our security agreement stands. Of course it stands. Listen. As I said, we *are* deploying away from Japan, to the Philippines and to the Korean peninsula. I forgot to mention Singapore and the northern coast of Borneo, because it is our genuine belief that the Islamist rebellion is a far more dangerous threat to world peace than North Korea. But the key element is that we're keeping our troops on the peninsula. That's 37,000 Americans in the front line. To supply them we need to keep our bases in Japan fully manned. We're bringing in more service personnel and equipment from the US and that means we are also in a position to defend any attack on Japan. So, please, tell your party not to try to make political capital out of this tragedy, or they'll provoke my wrath as well as yours.'

Sato inclined his head slightly, to catch a bead of sweat dripping from his forehead. 'Article six specifies that we must see evidence of a return to the status quo. What we are seeing, Jim, is the American war machine in flight because of a single North Korean missile.'

'Why don't you go get a job as correspondent for Fox News?' said West sharply. He drew breath, and Sato was certain he had rubbed a nerve. The United States and Japan shared common ground in Asia in that they were both used and despised. The difference was that the United States strove for love. For some twisted reason – as proven by their record of twentieth-century brutality – the Japanese almost strove to be hated. Perhaps they believed that loathing and not love led to respect. Their modern success, away from the battlefield, led to jealousy. They made no attempt to be understood. To outsiders, their society remained unfathomable. This was an element of deep national psychology on which Toru planned to write a book once he had retired.

'Fox News,' Toru repeated, balancing his tone between humour and irritation. 'They are great advocates of war, I know. It increases their advertising revenues.'

'Toru, I cannot emphasize enough the importance of you letting the US take the lead. Yes, Yokata was on Japanese soil. But it was an American base and American families that were killed. It is our tragedy and our conflict.'

Sato glanced over to Yamada. 'Do you mind holding for a moment, Mr President?' he said with emphasized formality. 'I must have a word with my Defence Minister.'

'Make the offer,' said Yamada, swinging his racket in his hand. 'If we don't take the initiative now, we'll lose it.'

'Precisely,' said Sato, taking his time to reconnect the line. 'Mr President, given your stretched deployment in the region, I suggest we send Japanese ships to monitor activities off the North Korean coast. We can then pool our resources, which will free up your forces should the worrying Islamic uprisings spread. I hope this will be helpful to you.'

'You can't,' said West. 'You mustn't.'

'Mr President, please think about it.' He beckoned to Kiyoko, who unfolded a fresh cold towel and laid it at the base of his neck. Sato smiled. 'My suggestion will help both of us.'

'It'll change the goddamn balance of power, and you know it,' said West, making no attempt to hide his anger. 'It'll do exactly what those North Korean bastards want us to do.'

'As democratically elected leaders, we have to take note of the wishes of our electorate,' said Sato, peeling the towel off his neck and handing it back to Kiyoko with a smile. 'My concern is to show that their lives are being protected in every way. The members of my party are reflecting their desire to maintain the status quo.'

'The status quo was that North Korea had a missile in a gantry tower ready for launch. What do you want me to do, ring them up and tell them to put another one in there?'

Sato made no reply to the outburst. Kiyoko threw him a tennis ball, which he caught on the racket and rolled around on the string. 'That is my point, Jim,' he said softly, slipping back into a more personal tone. 'The status quo has gone for ever. Every nation must reassess its priorities.'

It was not a good conversation. But then, Toru Sato had never intended it to be.

17

Moscow, Russia

President Andrei Kozlov paced his huge office in the Kremlin, head lowered, his thoughts private. Kozlov's appearance was of a man once exposed to all weathers and with a physique trained to optimum fitness. But in his late fifties, his age and cragginess were showing. He was at least six feet three and broad-shouldered, with thick, grey, messy hair, and sideburns shaved neatly to the base of each ear. He had a pale, chubby face, blotched with moles, a face more friendly and happy than you would expect from the leader of a troubled and wounded nation. It was a disarming image, which Kozlov rarely failed to use to his advantage.

Kozlov finished his conversation with Jim West and handed the encrypted portable telephone to his private secretary, Alexander Yushchuk. Yushchuk had been with Kozlov for more than a quarter of a century, and the President trusted him more than his wife, more than his four children and a lot more than any of the duplicitous colleagues who sat in his cabinet.

They had met in 1982 during the Afghan campaign. Kozlov, then a political adviser in Kandahar, had run under mortar and machine-gun fire to drag Alexander Yushchuk, a conscripted driver, out of an overturned and burning jeep. While Yushchuk had survived bruised but unhurt, Kozlov took shrapnel in the ankle, leaving him with a slight limp.

Kozlov was a high achiever. Yushchuk, tall, gangly and bespectacled, was an enquiring observer and a pacifist. He was intrigued that anyone would risk his own life to save the life of a man he didn't know. He attached himself to Kozlov out of curiosity. Having never known status, the lowest ebb of Kozlov's career had been normal for Yushchuk. He believed in Kozlov's policies, although he did not always agree with the detail. For Yushchuk, Kozlov was the only Russian who understood the stakes of what was happening to their nation.

Kozlov had recently swept to power after years in the political wilderness. A military historian with a degree in international relations from Moscow University and a master's in business administration from INSEAD in France, Kozlov had argued forcefully against the break-up of the Soviet Union.

Nothing was absolute, he had said. Nothing was clear enough to necessitate such a risk. There was no panacea, no perfect formula of government, and the sudden dismantling of the status quo was highly dangerous. Kozlov was ignored and Russia went on to witness the conflict and poverty that followed.

He had spoken out against creating a free-market democracy without the rule of law, but was derided while organized crime took over the country. He exiled himself to Vladivostok, as far eastward as he could go. On the long train journey there, over thousands of miles, Kozlov had seen the achivements of the Soviet system and how it had supplied housing, drainage, roads, electricity, healthcare and telephone lines to tens of millions. In India, Africa and Latin America, similar communities lived in dismal conditions, despite following the advice of Western democracies. From Vladivostok, he wrote against the triumphalism of the market economy, and watched helplessly as billions of dollars in foreign loans wrested economic control from Russians and gave it to foreigners.

He opposed Russia's acceptance as a partner in NATO,

but was ignored, and he watched as allies such as Yugoslavia and Iraq switched their allegiance from Moscow to Washington.

Kozlov had sunk deeper and deeper into poverty. His wife, Sonia, wavered but remained with him. His two sons ignored him. One of his daughters, Mariya, disowned him and emigrated to Paris. But Ekatarina, his youngest, and a talented cellist, knew nothing of politics, but everything of family love. She remained loyal, albeit ignorant as to the issues which Kozlov was fighting.

'What do you think?' said Kozlov, as he came to the end of the room and face to face with an oil on canvas by Isaac Levitan. Kozlov had pleaded with the Tretyakov Gallery to lend it to him in exchange for an old master from the Kremlin. Levitan called his work *Eternal Peace*. It showed a solitary church set against an expanse of lake and sky, and was meant to reflect the loneliness of the human soul in the vastness of the universe. There was a tragedy about it, as there was for much of that period of painting, where man was constantly shown as being in disharmony with his own environment. Kozlov turned and paced back along the length of the room.

'Tell me again what he said,' answered Yushchuk, leaning against the wall. 'Tell me how he said it, and I'll tell you what I think.'

'He wanted to know three things. One – did I believe there had been a military takeover in North Korea? I said I did, and I believed Park Ho was the man responsible. Two – could I guarantee him that North Korea would not fire another missile?'

Yushchuk, with his detailed knowledge of Kozlov's character, detected a deliberate pause. He stepped in. 'You told him no one was able to tell North Korea what to do, especially if the government had been overthrown and a rogue general was in power.'

'To which he asked a follow-up question – was Russia an ally of North Korea? And I said that it was an alliance that had long decayed. If he was looking for big-power allies, he should talk to Jamie Song in Beijing. Failing that, get the United Nations' list of the poorest and most unstable nations and work up from the bottom.'

Yushchuk laughed, pushed himself off the wall against which he had been leaning and lit a cigarette. 'Was it a good conversation? It sounds as if you were winding him up.'

Kozlov folded his large hands together, stretched them back and cracked the knuckles. 'He was wound up anyway. He had just got off the phone to that old snake, Toru Sato.'

'His third question?' asked Yushchuk, dropping his spent match into an ashtray on the table beside him.

'Did Russia regard North Korea as a vital and strategic buffer state?'

'Not if it's going to fire missiles all over the place. It switches from being a buffer to a liability,' said Yushchuk.

Kozlov nodded. Reaching his desk, he stopped pacing and ran his fingers along the crevice between the leather and teak. 'To which he added another supplementary—'

'Trying to slip it in unnoticed?'

'Yes. But I fear, like myself, the American president does not possess such subtlety of character.' Kozlov walked around the desk, sat in the chair behind it, pushing himself into it as if stretching his back. 'What would be Russia's reaction to a US strike on North Korea? To which I asked whether it would be to reprimand it or to collapse it. He wanted an answer to both options. To which I said a reprimand could be carried out without comment providing it was against a military installation with no civilian casualties. An onslaught to collapse the regime would destabilize the Korean peninsula and therefore the whole of the western Pacific rim. It would cause untold civilian casualties and a refugee crisis within Russia and China. Therefore, I would oppose it.'

Yushchuk drew on his cigarette. 'You are right.'

'He believes I have influence,' said Kozlov, tilting the chair forward and running his hands over the surface of the desk. 'He wants me to use it to stop Park Ho from doing anything that would provoke an attack.'

'He is clever.'

Kozlov shook his head. 'No. He is not clever. He is forcing me to take sides when I don't want to. He is assuming I will take his side. But this is not the nineties. Russia is not Japan. Nor is it Europe. We are no longer supplicants to defeat.'

18

Beijing, China

'Jim, how are you?' asked Jamie Song, the sharp, flamboyant, and media-savvy President of the People's Republic of China. 'Your call is a pleasure to receive, of course, but I can't say it was unexpected. Now before we go on, tell me: is this an official conversation, in which case I'll have to bring in an interpreter, or is it just a friendly chat?'

'Let's make it friendly,' said West.

'Very good. Fire away and don't hold back. The franker you are the better.'

Jamie Song's idiomatic English reflected his years of living in the United States, first as a law student at Harvard, then switching seamlessly between the roles of international businessman and diplomat, becoming China's foreign minister and eventually president. Song was a spiritual child of Deng Xiaoping, the leader who in the 1980s put China on the path to modernization with a speed that no nation had experienced before.

Shanty towns were ripped down to be replaced by highrise apartments. Swamplands became airports. Country lanes were turned into expressways. Whole areas were declared economic zones with their own sets of rules for creating wealth. While India and Russia foundered through lack of resources and conflict, China pulled hundreds of millions out of poverty and gave them a sense of their own destiny. It skilfully lured in foreign investment and allowed the wealth to spread. Yet it gave little heed to international opinion. Political dissent was silenced. Demonstrations were put down. Poverty was hidden. Books were censored.

Newspapers and television broadcasts were controlled. China apologized for none of this.

In China's eyes, Western democracy had failed the poor. China had developed a system that was working. Jamie Song, who so cleverly straddled all worlds, was now at the helm for the nation's journey forward.

'North Korea,' said West bluntly. 'What's going on?'

Song let the question hang on the scrambled satellite telephone line between them. He had perched himself on a window sill overlooking Zhonghai Lake in the secure and secretive compound where the Chinese leadership lived and worked. Through the misted glass, Song watched fresh snow turn the lake's dirty ice back into a brilliant white.

'We're almost certain there's been a military takeover, Jim,' said Song. 'Park Ho is in charge and he has the loyalty of the military. What we don't know is whether he ordered the firing of the missile, or whether it was done in the heat of the moment by someone else.'

'When will you know?'

'You're the one with all the gadgetry.'

'You have the border, Jamie. You have the trust—'

'Don't kid yourself,' Song laughed. 'They've been such a pain in the neck, I'm beginning to wish we had lost the Korean War.'

'We've got fifty-eight dead Americans, Jamie, killed by a North Korean missile,' said West, in no mood for jokes. 'You're the closest they've got to an ally. You're also a world leader.'

Song tapped his index finger lightly on the telephone. He didn't like being lectured. But he understood the high emotion of American society. 'OK,' he said with deliberation. 'How exactly can I help?'

'What influence can you use to stop Park?'

'Doing what?'

'Carrying out more hostile acts against Americans.'

'*If* he is in charge, we can try to persuade. In the present climate that would work more than threats. I understand your position has to be different. But ours will be a softly-softly approach. If you want, you could be the stick and we would be the carrot.'

'In what way?'

'Your electorate is demanding retribution for the deaths of its compatriots. Being the president of an autocracy, I have no such constraints. If you wish, Jim, you can threaten to obliterate North Korea. I will urge you to restrain, while between us we can broker a deal which will advance the situation on the Korean peninsula towards some kind of resolution.'

West was silent for a few seconds before responding. 'In reality, how far can we go?'

'If Park Ho ordered the firing of that missile, then you would have my private support to take out his missile launch sites. If he retaliates across the Military Demarcation Line, then you're on your own. Should you go beyond attacks on the missile launch sites, I will have to consider my support. Should you launch a military attack on North Korea designed to cripple its military machine, overthrow the present regime and either reunify with the South or install a government of your own choosing, China will oppose you.'

'If it self-implodes, then what do we do?'

Outside, a strong north-Asian winter wind blew through the barren trees around the lake. Soon the branches would be alive with spring blossom, but Song wondered what folly the leaders of the world might have imposed on their citizens before then. He leaned forward and rubbed a small, clear patch in the condensation on the window of the Central Committee Office. A silver-grey Mercedes limousine was drawing up.

'If it self-implodes – God forbid – you have to keep your troops off North Korean soil.'

'That sounds reasonable, but South Koreans?'

'No. They're too closely entwined with you. My military wouldn't stand for it either, specifically up near the border.'

'Who then?'

'A UN force led by Chinese and Russian units on six-monthly rotations, leading to a non-elected government of technocrats for the first five years of transition. South Koreans will have de facto control of the economy, but a World Bank panel, comprising Chinese, Russian, Singaporean and European Union delegates will oversee.'

'You have a blueprint?' said West, not hiding his surprise.

'We have a blueprint of more than a thousand pages translated into seven languages, Jim. The bottom line is no direct US involvement. A buffer state between great powers has to be deflated slowly and with deliberation.'

'Thank you, Jamie,' said West. 'Thank you for being so upfront.'

Jamie Song replaced the telephone in the cradle on the chair. Outside, a tall, brisk figure, dressed in a blue silk shirt and tie and a pinstripe suit cut by a Parisian tailor, stepped out of the Mercedes. General Yan Xiaodong brushed down his lapels and bounced energetically up the steps to the front door. Yan was the head of the Communist Party's International Liaison Department. His visiting card named him as executive director of the China Association for International Friendly Contacts. Its main mission was counter-espionage and to watch on Hong Kong, Taiwan and North Korea.

Jamie Song picked up the telephone. 'General Yan has arrived,' he said. 'As soon as you locate Park Ho in North Korea, put him through.'

An hour later, the call had still not come.

Panmunjom, Korean peninsula

At the truce village of Panmunjom, no fence separated the enemy troops. The actual line between the two Koreas ran through the centre of seven huts. Outside, it was marked by a strip of concrete. Inside, a microphone cable lay across a table covered in green felt where negotiations took place to end the war. The huts had a temporary campsite air about them.

Three of the huts were a pale blue, the colour of the United Nations, rectangular, long and narrow, pointing north–south, with aluminium chimneys for the winter and sloping, sharp-edged roofs with wide eaves that provided some shade against the overhead summer sun.

Lieutenant Lee Jong-hee, aged twenty-six, had been assigned to the centre hut, used by the Military Armistice Commission which handled the 1953 ceasefire negotiations. Outside the window were three North Korean soldiers, one looking south, the other two north. On the other side, the pattern was repeated with South Koreans. Soldiers from both sides took inspection tours around the huts.

Lee stood inside at attention precisely on the Military Demarcation Line. On both sides of the main negotiating table were smaller tables with hardback wooden chairs. The walls were plain blue with no posters or decoration. The windows had no curtains. In front of Lee were the UN and North Korean flags. Facing him directly at the other end of the table was a North Korean officer. It had been like this for more than half a century.

At the end of the Second World War, Korea had been divided along the thirty-eighth parallel between the United States in the south and the Soviet Union in the north. On 25 June 1950, North Korean troops attacked. Four days later they took Seoul. Five days after that, they were in combat with US soldiers. Then China's new leader, Mao Tse-tung, sent in his army against the Americans. The Korean War was the only conflict since 1945 when the armies of two formidable nations – China and the United States – directly fought each other.

America made its peace with China. The Soviet Union ceased to exist. South Korea became a great Asian economy. But North Korea, stubborn, unbowed, and bankrupt, remained a self-created prison camp, the ceasefire inconclusive and the conflict unresolved.

On the morning that Lee was on duty, fifteen tourists from Europe and the United States were shown into the hut on a tour that took place several times a day. Lee and the North Korean officer on duty with him remained stock-still in position, as a military guide, Captain Ed Hutton, explained the history of the war and the armistice.

'There have been violations, but none has led to war,' Hutton said. He ran his hand down the green felt, picked up the microphone cable and dropped it down again. 'You can now tell your folks you've stood on the last Cold War frontier in the world. Behind you is the success of democracy and freedom in South Korea. In front of you is a nation on the verge of collapse through poverty and communism. The succession of Kim Jong-il from his father Kim Il-sung was the only dynastic succession from father to son in the communist world. You may have read in the newspapers that a new, as yet unknown ruler, might now be in charge over there.'

'Was that why there was an attack on Yokata?' asked a German student.

Hutton faltered. Lee shifted ever so slightly on his feet, but his face remained concentrated and without expression.

'I am not at liberty to discuss that event, sir,' said Hutton, looking at his watch. 'Now, if you would, all file out the southern door of this building. You are not – I repeat not – allowed to cross the demarcation line outside.'

As the group left the hut, martial music from almost two kilometres away in Peace Village on the North Korean side stopped playing. The national red, white and blue flag hung from a pole 160 metres high. For the first time anyone could remember for that time of day there was complete silence from Peace Village.

Lee drew an automatic weapon from under his tunic and shot the North Korean officer three times, the first round in the right eye, the second through the neck and the third in the heart. The soldier collapsed face down on the table and slid to the floor, taking with him the microphones and the green felt, soaked in his blood. Lee walked out of the northern door of the hut, and, without looking back or changing his measured pace, strode across the narrow, open area into North Korea.

'**Lee Jong-hee** is a North Korean agent,' said Peter Brock. 'He had been in deep cover inside the South Korean military. He was used to murder a fellow North Korean in order to provoke an international incident.'

'I need to get this straight, one hundred per cent,' said Jim West. Peter Brock and he were standing by the study window in Brock's Georgetown home. 'The victim is North Korean. The assailant is North Korean but passing as a South Korean soldier. In other words, a deep-cover agent.'

'Right,' said Brock grimly.

'Now the North Koreans are accusing us of ordering the assassination of one of their officers.'

'Correct.'

'And are demanding an apology, compensation for the family and God knows what.' West slapped the window sill. 'How do they explain that the murderer is in their charge?'

'They say he fled to the North Korean side to escape the brutal punishment he was bound to receive on the South side. They say they will not hand him back because they need to interrogate Lee to establish whether he was acting alone or on the orders of the Japanese, South Korean or US governments. At least their response is diplomatically astute.'

'A euphemism, if ever I've heard one,' whispered the American President.

'They say, regardless of that outcome, they have the

right to punish the man who killed their soldier. Therefore they'll be keeping him.'

'What do we know about him?'

Brock looked down at a summary from the National Security Agency which drew together signals intercepts out of North Korea, CIA reports, together with reports from South Korea's National Security Council and Japan's Defence Intelligence Headquarters.

'He comes from Seoul, but his family's home town was in Kaesong. Contrary to our own propaganda, Kaesong was just below the thirty-eighth parallel before the 1950 war—'

'You mean it was ours and we lost it?' interrupted West.

'Yes, Jim, Kaesong was ours – the former royal capital – and it ended up in North Korea, above the armistice line in 1953. Lee Jong-hee's grandfather was lost on the first day of fighting in the Korean War. His grandmother somehow got Lee's mother and her sister to safety. But her brother and other sister went missing. Lee was brought up in Seoul. He is a child of South Korea's democratization and economic miracle.'

'But at the same time he was brainwashed by the North?'

'And brilliantly. To get to work in the Joint Security Area, you have to undergo rigorous psychological tests. Lee had no problem in passing them. He has a steady girlfriend in Seoul. He has an older brother who works for HSBC in Seoul and a sister who's training to be a doctor in Los Angeles.'

'Have we talked to her?'

'We're doing that now.' West walked back to Brock's desk, where they were sharing a pot of Chinese green tea. He topped up his cup. 'North Korea fires a missile into our base at Yokata. We threaten. The next thing we know is that a North Korean soldier is murdered at the most sensitive place in the most militarized area in the whole world. And we're being blamed for it.'

'A diplomatic neutralizer such as we've never seen before,' said Brock, leaning down and pouring his own tea.

'Like hell it is,' muttered West. 'You don't neutralize anything by spraying bullshit in our faces.'

West drained his tea and caught sight of Caroline Brock, smiling nervously. From the tense expression on Brock's face, West realized the discussion was far from over.

'It might not be that simple,' said Brock quietly. 'That's why I've asked Caro to join us.'

The three friends sat down, Brock at his desk, Caro and West in the leather armchairs.

'As you know, Jim,' said Brock, 'Caro's work has taken her inside the world of weapons of mass destruction. That's chemical, nuclear and biological weapons, together with their delivery systems – mainly missiles. Since the nineties, rogue states have been looking to procure the technology and raw materials to make them. Iraq, before we took it back, got its anthrax from the Soviet Union. Pakistan got its nuclear capability from China. One of the key methods of procurement is through universities where research is taking place. In post-Soviet Russia, they were strapped for cash, the staff was unpaid, and the odd sale here and there would keep them afloat. In China, there has been a long tradition of institutions becoming self-supporting without the help of the central government, meaning also that when you have a weak central government, other institutions can operate with impunity. Academics are a fairly tight-knit group. We use them to keep us up to speed on what's going on, who is looking to procure what and why. We've had some spectacular successes in stopping procurement. But we might have let two crucial ones through the net.'

Brock stopped his introduction and looked across the room to his wife. 'There's been a theft at the Pokrov Biologics Plant near Moscow,' said Caroline candidly. 'It's meant to be a vaccine factory for animals, but we have known for years that illegal supplies of smallpox are being kept there. During the Cold War Pokrov was what is known as a turnkey operation. It could do everything: research and grow viruses, weaponize them and stuff them in the bombs for delivery. There had been attempts before to take viruses out – strange Arab businessman, and that sort of thing, but none succeeded.'

'Until six weeks ago,' said Brock.

'Yes,' said Caroline softly. 'Until six weeks ago. Or to be exact, the same week the IL-4 agent was stolen from Canberra.'

'And we only know now?' said West.

'If you walk through the Pokrov laboratories, even today, you find rows and rows of incubators holding hens' eggs. This is a classic way of growing the smallpox virus,' said Caroline. It was important that he should know the whole story, so she didn't answer the President directly.

'A week ago, a night watchman working at Pokrov had a heart attack. He survived but apparently underwent a religious conversion where he confessed to the priest that he had taken 500 dollars to let a man into the laboratory. Another 200 dollars was paid to the scientist on duty that night. To put it in context, Jim, a night watchman earns about 80 dollars a month; the scientist about 200 dollars.'

'It wouldn't have cost a heap to put them on a decent salary,' muttered West.

'The virus freezers are secured with a simple padlock. There's a clay seal that indicates whether they have been broken into. When the night watchman's story was checked out, three freezers were found to have been secured with fresh seals: they had been tampered with. The eggs which were taken were being used in tests to stabilize the smallpox virus during the trauma of weapons delivery. They were the most dangerous and durable form of the virus.'

'Where'd they go?' asked West, putting down his fork and wiping his mouth with a napkin.

'We don't know,' answered Brock.

'Russian intelligence?'

'They don't know or they're not telling us.'

West looked towards his National Security Advisor: 'But you *do* know, or Caro wouldn't be here now.'

'The man who let the thieves into the Canberra laboratory is a scientist called Dr John Mason,' said Brock. 'He's young. He's brilliant. But he has a gambling, drink and unfaithful-wife problem. Lazaro Campbell has just come back from interviewing him.'

'I see,' muttered West. He shifted uneasily in his seat, crossing, then uncrossing his legs as if his body language was bracing him for what he was about to hear.

'Mason confirmed the story about the creation of IL-4,' said Brock.

'It's actually a thin jelly which coats the egg so that sperm can't get into it,' said Caroline. 'The plan in Australia was to spread it among the population with the mouse-pox virus, rather like was done with myxomatosis on rabbits years ago, in order to render mice infertile and cut down the population.' She shrugged. 'But IL-4 turned out to be a lethal catalyst. She shrugged, casting her eyes to the floor. 'A complete accident of science.'

'Mason maintains that he doesn't know who took it,' said Brock. 'He received money and instructions. That was all. They traced calls on his mobile and home and office phones, and found nothing. Then they were bright enough to check on the call boxes. A number of calls from two different boxes near his home and office matched. The outward calls went to Surrey University in England, a Korean–American organization in San Francisco, a similar society in Canterbury City near Sydney, Australia, where there's a big Korean community, and a Korean–Japanese scientific group in Tokyo. The single inward call came from a hotel lobby in Beijing, China.'

West drew his hands down his face. 'I get the point. But there's still damn all I can do.'

'This, the missile, the shooting,' said Brock, prompting West to glance at him, his eyes narrowed with irritation.

'No.' He shook his head. 'There has got to be another way that does not risk the lives of our troops in South Korea.'

'We're concentrating on the San Francisco call,' said Brock. 'If we can make something stick, we'll get Campbell and a couple of Australian ASIS officers to bring Mason over here, where we should be able to get more out of him.'

Beijing, China

General Yan Xiaodong stood in the centre of the room, holding a file open in his hand, like a priest at a lectern. Jamie Song was by the window, his favourite spot in the Zhongnanhai compound, where he could watch the changing seasons play with the trees and flowers around the lake. From time to time, he glanced across at the flickering pictures on a television set in the corner of the room. Coffins of the victims of Yokata were being taken by pallbearers off a transport plane at an American military air base, the Stars and Stripes draped over each one, and carried through a guard of honour to waiting vehicles. The sombre – often close-up – picture of the US President, hands crossed, head bowed, black tie and suit, standing completely still, intercut the ceremony.

Yan spoke with his back to the television, as if it was of no interest to him at all. 'We have a record of Lee Jonghee in the Investigation and Research Office,' he said, running his finger down the faded original sheets of paper in an intelligence file which dated back from before the Communist Party took power in China.

'His grandparents were loyal followers of Stalin and Kim Il-sung. They were infiltrated into Seoul after the Second World War as sleeper spies. They are here on our files,' he said, tapping the paper. 'During the Korean War, they managed to keep their cover and to stay in the south, with two children. The daughter, Lee Jung Hyun, registered the family as being separated through the war. It meant she would have legitimate access to organizations negotiating with the North for reunification. She made three trips to Japan, each to a different organization connected with the regime in North Korea. The last trip was in December 1999, where we actually tailed her. We believed she was involved in illegal money transfers through a company in Tumen on the border.'

'Was she?'

'It doesn't say.'

'But she was an active agent for the North?' asked Song, part of his attention suddenly attracted to a blackbird trying to land on the melting ice of the lake.

'The grandmother and the mother. Yes,' said Yan. 'She was active, then went quiet, then became active again. You never can tell with sleeper agents.' Yan brushed the lapels of his jacket and looked down at the file. 'Lee Jong-hee's upbringing was the same as any other South Korean child's. But at home, he was indoctrinated with the teachings of Kim Il-sung and the *juche* ideology. He was a North Korean agent.'

'And he murdered a North Korean soldier in cold blood.'

'Correct.'

'Passed down from generation to generation,' mused Song. 'How many like him, Yan?'

The general shrugged, closed the folder, walked across and handed it to Song. Jamie Song had asked Yan to bring him a file of raw intelligence so he could read the intercepts and HUMINT reports before they became distorted by analysts. But looking at it, Song realized that there was no such thing as raw intelligence. The documents and cables were there, but each was deciphered and explained. He leafed through the file, while Yan, standing close by, peered over his shoulder and explained.

'Over twenty years, Park Ho has built up his loyalty in the Reconnaissance Bureau. Once he had secured the support of most party and military leaders, he used it to seize power. Two generals, who opposed and had threatened to mobilize troops, were executed; one in Kaesong and another in Sinuiju while trying to escape across the border to us. The leadership is being held at a palace north of Pyongyang. Park has made no announcement of the change of power. The border is open. Train, rail and air services are operating normally.'

Song pointed to a paragraph on the report. 'So I can see. Who is this Air Vice-Marshal Qureshi from Pakistan who is on a train from Pyongyang?'

'He has just arrived in Beijing,' said Yan. 'I think it would be wise if you found a few minutes to meet him,' he said. Song detected a rare hesitancy. Yan spoke both softly and slowly, indicating that he was on unsteady ground.

Momentarily, Song saw Yan in a different light. His eyes were wide open, meeting Song's gaze, but looking beyond into something far more complex. He shifted his head to one side and let his mouth open, as if about to speak, but not sure what to say. Quickly, he recovered himself, straightening his tie. 'Air Vice-Marshal Qureshi ordered the assassination of President Asif Latif Khan,' Yan said, pulling down the cuffs of his jacket.

'I see,' whispered Song, putting the file on the window sill. 'Then he went straight to North Korea?'

'Pakistan is a very old friend of China,' Yan answered obliquely. 'It is better that you hear the facts from him.'

'But you knew, General?' Song's voice was both doubtful and angry.

'Of the assassination, I did not. I discovered it when Qureshi's aircraft flew into Chinese airspace without permission. The fighters scrambled to escort the plane down were picked up by Pakistani radar. The aircraft made no radio contact with us at all. Within minutes, though, I received a call on the military line from Islamabad. Our fighters escorted the aircraft to the North Korean border. In exchange for our hospitality, he agreed to return through Beijing to brief us.'

'Hence the train?'

'Correct. We would not allow him to return by air.'

Song made no secret of his relief. China was an unwieldy nation with many competing institutions and an appalling record of choosing allies. In the fifties it was insulted by the Soviet Union, paving the way for the supremacy of the United States. Had Moscow and Beijing sorted out their differences, the end of the Cold War might not have been so decisive. Its lesser alliances were equally disastrous. The Cambodian Khmer Rouge had turned out to be mass murderers. Burma was run by sadistic, drug-peddling generals. Pakistan, to whom China had given nuclear weapons technology, was an ungovernable morass of Islamic fundamentalism. Africa, where Chinese engineers had built railways, roads and socialism, had fallen back into tribalism and corruption. Only Cuba, nestled a hundred miles from Miami, had pulled through.

These relationships had been maintained because of the Chinese military. If Yan had chosen to keep Qureshi hidden from the President, it would have been easy to do so. Instead, he had gone to the other extreme of handing Song the file and insisting on a meeting with a man who had ordered the murder of a government leader and might well be connected with the Islamic uprisings that followed.

Out of the corner of his eye, Jamie Song saw a change of story on the television. It had moved from the ceremony in the United States to fighting in Brunei. He turned on the volume with the remote.

'Fleeing Islamic rebels have sabotaged oil wells around the western town of Seria, before heading for sanctuary in the Malaysian state of Sarawak, where they still hold territory,' said the presenter. 'Australia, however, says the situation is under control and within forty-eight hours the flaming wells should be capped.' The picture changed to amateur footage of the British-led raid to recapture Bandar Seri Begawan. 'But there's still no word as to the whereabouts of this man, Colonel Joharie Rahman, believed to be one of the three ringleaders of the attempted coup.'

Library footage showed Rahman at a military ceremony with the Sultan, King Charles of Great Britain and other dignitaries. He was a slight man, impeccably turned out, but as the camera moved closer, Jamie Song recognized a tightness and thinness of the lips, the head tilted slightly to the left, and the eyes cast down enough to make them look a little shifty. The face was one of a man with a troubled mind.

'Britain is coming under strong pressure to reveal the whereabouts of Rahman,' continued the presenter, 'and of this man, a British special forces colonel' – her voice accompanied the now familiar pictures of Burrows, pistol drawn, stepping over the prostrate bodies of the defeated Bruneian troops – 'who is believed to have led the attack, and is being accused of carrying out summary executions of the ringleaders involved. The British Prime Minister, Stuart Nolan—'

Song was about to mute the television again, when the presenter actually interrupted herself. 'I'm sorry we have to end that story for the time being to take you back here to the United States, where President Jim West, as you know, has been on the tarmac with the families as the coffins come in from Yokata. President Jim West is to make a live address.'

Jim West cut a defiant figure, standing without notes or a noticeable microphone, with the dark-green camouflaged tail of a military aircraft as his backdrop. His hair was wet from the rain, blown about, and water was dripping down his face.

'I share your grief,' he began, brushing away moisture with his right hand. 'To lose a loved one, to lose a child, to lose a wife or a husband, in such violent circumstances, is the most tragic experience any of us can imagine. When we grieve we like to both pay tribute and be with our loved ones, and that is why you are here, together, today. My job, as your President, is to tell you this. Right now, we do not know who is in control in North Korea. We believe there may have been a takeover of some kind. We do not know what, and we are asking our friends in Russia and China, who have a closer relationship with North Korea, to share their intelligence with us on this issue. We believe the missile was launched during the takeover. In other words, we do not believe it was deliberately targeted on Yokata or that any launch was authorized by the government of North Korea. Some of you may have seen that there has now been a shooting in the demilitarized zone at Panmunjom between the two Koreas. We are trying to get to the bottom of that incident as well. It shows us that things are not yet back to normal, and in this uncertainty I will not be authorizing any action that may result in the further loss of American lives. Having said that, I promise you that the person or people who caused that missile to kill your families will be brought to justice – or they will be killed while resisting capture. On that you have my word.'

As applause drifted across the airfield, Song muted the sound. 'China and Russia, Yan? I will ask you what you think, when we finish.'

Yan walked over to Song's desk and sat ramrod straight in an armchair on the other side. Song left the window for his desk as well. But he didn't sit down. He picked up two small marble balls resting in a tray there and rolled them around each other in the palm of his right hand. In late middle-age, it was a soothing technique to help him think.

Song had picked Yan as one of his advisers when China had changed the power structure at the very top of government. Song now shared power with the General Secretary of the Communist Party, whose job was to keep watch on China's ideological conscience, and with the Chairman of the Military Commission whose task was to keep the borders secure. To most of the world, Jamie Song was the leader of China, but inside Zhongnanhai the balance was far more precarious.

Song needed Yan as his eyes and ears of the military. He had brought the general into his trust precisely because he spoke his mind without airs and graces. Yan had cut his teeth in the 1979 war against Vietnam, taking shrapnel which was still in his leg. He had served in Xinjiang, forging an intelligence relationship with the corrupt police forces of Kazakhstan against the Muslim uprising of the Uigurs. In Tibet, he had destroyed cells of activists and even run special forces missions into Nepal and India to break up their sanctuaries. During the North Korean famine in the nineties, he had served on the border. It was then that Song, in his first spell as foreign minister, had noticed Yan. Song plucked him out and sent him to Hong Kong to teach him manners and etiquette, and then to serve as military attaché to Pyongyang. It was here that Yan had forged the contacts – shadowy as they might be – which were serving China so well today.

'We also have the report from the Air Koryo flight,' said Yan, offering Song a freshly printed sheet of paper. Song carefully rolled the balls back into their tray and took it.

'On its descent to Pyongyang, the aircraft suddenly pulled up, turned north, then dropped sharply to about two thousand feet,' said Yan. 'It maintained that altitude until it landed at a military airfield in Huichon. Two of our agents from the MSS were on board. They are alive, but they have not yet made contact.'

'These names you've underlined here?' asked Song.

'The interesting ones. Yes. The Iranians,' Yan explained.

'Do we know who they are?'

'We're still checking,' said Yan. 'One we know is Captain Mashoud Alband from the SAVAMA secret police. The two others we don't have. One was travelling on the passport of Mashhoud Najari, accredited to the Iranian embassy in Beijing. But Najari was seen inside the diplomatic compound with his children after the plane had taken off.'

Song glanced up. 'You're sure?'

'Yes, sir,' said Yan. 'We watch the embassy and the residences round the clock.'

'And the third?'

'The passenger register had him as Hossein Ansari.' Yan shrugged. 'No record of him anywhere.'

'The North Korean embassy must have issued a visa.'

'They've gone to ground.'

'Not surprising,' said Song, returning to the list. North Korea was a country entirely displaced by fantasy, whose people were still unaware that a man had landed on the moon. It was little wonder its diplomats hunkered down when cold truths were sprinkled into their world. Yet Jamie Song now had his own cold truth. With Park Ho in control, China had a most dangerous, but perhaps most useful, ally.

'I told the Americans we would accept a strike on the missile launch sites,' said Song, after a few moments. 'If they do, what will Park do? Go across the line?'

Yan shook his head. 'No. He's enjoying playing with them. He'd fire a missile from an underground silo. One the Americans couldn't touch with conventional bombing.

The problem the Koreans had in the past was with staging. They took years to get the second stage working. It was a problem with the starter motor and the solid fuel. They overcame it. With Yokata, he's proved he has a working three-stage rocket. That means it's conceivable that he could deliver a warhead to the United States.'

'Then Jim West will throw everything he has at him.'

'Precisely,' said Yan. 'And that is when he'll cross the line. But before that happens, comrade, there is a detail you should be aware of. Park Ho could launch from either Chunggan-up or Paekun, the two sites closest to our border with North Korea. It means that an American strike on him would be only miles away from Chinese territory.'

Song, a veteran of scores of boardroom and diplomatic negotiations, looked at his intelligence adviser with utter surprise. 'Do you mind, General, telling me how you know this?'

Yan remained deadpan. 'I spoke at length to Park. I have known him for many years. He is a formidable strategist.'

'Should I speak to him, too?' asked Song, refreshed and surprised by Yan's bluntness.

'Not yet,' said Yan. 'He already has a hostage with President West. As soon as you contact him, you become a hostage, too.'

Song nodded thoughtfully. A car door banged outside. Yan got up and went to the window. 'Qureshi has arrived,' he said, heading for the door, but then pausing and walking back to Song.

'I have revealed these things to you because you command great respect among us, comrade, as a political operator. I would trust no one more than you to see us through this great danger. I also would ask you to keep what I have told you completely to yourself.'

'Of course,' said Song softly, as Yan left the room. Song

moved to the window. The afternoon sun had broken up more ice on the lake and by leaning round he could see coloured kites being flown high in the distance in Tiananmen Square. So Quereshi's appointment had been made anyway. Song cleared the window of more condensation to get a better look, and saw Yan greeting the Pakistani Air Vice-Marshal, dressed in full uniform, a peaked blue cap under his arm, his eyes alive with colour and purpose, his hand gripping Yan's elbow, and looking around him in the heart of Zhongnanhai like a devouring force of nature.

Yan pointed towards the door, and leaned towards Qureshi, whispering. Song watched the two men and wondered who held real power in his nation.

Tassudaq Qureshi did not enjoy lying to Jamie Song. He also regretted the death of President Asif Latif Khan. He admired the courage of General Park Ho in North Korea. The sending of an unarmed missile into the Yokata base in Japan was an act of style and subtlety he found missing among his own colleagues. He was surprised the British had acted so decisively in Brunei, although he had never expected Colonel Joharie Rahman and his conspirators to hold Brunei for long.

Qureshi anticipated that territory in the other areas – northern Borneo, the Malaysian peninsula and the southern Philippines – would be lost again in time. The uprisings and the violent reaction to them would, however, have enough support to begin low-intensity guerrilla wars throughout that region, and that was what he and Memed had intended.

But most of all, he was appalled at the attack on the Indian Parliament. To gather a force of insurgents to act with such precision and skill would have taken years to plan. How did they get their vehicles? How did they get their aircraft? From where did the explosives come? Where did they practise? From where were they recruited? How would it change things?

The cordoned-off first-class compartment of an Air China Boeing 747–400, chartered for his exclusive use and heading through the night over the north Asian deserts and mountains, was as good a place as any to take stock.

At one stage during the day, Qureshi had wondered if he would ever get out of China alive.

On his way to the airport, he had been ordered back to Zhongnanhai after Song's difficult telephone call with Vasant Mehta. Yan was there, but distant, standing by the door. Qureshi, greeted earlier as a statesman equal to the Chinese President, was now made to stand in front of Song's desk, diplomacy thrown to the wind, and Song, his face blazing with anger, fired questions as if in a court of law.

'Did you know about this?' he began, throwing a newspaper down on the desk.

'Jamie, if you could just explain—'

But Song didn't. 'Answer me, damn you, or I'll have you dragged off right now, so you'll never be heard of again. Remember you're in China.' Qureshi's eyes darkened. There was something in the way Song issued the warning that sent a chill through him.

Song pointed to the newspaper again. 'Did you know about this? And I want yes or no answers.'

'No.'

'Do you know the group who carried out the attack?'

'Yes.'

'Is one or more of their leaders in Pakistan?'

'Yes.'

'Are they trained in Pakistan?'

'In Azad Kashmir.' Qureshi shifted awkwardly on his feet and brushed his hand down his moustache.

Song stalked round the desk. 'Don't mess with me, Qureshi. Azad Kashmir is your territory. So I will ask you again: Is the Lashkar-e-Jannat trained in Pakistan?'

'Yes.'

'Did you order the attack on the Indian Parliament?'

'No.'

'Do you know those who did?'

'No.'

'Do you know senior members of the intelligence agencies or military who would have supported the attack?'

Qureshi hesitated. He glanced round towards Yan, but Yan might have been a statue for all the support he was giving. 'Yes.'

'Did you know in advance about the assassination of President Khan?'

'No.' That was the big lie, and to tell it, Qureshi made sure his expression remained unchanged, his eyes lowered, his hands clasped in front of him, his head slightly tilted down. Gone was the ebullience and confidence of the former fighter pilot. In its place, Qureshi had installed humility because that was what Song in his present mood demanded.

'Did you know in advance about the uprisings in South-East Asia?'

'No.'

'Do you know the colonels who staged the *coup d'état* in Brunei?'

'No.'

'Did you transport any weaponry, nuclear, chemical, biological or conventional, in your aircraft to North Korea?'

'No.' And that was the second lie. Qureshi briefly closed his eyes and wondered if Song had noticed and if he had guessed. The next question took some time in coming. 'Do you support the assassination of President Khan?'

'No.'

'Do you support the attack on the Indian Parliament?'

'No.'

'Do you support the uprisings in South-East Asia?'

'I understand them.'

'Answer me, damn you. Do you support them?'

'Yes. But we have not sent any weapons, money, men.' Qureshi stepped forward, prompting Yan to stiffen. 'I support it because in my heart I believe the Islamic people have been suppressed and their uprising is a natural manifestation of that.' Now he leant on the desk, and Song let him. 'Your question is not one to which I can give a yes or no answer. You should know that, President Song. China is what she is today because Mao Tse-tung led her people against oppression.'

He moved back, his point made, his emotions displayed. 'And you have no right to treat me like a criminal.'

'Nor did I have the right to treat you like a national leader,' retorted Song. 'Yet I made the mistake of doing so.' He picked up the marble balls, testing their weight. As he rotated them in his hand, he walked over to Yan and spoke quietly to him so Qureshi couldn't hear. Yan nodded and left the room.

'Vasant Mehta has asked me to withdraw our technicians and scientists from your missile and nuclear programme within seven days,' said Song, pacing the room, keeping Qureshi with his back to him. Qureshi looked round sharply. 'Mehta wants us to share our intelligence,' Song continued. 'He wants a full arms embargo on Pakistan.'

'Impossible,' said Qureshi shaking his head.

'Not impossible,' contradicted Song. He moved round so that he faced Qureshi and sat casually on the corner of the desk. 'I want the men responsible for planning, ordering and executing that attack arrested and brought to China. I am providing you with a 747–400 and two companies of special forces troops who will secure the aircraft for the journey back. The men you deliver to me will match a list provided by India. I will give you three days. If you do not comply, I will accede to the Indian Prime Minister's request. China's alliance with Pakistan will be over. Should India have to go to war with you, we will support India. Am I clear?'

'Three days?' asked Qureshi. 'You said Mehta gave you a week.'

Song pressed a button under the ridge of the desk. Qureshi heard Song's voice from a speaker on a far wall: '. . . *China's alliance with Pakistan will be over. Should India have to go to war with you, we will support India. Am I clear?*'

Qureshi looked furiously at Song.

'Within half an hour, Mehta will have this recording,' said Song. 'You may have trouble convincing your fellow officers. So we have four extra days. For now, you can think of me as your friend.'

Qureshi tried to sleep, but the shuttling from city to city had left him without exercise and his body restless. Mehta had thrown down a gauntlet to Song, and Song had passed it on to Qureshi. The gauntlet would stop with whoever resisted taking it, and Qureshi's mind churned as to whether that should be him, and whether, even if he wanted to, he could achieve what Song had demanded.

Out of the window the night was absolutely clear, and he was able to see clusters of lights on the ground from 30,000 feet. The sky map told him he was above Xinjiang, China's own troubled border province where Islam was challenging the rule of the Communist Party.

There had been a deal, struck many years ago. Pakistan would stop insurgents being imported into Xinjiang. They could go to Afghanistan and to Kashmir, and after the 2001 War on Terror they were sent to Indonesia, Malaysia and the Philippines. But never would one trained Jihad fighter be allowed to operate in Xinjiang or anywhere that directly endangered Chinese territory. If they were found, they would be rooted out and executed. In return, Pakistan would receive unlimited military support from China.

Song must have calculated that the attack on the Indian Parliament was a greater threat to China's stability than insurgency in Xinjiang, and was, therefore, planning to break the agreement.

Qureshi would have faced down Song, and told him some cold facts of political life. But it was too early, and some elements of Qureshi's plan were not yet in place.

But Song was wrong. If the momentum was to have been stopped, it should have been in 1979, when Pakistan's democratically elected prime minister was executed by a military dictator; it should have been in 1980 when Pakistan became the launch base for the Islamic forces fighting the Soviet invasion of Afghanistan; it should have been in 1990, when the Soviet Union was defeated, American money vanished, and the money of extreme Islam poured into the schools, the military and the government. And when the 2001 War on Terror began, it was too late. To the outside world, President Khan had been a symbol of hope. But for Qureshi, he was an instrument of the Americans, placed there, bankrolled by them, and the ultimate weapon designed to destroy the vision for which Pakistan was created.

Yes, Qureshi had been right to have him killed. Had Khan remained in office, the nation would have slipped backwards again. America had never understood that democracy created tribalism; that the money needed for electioneering spread corruption; that broken promises of politicians created despair and resentment.

Strange. Jamie Song understood. He and his predecessors had kept China free of democratic institutions. Strange that he was acting as he was!

As Qureshi drifted in and out of sleep, his mind trying to run with the light turbulence and the change of engine sound, this was the question that perplexed him most. No nation destroys a historic alliance without having another to put in its place. But China and India could never be allies. Their borders, their beliefs, their ambitions would all make it impossible. So what was Song playing at, and would Qureshi be able to call his bluff?

The Air China plane landed and taxied to a remote area of the airport at Islamabad. Qureshi changed into a full dress uniform, checked himself in the toilet mirror, smoothing down his jacket and running a tiny comb through his moustache. A limousine waited at the foot of the steps for him, but no colleagues. He was driven alone to Chaklala, the military cantonment area of Rawalpindi. From the limousine's darkened windows, he was shamefully reminded of the filth and poverty in his country. However new a building, however freshly repaired a road, a beggar in rags would find his way on to it to remind him that whatever had been built was only a facade covering the real failed texture of his nation. China had not been like this; nor had North Korea.

As the car pulled up and the door was opened for him, Qureshi identified the distinct dark uniform of the Special Services Group taking up positions around his vehicle. He stepped out. The captain in charge saluted. He walked, unaccompanied, through to the General Headquarters. Staff stopped their work and stood to attention as he passed. The lift was ready for him, and took him straight down to the underground command and control room. As the lift door opened, Brigadier Najeeb Hussain stood at the head of a line of military officers, his hand outstretched.

'Welcome, President Tassudaq Qureshi of Pakistan,' he said, with a huge smile on his face. 'The destiny of our nation is now in your hands.'

23

Rawalpindi, Pakistan

Qureshi stepped across the threshold, finding his hand grasped by Najeeb Hussain, and hearing the rumble of outdated air conditioning in the silence which only military discipline could ever instil in Pakistan. Behind Hussain was Admiral Javed Mohmand, commander of the navy, a long, sinewy man, his hands rubbing together in front of him, his eyes blinking and wide, as if Qureshi was an apparition from the heavens. Next to him was General Zaid Musa, taller but more muscular than Hussain, smiling and welcoming, but his face a little too sincere, given that he and Qureshi had violently disagreed in the past.

As Qureshi moved down the line, shaking hands, squeezing elbows, patting shoulders, he understood how, at the precise moment of a military takeover, power was reversed. Momentarily it was being held by the men who greeted him. But when he reached the end of the line, Hussain ushered him through a door into a briefing room. Inside was a group of officers from all services, who, if he got it wrong, would be the ones to overthrow and possibly execute him.

Hussain moved slightly ahead of Qureshi and lightly held the back of a chair. 'We are military men, so I will not spend time on flowery words,' he said. 'As you may have heard, Vice-President Zafar has been taken ill with heart problems. This morning he left for medical treatment in Dubai.' Hussain paused as a barely detectable ripple of mirth spread through the audience.

'The new President of Pakistan is Air Vice-Marshal Qureshi. All of you know him, either personally or through his formidable reputation as a leader. We have chosen him because of his military record, his dedication to our missile and nuclear programmes and his determination to see our vision come to fruition. President Qureshi has, within the past hour, arrived back in Pakistan from China. He has also been in North Korea, which, as you know, has undergone a similar change of government as here.' Hussain let go the chair, clapped his hands together and stepped to one side. 'So without further ado, gentlemen, I present to you the President of Pakistan.'

Qureshi walked to the centre of a small dais in front of a blank, grubby white screen pulled down from the low ceiling. The room served both as a briefing area and a mess room. The central area was taken up with classroom-style desks and chairs. Around the sides were old sofas, armchairs and coffee tables, marked with cigarette burns. The badly circulated air smelt of stale tobacco. On the walls were a mix of posters and maps, some with Islamic slogans, some with military slogans. There were several montages of regiments on the front line in Kashmir and ships' crews out on exercise in the Indian Ocean.

He cast his eyes over his audience. These were the officers who still ran ships, submarines, aircraft, artillery and tanks. They knew where the fuel, the ammunition and the missiles were stored. They had the keys to warehouses. They commanded men in battle. They were colonels, squadron leaders and warship captains. Without their support the generals could not have acted as they did. What Qureshi once was, they were now, and as they sat, some with notebooks like students in a classroom, their expressions were not of the sycophancy and congratulations that had greeted Qureshi outside the lift but of judgement.

But how much did they know? Were they aware of the new missile arsenals under separate command and control structures assembled at five different sites in the country? Did they know that North Korea was now assembling a Pakistani tactical nuclear weapon to use, if necessary, against the United States on the Pacific front? Did they know that it was he, Qureshi, who had devised the assassination of President Khan and called in a favour from al-Qaida to carry it out?

'This room's a dump,' said Qureshi bluntly, putting his cap on the desk in front of him. 'As soon as I'm done, it will be cleared up, repainted and the air conditioning will be fixed.' He offered no charm, no courtesy. He stared down his audience, his eyes blazing with the irritation, until suddenly, a mask of change rippled across his face.

'My parents come from Delhi,' he continued, more softly. 'It was touch and go as to whether they would abandon their home at Partition and move to Pakistan. Or whether they would stay as part of the Muslim elite in a secular India. If they had, I might have become an Air Vice-Marshal in the Indian air force, priming the airborne Agni missile for launches against Pakistan. Such is the knife-edge of this damned situation we find ourselves in.'

He noticed the glances across the room, his analogy bringing flashes of doubt to the younger men's faces. 'I lost my family home in India and we endured the trauma of Partition in order to pursue a vision. It has been a long and troubled journey. But I have never—' he paused, using silence to underline his point. When he took up again he dropped his voice: 'I have never forgotten why my parents made that sacrifice. I am here with you today to ensure we finish it.'

He watched faces, challenging them to challenge him. But there was quiet. 'I trust that each of you knows why you are here today. I trust that when you tell your children and your grandchildren about the path we are about to pursue you can do so with your heads held high and that you can speak without shame or excuses.' He walked to one side of the room, turned on his heel and walked back, preparing his next line. 'Let me share with you what I hope to tell the next generation. That Pakistan was created as an Islamic state. For sixty years, it has dithered. Democracy creates tribalism and corruption because voters are loyal to their clan and money is needed to oil the machine of electioneering. But military rule destroys the imagination of the people. Science, arts, the ingredients of a great civilization cannot flourish from the barrel of a gun. This has been our dilemma, and this is what you and I are now going to solve. When you return to your commands bear in mind the great responsibility you have taken on by being with me today in this room.'

24

Washington, DC, USA

The Chinese ambassador to the United Nations in New York had lingered outside the Security Council meeting room. He had a message to deliver, informally, verbally and swiftly. The other ambassadors filed past him. North Korea had been at the top of the agenda, but nothing of substance had been discussed or decided. It rarely was in the UN. The ambassador stepped forward just as his American counterpart left the room. With a light hand on the elbow he drew him to one side. Back in his office, the American diplomat telephoned Mary Newman who arranged a meeting with the President and drove straight to the White House.

'Jamie Song's broken his word,' she told Jim West. 'China will oppose any missile strikes or air attacks by US, Japanese or South Korean forces on North Korean military facilities on a line between Anju and Hungnam. It's just below the fortieth parallel.'

'What does it leave us?' said the President, turning to Chris Pierce, who was unfolding a map of the Korean peninsula with missile launch sites marked on it, together with facilities for storing nuclear, chemical and biological weapons.

'There are six sites we know of above the fortieth parallel,' he said. 'Five if we exclude the test site at Nodong. Two of those have been designed for medium-range missiles targeting our military bases in Japan. They might have been modified for a launch on our west coast. In short, Mr President, if we can't hit them, there is little point in making any strike at all. Either we knock out all their launch facilities in one shot, or we risk them firing on us with whatever they've got left.'

'And we've got Japan threatening to send in an armada of warships,' mumbled West, looking around the hurriedly put together meeting of his Principals Committee. Only Pierce, Newman and Brock had managed to make it in time. He eyed each one individually. 'Can any of you tell me that your President hasn't been got by the balls?'

Brock smiled and Newman rolled her eyes, but before anyone could answer, the intercom lit up and Jenny Rinaldi's voice came over. 'Sorry to interrupt, Mr President. The National Security Advisor's office needs to speak to Mr Brock urgently.'

Peter Brock was on his feet. 'I'll take it outside,' he said, leaving the room.

A brief uncomfortable silence followed, with the President left between the two opposing views of his administration. It was Pierce who put forward a suggestion: 'Why don't we call Park's bluff, Mr President? We get South Korea to apologize for the killing at Panmunjom. We accept their explanation for the missile. The status quo resumes. Japan will have no reason to invoke article six. We turn the issue into one of development aid. They get no more until they abandon their missile programme and let in inspectors. After a decent interval we bring up the smallpox programme, and ask for access. If they comply, we build up a free North Korea, just like we have done with the whole of East Asia.'

'That's what we've been doing for years,' said Newman. 'And all it does is buy them time.'

'We might be buying lives,' snapped Pierce.

'Chris,' said West, wanting to avoid further confrontation. 'I need to be able to go with air strikes, bombing and missiles, on North Korea within twenty-four hours. Mary, can you work out a formula along the lines that Chris suggested and call in the Chinese ambassador? Tell him if Jamie Song doesn't want us to bomb those goddamn missile sites, we want China to do it.'

'China?' repeated Newman, about to object, but then thinking better of it.

'That's right,' said West. 'From where I come from, if one son of a bitch objects to your doing something, you tell him to either shut up or do it himself. Let's see what Jamie's answer is to that.'

The door clicked open and Brock stepped back into the room. 'Mr President. We have confirmation that there has indeed been a coup in Pakistan. The country is now in the hands of Islamist military commanders.'

25

Islamabad, Pakistan

After dining with his family in his sprawling house just outside Islamabad, Qureshi walked through the garden, past the unfamiliar sight of armed guards deployed everywhere around him, and climbed into the back seat of the waiting car. Below him were the glittering lights of the city. From their density, he could distinguish between the slums and the wide boulevards of the government buildings and Parliament. Only the slums existed as a real, functioning environment. The other half of Pakistan was a facade.

Qureshi had told nobody of the deadline set him by Jamie Song. Within the next six days, he had to arrest anyone involved in the attack on the Indian Parliament and deliver them to Chinese troops waiting on board a 747 at Islamabad airport, to be flown to a jail in China, where they would be held without trial. He respected Jamie Song for his imagination, but that was all it was.

Qureshi had showered, eaten supper with his wife, Tasneem, smoked, paced his garden and thought. He had not mentioned a word to Tasneem. Like most Pakistanis, she knew that their vice-president was in exile, but remained ignorant about the military takeover. And Tasneem would never intrude into her husband's work or his thoughts on such matters.

Their children were away from home. Akbar, Zeenat and Bashir were at boarding school. Javed was on a gap year in France, and Farrah, the oldest, had just moved out and set up in an apartment in Lahore.

It was this and not the unfolding political crisis that concentrated Tasneem's mind. Farrah, a beautiful and vulnerable nineteen-year-old, had defied her mother's wishes and had moved out of the house and out of the city in which they lived. Qureshi, with only a fraction of his mind on his daughter's wilfulness, had backed his wife by banning Farrah from leaving. To which she had said in English: 'No wonder this country's such a dump with people like you running it.'

With his wife in tears, Farrah had left. Mother and daughter had flung their arms around each other, reconciled to the inevitable, neither willing to sacrifice more than each already had. Qureshi had hung back in the hall, his pipe full but unlit. Uncoiling herself from Tasneem, Farrah had waved, like a showdancer in an American movie. 'Bye, Dad. Don't be a stranger. I love you. Remember that.'

And all Qureshi could manage was a quick smile and a wave, before retreating into the safety of a flaring match and the smell of freshly lit tobacco. In that moment he wondered whether he should ever have educated his daughter; whether he should have allowed her to grow up in a world of denim jeans and uncovered faces; whether he should have confined her forcibly; whether he had failed his wife; whether Farrah was an example of what his nation should never become.

He whispered the address into the ear of his driver. They retained their elevation, leaving the built-up residential area and the glow of street lights. The driver turned to the right, heading further north towards the Margala Hills. The road deteriorated. The car bumped over potholes hewn out by rain. The headlights lit up a shepherd, who froze for a moment, then bustled his flock to the side of the road, while the car passed.

Only Qureshi's driver of twenty years' service was with him. A sensible military leader, freshly appointed, would be unwise to trust his bodyguards with a meeting so sensitive.

The driver changed down to a lower gear to negotiate a rut. They turned a corner around the edge of a mountain. Qureshi pressed down his window. The air was colder and fresher. He could make out the shape of another car, parked just off the road, and a single, narrow flashlight beam, pointing down to the brown, grassless ground.

'Stop,' said Qureshi softly. 'And cut the engine.' He took his pistol out of the holster, put a round in the breech, but kept the safety catch on. Holding it in his right hand, hanging loosely by his side, he stepped out of the car and moved to the centre of the road. The flashlight ahead went off. On both sides there were static shapes of cattle grazing.

Qureshi walked forward until he saw the shape of a man leaning against the vehicle. He slipped off the safety catch of his weapon. The man opened the door and the interior lamp came on. The man leant inside, putting his face into the light, so Qureshi could see it.

He recognized him as General Wei Guo, the military attaché at the Chinese embassy to Islamabad. As far as Qureshi could make out, there was no driver. Guo had driven the four-wheel-drive Cherokee jeep to the spot himself. Guo slipped back out of the car and stood up again. He flared a match, lighting a cigarette, reaffirming his identity to Qureshi.

'General, thank you for coming,' said Qureshi, when he reached the vehicle. He shook his head, as Guo offered him a cigarette, and glanced inside the car to ensure that what he had come for was installed inside. Guo noticed. 'It's there,' he said, in Urdu with a smile. 'I will connect the line for you, then step away, so you have privacy.'

'Complete privacy?' asked Qureshi. He had worked with Guo for too many years for either of them to use diplomatic jargon.

Guo drew on his cigarette. 'From me, yes. I cannot guarantee what General Yan has arranged at the other end. My instinct, however, is that he would not wish anyone to know about this conversation.'

Qureshi put his weapon back in the holster and rested his hand on the bonnet. Guo opened the cover of the glove compartment to reveal a black box with a small screen, a keyboard and a dialling pad. He brought out a wire, with a rubber sucker on the end, pulled it to its full length and attached it to a precise spot on the roof, from which he extracted a metal antenna which looped around on itself. Then from inside the glove compartment, he took a box no bigger than a cigarette packet. Inside it were layers of folded aluminium, which Guo let drop down into a flat circular shape. He attached that to the antenna on the roof, making a small satellite dish.

'The NSA may pick up the actual transmission,' explained Guo. 'But they will not be able to penetrate the scrambler. Voice recognition will be impossible and they will have difficulty in pinpointing the location. Since their analysts are not looking for it, they will probably not even notice it.' A gust of wind struck up, blowing dust across their faces. Guo eyed the dish, satisfied that it swayed well but did not move. He opened the back door, where a telephone receiver was clipped into the back of the seat. Qureshi climbed in, just as the red light flashed silently on the handset. He looked up at Guo, who nodded. 'It's General Yan Xiaodong for you, sir,' he said. Guo slid off the seat, closed the door of the car and walked some way away, until his figure blended with the darkness.

Qureshi waited for static and white noise to clear from the line, indicating that the two scramblers had linked up.

'Thank you for speaking to me in these unusual circumstances,' said Qureshi. The last time he had seen Yan was on the steps of the Central Committee building in Zhongnanhai. He had said nothing beyond the formalities one dignitary would say to another. As Qureshi had watched him through the tinted dark glass of his Audi, Yan wore a crooked frown, and a look of genuine puzzlement. But he had given nothing away.

'It's always a pleasure to speak to an old friend,' said Yan. 'And while you may be in an unusual place, I am in my office where one telephone looks no different from any other.'

Qureshi paused, allowing for a delay on the satellite linking. If he read Yan correctly, the 'old friend' reference meant Pakistan still commanded the support of the Chinese military. The office location warned that others were listening in. The fact that Yan agreed to the call indicated that he knew the only topic of conversation was to be Jamie Song's ultimatum.

'You, too, are an old friend,' replied Qureshi, matching the veiled language. 'It has been a difficult half-century. We have fought wars against the same, common enemy. You and I have much shared ground.' He saw the glow of Guo's cigarette end far away from the car. Behind him were the sidelights of his own vehicle. His driver would be watching Guo through a hunting rifle with telescopic infrared sights. 'I have a problem and am calling to ask for your help,' continued Qureshi.

'I'll do anything I can,' said Yan, switching, like Qureshi, to the personal pronoun.

'I will do everything in my power to maintain the friendship between our nations,' said Yan. 'As you know, my power is limited, but I have one idea that might be successful.'

26

Chunggang-up missile base, North Korea

Park Ho, standing at the base of the inert launch pad, resting his hand on a piece of green canvas which covered the fin, looked skywards towards the heavy steel and lead doors which covered the top of the silo. Originally, the base had been designed to target the US military forces on the Japanese island of Okinawa. Park had also seen its potential as one of the key facilities for the long-range Taepodong-2 missile.

Among the trees, some buildings were visible, painted in a camouflage of green and brown. They were set apart from each other with good, sealed roads running between them. These were mainly administrative offices, staff quarters, an observation tower and a helipad. The key services of fuel storage, monitoring and tracking, assembly plant and test facility were all underground. They could withstand a direct hit from anything except a nuclear weapon.

Park stepped back as far as he could to get a better view. The rounded walls were made of steel, behind which was more concrete and finally the granite of the mountain into which the bunker was hewn. The circulated air had a dank, metallic smell to it. Hardened cables ran across the floor, through the side of the silo into a control room dug in several hundred metres away.

Right at the top, Park saw the lift jolt and begin its downward journey to collect him.

Had he acted and taken power earlier, the missile might have been ready earlier. His predecessor, obsessed with everything American, insisted on trying to develop three solid-fuel propelled stages powered by hydrazine and nitrogen tetroxide. But, knowing that the technology would remain beyond his nation for decades to come, Park had kept working on the less efficient liquid-fuelled engines powered by a mix of 20 per cent gasoline and 80 per cent kerosene.

His predecessor had insisted on testing. But the liquid fuel was so corrosive and toxic that after each test the engine would have to be stripped down and reassembled. Technically, with so many new components, it wouldn't even be the same engine. So each firing *was* a test firing. Park had developed missile delivery at its rawest. Against the psychology of the United States, he was sure it was lethal enough to win a war.

The lift was no more than a square platform, hauled up and down on cables and enclosed by a metal cage, whose door was kept closed with bent wire. Park stepped in alone, pulled on a pair of thin, rubber gloves and put on a hard helmet hanging on the side of the cage. As the lift ascended, Park followed the contours of the three stages of the missile. The first bulky stage rose up 16 metres. The second stage narrowed for 14 metres. The third stage was smaller and had been redesigned to take the small amount of solid fuel needed for the 100-second motor thrust. Nestling right at the top – 53 metres high – was the delivery capsule, where two technicians were working on installing the payload.

The lift stopped. Park unlatched the cage door but stayed inside it as he watched the two men position the final aluminium stays which would keep the weapon in place.

The potential of the missile as a weapon of delivery was awesome. Park thought back to his most vivid childhood memory – his first memory, because all those which preceded it became bland and forgettable. He was five years old. It was 15 March 1951 and all around him was devastation. No building was left standing except the railway station, as if the world had been ended by a cruel, dark cloud. Why he was there as American troops were advancing in Seoul, Park never found out. His mother, dazed and in panic, clutched his hand, and she dragged him towards the railway because she thought there might be trains to get them out.

But instead of finding trains, they came face to face with a column of American tanks. The GIs jumped down and separated Park from his mother. He was lifted up on to a man's shoulder and given a candy. He threw it to the ground and screamed to stay with his mother. But how would they know what he was saying? Why would they care? They had had their own feelings knocked out of them by the war. He watched his mother being dragged away. As she struggled, they tore her top, and soon she was exposed, flailing. They shouted in English. But he couldn't understand them. His mother broke free and began running. They caught her, hit her in the face and she fell. Then Park heard a phrase that he would never forget. 'Fucking useless whore.' And the GI who spoke it pulled out a pistol and shot her as she lay on the ground.

The soldier carrying Park said, 'Oh, shit. Come on, kid, let's get you somewhere better.'

The soldier had only taken a few steps when he crumpled silently, as if, while lowering Park gently to the ground, he had slipped and fallen. Park tumbled off his shoulders, ran and was whisked into the arms of the Chinese sniper who had fired the shot.

Back home, Park was brought up by his father, who spoke all the time about the glorious victory of the war. Park knew differently, and he set out to learn what had caused the terrible destruction of his country. He had listened and not argued. Once accepted by the elite, he had access to Western books and he studied international history, absorbing the nuances of politics and power balance. He emerged guided by a simple truth. With one intercontinental ballistic missile any nation, however small, could take on a superpower.

The nuclear research laboratories were set up at Yongbyon in the sixties, staffed by scientists trained in the Soviet Union. In the seventies, when Park became involved, they concentrated on refining and converting nuclear fuels. But it wasn't until 1982 that Park, aged only thirty-six, persuaded the Great Leader Kim Il-sung himself to begin building North Korea's own nuclear weapons and the missiles with which to deliver them.

Park pushed through the process of acquiring and reprocessing nuclear fuel. Nuclear reactors and reprocessing plants were built at Taechon and Yongbyon. When his government signed a deal with the United States to stop the nuclear programme in 1994, Park ignored it. He procured detonators from China and the guidance system from Russia. When the US ordered North Korea to dismantle its facilities, Park simply moved them. At that time, the United Nations weapons inspectors calculated that 24 kilograms of weapons-grade plutonium had been extracted from spent fuel rods at Yongbyon. The real figure was triple that. The US estimated North Korea could make three nuclear warheads, using 8 kilograms per warhead. Park's plan was to use just 2 kilograms a warhead. With the five higher-quality tactical weapons flown in from Pakistan, Park would be able to make forty warheads. The size of the explosion was irrelevant. Park knew he could never destroy America or Japan. But he could paralyse them with the terror of a nuclear holocaust.

One of the engineers stood up from leaning into the delivery capsule. He saw Park and saluted. 'We'll be finished in a couple of minutes, comrade,' he said, tapping his colleague on his shoulder. The second man lifted his head abruptly and took off his goggles. His was a face without subservience. There was no awe or fear of Park. 'So, we've done it,' he said with a smile. 'We've damn well done it.'

'Indeed we have, my friend,' responded Park.

'I have some final checks to make on the guidance system. We are checking the prevailing winds in the target area. Apart from that, it's done.'

Kee Tae Shin was the first scientist Park had picked out and sent to the Soviet Union in the seventies. Both were young, forceful and idealistic. After the death of Kim Il-sung in 1994, Park and Kee had urged his successor and son, Kim Jong-il, not to sign the deal with the United States. When Kim refused, Park, then a colonel, and Kee brought together sympathetic scientists and military officers in a highly secretive factional clique, ready to move if ever the new leadership came close to forging the sort of relationship with the United States that Eastern Europe and Russia had.

Park's faction had reaffirmed its commitment to the three founding concepts of the nation. There would be an eventual reunification of the Korean peninsula. Pyongyang would be the capital. Military force would be used to achieve it.

After the US campaigns in Iraq and Afghanistan, Park sensed that the American searchlight would again fall in his direction. They would demand that North Korea abandon its nuclear and missile programme; that it reform its political and economic system; that it allow itself to be swamped by South Korean money. Just a few miles across the Chinese border were factories built by Hyundai, Daewoo, Lucky Gold Star and others, waiting to move in on the collapse of his nation. Park planned for them to rot.

His predecessor was a weak man. He watched CNN and

Hollywood blockbusters, drank Jim Beam whisky and had bagels flown in from a bakery in Hong Kong. He passed secrets to the United Nations in order to win favour, and Park knew it might only be months before enough was known to destroy his programme by force.

It was then that Park contacted Qureshi, who gave him a simple solution. 'The Americans would have difficulty understanding nuclear conflict on one front,' Qureshi had argued. 'If they have two, they will withdraw. I would forfeit my life on it.' A year later, when they met briefly in Beijing, Qureshi said, 'When you are ready, let me know.'

Park did, and Qureshi put him in touch with Ahmed Memed. Park then wondered if he needed something else altogether, something that, without argument, would tip the balance towards indisputable victory. And even now, he wondered whether history would judge his decision as bold or rash.

Kee pushed back his hair to clear it of the straps and was about to slip the goggles down, when Park spoke again. 'You know, my friend, for more than five hundred years, from 1392 to 1910, Korea had the most stable system of government anywhere in the world. The Chosun dynasty taught us self-control, self-cultivation, benevolence, wisdom and propriety. We learned about loyalty to the ruler and to parents. We created a perfect world of strong and benevolent government. The Japanese invaders came, and we repelled them. Western missionaries arrived. We closed our doors to them. Everyone wanted to be in Korea, and we refused them. We became known as the Hermit Kingdom. We were the envy of many nations.'

Park stepped out on to the narrow platform encircling the head of the missile. Barely one foot above him was the sliding roof which if opened would let in a blaze of winter sunshine. Park raised his hand and ran his fingers down the wafer-thin gap dividing the two sides of the roof.

'But in the end we had a weak leader,' he continued, dropping his arm and letting his hand rest for a moment on the scientist's shoulders. 'He let in the Japanese. He trusted them. Our men were beaten. Our women were raped. We were not even allowed to speak our own language. It would have been better if we had fought and died than suffered such humiliation.'

Kee waited to see if his friend, now the new leader of the nation, had finished, or whether he would share more thoughts with him. Park touched the side of the missile head with his forefinger, gently, as if he was afraid of damaging it. 'Will it work?' he asked.

'It will work,' said the scientist confidently. 'But when, Park? When?' he added, using a familiar term of address.

'Very soon,' said Park.

'It will take four hours to load the fuel,' said Kee. 'After that we can be ready at any time.'

27

Washington, DC, USA

'Delay them, will you, John?' asked West.

'I can move them on fifteen minutes,' said Kozerski, gathering his files together at the end of his daily morning meeting with the President.

'That'll do,' said West, pensively. 'And, John, let's make that an undisturbed slot.' He briefly slumped back in his chair, then drew himself upright again.

'Jim, are you OK?' asked Kozerski, halfway out the door.

'I'm fine,' smiled West reassuringly. 'I need to make a couple of personal phone calls, that's all.' Before Kozerski could object, he added: 'To family, John. Not for fund-raising.'

With his Chief of Staff gone, West moved to his working office off the Oval Office, which was mainly a conference room. After Valerie had died, he had had his office redecorated in harsher, more masculine colours. The psychologists would have had a field day if he'd allowed them in. He had needed something to change, but it wasn't going to be the residence or the entertaining areas which Valerie had painstakingly designed with impeccable taste.

West pulled open a drawer under his desk, unplugged a video mobile from its charger, flipped down one name in the address book and punched in a call. He kept only two numbers programmed in. One was his son Chuck's in Oakland. They talked about once a week now, but never about politics. Chuck thought harshly of the government's policies which had forced him to shut down two depots and lay off hundreds of drivers and staff. The other number was his daughter Lizzie's roaming global mobile, which would find her anywhere in the world.

He sat behind the desk and set up the camera, waiting as Lizzie answered the call. When the screen flickered on, all he could see was her red hair splattered over the tiny lens while she tried to hook up the phone. Lizzie was walking with a weatherboard building behind her and a Chevrolet four-wheel-drive roaring past.

Once clear of hair, her face broke into a huge grin when she saw her father. 'God, Dad, you do choose the best of times,' she said sarcastically, stepping down what looked like a side street, and giving West a sudden and welcome drop in traffic noise. 'But hey, you look like you're about to address the nation. Loosen up, it's me, Lizzie.'

West loved Lizzie like nothing on earth. Lizzie had Valerie's wildness and independence: it was hard not to compare.

'How'd the conference go?' he asked, half-knowing the likely answer. His call had found his daughter in Jamaica, where she had been a keynote speaker on sustainable development. Some of the networks had run a short piece on her berating her father's own policies towards the developing world.

'It was great,' said Lizzie. West could see her secret service agents stepping back to let her talk in private. Word in the service was that an assignment with Lizzie was the best around. She was fun, yet disciplined, and she got to go to interesting places. The only country West had banned her from was Cuba, where the legacy of Fidel Castro teetered on. The US President's vivacious daughter heading there to look at health projects would not have gone down well with his party faithful.

'You should have been here, Dad. You would have got splattered with rotten tomatoes and I could have cleaned you up.' West laughed as Lizzie brushed her hair away from her long neck so she could signal to a car drawing up on her left. 'Give me a couple of minutes,' she shouted to the driver with a smile. 'Dad's on the phone.'

'Lizzie,' said West, as his daughter's attention returned. 'I don't know how to put this, and I don't know if I've ever asked you something like this before—' Even as he spoke, he recognized on the screen a soft sympathy flowing into Lizzie's eyes. Lizzie teased him and cajoled him, but never let issues get in the way of their relationship.

'I know,' she said with glint of mischief. 'You want me to join an oil company.'

'No, not quite,' he said slowly. 'It's getting a little lonely up here. You know, the place is pretty empty. You wouldn't have a couple of days—'

'Oh, my God,' she interrupted, putting her hand up to her mouth. 'I haven't been thinking. I've been so engrossed in the conference. That terrible attack. Everything that's going on. You must be— Forget it. I won't blabber. I'll be on the next plane.' She turned to onlookers whom West couldn't see on the high-definition but tiny phone screen. 'Smile, boys,' she shouted. 'We're going home.' Then in a flash back to her father. 'See you tonight, Dad, and just make sure there's no red meat on the menu.'

He returned the phone to the drawer and locked it. He would never tell anyone, save perhaps Lizzie, but it had been Vasant Mehta, calling him earlier that morning, who had persuaded him to call in his daughter.

The conversation with the Indian leader had begun routinely, but quickly became difficult when West asked Mehta to show restraint towards Pakistan. 'Don't go down that line right now, Jim,' said Mehta. 'I'm too raw for it. I'm in a "you're either with us or with the terrorists" mood.'

'We'll do everything we can to handle Pakistan,' pressed

West, trying to wring out a signal that the world was not about to be plummeted towards nuclear brinkmanship. He heard Mehta's sigh down the line.

'It doesn't work like that, Jim,' he said wearily. 'We trusted you with Pakistan after 11 September 2001. We trusted you as President Musharraf passed law after law legitimizing his dictatorship. We trusted you to keep a check on Pakistan's nuclear programme. The United States has let us down on all of those points, and more. We cannot trust you any more. If necessary, we will go it alone. But we would like to have your support in whatever we choose to do to safeguard our borders.'

'I'm with you,' said West. This was not the time to quibble. 'The American people are with you, Vasant. Believe me, we are. But don't take us by surprise.'

'You have my word,' said Mehta, and West thought he was about to end the conversation when Mehta went on. 'Jim, do you have any family with you there in Washington?'

Like most of the newspaper-reading world, West had seen the paparazzi photographs of Geeta Mehta on the ski slopes of St Moritz, and he had chosen not to mention it to the Indian Prime Minister. Mehta and West had only met once when both happened to be passing through London, but they had got on immediately.

In fact, they had shared West's most enjoyable evening since Valerie had died. In Downing Street, Stuart Nolan had dismissed his staff, kicked off his shoes, torn off his tie and opened a bottle of single malt whisky. Lizzie and Meenakshi had both been in Paris at a conference. They had met, liked each other, and when they heard their fathers would be in London, got on the Eurostar and hailed a cab to Downing Street. West had been on a whirl around Europe with Peter Brock and Mary Newman. Nolan played host to them all with his wife Joan. Mehta dropped by around 10 p.m. after a dinner at the High Commission, and no one got to bed until after 2 a.m. It was on that evening that Mehta had confided in West about the loneliness of high office.

'I've got a good staff around me,' answered West, a little too defensively, because Mehta picked him up straight away. 'It might get a bit rocky over the next couple of weeks,' he advised. 'Get Lizzie back there with you. She'll keep your feet on the ground.'

Outside the window, West saw the upright figure of his oldest friend, Peter Brock, wrapped up in a cashmere coat and scarf – both given to him by Valerie as Christmas presents. Brock stomped through a snowstorm, impatiently brushing the flakes off his shoulders as if there were no more to take their place. He needn't have gone outside to get to the West Wing, but he would have wanted the air and the distraction of the cold to freshen his thoughts.

Back in the Oval Office, West flicked on the television. The networks still seemed obsessed with the Yokata tragedy, which kept the political focus on Japan and North Korea. Britain's recapturing of Brunei had fired the public's imagination, but only briefly. The attack on the Indian Parliament caused cries of outrage and comparisons to Nine Eleven. A military takeover in Pakistan was a mere footnote, particularly as no one knew who was running the country. All West knew was that Pakistani Vice-President Javed Bashir Zafar had arrived in Dubai, asking for asylum in Britain and claiming to have been taken from his vice-presidential bedroom at gunpoint.

On his desk were files from Mary Newman and Chris Pierce, both of them read and endorsed by Brock.

Newman had pulled a brilliant diplomatic manoeuvre by persuading the South Koreans to issue a sympathetic statement over the murder in Panmunjom. The killer had, after all, been in South Korean uniform and drew a salary from the government. At the United Nations an agenda was being drawn up for official talks involving the US, China, North Korea, South Korea, Japan and Russia. Newman had got an agreement on the formation of an organization called the East Asian Economic Forum, and installed an extra vote on it by pulling in the bankrupt but compliant government of Mongolia.

Chris Pierce had delivered him a chilling war plan. It involved taking out North Korea's own military strike capability in a period of fifteen minutes. With amazement, West had looked at the ground-penetrating radar images deep inside the missile sites. The mouth of each silo was identified, meaning that the missile guidance could be programmed to strike exactly that spot. On impact, a chemical foam would be released to seep into the mouth and other crevices and gaps left after the explosion. Within three minutes, it would seal as hard as concrete. There would be no way in or out of the bunker.

Pierce would also use a high-intensity firebomb specially designed to warp rail tracks. The purpose would be to destabilize rail-based missile launchers. The bomb would send out explosive dust and liquid, like a detonator, for up to a mile from the target area, depending on the weather conditions and slope of the terrain. A fireball would develop, heating and twisting the railway track and rendering it unusable for up to ten miles in each direction. One aircraft dropping a single guided bomb at intervals of ten miles could easily cripple two hundred miles of track.

According to Pierce's satellite photographs, there were rail links to three missile sites, and tree cover affected only a small section of line. Pierce was convinced that any rail-based missile launch threat could be neutralized in a first strike.

On the border with South Korea, he would use thermo-baric bombs at the mouths of the caves which housed aircraft, armoured vehicles and artillery. Devastating shock waves would destroy everything, and everyone, in their path, as they swept through. At high altitude, he would deploy unmanned Global Hawk and Predator surveillance planes, which would call in missile strikes and relay back the successes and failures.

West regarded both his Defense Secretary and his Secretary of State as doing superb jobs, particularly as it was Pierce who wanted peace and Newman who believed in a pre-emptive strike. But still there was no answer to fundamental questions. How to stop the deaths of thousands of Americans in the human wave of North Korean troops that would cross the demarcation line? And how to keep China onside and stop her becoming a formidable enemy? Pierce suggested calling China's bluff, but West was not convinced.

Jenny Rinaldi's voice bounced out of the intercom. 'The Secretary of State is here, Mr President.'

'Thanks, Jenny,' said West. 'What happened to the National Security Advisor? I saw him fighting the snowstorm a couple of seconds ago.'

'He's taking a phone call from Langley. He'll be through in a moment.'

'And the Secretary of Defense?'

'Caught in traffic, but drawing into the driveway now, Mr President. This weather's snarling everything up.'

The door edged open and Mary Newman stepped in, patting down her hair which had been blown about in the wind outside. West was about to speak but he stopped himself when he spotted a flicker of regret cross her face.

Her hand hesitated on the handle, before closing the door softly behind her.

Newman smiled, but also cast her eyes down, as if contrite or shy. The President's earlier rebuke had altered the atmosphere of their personal relationship. For a moment it seemed she was guessing how much of his anger lingered; how much he was trying to hide; how much he regretted the way he had spoken to her; how much he thought she deserved it. It was rare that they were alone together, and the Oval Office was not the best setting for picking up the pieces.

'Good morning, Mr President,' she said, lifting up her head. 'Hell of a day out there!'

West stepped out from behind his desk, walked over and clasped both her hands in his. 'Morning, Mary. And you did one hell of a job with your diplomacy. It reminded me why I chose you as my Secretary of State.' He squeezed her hands, let them go, then leant towards her with feigned conspiracy. 'Now, before the others come, what's your gut feeling on India and Pakistan?'

She glanced at him sharply. 'With Zafar in exile, Pakistan is toppy.'

'To say the least,' agreed West.

'India is wounded,' she continued, stepping over to the floor-to-ceiling window at the side of the President's desk. It was being lashed by snowflakes which melted fast, leaving imprints of crystal on the bulletproof glass. 'My gut feeling is to hold back, Mr President.'

'And if India finds evidence of Pakistani—'

Jenny Rinaldi's voice interrupted. 'The National Security Advisor, Mr President, and I see the Secretary for Homeland Security and the Defense Secretary coming down the corridor.'

'—involvement in the attack?' continued West.

'Sure,' said Newman. 'They might. But look at South-East Asia. The last of the rebellions have been put down. Kota Kinabalu, Kuching and the main centres are back in government hands. But a rotten idea has spread there and will keep it dangerous for generations. It's the same idea as has destroyed Pakistan. It has turned people against us all over the world. Pakistan is a viral scab. Scratch it and the disease pours out. In North Korea, there's no virus. Whatever lethal doctrine Park Ho is preaching, it sure as hell isn't infectious.'

John Kozerski opened the door to let in West's inner circle, then stepped in himself and closed the door.

'Chris,' said West, before anyone had settled. 'What's your take on Pakistan and India?'

'You won't want to hear it, Mr President,' said Pierce, heading for the warm pot on the coffee table.

'One for me, too, Chris,' said Peter Brock, perching himself on the arm of a sofa. 'Before you answer that,' he said, 'I have an update on Pakistan. Yes, Zafar has been overthrown. Surprise, surprise. The man who has taken over is Air Vice-Marshal Tassudaq Qureshi.' Brock flipped open a folder he had with him and laid it on his knees. 'He's fifty-six years old, five children aged between nineteen and eleven. A career air force pilot. He pioneered the testing of Pakistani aircraft for the toss bomb technique of delivering a tactical nuclear weapon. Never been used yet, thank God,' he added, peering over his glasses. 'After Qureshi stopped flying, he became involved in negotiations with China and North Korea on upgrading Pakistan's missile arsenal. He is a practising Muslim. He prays five times a day and doesn't drink, but he is also – how should I put it – a man of the world. He is good company, intelligent and versatile in conversation. There are no political writings or speeches that we can pin on him. His views have been gathered mainly from human intelligence reports compiled by those who have met him. He is not a fundamentalist in the terms we understand it. But he believes Islam should be the bedrock of Pakistani society. I offer you this quote from the International Institute of Strategic Studies conference in Singapore in 2002. "We have muddled along for too long. There needs to be a showdown so that we can start again. Only after that can we move forward."

'My assessment of the man,' continued Brock, 'is that he is pragmatic rather than ideological or emotional. If he is set on creating an Islamic state in the fashion of Iran, then he might be a very difficult man to deal with.' Brock snapped shut the folder, slid himself into the sofa and took the cup of coffee which had been poured for him by Pierce.

'Is there anything that links him to the assassination of President Khan or the attack on the Indian Parliament?' asked Tom Patton, interested to know if any of those actions were likely to be transferred to American soil.

'Not specifically,' said Brock. 'But he is a part of the machine which must in some way have been responsible for both.'

'And he's the beneficiary,' mumbled Pierce.

'All right then,' said West. 'Since you kicked off, Pete, tell us your assessment of the overall situation.'

'A couple of other difficulties have been discovered,' said Brock, looking directly across to West. 'Zafar was deposed while Qureshi was out of the country. And where was he? According to the Indians, the new leader of Pakistan was in North Korea and then China, from where he was flown to Islamabad on an Air China Boeing 747–400 with a complement of Chinese special forces soldiers.'

'Shit,' said West.

'Exactly,' said Brock. 'We might ask what the hell is

going on.' He pulled out another sheet of paper from the file. 'Except – again from the Indians – Jamie Song apparently read him the riot act. Deliver those responsible for the attack on the Indian Parliament to Beijing or China severs its military relationship with Pakistan.'

'And what would that mean?' asked West.

'In the short term, Pakistan couldn't wage a war. No supplies. No spare parts. Its new fighter plane is made in Xian, central China, for example. No new fighter planes.'

'And the long term?'

'It'll have to look around for a new army supplier, particularly of nuclear components. Vasant Mehta told Jamie Song he wanted Chinese scientists and technicians out of there within seven days. Song gave Qureshi three days.'

West shook his head and chuckled. 'Jamie Song is a son of a bitch, but I like his style.' He pulled up a hardback chair and sat on it the wrong way round, leaning forward against its back. 'So we have a near-simultaneous military takeover in Pakistan and North Korea and evidence of direct contact between the two. Both nations have rogue missiles. Both have a nuclear capability. And we have circumstantial evidence that North Korea is developing smallpox.' He looked across at the Defense Secretary. 'Chris. Your turn.'

'In a nutshell. We should do with Pakistan what we've done with Afghanistan and Iraq. We use China as an ally in it and leave North Korea alone.'

'Mary?'

'I'd reverse that, Mr President. Go for North Korea and leave South Asia alone.'

'Tom?' said West, working round the sofa, tapping his fingers on the chair.

Patton shifted his huge frame so that he faced West. 'I go with Mary. If we hit Pakistan, there would be a backlash here.' Patton's experience of international affairs was limited. His expertise lay in banging together the heads of America's rival security agencies. 'We have a registered and monitored threat from the Islamic cause. Nothing from the Koreans.'

'Peter?' said West.

'If Jamie Song can handle Qureshi, I suspect he can handle Park Ho. Why should we do anything?' He shrugged. 'Let's wait and see.'

John Kozerski had not yet been consulted and usually the President kept it like that. Kozerski's job was to stay silent, listen, take notes, identify shifts of loyalty, and make sure the White House and the presidency came through unscathed. Kozerski had been West's second choice for the job. The first offer had gone to Brock, who had turned it down, saying his friendship with West was too valuable and his knowledge of day-to-day Washington politics too limited. But Brock found Kozerski for him, a Texan, whom West had never met and knew little about. He was a lawyer, an administrator and a political animal with antennae as sharp as anything produced by Pentagon technicians. 'You don't want a friend,' Brock had said. 'You need someone to tell you when you're being dumb and someone who'll stay with you through the storms.'

Kozerski had turned out to be straight-talking and unflappable. He kept his family and his private life to himself. The public barely knew who he was and he made it clear that Jim West was his boss, the US President, but not a friend or confidant.

'John,' said West. 'You got a view on this?'

'Fifty-eight Americans are dead because of North Korea, Mr President,' he said slowly. 'You go to war there, you'll get a second term and rid us of a threat to world peace. You pick a fight with Pakistan, no one'll know why you're doing it. If you wait to see what happens next, it takes a gloss off the leadership element of your charisma.'

West tilted forward on the chair. 'I like Jamie Song, but he runs a nation which one day will be at odds with our own. Like you said, Pete, what the hell is going on with Qureshi in North Korea one day, China the next, then coming back to overthrow a civilian government, but melting back into the shadows and not even declaring himself President? He needs more than a damn riot act read to him. Vasant Mehta of India is a friend and an ally. India is a democracy. If he needs my help, I have to give it to him. We should get a treaty going with India, just like we have with Japan. If there is evidence that this new bunch of generals in Pakistan had anything to do with the attack on their parliament, they should be hit and hit hard. So, Mary, tell me why we shouldn't?'

Newman's face clouded with reservation. Of all those in the room, she came across as the thinker, someone who would question her own beliefs at every stage of the way. It was what she had been doing in every telephone call to a foreign leader, in reading every editorial of a foreign newspaper. She took off her spectacles. Sometimes her face was unreadable. Sometimes it expressed a haunting vulnerability, as was happening now, which was part of her attraction for West. She picked up a bottle of mineral water, unscrewed the cap, poured a glass and sat back with it on her lap.

'The terror attack was on India, not on the United States. India is a powerful democracy. If it decides to punish Pakistan, then it must be allowed to do so without our interference. There is no threat from Pakistan to the United States. They do not have the military capability to hit us. The neat assassination of their leader might have thrown the nation into the hands of the politically irresponsible. But we should – as Pete said – delegate any action to India.

'North Korea, on the other hand, has a proven capability of being able to attack United States' facilities. It may even have developed a missile that can reach Hawaii or our western coastline. If we do not rid North Korea of Park Ho, Japan will carry out its threat to militarize. China will react and you have the scenario for a regional conflict.'

'As if you don't have a regional conflict in South Asia?' interjected Pierce.

'It has been going on for sixty years, Chris,' Newman shot back. 'Everyone knows the ground rules. On the Korean peninsula, we don't even want to get to the stage of setting ground rules.'

'What Mary's forgotten, though,' pressed Pierce, addressing the room as if Newman wasn't there, 'is that Pakistan is do-able. North Korea is not – without high casualties.'

'I don't think the President is asking for what's possible,' retorted Newman. 'He wants to know what should be done.'

'What should be done is the neutralizing of Pakistan,' answered Pierce brusquely. 'They have a nuclear weapon which is coveted by the fundamentalist Islamic world. On each change of government, those weapons get closer to the hands of terrorists. And now we have to factor in the probability that North Korea is transferring the long-range Taepodong-2 missile to Pakistan as well. That could give them a strike range to Europe.'

'You mean we should go into Pakistan?' asked West.

'We should neutralize their nuclear and long-range capability, Mr President. I can give you half a dozen options how to do it, starting with Kahuta.'

'Kahuta?' queried West, looking across at his Defense Secretary.

'Their nuclear research and reprocessing plant. Take out Kahuta and you cripple their nuclear capability.'

'Single strike?'

'Absolutely.'

'Then why don't we let India do it?' suggested West, half smiling. He motioned over to Brock. '*Delegation* seems to be today's catchword.'

Newman's eyes flamed. 'No, Mr President. No. We have to let the wounds heal, and India is too inflamed to be allowed to act on its own. It needs help.'

The President slapped his hands on his knees and broke out into a chuckle, taking everyone aback. They didn't know that Lizzie was on her way to Washington, and West was surprised how much that one telephone call had lifted his spirits.

'What gets me is this,' he said. 'Mary believes we should intervene in North Korea. Chris believes it would be a catastrophe. Chris wants to go into Pakistan. Mary says "hold back". Yet each of you has written the summary plan on how to execute the other's point of view. You know, one day I'll make a speech on this, because it's your flexibility of intellect that has made this the greatest nation on earth.'

West paused for moment, reflecting. 'Now, I just want to finish up with Mary, because as Chris says North Korea is a high-risk venture. Take me deeper into your thoughts, Mary.'

For one harrowing instant, as she brushed her fringe out of her eyes, she wondered if she should go down the road Jim West had thrown open to her. The memories of her rebuke at an earlier session were still fresh. The President wore a weatherproof smile on his face. The others waited like statues.

'The sad truth is,' she began, unable to stop herself swallowing hard. 'We know what happens when tyrants, dangerous tyrants, are left to their own devices, and left unchallenged. We know what happens when democracies cannot make a decision to act. We know what happens when international institutions are defied and don't act. We have a history with that and it is never good; a lot of innocent people end up suffering.'

Peter Brock was looking down at the notes on his lap. Chris Pierce's lips were parted in an indecipherable yet ghostly smile. Tom Patton stared at some far-off place outside in the snow. John Kozerski's eyes flitted between her and the President, who himself had barely moved. She pressed on.

'Park Ho believes he can win because he doesn't think we will act. He believes the hype about the hatred around the world for the United States. He thinks that Afghanistan, Iraq, the War on Terror have left us with an exposed flank, that there is a flood tide of loathing which we should ignore at our peril. Park Ho, closeted in his madness in North Korea, thinks that those governments which are our closest allies will turn against us. He believes they are deeply suspicious of us – which they are, Mr President, except Park Ho believes that that suspicion could be turned into a strategic alliance against us. He is probably on the phone right now telling big hitters like Jamie Song and Andrei Kozlov that he can start the ball rolling to end the world of the lone superpower. To Song, Kozlov and anyone else from Cuba to Libya to Iran who'll listen to him. He's probably boasting that finally there's a guy out there with the balls to drop a missile on an American base. Not a terror bomb, but a missile from sovereign soil. And those leaders have problems with their own people. They *are* suspicious of us. They *do* loathe us. There *is* envy. And there is something deeper, too – a belief that the path of following the United States is a path to damnation. They simply do not want their own societies to go in that direction. We are no longer their role model – if we ever have been.'

She glanced at West's face, and there was a hint that she was breaking through. In John Kozerski's eyes was a glimmer of respect and Pierce's smile had faded.

'Park Ho might be a fly-by-night. He might be dead in a month. But he'll have opened a can of worms, Mr President, about our power, our loyalty and our legitimacy. He is a direct and real threat. The only one, Mr President, that I can see facing us at the moment.'

'Why are you asking me not to accept China's offer?' asked Vasant Mehta bluntly on the hotline to the White House. 'Is it because it won't work, or because it erodes your own influence? Jamie Song has made an offer to take the terrorists out of Pakistan. No one else has, so what's your problem?'

Jim West shot a look across to Peter Brock. He had been told this would be an easy call to make. Something had dramatically changed. 'That's not what I meant, Vasant. I asked if you wanted to have the tape checked against voice verification with our people. We have the equipment to do it. You don't.'

'Thank you, but no.'

West breathed deeply. 'All right. Then – assuming it is genuine – what happens if Qureshi does not deliver? Does that mean you will invade?' West held up a satellite photograph in front of the camera, so that Mehta could see it. 'This was taken yesterday, Vasant. You are piling artillery, tanks and troops into the Punjab. You're moving aircraft from your eastern airfields to those closest to the Pakistan border.' Brock handed him another image. 'You've got big guns up there that could hit Lahore. Everything here points to an invasion of Pakistan.'

The satellite link faltered and the whiff of a shadow distorted Mehta's face. The screen shuddered. When it recovered, Mehta was leaning away from it, the camera showing the back of his head and the blurred background of his office. Then he reappeared holding up a CD-ROM in his hand. 'This is the interrogation of the terrorist who survived the attack,' said Mehta. 'You can have it. I'm sure he's on your files. You can match his fingerprints and voice signature.'

'Can you give me the crux of what he says?' said West, cautiously. Brock moved closer to the speaker phone. John Kozerski hung back by the door, a notepad in one hand and turning a ballpoint pen in the other.

'Before they were deployed, the terrorists were briefed by a senior Pakistani officer,' said Mehta.

'Qureshi?'

Mehta smiled and shook his head. 'No. It was Najeeb Hussain. It was Qureshi who ordered the assassination of Khan. But we can't pin the attack on the Parliament on him.'

'What a goddamn mess!' muttered West, his eyes leaving the screen for a second to look to Brock for advice. The National Security Advisor shrugged and mouthed his reply that the President should keep listening.

'Qureshi is now the de facto president,' agreed Mehta. 'But Hussain put him there. When Qureshi stepped off the plane from China he was told he was the new military leader. To have refused would have meant a bullet in the head.' The video link could not hide Mehta's fatigue. He rubbed his hand round his chin, then suddenly sat upright and stabbed his finger towards the camera.

'You have to be with us on this, Jim. Listen to the interrogation. Hear the evidence, and always remember that India is a democracy. Pakistan is a dictatorship. Don't be neutral. If I decide to go in and destroy that nation, India expects your unquestioning support.'

With the conversation over, black and white lines flitted

across the screen. Kozerski stepped over and turned it off. West turned to Brock who was staring out of the window, where a grey winter's evening was closing in early, accompanied by a swirl of rain. He stepped over to the window to join Brock, but it was Kozerski who spoke. 'If I may, Mr President,' he said, taking advantage of the silence.

'Sure, John,' said West.

'The Indian community in the United States is the single biggest immigrant economic grouping. Whatever decision you take, you should talk to them, get them on board and pay them some attention. Make them understand they are Americans first and Indians second.'

West knew he could only ignore Kozerski's political antennae at his peril. He glanced sharply across at his Chief of Staff. 'You saying we might end up on different sides of the fence?'

'That's what it sounded like to me,' said Kozerski. 'Your voice gave you away, that's all.'

Brock turned back into the room. 'I can't think of any nation, apart from the United States, that has succeeded in overthrowing a regime by force since the Soviets went into Afghanistan in 1979.'

'Either Mehta is calling everyone's bluff,' said West, 'or he believes he can win.'

'He can win,' said Brock. 'But it would take nuclear weapons to do it.'

'The decision is easy,' said West, glancing first to Kozerski and then to Brock. 'We can't let Mehta go into Pakistan.'

28

Beijing, China

'I think we should walk outside,' said Jamie Song, as General Yan began on a subject he did not want to hear and had hoped would not come up. He looked out the window, welcoming the ice-cold air. Fresh snow was falling. He took his black cashmere coat from the stand in the corner of the office. Yan was still wearing his military olive-green greatcoat and leather gloves. Outside on the steps, Song pulled on his own gloves and put on a cat-fur hat with flaps which covered his ears. It was a windless sub-zero day. Their breath hung in a cloud in front of them. They crossed the road, careful not to slip on ice underneath the snow.

An expression of irritation crossed Song's face as his private mobile telephone rang. But he relaxed when he recognized the mischievous face of his son, Yun, on the screen, in shirt-sleeves, and positioning himself so that his father would have a brilliant sun-swept view of Hong Kong harbour in the background.

'Dad, have you got a moment?' said Yun, smiling, then waving his hand back. 'You like my new office? I moved in last week.'

'It's Yun,' whispered Song to Yan, who dropped back to allow the Chinese President privacy.

'It's great,' said Song. 'And you're looking very well on it. Business must be good.' Song stepped on to the paved edge of the lake, looking across, and keeping the drab, low-rise buildings of the compound behind him.

'Business is always good down here,' said Yun, switching

to English and imitating the accent of a New York fund manager. Then effortlessly he switched again into an Italian accent to imitate a Mafia don. 'Give up all your meetings and come and join us. I will make you an offer you cannot refuse.'

Song laughed. Yun, his only child, had just turned thirty. Song had managed to fly to Hong Kong in secret for the celebrations. It had been a magnificent party in a friend's house overlooking Deep Water Bay, and for one evening, at least, Song had been free of the constraints of office. His wife, Xiaomei, with her delicate fine-boned features, had looked as glamorous as twenty years earlier, and the invitees had been their own friends from the international business community and Yun's friends from London, Hong Kong, China and New York.

On becoming president, Song had put some of his businesses into a blind trust, but had sold off others to raise cash and give Yun a head start. Yun had used it well, taking advantage of low prices during the downturn and turning a few million dollars into assets now worth much more.

Xiaomei and Yun kept out of his political work, although as the family of the President, they were courted and feted everywhere they went. The only thing that Song insisted on was that every purchase Yun made and every deal he struck was vetted by compliance and monopoly experts. It had been a wise move. On several occasions, his enemies had tried to get to him through his family. Allegations of insider trading, fraud and favouritism had been made but had never stuck. Song hoped that his example could be replicated bit by bit in every element of the new system of government he was trying to create in China.

Yun now put on a pompous English accent, picked up from his postgraduate days at Oxford. 'Mother and I have been talking about a weekend visit, and wonder what dates would be convenient for you.'

'Any time, as you know,' chuckled Song, unable to mimic as Yun could. 'My doors are always open.'

'Your doors might be open, but the last time I came up you had buggered off to Bangkok for an ASEAN–EU conference.'

'Something cropped up,' said Song. 'We should get our secretaries to copy each other's diaries.' He sensed Yun was heading somewhere, but couldn't work out where.

'Dad,' said Yun, dropping his voice. 'I shouldn't have to tell you this, but it's for your wedding anniversary.'

'Oh my God,' exclaimed Song, smiling. Out of the corner of his eye, he saw Yan, deliberately, yet discreetly, shifting himself into his line of vision. 'You are a true son. Of course. It's a date. We'll do it. But I've got to go now. Technically, I'm in a meeting.'

'A meeting by a lake in below zero temperatures? I'd get a new job, if I were you.'

'Look after yourself,' said Song jovially. He shut down his telephone and spent a moment gathering his thoughts, while examining a pattern of broken branches trapped into the lake's ice. He felt more than saw Yan silently bringing himself beside him, keen to finish the conversation they were not able to have in the office.

'Yun is well?' Yan inquired politely.

'Very well,' said Song, not wanting to linger on the subject of his family. 'Now, you were suggesting that if we don't find a way through this we would be, as you put it, blackmailed.'

'Yes,' said Yan, his face unusually drawn.

'My dear Yan,' said Song. 'Whether you are a mosquito,

a tiger or a human being, life is a relentless series of compromises. Blackmail is the only certain companion which will accompany you from cradle to grave. It is simply a matter of recognizing it and not fighting it.'

With an incredibly slow movement, as he was trying to work out Song's meaning, Yan stopped and turned to him. 'Did you anticipate this?' he asked softly.

Song squatted down, picked up a twig, snapped it in two and tossed the pieces into the air towards the lake. They hit the ice slightly apart, but skidded away in different directions. 'See,' said Song, pointing. 'You never can tell exactly what will happen. If you anticipate ten threats coming towards you, nine will fall into a ditch before they get to you. Yes, I did anticipate it. But I put it to one side. Now it has reached us, we must deal with it.'

Yan snapped his own twig in three and tossed them in the air. They slid in the same direction ending up side by side. Song chuckled. The grounds of Zhongnanhai relaxed him. The compound, the Forbidden City next door and Tiananmen Square nearby acted as a natural lung to the pollution of Beijing. The air was far from fresh, but at least it was breathable.

'Was it a threat?' said Song, starting to walk again. 'Or did he say it was out of his control?'

'He said it is out of his control,' replied the general. Even when strolling, he moved as if on a parade ground march.

'But to his advantage?'

'If Pakistan is defeated, if either the Americans or the Indians dismantle the security system, hundreds of trained terrorists will look for new sanctuary. From Afghanistan they fled to Pakistan. Some went to South-East Asia. You have seen the result. But they are now being routed from there.'

'And you believe the new sanctuary will be Xinjiang on our western border?'

Yan nodded. 'Yes. I do.'

'Then we smoke them out, too.'

'We can't, Ligong,' replied Yan, using a familiar term of address. 'Pakistan has been our protection. It has prevented terror attacks within our own Muslim areas. It physically stops the terrorists from going there. It shares intelligence with us. Pakistani agents help in interrogations. If we end our alliance with Pakistan, we lose that protection. Our western flank will be wide open.'

Jamie Song looked skywards towards Tiananmen Square. The day was too cold for the kites to be out and the air was too still for them to fly well. He walked on ahead, keeping his thoughts to himself. Yan had spoken for China; blunt, unsubtle and without frills. Years ago – and it must have been an act of the subconscious – Song had spotted the candid but sophisticated Yan to use as his sounding board. Today, Yan was earning his pension.

Song himself was a child of globalization. He had believed he could be President of China and a citizen of corporate America at the same time; a champion of the developing world and the master of blind-trust companies which, with the help of visionary lawyers, had been made safe from all avaricious hands, including crippling taxation, asset freezing and international sanctions.

For too many years Song had straddled both worlds with the ease of a broad-minded man, always believing that compromise was possible. He had brokered peace with the United States to neutralize any pending conflict. He had earned a reputation as a bridge between the developed and developing world. He was a favourite in the contacts books of BBC and CNN producers for his forceful and well-argued thoughts. He was the respected and successful voice in the secret debates behind the walls of

Zhongnanhai. He was a popular figure, but not a man of the people; privately, he remained torn between his native culture and the one across the Pacific that had spawned his wealth and educated his son.

'We have to keep control of our oil,' said Yan softly, catching up with him. 'With Russia, we can control that area. With the United States we will have to fight for it.'

'Yes,' said Song. 'I know.'

China was using six, maybe seven million barrels of oil a day, 50 per cent more than a decade ago. Half was produced in China. Half was imported, and as oil consumption grew, so would the imports. Its suppliers had become its allies. The more wretched the country, the more China could step in with aid and weapons and cut deals for oil. Yemen, Iran, Sudan and Libya were among the unhealthy relationships Jamie Song was nurturing to fulfil China's energy needs.

But real long-term security lay in securing access to the oil and gas fields in Xinjiang, Kazakhstan and the rest of Central Asia. It meant building eastbound pipelines from there to the great trading centres of Hong Kong and Shanghai on the southern and eastern coastlines. It would spread wealth to Xinjiang and draw it into China's own economy, but it needed peace for a quarter of a century at least for it to work.

If Song carried out his threat and ended China's alliance with Pakistan, all that could be put at risk. His footsteps disturbed a lone winter bird from its tree. Where did it come from? Song remembered a sparrow he had killed for food as a young man. It had filled him with shame. China had no birds left, because no one had enough to eat. This bird – and he didn't even know what species – flitted in front of him, dipped down to skim the ice, found it too hard and decided on a bush, thick with icicles and stark branches, on the other side of the lake.

In watching it, Song envisaged a tawdry mess of political misjudgement all around him. It was a picture of madness, filled with black waters, icy and unbreakable, and cries of distress from ships all around. There was no voice of sanity. Each was sinking; each determined to save itself, and, in doing so, each destroying the other.

In the tranquillity of Zhongnanhai, the fury of Vasant Mehta rang in his head. *What you owe this country after supporting those bastards for forty years*, the Indian Prime Minister had shouted.

Yes, China had bankrolled Pakistan, allowing it to create havoc in Kashmir in order to keep India weak. The more Indian troops were tied up there, the fewer China would have to deploy on their own disputed border. The more the spectre of war hung over India, the less chance it would have to grow into a powerful nation. While India and Pakistan fought, China was able to modernize and become the Asian superpower.

But now, supposing Pakistan turned its wrath on China? Suppose the United States used Pakistan to weaken China as China had weakened India? What if Xinjiang echoed with car bombs, firefights and the cries of torture victims as the Kashmir Valley had for two decades? What would happen to the money and expertise China needed for her pipelines? What would happen to her influence in the Central Asian states who, mistrustful of Russia and sceptical of America, saw China as a beacon of stability? What would happen to her eastern and southern flanks, with arrogant Taiwan, and with the wealthy provinces restless for independence?

Yes, he felt for Vasant Mehta. But to help him would be to hurt China. In threatening Qureshi, Song had acted out of guilt, out of compassion, out of a naïve vision. But he had not acted as a statesman.

Yan, the reliable sentinel, allowed Song a few seconds

to languish in his complex and dark vision, before touching him on the elbow. 'We can't do it,' he said cryptically, offering no reason, except that he knew Song would agree with him.

'Is our aircraft still in Islamabad?' asked Song firmly.

'It is,' said Yan.

'Tell Qureshi to load it up with any activists who have links with Xinjiang. They can be our sacrifical lambs.'

'Excuse me?' said Yan, querying Song's terminology.

'It's a phrase. I need terrorists to present to Mehta.'

'Very well,' said Yan, doubtfully.

Song began to walk on, but stopped after a couple of steps and turned round. 'Do you have a telephone on you?' Yan brought a handset out of his greatcoat pocket and handed it to Song. 'Give me a bit of space, will you?' asked Song. 'I need to talk to Kozlov privately.'

Song didn't bother with the video link. The screen on a portable satellite telephone was not clear enough to make it worth it. And besides, he had no wish to have to interpret the facial nuances of the Russian president, distorted by difficult light and technology.

'Andrei,' said Song, in Russian, as he was put through. 'Is India going to war with Pakistan?'

'It may, but I hope not,' said Kozlov.

'If it does, you will guarantee India's arms supplies?'

'Of course, as you will to Pakistan no doubt.'

'Of course,' agreed Song, although Kozlov may have picked up his split-second hesitation as he was meant to.

'As we would guarantee our arms contracts with China, Jamie,' added Kozlov pointedly.

'Providing we weren't marching on Moscow,' joked Song.

'Or Delhi,' said Kozlov, spicing his quip with a hard fact.

Song liked Kozlov, and had befriended him long before

he came to power. When Song was steering his software company through stock market listings in the United States and Europe, Kozlov was living in poverty in an unheated apartment in Vladivostok. In the late nineties, Song had read one of his provocative papers, published only on the Internet, warning that the Russian Bear was being tempted into the claws of the American Eagle. He kept track of Kozlov's writings through the precarious last years of Boris Yeltsin, the election of Vladimir Putin and the rapid swing behind America in the War on Terror.

'Large sections of the Russian public do not share Mr Putin's confidence that Russia will be rewarded for its support of American interests,' Kozlov had written. 'US troops now surround our nation. From western Europe, through the Middle East, to Afghanistan and Central Asia, Moscow has surrendered influence to Washington.'

One argument specifically caught Song's attention. 'America has a military presence in 132 of the 190 member states of the United Nations. Each of the emerging powers, Russia, India and China, find American armour closer and closer to their territory. Whether they are warships in Sri Lanka, airbases in Pakistan and Kyrgyzstan, or sales of hostile submarines to Taiwan, the encroachment of the American empire is reaching areas we had never thought possible. Unless it is stopped, the pressure to follow American cultural and political values will become overwhelming.'

Song immediately arranged for Kozlov to come to Beijing as a guest of the China Association for Friendly International Contacts, which Song had adopted as his own intelligence-gathering think tank. Song learned about Kozlov's difficult family life, the desertion by most of his family, the loyalty of his gifted musical daughter, the friendship with Alexander Yushchuk. Kozlov's conversations were taped. His room was bugged. His telephone calls back to Yushchuk in Vladivostok were recorded. Song used his private resources in the United States to put together a psychological profile of Kozlov. The profile found Kozlov was determined, stubborn, arrogant and had a high regard for his own beliefs. He was not a team player and spoke his mind, often to his own detriment. It was enough for Song to ask Kozlov, a discredited academic, to share a drink with him, then Foreign Minister of the People's Republic of China.

Song rarely drank. At diplomatic receptions, he nursed a single glass of wine throughout, barely sipping it. But for Kozlov, he threw all that to the wind and got drunk with him. They discussed how Russia and China could develop, free of American pressure, and how it could be done without war. Kozlov quizzed Song about China's economic success. He asked how it could be applied to Russia. They talked about political dissidents, freedom of the press and underworld corruption. Nothing was decided, but Song had forged a bond with the Russian. Kozlov had turned down his offer of money. He wanted no political support. He had insisted on fighting the campaign for Russia's soul with his own resources. Yet, within an hour of his election victory, Kozlov had called Song and thanked him for his foresight.

'Andrei,' said Song, his voice becoming quieter and more serious. 'We need to meet privately.'

29

Delhi, India

The passengers from the Singapore Airlines flight clustered at the end of the escalator and shuffled slowly towards the immigration desk. A faded sign, high up and hanging crookedly on the dirty cream wall, welcomed them to India. The hall smelt faintly of spices and carried something of the night about it. Indian international air travel revolved around the hours when the human body was at its weakest.

The man whose British passport described him as Jonathan Desai said nothing as the officer, his fingers yellow with tobacco smoke, flicked through the pages, looking for the visa. When the officer looked up to check the passport photograph, Desai tilted his slightly tinted spectacles downwards to show his eyes, but not enough to reveal a cut under his right eye which was still bruised. With the thud of the stamp, Desai took his passport back and moved through.

He carried only hand luggage, a worn, black canvas briefcase and a laptop in a black case, both slung over his left shoulder, leaving his right hand free. He eased his way through the melee in the baggage hall, nodded at the customs officer who waved him on, and raised his hand to the moustachioed attendant from the Imperial Hotel holding up a sign with his name on it.

Outside he was engulfed by the chill of winter, the cold air, acrid with the smells of cheap burning coal and wood smoke. The attendant made small talk, and Desai obliged. It was a long time since he had been to India, he said. He

ran a business from London. Was business good? No, said
the concierge, it had never recovered to the glory days of
the 1980s. The War on Terror and the conflict in Kashmir
had made life difficult. Desai slipped him a 1,000 rupee
note, just as the jeep pulled round and the driver opened
the door, offering a hot face towel.

In his first-floor hotel room, he pushed open the
windows, which looked out over the kidney-shaped swimming pool and a row of palm trees in the garden. From
somewhere beyond came the sounds of holy men, beggars
and those who slept on the streets. But the driveway
beneath was empty apart from the beam of a nightwatchman's flashlight.

Desai kept the main light of the room off, and used
the fluorescent lamp over the bathroom mirror. He
undressed, hanging his beige cotton trousers and light
checked shirt in the wardrobe. He showered, shaved, put
on the white towelling hotel robe and fixed himself some
coffee.

The hotel safe in the wardrobe was closed with a code,
known only to Desai and the hotel room boy, who had
punched it into the safe's memory. Desai opened the safe.
Inside was an Australian passport in the name of Ben
Dutta, a driving licence and two valid credit cards,
MasterCard and American Express. His date of birth was
given as 22 April 1977. Place of birth was Manly, New
South Wales, Australia. A box of business cards described
him as Managing Director of Maximol Computing, with
an address in north Sydney. He felt towards the back
of the safe where he found a black box the size of a
cigarette packet with the battery unattached and the aerial
wrapped in polythene beside it. He felt around for the
weapon he had asked for, but it wasn't there. A message
to tell him the location and the identification features
of the vehicle being used was also missing. The back-up

for it was to have been sent by email. For under no circumstances should the telephone, mobile or landline be used.

Working on the lowered lid of the toilet seat, he opened the laptop case and removed the computer. He unfurled a telephone cable and ran it to the socket under the desk. While it was booting up, he drew the curtains across the window and wedged a hardback chair against the handle of the door. Before boarding the plane in Singapore, he had reformatted the computer's hard disk and reinstalled the factory software, together with the latest AOL programme, to which he had signed up using the name and credit-card number of Ben Dutta.

When he logged on, one message was waiting. It told him the operational names of the men with whom he would work, and the schedule of the Indian Prime Minister.

Desai, Dutta, or in fact the man who thought of himself as Hassan Muda, put on a beige loose-fitting top and pants, a common dress for all classes and castes in India. He slipped his identity documents into an inside pocket, took the reformatted computer hard disk, left it in the safe and closed it using the same code. He pulled off the bed covers, crumpled them and dropped them back to give the bed the look of having been slept in.

He unfolded a detailed street map of Delhi. He preferred to walk, rather than leave a witness by taking a taxi ride. Security around the parliament compound was still tight. But it also attracted the curious, as had Ground Zero in New York. If he was stopped, he had his reasons, his passport and his hotel key. His only risk was to be his exit from the hotel. Muda drew back the curtains. The driveway was still empty. He waited five minutes and saw no sign of the nightwatchman.

With his bag slung over his back, Muda eased himself

out and jumped one floor down on to the grass. This was the back of the hotel, with kitchen flues and rubbish carts. He walked quickly past them. The gate at the end was ajar. Once through it, he was on the streets. It was peppered with sleeping bodies and the odd car, shrouded in a mix of early-morning mist and pollution.

Vasant Mehta looked across the table with incredulity at what he was hearing. He brushed his hand over the linen tablecloth, then glanced out of the window where grounds-men were lighting a fire of dead, dried leaves at the bottom of the garden.

'No brown faces at all?' he said, repeating it in order to clarify it.

'That's right,' said Lazaro Campbell. 'All volunteers. All Caucasian. No documents. No traceability.' Campbell buttered a piece of toast. He had flown to Delhi from Australia and had been holed up in the US embassy for the past two days, discussing the plan with Brock and finally confirming how to handle it on a conference call with Jim West and Chris Pierce. Campbell's idea had just been to go in. But Brock, judging that his protégé was still fired up with the success of Brunei, argued that Pakistan would be a much more difficult target. And Jim West insisted that Mehta be brought on board. He would not do it without Mehta's agreement.

'No accountability. But the job will be done,' assured Campbell.

'Deepak,' said Mehta. 'You are very quiet.' His face carried a barely detectable expression of understanding, that here in front of them, there might be a way out, if only it could be made politically acceptable. Mehta had invited his Chief of Defence Staff to the breakfast precisely because he expected Suri to disagree with him.

'I am quiet because it is for you to determine the political fallout from such an action,' said Suri slowly, nursing a cup of tea in both hands. 'And by fallout I mean the reaction to allowing another nation to fight a war that should be fought by India. The all-white-skin scenario may leave a bitter taste.'

'With all due respect, Mr Campbell, you don't look that white-skinned yourself.'

All three men turned to see Meenakshi walking quickly into the room, carrying a heavy cardboard box in both arms. A corner of the box had become caught on her blue sari, and it was skewing across her shoulders. Campbell stood up, freed it and helped her lower it on to the table.

'Thank you,' she said, smiling.

'A pleasure, ma'am.' Campbell had seen Meenakshi briefly earlier that morning. While he was walking round the garden with Mehta, she had appeared on the back verandah, sleepy-eyed in a nightdress, her hand on her forehead, shielding her eyes from the sun.

She had filled a bird tray with water and sprinkled food grain on it, before examining the unexpected guest from a distance and stepping barefoot on to the lawn to introduce herself.

'I've never seen anyone out here with father so early in the morning before,' she had said, shaking Campbell's hand. 'You must be a very special visitor indeed, Mr Campbell.'

With that she had vanished back into the house, and, thought Campbell, off the agenda. Except, now, she must have been listening to some, if not all, of his highly classified conversation with the Indian Prime Minister and his Chief of Defence Staff. Campbell, younger than his hosts by a generation, glanced at Suri for guidance, his eyes reflecting the uncertainty he felt at Meenakshi's presence.

But it was Mehta who spoke. 'She's fine, Campbell. She might even knock some sense into your damn head.'

Meenakshi picked up a breakfast knife and sliced open the box. 'You're from Washington, I understand,' she said, carefully unpeeling the lid. 'Do you know Lizzie?'

'Lizzie?' asked Campbell, hiding his irritation that the meeting was so abruptly being disturbed. In ten minutes, Mehta was due to leave. Once gone, the momentum would be lost.

'Lizzie West. Jim West's daughter,' smiled Meenaksi. 'She thinks the Pakistanis are going to gas us, so she borrowed these from the White House secret store and FedExed them over. Apparently, they're better than ours, Deepak,' she finished, looking reprovingly at the Chief of Defence Staff.

Her hands plunged inside pulling out air-bubble padding. On the top were three masks. Below that four pairs of rubber boots and at the bottom was a pile of vacuum-packed nuclear, biological and chemical warfare suits.

'Good God,' she exclaimed, reading from a note. 'Lizzie says they're the best around. We can keep them in a cupboard and they'll last for years.' She recited the label on the olive-green suit. 'See here. This suit is computer-designed and impregnated with charcoal to withstand the most toxic threats in an NBC environment. Two-piece suit with pants, top and attached suit, cuff closures and pull-string adjustments.' She dropped the packet on to the table. 'Is that what does it, Mr Campbell? Charcoal?'

'It helps,' smiled Campbell. 'But best not to be there anyway.'

'Quite right,' she said firmly, becoming distracted by the packet at the bottom. Her face broke into a huge grin. 'Lizzie!' she exclaimed to nobody in particular. 'My dear Lizzie, you are so mischievous.' With packet in hand, she walked over to her father, leaned on the table and read him the description. 'Listen to this, Father. Designed for infants up to three years of age. The finest infant protective suits on the market today, blah, blah, blah. Reduces stress by providing a constant airflow to the infant.'

Mehta patted his daughter on her leg, chuckled and made a show of inspecting her waistline. 'So the President's daughter doesn't think there'll be a war for at least nine months,' he said.

'Wishful thinking, if you reckon on nine months,' quipped Meenakshi. 'And if you get us into a war, I will personally kill you. That goes for the two of you as well.'

'Exactly what we're discussing,' said Mehta, handing his daughter back the infant's NBC suit.

'So I heard. Well, a bit anyway.' Meenakshi pushed her hair off her face, looking straight at her father, but pointing to Campbell. 'If what he's suggesting is going to work, Father, do it. Don't for God's sake stand on any high-minded philosophy. It's not who fights wars that is important. It's who is clever enough to stop them happening in the first place.'

'You should be knocking sense into *his* head, not mine,' said Mehta. He still wore a smile, but his tone indicated that the cheerfulness that Meenakshi had brought to the room was fading.

'Why don't you meet halfway? In my job, it usually works,' replied Meenakshi brightly. 'I'll leave this stuff here for now,' she added in a tone that dismissed herself from the meeting. 'Mr Campbell, if you're going back to Washington, could you take Lizzie a thank-you note? If you're important enough to have breakfast with my father, I expect you could drop by the White House.'

'It'd be my pleasure, ma'am,' said Campbell, knowing that he would deliver it straight to the embassy and it would be couriered over for him.

Meenakshi left a lingering silence behind her as the mood shifted back. The box of NBC equipment remained as if symbolic on the table. Its smells of polythene and rubber mixed with the fresh flowers on the table and faint fire smoke from the garden.

'No dog tags,' resumed Campbell. 'No documentation. The men are trained to withstand torture. They've all been through the polygraph detector. They've been tested with sodium pentothal.'

'Foolproof?' asked Suri.

'Nothing's foolproof, sir,' said Campbell. 'But we think it will work.'

Mehta stood up, walked to the door and stood right in the entrance, leaning on the frame looking into the garden. 'Deepak, give me your thoughts again.'

'I'm pretty certain we can shoot down nuclear-armed aircraft before they launch. But against missiles we have no real defence. I understand that Qureshi will soon announce himself both as president and commander-in-chief. Hussain is chairman of the National Command Authority, which means he directly controls the ten corps commanders, and it is they who would have the autonomy to launch in a time of war.'

'Without the authority of the NCA?' said Campbell.

'Correct. The thinking behind that is that if India captures Rawalpindi and Islamabad, the commander in, say, Karachi can order nuclear retaliation without authority from the centre.'

Mehta turned back into the room. 'The criterion for a launch, Mr Campbell is – or *was*, because the coup might have changed things – that the NCA no longer existed. In other words it was wiped out.'

'It could equally mean that if the commander disagreed with his orders from the NCA he could do what the hell he liked,' said Suri, shooting a hostile look in the direction of Campbell. 'If we went along with you, you would have to take out each military commander in each district. Then you would have to get access to the missile areas and neutralize them. That's not to mention whatever short-range missiles they might have on rail tracks or on trucks.' He shook his head. 'It can't be done. If it was that simple, don't you think we would have done it by now?'

'Tell me, the Taepodong-2 missile from North Korea – what difference does it make?' Mehta asked Deepak directly.

'They can strike anywhere in India.'

'Correct. But with a smaller warhead they can reach Europe and South-East Asia. Which means that the threat is not just to India.'

'That's why the President has sent me, sir,' said Campbell.

Mehta lifted his jacket off the back of the dining chair, slipped it on and addressed Campbell. 'I want you to come to our Cabinet Committee on Security meeting. Travel with Deepak, and meet me there. I believe your special forces concept would fail. But you could succeed with your white-only faces in assassinating Qureshi, Hussain and probably a handful of others. If we eradicate that level of the new Pakistani leadership, then we might find someone underneath who talks some sense.' He glanced out of the window which had just become spotted with raindrops, and waved at Meenakshi who was in the garden, gathering her sari around herself, and walking briskly towards the house so as not to get caught in a downpour.

By the best of Muda's estimates, the Indian Prime Minister would be in the dining room between 08.00 and 08.30. He usually attended breakfast dressed and ready to go to work.

He would either breakfast alone, with his daughters Meenakshi or Romila, if they were staying with him, or very
occasionally with senior advisers. Today, Meenakshi was to
chair a workshop in Old Delhi on the communal integra-
tion of the urban poor. The Prime Minister was due at his
office in South Block at 09.15. Mehta had a reputation for
promptness, meaning that his motorcade from Race
Course Road would leave by 08.45. Ashish Uddin, his
private secretary, would brief Mehta and any other aides
in a small office off the entrance to the residence for ten
to fifteen minutes before the convoy left.

Muda took a three-wheeler to India Gate and was
dropped off just past the National Stadium on the corner
of Pandara Road. He paid the fare, tipped moderately and
idled until the driver disappeared from sight. Rajpath, the
stately boulevard which ran between India Gate and the
government buildings, was shrouded in winter fog. Since
the attack on the Parliament, no one had been allowed
there except the police. Onlookers still gathered against the
cordon ropes. India was a place where too many had too
little to do, and disaster was always an attraction. The
traffic was thin, with the city slowly waking to a misty,
chilly morning, and the cordons up to Raisana Hill and
around the parliament building were heavily fortified but
lazily manned.

He quickened his pace, turning left in Akbar Road,
where four schoolchildren with their maids waited on the
corner for a bus. Up ahead a sweeper, caped in blue
chiffon, threw dust into the air, and Muda stepped into
the empty road to avoid it. As soon as the morning got
under way, there would be a roar of white Ambassador
cars, some with the flashing lights of dignitaries and
ministers. But at this time, a quietness hung over the big
houses set back behind gates. It was a neighbourhood of
wealth and high office.

He passed the Congress Party headquarters on his right, with a poster of Indira Gandhi, grey hair swept back, her confident eyes showing none of the failure of her rule. To his left, set back from the road, was the house of the Air Chief Marshal.

At the second roundabout, he lingered just for a second by the memorial to Mahatma Gandhi. Two cars appeared through the mist, the grubbiness of their windows shown up by the sun, which was breaking through in slatted rays. At the next junction he passed the sign for the Indira Gandhi Memorial Trust and, suddenly, he felt surrounded by the history of what he was about to do.

India's leaders often met violent deaths. His action seemed natural, given the character of the nation. As he walked on, stepping on to the road to avoid a leaking water pipe, a mask of relaxation drew across his face.

By the time he reached the next roundabout, the traffic had become busier and fine needles of rain were falling on the dry road, creating a small rainbow over the cordon set up across Race Course Road. A four-wheel-drive police jeep was parked at one end of the cordon, with two men, leaning on the metal barriers, smoking. At the other end, the door of their small hut was open, their tunics hanging in the window, with their weapons carelessly left in their holsters.

Muda walked purposefully into the junction, crossed Safdarjung Road, turned left and then right into the entrance of the Gymkhana Club, nodding at the guard with an expression that allowed no room for a response. Muda kept going past the main buildings with the club-house on his right, and on his left at first the library and then the expanse of playing fields and open space which stretched to the gardens of the Prime Minister's house and offices along Race Course Road. He estimated the distance to be just over five hundred metres.

At the tennis courts, he turned left, keeping up his brisk pace, until he spotted the vehicle, a grubby delivery truck, its logo covered in grime and a rattling freezer unit belching cold air on the roof. It was backed up against a trade delivery entrance of the clubhouse.

An email to the club, one week earlier, had booked the Kashmir Room for a private party, citing membership of one of the Gymkhana's reciprocal clubs in London, the Royal Over-Seas League. The reservation had been followed up by a faxed menu request, specifying a special delivery of frozen Irish wild salmon would be flown in that morning. The number plate of the van was on the fax, a copy of which the driver produced when he had arrived at the entrance. He had been early, and told to wait until the staff arrived for the morning shift.

Once inside the gates, the van was free of random police checks. The hallowed grounds of the club itself were beyond suspicion. From far away in the Philippines, Memed had drawn up the plan, and Muda refined it.

Inside the cab, two men were smoking cigarettes. The driver's window was down, his elbow resting on the door. A third man was at the open back door of the refrigerated unit, sorting through frozen luxury food.

Once past the tennis courts, Muda stopped to flick a stone out of his sandal. The truck driver brought his elbow in and started the engine. The doors at the back were closed and the van set off, driving the short way to a spot in a large car park, and pulling up as far away as possible from the target, adding another two hundred metres to the range. Muda felt the inside pocket of his loose-fitting shirt. With one hand he eased up the aerial, making enough space for it to be extended inside his clothing. He brushed his fingers over the control panel, pressing the single button on the right, which let out a complex series of directional radio beams.

Muda strolled, watchful and undisturbed.

He never needed to be closer than fifty metres to the van. The windows were up. They were so filthy it was impossible to see through. Muda knew the other men would have a false partition in the cab to hide the mortars in the back of the van.

He had designed the mortars at just over 120mm and ordered them to be set for a range of seven hundred metres, with enough altitude to connect with the radio signals. He had instructed that heavy steel plates should be welded into the base of the van and for each mortar stand to be wedged in with sandbags. The three firings had to be carried out in quick succession, before the heat caught the fuel tank of the van and blew it up.

The mortar had been Muda's weapon of choice because it need not be in the line of sight of the target. Nor did anyone have to infiltrate the target area to plant a bomb or carry out an assassination. The aeronautics had been the main challenge. It had taken months to get right, but with Muda's remarkably simple electronic guidance system, pinpoint accuracy on trajectory was no longer essential.

As long as the mortar was fired in roughly the right direction, it would find its target. Until now this type had never been used by any guerrilla organization anywhere in the world.

Instead of being a free-flying bomb, Muda had experimented with aluminium fins, a tiny motorized propeller, a radio-signal receiver and technology from the hand-held Stinger surface-to-air-missile which locked on to heat given off by aircraft.

After dozens of practice sessions in the Philippines he had created a mortar that could be coaxed down in the right direction. On the mortars themselves, he installed a Global Positioning System tracker. To make it work, he only needed it to fix on a target which was linked to a satellite. He did not expect there to be a GPS on the Prime Minister's house itself. But there would certainly be one attached to his car and the chase cars of the convoy. If he tilted the trajectory slightly beyond the vehicles, he should be able to guide the mortars through the roof of the house.

He had chosen one to be airburst, one to detonate on impact and a burrowing one to explode several seconds after impact and filled with phosphorus which would act as a firebomb sending out toxic smoke.

What Muda did not know was the sophistication of the anti-mortar defences around the Prime Minister's residence. But he doubted they had the ability to create the defensive shield needed to withstand a three-mortar attack.

Inside his clothes, his finger slipped to the second button. The small vibration of the box confirmed that the radio signals were running at full strength. The top of the van slid open like a sun roof. For a second, the sharp crack went unnoticed. Muda pressed the button and the vibration stopped, indicating that the signals had locked on. The mortar was travelling too fast for him to check. Another crack. Then another. A cry from the tennis courts. A guard running forward. Muda broke his stroll into a half-run, looking towards the confusion among the handful of people in the car park, his eyes following everyone else's, quickening his pace with their mood. Then the withering explosion of the first mortar round finding its mark, and almost simultaneously a ball of fire rising out of the van which had launched them, killing the three men inside.

Muda let the crowd gather around him, and he stayed with it, until the first police car arrived, when he walked out of the gates, exchanging expressions of shock with the guard. Once clear, he hailed a taxi to take him south, away from the government houses, India Gate, North Block,

South Block, the parliament building and the Imperial Hotel. He got the taxi to drop him off at the neighbourhood known as Defence Colony, and an hour later took another taxi to the domestic airport.

His hotel room would have been cleaned out and wiped clear of fingerprints. The phone record of the call to AOL would have been destroyed. The bill would have been paid by the imprint of the credit card of Jonathan Desai. Memed's orders had been for Muda to be on an afternoon flight to Mumbai and to lie up there for a week. Then he would receive his next instructions.

'Mortar,' yelled Mehta, throwing himself at Suri and pulling them both to the ground. Flame shot down from the roof. A searing explosion tore the ceiling, hurling down chunks of plaster like missiles. The blast threw Campbell against the wall. As he crashed to the ground, he saw an unexploded mortar embedded in the lawn outside. Behind him, there was a second explosion. The door to the hallway was flung open amid a mass of smoke and fire.

Meenakshi, in the garden, was running away from the burning house towards the unexploded bomb. 'No,' screamed Campbell, scrambling up, toxic fumes choking his throat. He threw himself through the door frame, slashing his face on jagged glass, running, arms waving, blood on his face, tripping over himself, his voice screaming out. 'No, no, get back, get back—' as the mortar exploded, smashing him down against the ground.

30

Rawalpindi, Pakistan

'**Mehta will probably** not survive,' said Brigadier Najeeb Hussain. 'Meenakshi, his daughter, was also there. All India Radio is reporting that she is dead. Suri has shrapnel in the leg and a broken arm. Uddin, the private secretary, escaped unscathed. Four of the household staff are dead. Three others in the vehicles outside, also dead. There was also an American there. We don't know what happened to him.'

General Zaid Musa, sitting furthest away from Qureshi, tilted his head in respect. 'Dead or alive, doesn't matter. It was the accuracy of the mortar which counted.'

'Dead would have been better,' said Admiral Javed Mohmand. 'Mehta is a charismatic leader. If he survives, he will remain a formidable opponent.'

Qureshi's living room was tastefully decorated in minimalist style, with a suite of sofas covered in white brushed linen and brightly coloured cushions. Here there were the ornaments and art of a man who had travelled widely, but he had displayed only a fraction of his collection, preferring to leave the room fresh and uncluttered. The two oils on the walls were of modernist Islamic art and the controversial small bronze statue on the coffee table was of a woman crashing to the ground from the World Trade Center towers in 2001. Hardline Islam might prohibit the artistic depiction of any human form, but Qureshi had acquired it at some price through a dealer in New York because he thought it so precisely summed up both his religion and his politics.

General Musa's nod to him had sealed his presidency. The attack on Mehta's residence had been Qureshi's rite of passage, just as the attack on the Indian Parliament had belonged to Najeeb Hussain.

Not that Musa, a highly decorated infantry general, had been in favour of the continuation of civilian rule. His concern had been that men of the right metal should take over. Without Musa's support the coup would have been impossible. He commanded the loyalty of the corps commanders to whom Qureshi would cede nuclear strike control in the event of conflict.

Out of the corner of his eye, in the shadows of the encroaching darkness, Qureshi spotted the Cherat Special Services Group installing anti-terror equipment in the garden. This was what life would be until the conflict was won. Farrah had been wise before the event to move to Lahore. Tasneem would have to stop berating him for letting her go. She was safer there.

'Then the man I should talk with is Suri,' said Qureshi. His face was intense as he kept an eye on the men working outside, and listened to the rhythmic hum from the generator at the back of the house. 'It is right it should be Suri,' he said out loud, but really confirming it to himself. 'A military government should negotiate only with the military element of a civilian government.'

In the short time since the three other military officers had arrived, the sun had vanished over the edge of the hills, taking with it warmth and light and leaving in its place a quickly darkening dusk and the sudden sounds of nocturnal insects.

'As a mark of respect for this second terrible act of terrorism in such a short space of time,' said Qureshi, lacing his voice with irony, 'Pakistan will fly its national flag at half-mast on all government buildings. Our ceremonial troops will not partake in the face-to-face border rituals. They will instead go to the ceremony unarmed and will salute the Indian troops on the other side. At first light tomorrow, we will withdraw our armoured columns and artillery right along the joint border with India to create a demilitarized zone on the Pakistani side stretching at least ten kilometres. Through an unspecified agency, I have commissioned a commercial satellite to photograph the withdrawal and post the images on the Internet. This is in case the Western intelligence agencies choose not to publish their own images. The only place where India might immediately respond is with artillery on the Siachen Glacier. Pakistan will not fire back, regardless of the casualties. In the absence of Vice-President Zafar, power naturally goes to the Speaker of Parliament. That process will continue. The press can report freely. We will not comment, of course. If any member of the armed forces does, he will receive a summary court martial.'

Qureshi paused and took some nuts from a bowl on the table. Hussain and Mohmand were silent. Musa, as always, jousted. 'We would, in effect, cede ten kilometres of territory to India. It would take months to rebuild our defences in new positions.'

'And it would take only hours for India to destroy them wherever they were – if it so wished,' responded Qureshi, crunching the nuts noisily between his teeth. 'The day India went nuclear was the day we won the right to defend our nation by whatever means possible. I am proposing that we make our last resort our first resort. If it works, it means we can wind down our costly conventional war efforts, and rely solely on our nuclear deterrent. If India – or any other nation – puts one foot into Pakistan, it will know what will happen.'

'My God,' said Musa. 'It is both insane and brilliant.'

'It is not insane,' said Qureshi, shaking his head. 'It has

been unspoken since the nuclear tests of 1998. We could never win against India in a conventional war.' He looked around to meet the eyes of each of the other three. 'As is known only between the four of us, I have delivered five tactical nuclear warheads to General Park Ho in North Korea. He had already shipped to us the components of the Taepodong-2 long-range nuclear-capable missile. These have now been assembled and are ready to launch at any time we need them. North Korea and Pakistan have forged an inseparable alliance. Yes, we can now take on India in a city-for-city exchange. Let us hope that will deter war. But should any other nation intervene against us, it will also be in range of our nuclear weapons. That, gentlemen, is the nature and power of our deterrence. Together, we have changed the balance of power against small nations for ever. Now,' he concluded lightly with a smile, 'all we have to do is explain it to the world.'

'Who should explain it?' said Hussain. 'It is far more likely to be accepted from a civilian leader than from us.'

'Musharraf was accepted,' said Mohmand. Apart from Qureshi, Mohmand had the most complex and sophisticated mind in the room. He had risen to head the Pakistani navy by being both a skilful naval commander and a careful diplomat. 'Yet Musharraf ended up being discredited.' He smiled self-effacingly. 'So my point is, that it's impossible to tell. Certainly you, Tassudaq, would have more authority, but that would not necessarily give you credibility among the western democracies.'

'We should bring Zafar back,' said Qureshi, sprinkling nutshells on to a saucer.

'Would he come?' said Hussain.

Qureshi laughed quietly. 'Of course he would.'

'Who could resist becoming the president of the most powerful Islamic nation?' agreed Musa, sarcastically. The general stood up and clapped his hands together. 'Are we decided then? If so, it seems I am to be the busiest, so perhaps I should get going and start the ball rolling.'

Qureshi was on his feet. 'Just one other thing. Mehta, before he – well, we don't know how he is exactly – but he gave Jamie Song a hard time about China's support for Pakistan. Song gave me a hard time when I passed through Beijing. If Mehta dies, I don't think we have a problem. If he survives, we will have to hand over some men to be flown to China as a token of—' Qureshi shrugged, and it was difficult to tell how much was a show and how much was heartfelt. 'I think you all know as well as I that we have to give face to China if we are to retain the technology we need. So whatever it takes, we'll do it.'

31

New York, NY, USA

The murmuring of low, disciplined voices faded into silence as the side door of the United Nations General Assembly Hall opened near the podium. For a moment, a cluster of people gathered at the entrance, half-exposed, half-hidden, dark-suited men, security guards, assistants with speech notes and files. Their feet shifted, heads tilting to pick up whispered conversations. The 1,743 delegates and their staff from 192 nations craned to see what was going on. This was a special emergency session called after the two terrorist attacks on India. Ambassador after ambassador, summoned in alphabetical order, had spoken about the need for dialogue and international cooperation. Then, just over an hour earlier, the Secretary-General had been notified that India wanted to speak immediately. Unbeknown to most, the leaders of China, Britain, Japan and Russia were also flying into New York. At first, the request from India had been denied, until Mehta's private secretary, Ashish Uddin, had telephoned John Kozerski, who then spoke directly to the office of the UN Secretary-General. 'India very much wants to retain the authority of the United Nations,' Uddin had said. 'For security reasons, which you will understand, we could not announce the movements. Nor do we have time to linger in New York and wait our turn. So either the announcement will be at the UN, immediately, or we will give a live address to be broadcast on both CNN and BBC.'

Uddin had swiftly won the argument, and now the cluster of people in the wings of the assembly hall melted

away, leaving two figures exposed in the doorway. One
was in a wheelchair, with a medical dressing covering the
left eye, and the right leg protruding out and wrapped in
bandages. The second person walked with one hand on a
cane, the other balancing on the handle of the wheelchair,
pushing it from behind.

To have walked it at a normal pace would have taken
only a few seconds. But for Vasant Mehta and his daughter
Meenakshi the journey to the podium took two minutes
and seventeen seconds. Within seconds of starting out, as
the two figures made their way under the huge UN
emblem of an image of the world, flanked by olive wreaths
as a symbol of peace, a murmur rippled through the
historic General Assembly Hall. Father and daughter, lit
up by spotlights, their images thrown on to two massive
screens, looked out across the expanse of people. The
murmuring dropped to a silence. The television networks
cut into their normal programming and transferred to the
stark image. The commentators spoke sparingly because
the picture told all. In the hall, clapping began, a solitary
staff member in one place, picked up on the microphones,
and copied, louder and louder, until applause rose like
a surging wave. As Mehta and Meenakshi reached the
podium, the United Nations stood up, delegates rising to
their feet like a Mexican wave, peppered with wolf-whistles,
cheers, the slapping of desks and the shaking of papers.

Vasant Mehta turned the wheelchair to face the hall.
He leant down and locked the wheels. Meenakshi handed
him a file from her lap. He limped on to the podium and
raised his hand in appreciation, just a single hand, palm
outwards, diffident and quickly. He waited for the applause to fade. He stared out, unblinking, unsmiling, until
the chamber returned to absolute quiet. Only then did
he drop the cane at his feet. The noise echoed in the
quiet. He kicked the cane away, and the image of it sliding

across the polished stage came to symbolize the anger of India.

'None of you here will welcome what I have to say,' he began. 'I have come because my Parliament is in ruins and my house has been destroyed. My staff who protected me are dead. My daughter is in a wheelchair.' He glanced down at Meenakshi who raised her hand to him. He took it, squeezed and smiled. It had taken a lot to persuade Meenakshi to come with him.

'She is here not as a mascot, but as evidence of what you and I and the citizens we represent are ultimately working for – the protection and the future of our children and our families. There is nothing in the world more simple to understand.'

He paused to allow another wave of applause to break out. He let it die naturally, resting, two hands on the stand, absorbing the stabbing pain which seared through his right leg. As a stillness again took over the hall, Mehta said: 'I have failed in that simple duty. I have failed abysmally.'

He dragged his leg forward to try to ease the pain. His face creased up. The ache he could withstand with a poker face. The sudden jabbing of torn nerve ends still took him by surprise. He gripped the stand. 'In due course, I will take the honourable path and resign. India is a democracy and we have institutional machinery which will make the transition seamless and transparent. But before I go, I will announce to this assembly my nation's new doctrine, which is being implemented to protect our people, and I will explain why we are doing it. And when that is done, perhaps the television reporters will ask the White House whether or not it believes I am an honourable man or an enemy of the United States.'

32

Washington, DC, USA

'**You can't go** in, John. He's got five minutes to go,' said Jenny Rinaldi as Kozerski burst into the outer office where she sat. He pointed to the screen where the General Assembly meeting was being broadcast live. Kozerski slowed his pace. 'No,' he said, filling a paper cup from the chilled-water dispenser. 'Tell him I'm coming in. And turn that thing up and listen.'

Kozerski drained his cup, waited for Rinaldi to start speaking through her intercom, then went straight into the Oval Office. 'I'm sorry to interrupt, sir,' he said, taking in the half-dozen senators whom West was meeting. 'But you've got to see this.' He picked up the remote, flipped on the television, and stood, arms folded, by the door. Jim West got to his feet, and concentrated, hands on his hips, in the middle of the room. One senator got up to leave, but West waved him back down.

'. . . and you may ask, why I use such an emotive term as enemy of the United States,' Mehta was saying. West shot a perplexed look across to Kozerski.

'I will explain.' Mehta paused to grip the stand and balance himself in a more comfortable way. The camera was close on his face, showing the creased brow, eyes blinking and watery. Kozerski stepped over to be next to West. 'He's also announced he's resigning,' he whispered.

'Those young men who attacked my parliament and my house were terrorists,' said Mehta. 'They were a product of Pakistan. Pakistan is a strange and unfortunate product of many nations. From Saudi Arabia it imported an extreme form of Islam. China and North Korea gave it its missiles and nuclear weapons. The United States flattered, scolded but ultimately built up Pakistan to what it has become. It trained its shadowy and evil institutions; it applauded its dictators; it has been there at every stage of the journey and has made Pakistan what it is today. Every action the United States has taken regarding Pakistan has been for nothing except its own short-term national interest.

'Those of you from smaller nations, trying to determine a way forward, will know how brutalizing it is to have the forces of the United States government lined up against you. Believe me, it is not much better if you are the world's biggest democracy.'

The camera, picking up applause again, shifted to a wide shot as dozens of delegates clapped. It settled on the unmoving hands of the US ambassador, eyes down as if reading notes.

'Why, you might ask, am I fingering the United States? Why not China? Why not Pakistan itself? Why not Russia? It is because—' Mehta shook his head and tapped his file. 'What can I say, without surrendering my self-control to anger? It is because in 1998 when we declared ourselves a nuclear power with underground tests, we were punished by America with sanctions designed to slow down our development. In 1999, when Pakistani troops invaded our territory in what is known as the Kargil war, President Clinton urged us to be patient. In 2001, when the United States began its War on Terror, we were asked to absorb provocations and not respond. Our Parliament was attacked back then. We had evidence of Pakistani involvement, but we did not go to war. There were other assaults, and we trusted the United States to bring Pakistan under control.

'In 2002, when President George W. Bush announced the US's new National Security Strategy, it laid out a doctrine, and I am ashamed to say we trusted that as well. It told us that America would help all nations that needed its assistance in combating terror; that the allies of terror were the enemies of civilization; that the United States would work to bring the hope of democracy, development, free markets and free trade to every corner of the world. In order to achieve this, it stated that it had no intention of allowing any foreign power to catch up with the status America had created for itself since the fall of the Soviet Union. Never again would there be parity. There would be only one power and one set of values and all of us, including a great democracy and culture like my own, would have to live within it. And I am ashamed to say that we accepted that doctrine. I am sure each of you have stories to tell of how it has actually worked for you.'

He stopped speaking to rearrange his notes. Unsteadily he picked up a glass of water and drank.

'Where's he heading with this?' whispered West to Kozerski, who shrugged, keeping an eye on the UN General Assembly Hall which was completely quiet waiting for Mehta to continue.

'With that doctrine, America took on the responsibility of keeping our nations, our institutions and our families safe. It told us that there was only one way forward and that was the American way, that either we were with the United States or we were against it, and that there was no middle way. It told us that it would not hesitate to act alone and that, if necessary, it would exercise its right of self-defence by acting pre-emptively.'

Mehta put his hand up to his eye. The camera showed cuts and bruises still unhealed on his face. He let go of the rostrum and leant down towards Meenakshi. She handed him a laptop computer. He opened it up and slotted a plug on to the side. 'Son of a bitch,' muttered West. 'What's he doing now?'

'Visual display of some sort,' said Kozerski softly.

'Can you switch us to the main screens?' asked Mehta into the microphone. The camera cut from Mehta's face to the strange sight of the black and white booting of a laptop, following each step until it settled on the blurred image of a man in a hospital bed – a video sequence on pause. Mehta pressed another button. 'For the benefit of the interpreters, what you are about to hear is in Arabic,' he explained. The now world-famous photograph of Meenakshi and Mehta in the middle of the assault on the Parliament building came up on the screens. 'Most of you will be familiar with this,' said Mehta. 'I am showing it to you now to explain that the terrorist my daughter is tending in this photograph is named Ammar Abu Taleb. He is from Sana in Yemen. He was trained by al-Qaida in Afghanistan in the late 1990s. His voice print is known to the US National Security Agency, who if they wish can verify at least his identity. He was interviewed at a military hospital in Delhi, where he remains now.' Mehta tapped a series of buttons on the laptop. 'I will now play a key part of the video,' he announced.

The first scene was a wide view of the hospital room, showing the backs of two interrogators' heads. An armed guard in silhouette was at the side of the frame. Taleb himself sat up in bed. His neck was in a brace which seemed to come up over his head and cover his eyes in a blindfold, making it obvious why Mehta had challenged the NSA to make a voice identification as well. Taleb's left hand was free. His right was handcuffed to the bed frame.

The first voice came from the interrogator on the right. His colleague never spoke at all.

'When were you told to carry out the attack?'

'We were never given a date,' Taleb replied. The camera moved closer in to show the synchronization of the voice and the lips.

'You mean you could have attacked any time you wanted,' pressed the interrogator who was now off screen.

'Not any time.'

'What, then?'

'It was to be a certain time before President Khan's visit to Malaysia. That is all we knew.'

'So you knew he was to be murdered?'

'We knew?'

'All of you.'

'No. I knew and Khamis, who has been martyred, knew.'

'Who is Khamis? Is he the one who flew the plane?'

'Yes.'

'Who told you?'

Silence.

'Who told you?'

Silence again. The camera returned to a wide view. A guard stepped in and roughly pulled away the cover on Taleb's eyes. The interrogator leaned over the bed and thrust a photograph in front of Taleb's eyes. 'Do you know this man?'

Taleb didn't answer. His face gave nothing away. The interrogator turned the photograph to the camera. He put another one in front of Taleb, who remained expressionless. Then with a third one, he blinked and swallowed. A fourth, nothing again. On the fifth, his eyes reacted harshly, flaring at the camera with hatred. And on the sixth, whether on purpose or by instinctive reaction, he tilted his head to say he knew the identity of the man being shown to him.

Each picture was also shown to the camera. The third was of a woman with whom Taleb was known to have been in love, kneeling on a bed, naked and kissing another man with her hands draped around his neck. The fifth was of Taleb's father, an elderly man, his head yanked backwards, being marched away by police, and his mother, her hands held helplessly in front of her, standing at the door of his childhood home. The sixth photograph was of Air Vice-Marshal Tassudaq Qureshi, in full uniform, against a backdrop of a line of F-16 fighter aircraft.

'And him?' said the interrogator, showing him another picture. 'Do you know who he is?'

A tilt of the head again.

'Who?' pressed the interrogator.

'Qureshi,' whispered Taleb.

'Have you met him?'

'He talked to us. Yes.'

'When?'

'Before the death of Khan. But I met him before that even, during the Kashmir Jihad. He talked to us then as well.'

Mehta turned off the video. The screen went back to him. He unplugged the laptop and handed it down to Meenakshi.

'Do any of you know these guys?' West asked the senators in the Oval Office. 'Pat, how about you?' he said, looking at Patrick Chase, by far the oldest politician in the room, who had made his career by speaking on security and intelligence issues. 'A bit, Mr President. They're guys we've used and abused over the years, just like Mehta said.'

'Get Peter Brock up here,' said West to Kozerski.

On the screen, Mehta took another drink of water. 'This General Assembly is not a world government and its resolutions are not legally binding. So I am not here to ask for any of that. I am here to use this forum to give a message to the United States of America. You know Najeeb Hussain and Tassudaq Qureshi. Like Pakistan itself, you have helped mould these men into what they are. If you are to retain your position as the only world superpower, you will dismantle the authority of these men and everything they represent. You will do it swiftly, without debate and with whatever means necessary. You have failed to protect our nation, and India is giving you one last chance to prove you are worthy of the great responsibility you volunteered to take on. If you do not act, India will go it alone. If you do not back us, we will consider you to be against us. Mr Secretary-General, thank you for allowing me the floor.'

Mount Kanggamchan missile base, North Korea

Park Ho caught Vasant Mehta's address on BBC World just as he was leaving. He heard the helicopter coming in to land and listened to the throb of its engines from the roof as the Indian Prime Minister flung down the gauntlet to the United States. When Mehta finished a few delegates clapped, but their efforts were soon lost in the confusing silence which followed the end of the speech.

Park watched the transmission, transfixed by the event. He was trying to work out how much Mehta knew and how much America knew. How much would Mehta still be hiding? And how seriously was he challenging Jim West to back him in a war to destroy Pakistan?

On the screen, in the UN Assembly Hall, carefully, using the rostrum for balance, Mehta stepped down and rested his hands on Meenakshi's wheelchair. Someone ran across the stage this time and handed him the fallen cane. And when Mehta and Meenakshi started their slow journey back, a hum of voices began around the hall, getting louder and louder until the presenter cut in, eyes down on her notes to recite the main points of Mehta's speech.

Mehta had exposed Qureshi. He had named China. But North Korea had not been named. Park had just taken his coat from the back of the door when the weathered face of Senator Patrick Chase appeared on screen, his plentiful grey hair blown about in the wind. The shot widened to show the senator standing on a spot just inside the White House grounds reserved for press interviews.

'Yes, I did watch it with the President,' said Chase

when asked. 'And it's for the President to give his own reaction. I have just this to say. America feels for the Indian Prime Minister and his family. Both he and his nation have been through a terrible tragedy. But it is wrong to turn on your friends. America is a friend and ally of India. We will do everything we can to help it through this difficult time. But we do not enjoy being threatened by any nation at any time, regardless of what ordeal it is recovering from.'

Park turned off the television, locked the door behind him and took the lift to the roof. Outside, the helicopter rotor blades threw a rush of cool air towards him. Park broke into a jog. As soon as he was on board, the pilot lifted off, turning south and climbing to clear the mountains ahead. The journey did not take long, but it was enough time for Park to change from military uniform into a suit and tie. The helicopter dipped through a cloud which hung between peaks and juddered down to a helipad on top of an octagonally shaped building, next to a fast-running river and flanked by high trees.

He was met by the virologist, Li Pak, who escorted him down to the hotel grounds, with its manicured gardens, tennis courts, a golf course, swimming pool and riding stables. For anyone who didn't know better, it was a remote luxury resort, hidden away in pristine mountains.

Underneath was a vast military complex, completely invisible from above ground.

A line of Mercedes limousines curved round the driveway, together with two coaches displaying a local tourism logo. From a frozen fountain in the centre, craftsmen were sculpturing the image of a missile in the ice. Inside, the foyer was a ten-storey atrium. A statue of Kim Il-sung, dressed in casual slacks and a short-sleeved shirt, was suspended from the ceiling. Mingling with the guests and staff were members of Park's own Reconnaissance Bureau protection unit, trained to such sophisticated levels that they could be infiltrated into almost any society anywhere in the world with little risk of detection.

Park in his suit and Li Pak in his open-neck blue shirt attracted no undue attention. Sitting or wandering between the armchairs, the bar and the coffee shop were some of the passengers from the missing Air Koryo flight – two Chinese, a Pakistani and two Russians, all of them concentrating on a BBC World television interview with the Chinese President Jamie Song.

Park wanted to go into the bar to watch. But the men off the flight were still alive and not in a prison cell precisely because they belonged to the intelligence agencies of friendly governments. If they saw Park, they would recognize him. Park held back in the lobby, the picture distant but clear enough to see the Chinese President speaking against a studio backdrop picture of Tiananmen Square.

'Yes, I have spoken to Vasant Mehta about our alliance with Pakistan,' said Song. 'Our conversations have been confidential and – as a matter of detail – I can tell you they are conducted in English without interpreters.'

'But the point surely is, President Song,' interrupted the presenter, 'that the Indian Prime Minister made a direct accusation about China's involvement in terrorism which originates from Pakistan.'

'You have a vivid imagination,' laughed Song, genially. 'Although, in a broad-brush way, you could be partly right. Pakistan is India's enemy. They have been at war on and off for more than sixty years. China is an ally of Pakistan. We supply it with *conventional* weapons, not, I stress, with *nuclear* weapons. All this is a matter of record. We are trading partners. And I might add that our trade with India has also grown tenfold in the past decade. Now, India believes that if we stop giving Pakistan military support, its troubles would end. This, I am afraid, is not the case. Indeed, if you follow India's argument to its conclusion, every government-to-government relationship would be determined by the arms trade and that simply is not the case. What must be addressed is not the weapons supply but the causes of conflict.'

The picture turned back to an impatient presenter, now captioned as Susannah Sampson, her blonde hair hooked back behind her ear revealing the earpiece through which she was getting instructions from the studio.

'All right, then,' she said, with an engaging smile that Song could not see. 'To a related subject: do you know either General Najeeb Hussain or Air Vice-Marshal Tassu-daq Qureshi?'

'Qureshi, I know,' said Song, his face deadpan and throwing the presenter off balance.

'Er, you said you know him?' she managed.

'He was passing through Beijing recently. It happened after the attack on the Indian Parliament. He had a long-scheduled appointment with our military, and I took the opportunity to call him into my office in Zhongnanhai.'

'Zhongnanhai being the complex of offices at the heart of Chinese government,' Sampson commented to remind her viewers. 'And what did you tell him?'

'We had what you might call a full and frank exchange of views. I sent a recording of the conversation to Vasant Mehta. It is up to him to disclose its contents.'

'Are you saying you have taken measures to help India?'

'I will only say that no nation can take its alliance with any other nation for granted. There are some boundaries which must not be crossed. Prime Minister Mehta has given the United States a similar message in his address today. It is one which China has much empathy with.' Song leant forward in his seat. 'Now, I do apologise to your viewers around the world, but I have a pressing schedule which I must now get back to.'

He was unplugging his earpiece when Sampson threw in one more question. 'Mr President, what about North Korea? What can you tell us about what's happening there?'

Rather than be filmed disentangling himself from earpieces and microphones, Song chose to answer. 'There's been a military takeover in North Korea, Susannah,' he said authoritatively. 'We are not certain who is in charge. Americans are grieving their dead from Yokata. We all feel so much for them. Jim West and his team have done a brilliant job in defusing a world crisis. South Korea has acted in a statesmanlike manner by apologizing for that dreadful shooting at Panmunjom. China is party to the talks going on now at the United Nations in New York to make sure no such tragedy happens again.'

'But if the US strikes North Korea—'

'Susannah,' smiled Song, with visible impatience. 'If you were party to my conversations with Jim West, you would not even be asking that question. There will be no strike.'

Park slipped away before the hotel guests turned their attention away from the television. Li led him downstairs to the basement, and they took a lift two more storeys down. They stepped out on to the top floor of another atrium, carved deep into the ground.

'You've taken them to a different place?' queried Park, as Li ushered him along.

'Yes, General,' said Li. 'This is a totally new series of experiments for us. We have to test contamination areas, which is why the subjects are kept in different areas. For example, at one time in a hospital in Germany the cough from one patient with smallpox contaminated patients on three other floors of the building. So we are looking at that, together with the survivability of the virus in varying temperatures. Whether ethnicity is making a difference in the fatality of the disease. That sort of thing.'

Li Pak, having been left alone with his science, was more relaxed with Park Ho now. He handed the general a white coat from a cupboard, put one on himself, then opened the door into an observation room. Two scientists were working at computers. Another two looked through a floor-to-ceiling glass panel, checking what they saw on high-resolution video monitors at their desks.

'We have conducted one experiment using the variola major virus and IL-4 on a Caucasian,' explained Li, offering Park a chair at the end of the room. 'He died within two days. It was astonishing. Even with haemorrhagic and malignant forms of smallpox death usually takes at least five days after the onset of the rash.'

'What about normal smallpox?' said Park, becoming absorbed with what he saw on the other side of the glass.

'The incubation period is up to fourteen days after infection,' said Li. 'Patients rarely become infectious themselves until the appearance of the rashes. Six days after that neutralizing antibodies are detected. Then—'

'How do we distribute the weapon?' interrupted Park, his back to Li and his head resting on the glass.

'We have a window of only a few weeks to decide. Once summer comes in Europe and the United States, the virus will survive only a few hours. In temperatures of 31 degrees, it will be less than six hours. If we strike in colder temperatures – no more than 10 degrees Celsius, with humidity no more than 20 per cent, the virus will have a lifespan of at least twenty-four hours, more than three times longer.'

'I asked *how* do we distribute, not how long it would take,' snapped Park.

'We are still experimenting with the aerosol,' replied Li,

contritely. 'So far we have been unable to stabilize the virus enough to survive the pressurized delivery. If it did work, it would infect between fifty and a hundred people. The second generation would expand ten or twenty times, say the infection of 2,000 people, and the third generation would infect 40,000 and so on. But with the normal incubation rate, General, I do not believe we would achieve what we want. After the first generation, the whole population would be vaccinated—'

'I thought you said the IL-4 agent would neutralize the antidote,' said Park, turning round and looking Li straight in the eye.

The scientist hesitated: 'They know the IL-4 mousepox agent is missing from the Canberra laboratory. They also know about the theft from the Pokrov laboratories near Moscow. They don't know where it went, but they will be manufacturing new vaccine. Again, the longer we wait, the greater the chances are they will have a vaccine.'

Park glanced sceptically across at Li. 'This is a military offensive, not a scientific experiment.'

'General, I understand it better than most. If we deliver this weapon so that it is neutralized within a few days and if our second or third missile launches fail, then the whole project will fail. We will be conquered and the United States will be stronger than ever. The only way we can win is by using the weapon of fear and by showing we can deliver it. This is your campaign, General. You have others working on the missiles. For my part, I will guarantee you the best and most widespread delivery. But you have to trust me.'

For a second, Park hesitated, enough to let Li know he had broken through the outer membrane of this most impenetrable military leader. Park coughed, brought out a packet of cigarettes, then had second thoughts. 'All right, comrade,' he said slowly. 'What do you propose?'

'We will carry out simultaneous experiments with aerosol and human delivery. Once we know the exact contamination strength of the IL-4/smallpox virus, we will attack. If the aerosol is unreliable, we will have to use a human delivery mechanism. It will not be so effective, but with the speed of fatalities from the IL-4 agent we will be able to achieve our objectives.'

Park nodded and turned back to watch what was happening on the other side of the glass. Scientists moved around in biohazard suits. The body of a blonde woman – the Swedish aid worker, Agneta Carlsson – lay on a marble slab. She had been stripped of her clothes. Her skin was covered in scabs and lesions, from which one scientist was taking samples.

To the left, but separated by a wall of reinforced glass, were two middle-aged Caucasian men. The British ambassador to Pyongyang, Bob Robertson, and the Hungarian ambassador, Jozsef Striker, were sitting at a desk, drinking coffee. They glanced up from time to time at the two-way mirror, and it was then that the apprehension showed in their faces. They were confined but not handcuffed or restricted.

In the section with Anita Carlsson's body was her partner, Jonas Wallen, out of view of the two diplomats and huddled in a corner, unable to look at her corpse. Wallen was whimpering and shaking.

'She died three hours ago,' said Li, 'less than twelve hours after being infected. It was astonishing. We want to see how long it will take for the disease and fatality to strike the man.'

'And the other two?' said Park.

'We will refine our experiments using the Korean passengers. After that, we will carry out our final tests on these two men.'

'Very good,' said Park, getting up to leave.

'It is apt that the British ambassador is here,' said Li, with a new-found confidence. 'The British were the first to use smallpox as a biological weapon, against the French and native Americans between 1754 and 1767 in North America. They deliberately handed out contaminated blankets which had been used by smallpox patients.'

'**If you lose** India, you lose,' said Lizzie West, pacing hands on hips around the middle of her father's living room in the White House. Jim West sat at one end of the sofa, his legs up on the coffee table, with a lukewarm cup of black coffee in his hands. He controlled his irritation as he listened to his daughter.

'You know why people hate us?' continued Lizzie. 'It's because we offer this great brand name, and when things get difficult, we turn round and say . . . "Yeah, but you didn't read the small print." She stopped in front of him, glaring down. 'They don't hate us because we're rich. They don't hate us because they're jealous. They hate us because we don't tell them the rules, and we don't tell them because there aren't any and there aren't any because you, the President, and those who came before you, haven't bothered to make them up. And why haven't you? Because it makes it easier to keep control.'

That smarted. The last person he wanted to fight with was Lizzie. She had none of her mother's tact and gentleness. That had gone to Chuck who, far from wanting to change the world, was happy with his family in Oakland. Lizzie had inherited high ambition and moral values from West, and was now using them against him.

West shook his head. 'It's not that simple, Lizzie,' he said tiredly. 'Not that simple at all.'

She stepped over his legs and sat down next to him. 'No, Dad, it is. Imagine that you're a farmer in Argentina or Nigeria. Everything you do is infected with inefficiency and corruption. Suddenly, the HSBC or Citibank opens a branch in your town. Or Nestlé comes along and suggests you change from growing rice to coffee and cocoa. You see hope. You see honesty. You see a future for your children. You do as they say. You put your money in their banks. You grow the crops they want. Then, one day you wake up and find there's been a coup or the government's declared bankrupt. Your accounts are frozen. There's no market for your crops. You go to the bank, which says it can do nothing to help. You go to Nestlé and they say, "Free market, you're on your own." They pull out of your town and set up somewhere else across the world, until there's trouble there, too. Then, they pull out again.' She turned in her seat so that West felt the full force of his daughter's onslaught. He understood how her reputation in her field had become so formidable. 'That's why they hate us, Dad. Because it's happened too many times.'

West swung his feet to the ground and put his cup on the table. 'So what should I do?' he asked lazily.

'The multinationals must not use weak government to make profit and they must take responsibility for the lives of the people who earn them their money. Believe me, Dad, if they did, there would be more wealth and fewer wars.'

'Nice thought,' said West, to which Lizzie rolled her eyes.

'I know, call me naive. Call me simplistic. But if *you* don't do it, no one will.'

West laughed. 'You're unique, Lizzie. You know that? An Islamic uprising in Asia, on the brink of an Indian–Pakistan war, American body bags in Yokata, and you want me to announce a new global charter for international business. Nice thought.'

'Why not?'

He glanced across at her incredulously, then recognized the challenge in her flaring eyes.

'Time's not right,' he said flatly.

'When is it right?'

But before West could answer, there was a rap with a cane on the double doors. Lizzie looked behind her, smiled, gave her father a peck on the forehead, jumped over the back of the sofa and opened the doors. Vasant Mehta, stick in hand, kissed her on the cheek, refused her hand on his elbow, and limped in.

'That was one hell of a speech, Prime Minister,' said West, standing up. Mehta let the President help him into an armchair.

The night had settled, but lamps in the White House grounds sent patterns through the corner windows, making the room ripple with light across Valerie's textured blues, greens and reds. West rarely used the room for entertaining, but Lizzie had insisted on it. If Meenakshi was in town, she said, they weren't going to sit with her in a stuffy state room.

Meenakshi appeared at the door, still in her wheelchair, pushed by Mary Newman. 'I don't know how anyone can look so delightful, having been through your ordeal,' said West with a smile. 'Now, do you want to get out of that thing or stay where you are?'

'I'm sure Secretary Newman'll help me hobble out,' said Meenakshi, turning round and jokingly raising one eyebrow at the Secretary of State. 'We couldn't work out which one of us should use the wheelchair. But Dad absolutely refused. He would rather have crawled to the podium than be wheeled.' She leant down, cleared the bottom of her sari from her ankles, lifted her wounded leg to the floor and pushed herself up. Newman took hold of her elbow. Meenakshi rested her other hand on Newman's shoulder and manoeuvred herself into an armchair.

Lizzie headed straight for Meenakshi to give her a big hug. 'You are so, so brave.'

'And I never managed to put on one of your suits,' laughed Meenakshi. She pointed to her bandaged leg. 'Don't worry, it's only for a few days. There's nothing like getting blown up to get a good rest, which is what my doctors *had* ordered. Then my father, who's far more badly hurt than me, insists we both get on a plane and fly over to the Big Apple.' She screwed up her face. 'Air India, too. We don't even have an Air Force One.'

'I would have sublet you ours,' quipped West, 'if you'd told me you were coming.'

'What, and given you notice?' said Mehta, shaking his head. 'We have to keep our American allies on the ball.'

John Kozerski appeared at the door, a confused expression on his face. 'Prime Minister, sir, two phone messages.'

'Keep going, John,' said Mehta. 'Whatever it is I can take it.'

'Your daughter, Romila, called from Buenos Aires. She's at a NAFTA banking conference and wants to know if you'll be here for a couple more days. Otherwise she'll break off and fly up.'

'Impetuous woman,' muttered Mehta, unable to hide his pride. 'I'll call her shortly, John. Just tell her to stay where she is and keep making money. Her father will need it one day.'

'If someone throws me a phone, I'll call,' said Meenakshi, glancing over at Mehta. 'You've thanked her for the flowers, have you, father?'

'Indeed. Many times over,' said Mehta.

'And the second message,' said Kozerski, reading a piece of paper in his hand as if he couldn't remember straight off. 'Your wife has just flown into Washington. She wants to join you this evening.'

Mehta's face became a shadow in a storm. He shook his head, but didn't reply.

'I'll call her,' offered Meenakshi softly.

Seemingly out of nowhere, an intercom started up. 'Mr President, the National Security Advisor is ready.'

Mehta recovered immediately and eyed West. 'I thought this was a friendly evening gathering.'

'Pete Brock's an old friend,' said West, pausing for a second. 'You know that, Vasant. At the risk of incurring your wrath, why don't we head next door with Mary?' He nodded in the direction of Meenakshi and Lizzie. 'You two stay here and we'll all meet up a bit later for something to eat.'

With his cane in one hand and gripping West's arm with the other, Mehta walked slowly out of the room. He didn't attempt small talk. West recognized the face of a man who had taken too much in too short a measure of time. Nor did West humour Mehta with his usual patter about the history of the White House and the great men and women who had walked through its rooms. It would have been especially out of place to a man whose official residence lay in ruins.

Instead West said: 'Thanks for the advice. Of the billions of dollars I spend on advice a year, that was the best I've had for some time.'

'Did I give you advice?' asked Mehta. His head was bent. His eyes were on the floor. His fingers curled tighter around West's arm as a spasm of pain shot through him.

'You told me to get Lizzie up here.'

'That's right, I did.' Mehta managed a smile. 'I had forgotten about that.'

Newman, who was following a couple of steps behind, moved ahead of them and opened the door to the President's study in his private quarters. There was a small desk in front of the windows overlooking a back garden, hidden from public view. The walls were lined with books West had collected since childhood. One shelf was used for reference and business books. The rest were those he had read for pleasure, ranging from Henry Kissinger's *Diplomacy*, through Paul Kennedy's *The Rise and Fall of the Great Powers*, Vaclav Havel's *Living in Truth* and on to novels by Graham Greene, Aldous Huxley and John le Carré, and poetry by T. S. Eliot, Ruth Fainlight and Lawrence Ferlinghetti.

Newman turned on the side lamps and one lit up a framed photograph in between the two windows. It had been taken one Saturday during an open day on the railroad in Oregon, when West's father, Michael, had taken the family out. West's mother, Nancy, had a proud arm around her husband's waist. They must have been in their mid-thirties. His little sister, Barbara, and his older brother Henry stood raised behind them on the slatted bed of a rail truck. West had lit the picture and arranged the study to remind himself of where he had come from. There was nothing in the room to suggest high office.

Newman arranged cushions in the corner of the sofa for Mehta. Together with West she helped him down. 'Can I get you both a drink?' she asked, opening a small fridge in the wall by the desk.

'Scotch and water, please,' said Mehta.

'Same here,' said West, sitting in the swivel chair at the desk, and turning it in to face the centre of the room, just as Peter Brock and Lazaro Campbell opened the door and stepped inside. 'You'd better make that four,' added West. 'Gentlemen, welcome. Prime Minister, you know Mr Campbell, of course. The elder and more distinguished gentleman is Peter Brock, my National Security Advisor.'

Brock sat on the sofa next to Mehta. Campbell walked across to Newman. 'Secretary of State, ma'am, let me do that for you.'

'A woman should never think herself too important to pour the men a drink,' said Newman lightly. She held out two glasses ready to go. 'But you can hand them round, Lazaro.'

When he had done that, Campbell chose the smallest chair set back in a alcove from the rest of the room. Newman, also with a whisky and water, took a hand-carved rocking chair, kicked off her shoes and tilted herself back in it.

'To you, Prime Minister,' said West, raising his glass. 'And to your brave daughter.'

'Thank you,' said Mehta, sipping his drink and resting the glass in his hand on the side of the sofa.

'This is an informal meeting,' said West, although his change of tone concentrated the atmosphere. 'Both Peter and Mary are close friends. Mr Campbell, as you know, was halfway through an idea with you in Delhi when the terrorists struck. I asked him to join us so we can see this through. Mary is against us interfering in Pakistan. I'd like you to hear her argument. Nothing need be decided, and' – he checked his watch – 'after we've finished our drinks, we're all going to have dinner together. In essence, if between us we can achieve a regime change in Pakistan, and take that nation's nuclear weapons facilities out of its control, then we have achieved our immediate objective. Once that's done, Prime Minister, we will pass legislation committing the United States to a twenty-five-year aid and construction programme for Pakistan. We'll give that damn country a generation to rescue itself.'

Mehta drank slowly, taking an ice cube into his mouth and crunching it. 'I'm not sure you've really grasped it, Jim,' he said resignedly. 'Whether a corrupt democracy or an unimaginative military dictator runs that damn country, India will still be a victim of terror attacks. If I let it go on, Hindu–Muslim violence will increase in India itself and thousands more will die. If I go to war, Pakistan will use a nuclear weapon. I am caught between a rock and a hard place. I am sure Mr Campbell is a skilled soldier and can take out Qureshi and his henchman if ordered to do so. I am sure you have a plan to neutralize Pakistan's nuclear weapons systems – although I am not so convinced that will be successful. But even if that works, who will stop the terror attacks? And if they're not stopped—' Mehta shugged, crunched the final bit of ice and swallowed it.

'Could you give Jim's suggestion a chance?' prodded Newman who, with her left foot curled up under her in the rocking chair, looked a world away from her usual ordered image of Secretary of State.

'There's only one way you can do it, Mary,' said Mehta, 'and that's to occupy the country, take over its security agencies and root out the terror elements. Do an Iraq.' He took another sip, unable to hide his frustration.

'Prime Minister,' said Brock. 'You've vividly explained the position you are in. Do you have a solution, any policy which you believe will work?'

Mehta nodded and looked straight at the President. 'I have thought about this long and hard, Jim. You won't like it, but I see no other way out.'

'Trust me,' said West, forcing a smile. But even then, with scenarios swirling around his mind, he had never

envisaged the one Vasant Mehta laid out. And as soon as
the Indian Prime Minister had spoken he understood why
Mehta had given his global audience the choice of deciding
whether he was an honourable man or an enemy of the
United States.

35

Dukchun Palace, Pyongyang, North Korea

Through the secured glass, Park Ho watched as two overweight middle-aged Caucasian men negotiated for their lives. Three guards lifted the British ambassador to his feet, walked him to an area next door, unlocked his handcuffs and pushed him inside. Bob Robertson, who had been posted to Pyongyang only two months earlier, tripped but managed to block his fall against the wall. A door slid across to secure the area into a separate room.

Jozsef Striker, the second man, was kept back, handcuffed to a chair. He had been in North Korea for more than five years. Park used to meet with him regularly. As Striker pleaded with the guards, Park heard his name mentioned: Park was the man the guards should contact to secure his release. If Park had been a sadist, he would have gone through and taunted the Hungarian ambassador. But he was not. He was a tactician, and inadvertently and unfortunately Striker had become a cog in the wheels of Park's war.

Robertson had been chosen to go in first because he was younger and fitter, although neither man was in good shape. He steadied himself and leant against the wall. The room created for the experiment was a mix of strange objects: bed sheets, writing paper, kitchen utensils; different flooring of concrete, tiles, carpet and other materials; a wardrobe of clothes; a tube of toothpaste; poured glasses of whisky, water and beer; and other examples of everyday life in the West.

Robertson tentatively stepped around the room, touching and examining. 'There'll be comeback, you know,' he shouted, his head automatically turning up towards the ceiling, where various curtain fabrics had been hung. 'Whatever you're doing violates every international law. We'll throw the book at you for this.'

'Just relax, Ambassador,' said Li in softly spoken, accented English. 'We have to conduct some more medical tests, then, of course, you can return home.'

'Bullshit,' muttered Robertson. He flung himself into an armchair, and stared at the wall as if he could see right through it. 'If you're going to execute me—' he whispered, not finishing his thoughts.

The nozzle of a household aerosol can was inserted in the partition. But just as Li gave the signal for it to be sprayed into the room, a radio crackled, calling Park Ho urgently to the telephone. Park raised his hand to delay the experiment and took the call.

The call had been directed to Park on a military line from the Chinese city of Yanji close to the northern border with North Korea. 'Mason is being sent to the United States to be interrogated with sodium pentothal,' said the caller.

'Thank you,' said Park, ending the call. If anyone had succeeded in knowing the general intimately, they might have detected a look of satisfaction.

Park himself had ordered the theft of a bioterror agent from a country where the rule of law remained intact and effective. Not only would Park get his hands on IL-4, but also he would sow confusion among the Western democracies. Yes, they would trace telephone calls and interrogate suspects. The more they suspected, the more the international media would play up the need for a military strike on North Korea. And, then, the more reason he would have to defend his nation.

'Go ahead,' he said to Li, pushing back the chair and standing up as the aerosol spray was released into Robertson's prison cell. By the time the virus took effect, the ambassador would be tired of his own whimpers and threats. Park would return shortly before rashes were due to show. If the IL-4 formula was working, that would be in less than a day. Once the rashes had broken out, Robertson, at his most contagious, would be put back in with Striker.

Key to the experiment would be the speed with which Striker was also infected. If it took several days, then the IL-4 agent would only be effective for the primary infection. But if Striker fell sick within twenty-four hours, the agent would remain with the virus, through secondary and tertiary infections and beyond, and Park would have at his disposal a genuine weapon of mass destruction.

Park had chosen smallpox precisely because it represented the dark unknown of bioterror. In 1995, after years of planning, a Japanese religious cult released the chemical nerve agent Sarin on the Tokyo subway. But only eleven people died, not exactly wholesale slaughter. In 2001, after the 11 September attack on New York, highly contagious military-quality anthrax was sent through the post to a senior politician and journalists. Only five had died.

The initial smallpox outbreak itself might be enough to paralyse America and Europe's health-care systems. If it spread, tripling and quadrupling from infection to infection, Park would regard it as an added bonus.

But at which stage should he hand over the vaccine? He was undecided. He was sure only that Robertson should be given it at the earlier stage, because he would need his testimony of both the brutality of the disease and the swiftness of the cure. Striker would get it later. And if it was too late, so be it. His English was heavily accented and would not be so well understood on television.

Deep in thought, Park took the lift and walked across the hotel lobby, alone and ignored by guests and staff. One day, he would be recognized. But at the moment, it was more important that he be proved right.

36

Washington, DC, USA

Lazaro Campbell helped Mehta out of the President's study. As they slowly made their way to the door West, Newman and Brock sat without speaking, stunned at what they had been told. West had suggested a fifteen-minute cooling-off period before getting together again with Lizzie and Meenakshi. He understood exactly Mehta's point. He could see how it would secure India's borders and allow its economy to grow without the constant threat of war. But as President of the United States, charged with protecting American interests, there was no way he could allow it to happen.

'I'm not having the damn Chinese in Pakistan, and I'm not having them in Camp David,' snapped West, as Newman asked the switchboard to connect her to Zhongnanhai in Beijing.

'You can't not,' answered Newman. 'It'd be the diplomatic equivalent of an act of war.'

'We're not asking the Brazilians?' said West, mockingly. 'They've got a big country, too.' His neck was bent down to hold the receiver as he waited to be connected to Stuart Nolan in Downing Street, hoping that the grizzled British Prime Minister was enjoying a nightcap and not asleep in bed.

'Very helpful,' said Brock, supporting Newman. 'I'm sure China would be flattered to be compared to Brazil.'

'Don't insult Brazil.' West was about to say more, when he was connected. 'Stuart, you got five minutes? I need a favour, and I hope your diary's flexible.'

As West hung up, Brock was talking to Alexander Yushchuk, the Russian President's adviser. 'Alex, if he feels it'll leak out, we can send Air Force One for him, and pick him up in Helsinki or something ... Yeah, just don't get ... and no, we won't bill you in six months' time like the IMF does.'

Newman was through to Germany, where the Japanese Prime Minister was overnighting on a tour of Europe. 'I can't give you the specifics now, Toru, but Japan's presence is needed ... yes, I know you have a full diary, I know it is far away from your sphere of influence, but if China's here, I think you should be here.'

'Mary, you haven't confirmed that,' said West, as Newman finished the call.

Newman shook her head. 'Not yet, but Zhongnanhai is on the line now, and you've got to speak to him, Jim. This isn't one to delegate.' Newman thrust the telephone receiver in front of West. 'And don't forget,' she added with a smile, 'be humble and polite.'

'Jamie, sorry to chase you so early in the morning,' said West at his most modest. 'You were excellent in your BBC World interview. I envy you your polish ... Thank you. Thank you ... The reason I'm calling is that Vasant Mehta is with me now. Stuart Nolan is in town anyway as is Toru Sato ... Yes, yes, one hell of a coincidence. Andrei Kozlov has agreed to come over, and I know you're busy, but if you've the time, I think we could all have a useful meeting, get this India–Pakistan issue dealt with once and for all and maybe, with you and Toru here, we could tackle North Korea as well ... No. Absolutely private.'

He handed the receiver back to Newman who dropped it on the table, perched on the edge of the President's desk and sighed. 'Thank you, Jim.'

West took Newman's hand, squeezed it and withdrew.

'I hope, sometime soon, I can thank you for making me ask him.'

Newman dropped her head, not wishing the President to see her eyes aglow. Without Pierce, the atmosphere was completely different. She didn't know why West had excluded his Defense Secretary now. She didn't even ask. But she chose to enjoy it.

'You think Mehta's plan will work?' asked Brock.

'Sure it'll work,' replied West, full of sarcasm. 'Like Vietnam worked for us and Afghanistan worked for the Soviets.' He drained the last of his whisky. 'But we can't wait to try it and fail. We can't allow China to walk in and run Pakistan like a goddamn colony.' He stood up and slipped on his jacket. 'Mehta knows it won't work. But he's said to us: "Go in and take over Pakistan." We've said we won't. Now he's going to say to Jamie Song: "She's your monster. Go in, educate her, control her." But he knows that if we agree to that, we'll be handing China one of the most strategic pieces of territory anywhere in the world. And we can't do that for a nation that one day may be truly hostile to us. Never. Not in my presidency. Then, if China refuses – and this is what Mehta is telling us – India will risk a nuclear war with Pakistan in order to destroy it.'

He had his hand on the door handle. 'Mary, walk with me, will you? A woman's company makes me feel like a human being.'

Newman and West walked together down the corridor to his private sitting room. Brock ambled behind, giving them space. Campbell, coming from the washroom, fell into step with him.

'There's a plane for you at Andrews,' Brock instructed him quietly. 'It'll take you to Islamabad. The President wants you to be ready to go – the job done by the time this summit meets.'

As they stepped into the room, West turned and spotted Campbell. 'Meenakshi,' he said, 'this is a young protégé of mine, Lazaro Campbell. I've asked him along to close the age gap with you two young women.'

'Protégé? I hope so, Mr President,' said Meenakshi, wheeling her chair towards Campbell. 'Actually, Mr Campbell and I have met before. If it were not for him, I would now be dead.'

37

Islamabad, Pakistan

Lazaro Campbell lay face down on the grassless earth,
listening to the fading throb of the helicopter. The dim
shape, flying low against the rise of the hills, blended with
the darkness and became invisible. Fifty-six thousand feet
in the night sky above Islamabad, high enough to observe
the curvature of the earth, a Global Hawk Unmanned
Aerial Vehicle, or drone as it was more popularly known,
loitered, its cameras fixed on one specific target. It sent
back spot images which were relayed simultaneously to the
United States Central Command at MacDill Air Force
Base, Florida, the National Security Agency, the National
Security Advisor's offices at the White House, the Defense
Secretary's office in Room 3E880 in the Pentagon and the
Oval Office in the White House.

Intercepts were running through voice-identification
and code-breaking computers in real time. With the new
Pakistani military command speaking on secure lines, the
super-computers had now been programmed to find elements within the scrambled code. Each scrambler threw
up its own distinct signature, which identified the single
handset being used. With that they could pinpoint the
location of the speaker, a probability of who it was and
with whom he or she might be talking.

Using radar waves thrown out by the telephone signal,
they could distinguish the shape of the person making the
call and match it to shapes in the NSA database. It did not
guarantee identification, but it was used with other evidence to try to confirm that the right target was being

tracked. But as of yet, not even the NSA could determine what was being said.

As Campbell, John Burrows and twelve Ghurka special forces soldiers moved over the rugged terrain towards their target, analysts at the NSA picked out the call they were looking for. It was made from just outside the Chaklala cantonment area of Rawalpindi. The signal moved at vehicle speed along the main highway between Rawalpindi and Islamabad. Just before Constitution Avenue it stopped. Thirty seconds later, the caller dialled another number, this time to Karachi. The call lasted just over a minute, long enough for one of the cameras on the Global Hawk to pick out the moving vehicle in the traffic. Once locked on, it followed it to its destination.

Another of the Global Hawk's infrared lenses sent back images as fine as 0.25 metres in resolution. They outlined the contours of Tassudaq Qureshi's house outside Islamabad and the vehicles parked in the compound. Thermal imaging picked out the special forces commandos deployed to secure the property. Ground-penetrating radar showed the layout of the rooms inside and the image of Tasneem Qureshi in an armchair, with the television on, waiting for her husband to return home.

'Campbell's moving,' muttered West to Kozerski as, in a blur, one of the Pakistani guards disappeared from the screen. His principal advisers were in their own offices. Each was holding a meeting on an issue unconnected to the crisis in India. West had ordered them all to have viable alibis in case the political fireworks began.

On the ground, Campbell held back, while Burrows led his Ghurkas to take out the six guards on duty outside Qureshi's house. Burrows had decided the method – a knife across the throat, a hand over the mouth, two men simultaneously, and knife through the radio connection. A sniper was ready with a silenced rifle should anything go wrong.

The job was over within a minute. The bodies were pulled into the undergrowth, the Ghurkas, in replica guards uniforms, took positions throughout the grounds. Burrows, also in uniform, his face and hands blackened, a dark beret on his head, waited in the shadows, as Qureshi's Mercedes turned through the gate, crunched on to the gravel and pulled up to a halt. The driver got out, walked around the side of the car and opened the back door. Qureshi stepped out with a briefcase in his left hand and threw a cigarette on to the gravel. A light cast from inside the house dimmed as Tasneem passed across it to greet her husband at the door. Qureshi breathed the fresh hillside air deeply. The driver reversed the Mercedes to a covered but unlit part of the forecourt. Behind it was a small room which was his quarters.

As the driver stepped out of the car, a pistol muzzle was put to his head, a hand clamped over his mouth and a hypodermic needle pressed into his arm. He slumped and was gently lowered to the concrete floor.

Qureshi turned to look across at the lights of Islamabad and came face to face with Lazaro Campbell, dressed in a dark linen suit and open-neck shirt, his weapon concealed.

'We don't want to have to kill your wife,' Campbell said softly, pointing to the tiny spot revealing a sniper's infrared sights which danced across the wall of the house towards the door that Tasneem Qureshi was about to open. 'As soon as you see her, tell her that you will be with her in a minute.'

Campbell melted back, and heard the US President's voice in his earpiece. 'So far so good, Lazaro?'

'Yes, sir,' he whispered, knowing that on a clear, cloudless night like this the movement of all the figures would be picked up by the Global Hawk – even the appearance of Tasneem Qureshi at the door.

'I'm getting some air, darling,' said Qureshi. 'I'll be inside in a moment.'

'Farrah called,' said Tasneem. 'She wants to speak to you.'

For a moment, she lingered. Campbell was worried she would step out, mobile phone in hand, insisting that father speak to daughter. Burrows was under orders *not* to kill her. But if she did come outside, she would have to be dealt with.

Qureshi twisted round in the gravel, his feet loud on the tiny stones. 'Please, Tasneem. I need to be alone to think. Go inside.' She obeyed, quietly closing the door without another word. Qureshi looked to his left and right, confused at the stillness around him, a realization dawning on him that his guards were nowhere to be seen. He walked out of the area of light towards the darkness of the undergrowth. The sniper's spot left the house and picked out Qureshi's chest, flitting from the area of the heart to the forehead and back, making the target well aware how close he could be to death.

'Well done,' said Campbell, emerging again so Qureshi could see him.

'What do you want?' asked Qureshi brusquely. 'And who are you?'

'Before I answer that, have you alerted any other party that we are here?'

Qureshi shook his head and waved a hand towards the bushes. 'If I had, it seems I would have written my own death warrant. Now, tell me who you are.'

'I am representing the President of the United States,' said Campbell. 'He is listening to this conversation. He is watching images of us right now as we speak. You are the military ruler of Pakistan, yet you have not yet announced it.' Campbell pulled a tiny aerial out of an earpiece and handed it to Qureshi. 'Put this on. President West wants to talk to you.'

Qureshi fumbled with the unfamiliar equipment. When it was wrapped around his ear, Campbell turned it on by remote sensor. 'Mr President, Air Vice-Marshal Qureshi is now available to speak with you.' For a moment, Qureshi's mask dropped. He hesitated before he spoke, his eyes uncertain and looking towards Campbell for more confirmation.

Then he heard the voice. 'Qureshi. This is President West here. Do you know a man called Colonel Joharie Rahman?'

Immediately, Qureshi returned to his public face. 'Mr President. What a privilege to speak to you – albeit in such strange circumstances.' He looked down at the red dot hovering over his chest.

'Answer my question, Qureshi.'

'I can't recall,' said Qureshi.

Campbell took a step back. His orders were starkly simple. If Qureshi messed around, kill him. Both Campbell and Burrows were listening across the conversation. The President would speak three words in code – *enough is enough* – and that would be the sniper's signal to shoot.

'Rahman knows you,' said West. 'He knows the furniture in your house. The pictures on the walls. He knows you have a World Trade Center sculpture in your living room. Because he's been in your house, Qureshi. So don't fuck with me, because he's been singing like a canary about you and everything you plan to carry out.' West let it hang there. Campbell kept his eyes on Qureshi. He had been a pilot, for God's sake. He knew about risk. Qureshi had tested both the American F-16 and the French Mirage 111 for toss-bomb attacking with a one-kiloton tactical nuclear weapon – before anyone else had tried it out. Qureshi devised how to keep the aircraft in a steep dive after releasing the bomb, so as to put as much space as possible between the pilot and the bomb. Once clear, the pilot would pull the aircraft up and avoid the impact of the nuclear explosion. Only a man with rock steady-nerves could carry out such a test.

Qureshi kept his poise, but completely changed his approach. 'Yes, Mr President. I know Colonel Rahman. We planned the coup in Brunei together. You probably know that I also ordered the assassination of President Asif Latif Khan. Khan was salting money away into bank accounts in Dubai and Luxembourg. Would you like me to give you the account numbers? Or does the CIA already have them, but has chosen to ignore them, just as long as you have your puppet in place, stealing from the country in the name of democracy?'

'Were you responsible for the attack on the Indian Parliament?' pressed West.

'I haven't finished, Mr President,' said Qureshi, letting sarcasm drip off his pronounciation of the title of the world's most powerful leader. 'You lead a nation paralysed with fear which pushes weaker nations like mine towards an abyss. So this is what I say to you. If you let me take power unhindered, I will rein in these terror groups. I will bring peace between India and Pakistan. But it will be done from a position of strength and not from fear of being an enemy of the United States.'

'Were you responsible for the attack on the Indian Parliament?' repeated West.

'I was not,' answered Qureshi, maintaining his confidence. 'The group responsible for that was nurtured under the rule of Prime Minister Nawaz Sharif and President Musharraf. Both were staunch allies of your country. If you want it stopped, listen to what I have to say.'

Briefly the sniper's dot left Qureshi's chest, flitted to the gravel and returned, signalling Campbell to switch channels to the Central Command in Florida. 'Army truck approaching three miles away, heading in your direction.'

Campbell flicked the channel back to the White House. He looked slightly to his left and picked out the moving shadow of Burrows.

'To be frank, I'm a little short on rhetoric today,' said West, 'and I'm not in a mood to make deals with dictators. I need you to mothball your nuclear weapons facilities. All terrorists must be pulled in. A complete dragnet against them. You do that, and I'll do my damnedest to help you. You have my word on that. If you don't, I can't guarantee the future of your nation. Mehta will destroy you. That's your choice, Qureshi. That's why I've chosen to speak to you like this. Either Pakistan gets taken over by India, or you mothball your nuclear arsenal.'

Campbell switched over to Central Command, so he could listen to the data sent down from the Global Hawk, together with Qureshi's reply.

'. . . identified as one armoured personnel carrier and one troop carrier truck – maybe a company of men.'

Qureshi looked down and shuffled his feet on the gravel. In the dim light thrown off from the house, Campbell identified something uneasy in his face. He switched channels.

'There are troops on the way to your house. Did you order them in?' said West.

Qureshi looked up. His face had settled now. There was a curious stillness in it which suddenly transformed him into a threat. 'Yes, Mr President. I did.'

'. . . two miles, and slowing. Curves in the road. They should be with you in three to five minutes. I suggest you get the hell out of there.'

Campbell's eyes didn't leave Qureshi's. He was trying to read the man's face. First he detected smugness; then indecision. Qureshi met Campbell's stare and shrugged: he couldn't stop them if he wanted to.

'Why don't you put your policy to the United Nations, Mr President? Get a resolution passed against us,' said Qureshi with a sigh. 'I cannot and will not make a decision on the future of Pakistan in the cross-hairs of a sniper's rifle.' He brushed his hand across the red spot in disdain.

The silence around the house was broken by the throb of a helicopter engine. It swooped in and turned sharply on itself. The green glow of the pilot's night-vision goggles was relayed back to Florida, where commanders saw what he saw – a clear patch on which to bring the aircraft down.

Campbell was on dual channel now. 'Evacuate,' came the order, cutting through the President's conversation. Burrows broke cover, running fast and clear across the courtyard to the helicopter. From the undergrowth, down from the roof and out from behind the carport shelter came the Ghurkas.

Dust blown up by the rotor blades flew into their faces. A hand moved back a curtain in Qureshi's house. Campbell alerted a sniper. Tasneem would be looking at the Ghurkas, but in the dark, and with their Asian complexions and their familiar uniforms, she would not know who they were unless her husband told her. They ran across the compound to where the helicopter skids were just brushing the flat, dry landing spot. Burrows was first there, holding on to the metal, as if he was keeping the aircraft down. He counted all twelve Ghurkas in and gave a thumbs-up to the pilot. As it lifted off, just a few feet off the ground, before heading into the gloom, Burrows ran back to the house and kicked open the door. Tasneem Qureshi managed a spurt of a scream before he silenced her.

'Take them out,' said Campbell into his mouthpiece.

Far above, unseen by anyone on the ground, the Global Hawk made a graceful curve. From underneath its sail-like wings two air-to-surface missiles sped off towards the ground, leaving a silver trail through the sky. Seconds before they reached their target, they separated to hit the armoured personnel carrier and the truck with armour-piercing high explosives. A ball of fire shot up through the night, lighting up the sparseness of the area around it. Burning debris set light to scrubland and sent cattle scampering away.

Qureshi turned first to the door hanging open in his house and the sight of his wife, held by Burrows with one hand over her mouth. Then he spun back as the roar of the two explosions rippled across to him. He lowered his eyes, checking and confirming that the red dot had gone. He put his hand against the earpiece, glaring incomprehensibly at Campbell. 'You poor fool,' he muttered. 'You don't understand.'

By which time Campbell had a pistol levelled at his chest. 'Then why don't we go in so you can explain it to me?' he said calmly.

Inside the house, Tasneem sat, arms folded, in an armchair. Burrows had taped over her mouth. Three servants, the female cook, and two male housekeepers, lay prostrate on the floor with their hands tied behind their backs.

Campbell and Qureshi watched the ebbing glow of the burning military vehicles. Burrows locked the door and drew the curtains. Unlike Campbell's, Burrows's face was blacked, his dark uniform hung with weapons and ammunition. He stayed by the window, while Campbell moved to the centre of the room.

'Call the General Command at Chaklala and tell them everything is under control,' said Campbell.

Without hesitation, Qureshi drew a mobile phone from his pocket and made the call in English. As far as Campbell could tell, it was straightforward, with no hidden code.

Qureshi then sat on an armchair opposite his wife. 'Tasneem, darling, they will remove the tape from your mouth. If they do not, I will not cooperate with them,' he said, looking harshly at Burrows. 'But you must not say a word. Do you understand?'

Tasneem nodded. Burrows glanced over at Campbell. 'All right,' agreed Campbell hesitantly. Burrows stepped over to her. 'You must understand, madam, if I take this off and you utter a sound, I will shoot you. Indicate that you understand.'

Tasneem, her eyes both wrathful and confused, nodded. Burrows tore the tape, screwed it into a ball and dropped it into a waste-paper basket under a bamboo table by the door.

'Is the President still listening in?' asked Qureshi.

'Do you want him to?' replied Campbell.

Qureshi took off his earpiece. 'He can listen to me. But I won't listen to him. What I have to say, I will say to you. Then, if you want to stay alive, call back your helicopter. They will send reinforcements. They will get through and they will not appreciate stumbling over the bodies of their slain colleagues.'

'How long?' said Burrows, walking across the room to the back window.

'Thirty minutes. Maybe fifteen. It's impossible to say.' A sullenness took over Qureshi's face. He had the look of a strong man in despair. A few minutes earlier, Qureshi had used the word fool, as if Campbell had no idea of what he was dealing with, as if he was meddling in something too complicated, and for a moment Campbell wondered whether Qureshi knew the workings of his own agonized brain.

'John, go check on the driver. He should be coming round,' said Campbell. With Burrows gone, he sat back in his seat, crossed his legs, and balanced his gun hand on his knee with the weapon pointed at Qureshi. 'A few hours ago, I was at a meeting in Washington between Vasant Mehta and the President,' he said. 'Mehta has thrown down an ultimatum. Your conversation with the President was cut short. So I'm going to fill you in with what was missing. The choice is that either we, the United States, take responsibility for your nuclear arsenal or Mehta is going to ask China to do it. If neither of us agrees, he will come in himself. Whether it was you, Air Vice-Marshal, whether it was Najeeb Hussain or any of the others on your junta who ordered the attack on his house, I don't know, but it has solidified Mehta's resolve to rid India of Pakistan altogether. The President wants a way out of this. He wants you to give us that responsibility. So that's your choice: the United States, the devil you know; China, a completely unknown quantity; or India, which would end any semblance of independence and be as good as a military and political defeat.'

Qureshi ran a hand through his hair, and when he spoke it was with his head turned partly away. 'There is always another way. You westerners don't realize how grave the situation in Pakistan has become and how determined we are to make sure we come through it with our culture and sovereignty intact. Every year India is more bellicose towards us. Islamic terror is firmly planted within our society. Law and order has broken down. Our economy is in acute recession. Seventy million live below the poverty line.' He turned towards Campbell and smiled out of the corner of his face, just for an instant, to show Campbell a fraction of the power he still retained. 'Do you seriously believe that either China or India wants to take us on at the precise time they are competing to become the superpower within Asia?' He shook his head in feigned disbelief. 'You might want to move in further. But we won't accept you. Not any more. India wants a guarantee that conflict will stop. I can deliver that to them. You can't.' There was a sympathetic look in his eyes, and he shrugged. Perhaps he wanted to gain Campbell's trust. Perhaps he was being patronizing. Campbell couldn't tell.

The door opened. Burrows pushed the driver inside.

'He's fine,' said Burrows, stepping inside himself and closing the door.

'You will drive us down to Islamabad, avoiding the wreckage,' said Campbell, standing up.

'To where?' said Qureshi, staying in his seat.

'The US embassy.'

'Am I your hostage?'

'No. We need to talk more, but we also need to get out of here. If you have another way, tell me.'

Qureshi got to his feet and took charge. 'Start the car and bring it round to the front door,' he said to the driver, adding to Burrows: 'Let him go. Don't worry, we do not speak in secret codes.' He moved over to Tasneem and kissed her on the forehead. 'I will be back soon. Not a word to anybody about this. Not a word.' He squeezed her hands, looked up at Burrows, then back at his wife. 'Darling, go to my room and get this man a shirt, some trousers and a pair of my sandals.' He indicated to the washroom by the door. 'You can clean up your face in there. That is, if you are coming to Islamabad with us.'

As Burrows was changing, Tasneem Qureshi gave the driver, still groggy from the tranquillizer, tea from a Thermos.

'Let's go, then,' said Burrows, emerging. Outside in the chill of the night, Qureshi hesitated before getting into the car.

'Back seat,' said Burrows, letting Campbell through and shutting the door.

'Yes, I know,' said Qureshi. 'But I was wondering why,

if you didn't kill my driver, you had to kill my guards.' He shook his head. 'It seemed so unnecessary.'

Neither Burrows nor Campbell answered. Qureshi, the airman, might not have known that millisecond between the success and failure of a military operation, made more acute when trained men on both sides are in conflict. In the lull after action, there is often doubt, and perhaps Qureshi wanted to exploit it. The turn of his head towards Campbell was weary, but his eyes flared with anger as he climbed into the back seat of the Mercedes.

Tasneem pulled back the curtain to watch, and a beam of wavering light from the room fell on the bonnet. The car turned on the gravel, and took the left-hand fork outside the gate away from the main road where the troops had been stopped. The surface deteriorated and the driver shifted from automatic to a low gear. Rocks on the road scraped the underbelly of the chassis. Qureshi was in the back with Campbell, Burrows in the front with his weapon on the driver.

Far above, the cameras of the Global Hawk predator locked on to heat from the exhaust of the vehicle and sent back pictures of its journey to Islamabad. President West, with only John Kozerski in the Oval Office, watched. Like Campbell, he still had no idea whether the mission was going to be a success or a disaster.

'Tell President West that nations do not change their character, and that is why Pakistan is as it is,' said Qureshi, his head turned away, looking out of the window and the dark, shadowless land. 'Washington has always preferred working more with one-man dictatorships than the divided authority and debate that accompanies democratic decision-making. If it did not, Pakistani dictators would not have survived for so long. You must concentrate on restraining Vasant Mehta. I will bring Pakistan into line.'

The road dipped and curved towards a hillside, where the headlights picked out a formation of rocks. Beside it were two boys, sleeping next to a herd of goats. Burrows raised his weapon. One boy stirred, putting his hand to his eyes, then rolled over to sleep again.

'Tell West,' said Qureshi, 'that if forced, we will not hesitate to use our nuclear arsenal to protect our national sovereignty.'

'And if China withdraws its support?' pressed Campbell.

'It is more complicated than that.'

The car bumped off the track on to a smoother road. The driver dipped the lights, waiting for three trucks to lumber past, ablaze with coloured lights and garish paintings on their side. Their wheels threw dust up to the Mercedes. Soapy water jets came up from the bonnet, and the windscreen wipers started up. Across the road, a single light bulb glowed above a stall selling drinks chilled inside a block of melting ice. As they joined the main road, Campbell knew he had all he would get. The impenetrable Qureshi wanted to do business, thought Campbell, but the reference to the dead security guards reminded him of the bad taste the mission had left in his mouth.

'I know he's heard this before,' continued Qureshi, 'all politicians have. But there are people who want to act more quickly and with less flexibility than I do.' He wound down the window. The night air was warmer. He breathed it in and turned to face Campbell. 'Tomorrow, or next week, you might find you've been talking to the wrong man.'

'I'll pass on your message,' whispered Campbell.

'Thank you.' Qureshi leant out so that the airstream hit his face. Then he closed the window. 'I think we've said all we have to say. I will get the mess around my house cleared up. You will hear nothing of it. You have met me. I trust you to tell Jim West that I am a straightforward

man who has inherited a conundrum, partly of his government's making.'

His hand squeezed Campbell's shoulder, and he smiled.
'Now, without sounding bizarre, do you mind if I drop
you at the Marriott Hotel, from where you can get a taxi
to the embassy? The last thing I can afford to be seen
doing right now is consorting with anything American.'

As the Global Hawk tracked the vehicle back, the
National Security Agency intercepted two calls each from
a different telephone. The first lasted five minutes and was
on an open line to Qureshi's daughter, Farrah, in Lahore.
The second, lasting twenty-eight seconds, was to a satellite
phone in Pyongyang, North Korea. Instead of going home
to his wife, Qureshi's vehicle headed for the military
cantonment area of Rawalpindi just a few miles away.

38

Washington, DC, USA

'No, we don't know what was said,' said Brock. 'But we do know it's a number used exclusively by Park Ho. He travels with three satellite phones and that was one of them.'

'In Pyongyang?' said Jim West slowly, allowing himself time to think. He sat back on the sofa, jacket off, with his feet up on the coffee table. Brock leant over the back of an armchair opposite, having just walked in from his office. Mary Newman stood quietly by the window looking at the melting snow.

'John, how long have we got?' asked the President.

'Toru Sato has arrived in Camp David,' said Kozerski, standing by the door. 'Mehta and Meenakshi are already there with Lizzie. Marine One should be back here any moment now to take us down. The helicopter will return from Camp David to pick up Andrei Kozlov and Stuart Nolan who are getting in within fifteen minutes of each other. They'll be choppered down together. Jamie Song won't be with us until tomorrow.'

'Do you mind meeting him?' West asked Newman, swinging his feet off the coffee table and slipping on his shoes. Then, recognizing disapproval on Newman's face, he quickly added, 'I'll ask Lizzie to go with you as my personal emissary if that helps.'

'That'll help, Mr President, thank you,' said Newman. 'I know it's informal, but the Chinese are very sensitive on protocol.'

'Chris, where's Campbell?'

'On his way back, Mr President,' said Pierce, putting his electronic organizer back into his jacket pocket. 'Qureshi must have thrown a blanket right over the unexpected collateral damage we left behind. Not a squeak.'

'He's keeping our options open,' said Brock, his hand on the door to open it.

'Why blow everything because of a couple of military vehicles and a half-dozen security guards who didn't do their job properly,' said West putting on his jacket. 'The key element is that he must also have the support of the rest of his junta.'

'You know what's really troubling me, Mr President?' said Newman. 'He made the call to North Korea *before* he got to the bunker in Chaklala.'

'And that, apart from his daughter,' said Brock, 'contacting North Korea was uppermost in his mind.'

Brock opened the door and let the others file through, with the President going through last. 'Scares the shit out of me, if you want an honest reaction,' said West.

39

Camp David, Maryland, USA

Camp David, on the Catoctin Mountain in Maryland, was a thirty-minute helicopter journey from Washington. In winter Aspen, the presidential lodge, a single-storey, four-bedroom stone-and-timber building, sat on a bed of snow amid clusters of stark, leafless trees. It was created by Franklin Roosevelt and over the years each president had added his own touch. Jim West had yet to do so.

Their first winter in office after the inauguration was so harsh that the Wests never made it to Camp David. The mountains kept the temperature five to ten degrees colder than in Washington, and snowstorms made helicopter landings precarious. Then, in the spring, Valerie was diagnosed with ovarian cancer. Secondary cancers were found in the lymph nodes. As she became more ill and exhausted from chemotherapy, the constant presence of the secret service began to irritate her. Rather than rest in unfamiliar surroundings, Valerie chose to stay either in the White House or go to their family ranch in Virginia.

As West changed out of his suit in the bedroom with its spectacular winter mountain views, he was glad of his decision to bring everyone down here for the summit. Valerie's voice and presence was everywhere in the White House. During their long marriage, they had talked constantly about the presidency. As a young politician, he had taken her around the White House rooms and, as he became more successful, they frequently found themselves as guests there. Her death, sudden but painful as it was, had probably affected him more than he allowed himself to examine. To lose a soulmate of more than thirty years had to change a man. Was it madness when he found himself making a cup of coffee for both of them, or when he spoke aloud while reading a newspaper article on something that would have interested Valerie? Was it forgetfulness? Or was it wishful thinking?

Whatever the answer, he felt the unfamiliarity of Camp David was helping. There was a sense of stepping into a hotel more than a home. They had never slept together in this bedroom. Her clothes had never hung in the wardrobe. He had never watched her walk around after an evening with guests, smelling her perfume and watching her slip off her dress and kick off her shoes. Perhaps, he thought, he would note in his diary that the summit of world leaders at Camp David would be the weekend that he was able to move on; not to forget, nor to end the love, but to stop grieving and start living again.

He opened the door and stepped into the narrow, short corridor down to the long reception room, elegantly but sparsely decorated by his predecessor, with its floor-to-ceiling windows and freshly fallen snow on the patio outside.

The small, energetic figure of Toru Sato was bent over a telescope as Mary Newman explained quietly in his ear the history of the Monocacy Valley spread out in the national park below them.

'Prime Minister,' said West, speeding up his step and stretching out his hand. 'I do appreciate your coming. I hope it's not too cold for you.'

If Sato retained any ill will from their earlier blunt exchange, he didn't show it. 'Japan has inhospitable winters as well,' he replied, taking the President's hand. 'But I do not have any place as beautiful and as close to Tokyo to retreat to in times of crisis.'

'Come,' suggested West, ushering Sato to a sofa and

taking the one at right angles to him. Newman quietly slipped away leaving the two men together, having made sure pots of tea and coffee had been delivered to the table, together with a jug of water and notepads and pencils.

'I wanted to have a private word before the others arrive, Prime Minister,' said West. Sato had not invited him to use any other more familiar term of address, so West stuck to the formal approach. 'India and Pakistan are on the verge of war. We believe Pakistan has some kind of new practical support coming from North Korea, but we have no idea what it is. We do know, however, that both countries are under new military rulers.'

'And North Korea has killed fifty-eight of your citizens by firing a missile on to Japanese soil,' reminded Sato.

'Correct,' said West. 'In complete confidence I tell you that Jamie Song, having agreed to our carrying out pre-emptive strikes on North Korea, has now said we *cannot* strike above the fortieth parallel which would leave many of the launch sites intact. You know that Vasant Mehta has thrown out a challenge to us – either go in and take Pakistan or he's going to offer it to the Chinese.' West, his brow deliberately furrowed and his hands clasped together, looked straight at Sato. Newman had advised him to express humility. West hoped it was showing through. 'Prime Minister, I need your advice and your help. This is why I have come to you first.'

For a long time, Sato sat upright, looking out the window and saying nothing. He leaned forward and poured himself a cup of green tea from a pot. He drank it slowly, holding the cup precisely by the handle and keeping it close to his lips for each sip. When he had finished, he returned it to the saucer and wiped his mouth with a paper serviette.

'Really, you are talking to me about China, Mr President,' he said. 'If China was our ally, we could close down

North Korea tomorrow. But it is not and that is where the problem lies. If China was our ally, in that it had the same goals as us, we could have negotiated an end to its military support for Pakistan and none of this terror culture would have been able to grow. But China is not our ally. In all my time in politics, Japan's relationship with China has remained haunted by the past. Our nationalist politicians continue to visit the Yasukuni Shrine, which honours men who were war criminals. We have had issues with our history books which sanitize the brutality of our occupying forces in China and elsewhere in Asia. But they are no different from American history books which gloss over your government's treatment of the native Americans, or the British who glorified their era of colonization.'

He stood up and moved to the window, then turned to face the room, showing an alertness in his eyes and remarkably swift movements that belied his age. West watched, but stayed silent.

'There is nothing we can do to rid ourselves of our history. China knows that, which is why it is using it,' said Sato, flipping his hand over as if to dismiss that section of his argument. 'But there is something far deeper and far more dangerous. We have a profound mutual distrust for each other because we are rivals for regional leadership. In the past century, with China's weakness, this has not been an issue. But she is no longer weak, and never in our history have both Japan and China been so powerful at the same time. China is wary that we are building a stronger military and that we are planning to project power again. It is also concerned about our alliance with the United States, our technology exchanges, our joint missile programme. It is suspicious of anything that would help Japan rid itself of shame. Yes, China and Japan have common ground, but it is limited. We are all part of the global economy. We are both big players in it. We both want stability on the Korean peninsula, but I doubt we will ever agree on how it is to be accomplished. Neither of us want nuclear war between India and Pakistan, but again, will we ever agree on how to create peace there?'

Sato paused again, wiping his finger down the condensation on the window, and touching his face with the cold moisture.

'What would you do if you were Jamie Song?' prodded West.

Sato laughed softly, glanced at West and then concentrated back on the window. 'A statesman has to decide who he is. Is he a statesman? Does he protect the interests of his state? Is he a philanthropist? Does he hand out largesse to societies less fortunate than his without asking for anything in return? Is he a humanitarian? Does he cast a searchlight around the world and find societies that need saving from their own stupidity or lack of luck? In order to recover from the loathing showered upon us, Japan has been both philanthropic and humanitarian. But I believe, Mr President, we should accept that all of us ultimately are simply statesmen. Therefore the bedrock of our interest is what is best for our nation, and,' he added with a quick smile, 'our own reputations.'

'I'm not sure you have completely answered my question,' said West.

Sato returned to the sofa and leant on the arm, bringing himself closer to the President. 'Yes, of course. You want me to read the mind of Jamie Song. If I were him, I would do everything to drive a wedge between the US and Japan,' he said, pointing his finger back and forth between the two of them. 'If he breaks that, he breaks everything that has underpinned our success since the Second World War. Also, if I were Jamie Song, I would calculate exactly when the conditions would be right for China to make the move to be the top dog in Asia. Is it now, when India is weakened by Pakistan, and Japan and the United States are threatened by North Korea? Or should China wait another fifty years, when he is long dead and the next opportunity arises?' He shrugged. 'Would I, if I were Jamie Song, make a move now? Of that I am not sure, as I suspect he is not sure.'

'And what would you do as Prime Minister of Japan?' nudged West.

'A good statesman will take any opportunity to make his nation great. I am an elderly man now, Mr President, and I know my people. I sense perhaps they feel that they cannot rid themselves of the legacy of the bad war of the last century without fighting a good one. There is an idea among us that we have to become a complete nation once again and put the spectre of our brutal past behind us.'

'By fighting another war?' asked West sceptically.

'Our economic success didn't do the job,' Sato answered with a regretful smile.

'And in order to stop that, I have to go to war with North Korea?' said West, his voice hardening.

'And take us as your ally. Yes. But China will never allow it.' Sato shook his head and clasped his hands together. 'I cannot tell you how to run your foreign policy,' he said. 'I am only telling you the pressures on me.'

'I'm not sure exactly what you are implying, Prime Minister,' said West, holding Sato's gaze.

'I'm implying that Jamie Song might have won already, and Japan might soon have to act on its own. Sitting in the security of Camp David is very different from sitting in Tokyo where a missile could strike us at any time. Don't forget, Mr President, that the Japanese are the only people who know what it is like to be on the receiving end of a nuclear explosion.'

Sato's eyes bored into West, sending a chill through the

room that made the ravaging cold outside a more hospitable place to be.

'Where's Sato now?' asked Stuart Nolan, making sure no more than three drops of water fell into his glass of malt whisky to release the peat aroma. He took a sip, cupped his hands around it and leant back on the sofa.

'We put him in Birch,' said Newman, referring to one of the guest chalets. 'He has a young assistant with him by the name of Kiyoko Miyake. She's in Dogwood. Both chalets have just been done up and are a few yards apart.'

Nolan chuckled. 'No wonder the wily old bastard looks so young.'

'I hope you have the finer brain,' said West. 'Tom Patton's running late. Something's cropped up, and the Homeland Security Secretary is one person even the President doesn't prise away from his job.'

The US President and the British Prime Minister sat at opposite ends of a long sofa. John Kozerski and Charles Colchester had taken hardback chairs side by side in front of the window. At a dining table at the other end of the room, Brock, Newman and Pierce, who had just arrived from the Pentagon, worked on office papers, while occasionally chipping into the conversation. A faint smell of wood smoke wafted through the room from a log fire in the stone grate at the end.

'While we're waiting for Tom, tell me what you make of Sato,' said West.

'From the way you told it, Jim,' replied Nolan, 'I think he was giving it to you pretty straight. He's giving you a choice between Japan and China, and he's saying that, if needs be, Japan has the wherewithal and political motivation to go it alone.'

'What do you mean by wherewithal?' said West uneasily.

'Military muscle. That's what underscores it all.'

'Sato was talking about their nuclear capability,' said Brock from behind them. 'Declaring nuclear weapons has been linked before to the line about the bad war–good war.'

'That's all we need,' said West. 'India and Pakistan blowing each other up and China and Japan doing the same so they can become "complete nations" again. I've never heard so much bullshit.'

'If he sees it through, Mr President, it could mean an end to our bases in Japan,' said Chris Pierce. 'Anyone wants to weaken our presence in Asia, the Japanese only have to throw us out.'

'Would they ever do that?' wondered West aloud.

'The Philippines did,' said Nolan, pushing tobacco down into his pipe with a broken match, but not seeming to want to light it yet.

'We got thrown out of Vietnam. But it didn't make a damn bit of difference,' growled West.

'Good point,' muttered Nolan, interested as much in his pipe as in the conversation.

West cocked his head and turned round to look behind him. 'Chris, what's your take on what would happen if they threw us out?'

'It wouldn't be good, but we would manage,' said Pierce. 'We went back into the Philippines during the War on Terror. The Vietnamese would be happy to have us. We could increase our presence in South Korea. We've got ship repair facilities in Singapore. It wouldn't be the weakening blow the press would make it out to be.'

'Do you agree with that, Mary?' said West, squinting against a shock of sunlight which had broken through the thick blanket of snow falling on the lodge, spilling light on to the President's face.

'Our trade and diplomacy would continue,' said Newman, 'But our relationship with Japan would be more bland. I imagine our natural emphasis would shift to China.'

'Pete?'

'When New Zealand refused us ship visits in the 1980s, we cut them out of the intelligence loop. We would do the same with Japan. If they threatened to go nuclear, we would stop dual-use technology transfers. There's a heap of things which would run against them. I can't see what they would gain from it, frankly.'

'Let me say this,' said Nolan, putting his pipe face up in the clean ashtray. 'If we threw you out, closed the airbases, mothballed Menwith Hill and Fylingdales and all that, Britain as a nation which punches above its weight and – if I may say so – so skilfully provides that bridge between America and Europe, would be stuffed. The only reason to do it would be ideological, not pragmatic. In Britain, we were driven by ideological strains in the sixties and seventies. I was a young politician then and, believe me, you ignore them at your peril. Japan is suffering the same fate now. What I might suggest, Jim, is that you challenge Sato to say exactly where his leadership lies on this. If it's a case of him facing down his electorate and the Young Turks in his party, he must do that. If he himself is leading a pro-nuclear, pro-military, anti-American movement, then you must find another ally.'

'Well put, Stuart,' congratulated West, turning back on to the sofa again. 'Now in your inimical and avuncular style, tell me what was said between you and Andrei Kozlov on your trip down.'

'Marine One is not the quietest of aircraft,' replied Nolan. 'He had Alexander Yushchuk, his intellectual muse, with him. Charles dealt with Yushchuk mainly.'

'Yushchuk kept his own counsel,' said Colchester. 'The most I got out of him was a comparison of winter temperatures between Washington and Moscow.'

'And the only nugget of interest Kozlov said,' continued Nolan, 'was – and I'll quote him directly – "Have we been summoned because Jim West realizes his country's super-power shelf life is almost over?"' Nolan picked up his pipe and flicked on his lighter. Just as he was about to touch the tobacco with the flame, he flicked it off again. 'That from a man whose nation has seen its empire come and go a couple of times. So I replied – and what a pompous ass I am sometimes. I said, "Democracies are like rechargeable batteries, Andrei. There's no such thing as a shelf life."'

He lit his pipe, drawing on it as a blast of cold air swept through the room, blowing around sheets of paper from Colchester's file.

Tom Patton appeared before the staff could close the outside door of the lodge, bringing the rush of weather inside. The Filipino butler helped him off with his coat and shook the melting snow on to the stone tiles in the hallway.

'Sorry I'm late, Mr President,' said Patton, brushing down his lapels. He ran his hand through his hair, shaking the water on to the floor tiles. He turned to look behind him and stepped to one side to let through a less ruffled Caroline Brock. Peter Brock stood up, eyebrows raised. He had had no idea his wife was coming to Camp David in an official capacity. The others, including West, Nolan, even Newman, were all on their feet. Caroline Brock often had that effect on a room.

'Stuart, Charles,' said West, 'Tom Patton you may know from his regular television appearances. Caroline Brock is the better half of Pete over there. But I suspect her being here is to do with something altogether more sinister.'

Patton put his briefcase by the side of the coffee table and took a seat next to the President. For a moment

Caroline was left unsure of where to sit until Nolan said, 'Mrs Brock, it would be my pleasure to have you next to me.'

'Is Campbell here yet?' asked Patton.

'On his way,' said Brock.

'Good. And Mason?'

'If it's Mason, the Australian virologist, you're after,' replied Brock, looking to Pierce who nodded his confirmation of what he was about to say, 'he's still at Guantanamo Bay under interrogation.'

'Tom,' suggested West gently, 'why don't you settle and tell us what all this is about. Join us in a Scotch.' He jerked his thumb behind him. 'They're not drinking because they're meant to be in their offices. But on this side of the room, the whisky's free and you look as if you could do with one.'

Patton let the President pour a glass and accepted the cubes of ice taken out of the holder and dropped in by hand. 'I don't think any of us are going to want to hear this,' he said, pulling a file out of his briefcase. He opened it on the coffee table, and glanced over to Brock. 'Lee Jong-hee, the South Korean officer who shot the North Korean in Panmunjom.' Patton took a sheet from the file and looked around the room, checking that everyone knew what he was talking about. 'Well, the NSA have intercepted three calls in the past day. One to his home phone number in Seoul. One to the barracks pay phone. And one to his cell phone. They were made one after another and came from a landline at a Korean community centre in Canterbury City, near Sydney, Australia. When Lee didn't answer, the caller hung up. It was the same number which Mason himself called from a phone box near his laboratory before the theft of the IL-4 agent.'

Patton handed the President a classified log sheet bearing the white-headed eagle logo of the National Security

Agency. He patted down his hair, still wet from the snow. 'We have established a link between Mason and a Korean organization. The action of Lee Jong-hee at Panmunjom indicates there could be – and I don't want to sound over-dramatic – but there could be North Korean sleeper agents like him embedded in Korean communities all over the world. I hope to hell I'm wrong, but my job is not to take risks.'

He stopped to take a long drink of his whisky. West had appointed Patton because of his legendary list of contacts on Capitol Hill and throughout the state legis-latures. He was the only candidate who West knew would smash down, physically if necessary, the walls that Amer-ica's numerous security agencies built around themselves. Word had it that Patton was owed more favours than any other player in Washington, and could bully like no other man around.

'I need to get inside the Korean community in the United States,' Patton continued, keeping the glass in his hand. 'And we need to begin immediate work on a new smallpox vaccine, one that takes into account the IL-4 agent.'

West looked sceptically at Patton. 'What you're saying is that we have to revive our own biological warfare programme in order to combat this new threat.'

'Nixon's 1969 ruling did not prohibit work on offensive applications necessary to develop defensive measures,' said Patton. 'We would not be breaking the law. I've already spoken to Matt Lemont at Fort Detrick and Claire Glasse at the CDC in Atlanta. I explained the urgency. On your word, Mr President, they'll get to work.'

'How will we know if a vaccine will work?' said West, glancing towards Caroline.

'When it's tested on a human being with smallpox,' said Caroline. 'And since smallpox has been eradicated, the answer is we won't. Ideally, the tests should be ethnically categorized. The immunization system of a Caucasian is different from that of an Asian-American, African-American or Hispanic. If Park Ho has indeed obtained the IL-4 from Canberra and smallpox virus from Pokrov, he would be well under way with tests. Let us assume those tests began immediately, and that they have been conducted on human beings – which we can't do. Then they're already way ahead of us, Mr President.' She covered her face with one hand and shuddered. 'It's frightening. It's really frightening,' she whispered.

West handed back the NSA log to Patton. 'Go ahead,' he said softly.

The noise of a helicopter sounded over the lodge, the machine's searchlights flashing from the skids and lighting up the snow. Newman stood up, gathering her papers together but leaving them on the table. 'That's Marine One,' she said. 'I have to go meet Jamie Song.'

'Song,' mused West. 'North Korea's his turf and it's running out of control.'

'If you would like me to go instead and read him the riot act, I'd be more than happy,' said Nolan.

'Nice suggestion,' smiled West. 'But I feel Mary might be a touch more diplomatic.'

The helicopter became less audible, as it climbed to avoid a hazardous peak, its lights fading, then the noise was full on again as it came down on the helipad not far from the lodge.

'Lizzie's not going,' said West to no one in particular. The decision was personal. It didn't need explanation. 'And Mary, nothing of this at all. Everything's fine between us. Talk about ice skating in China. The World Trade Organization. The latest coup in Africa. But not a word about this or anything to do with North Korea.'

'Yes, sir,' she said, putting on her coat, slipping a woollen hat on her head and pulling the flaps over her ears. Her cool blue eyes smiled at him, but her face was serious. He could trust her. He should have trusted her before and, for a moment, as the enormity of what Patton had told him began to sink in, he thought himself unchivalrous for not going with her.

'Mrs Brock talked about ethnicity,' said Nolan, as Newman left. 'Charles, I might be completely wrong, but remind me of that scrap of intelligence on the disappearance of the Air Koryo flight.'

'A photograph in a North Korean newspaper showed an engine casing which was meant to be from the crash site,' said Colchester. 'One of our aircraft buffs simply spotted that it was not from a Tupolev, more likely one of their Ilyushin 62-Ms, which have the engines mounted at the back and the high tail fin.'

Nolan drew on his pipe and looked straight past the President to the views of the valley. 'So that's it. What a bloody monster! The Caucasian passengers on board have been harvested for biological weapons testing.'

'And we ignored it all the time,' muttered West, looking towards the door through which Newman has just gone. Among all of them, Mary had understood the danger.

'Caroline, how long to get a vaccine?' asked West

'Six months at the earliest. We'd be building on what we've got.'

'Do we have this IL-4 agent to work with?'

'We got some flown up as soon as the theft was reported,' said Patton.

'Chris, is our strike plan ready to go?'

'Any time, Mr President,' said Pierce.

'Land invasion, too?'

'Correct.'

'John, make sure Tom gets whatever he needs,' he instructed Kozerski. 'No leaks. No hint of what we're doing to anyone.'

Camp David had two helicopter landing sites, one which brought Marine One down inside the camp itself, and another at a lower altitude some miles away used when the weather was particularly bad. West had chosen to deliver Jamie Song to the lower one and was waiting on the helipad, snow sweeping across his face, wondering if the pilot would judge the weather too harsh and return to Washington. He stamped his feet against the cold and slapped his gloved hands together, but he stayed in the wind chill from the rotor blades as he watched Marine One inch its way to the ground. Jamie Song stepped out with Mary Newman by his side; then Newman, as pre-arranged, excused herself, ducking under the front of the aircraft to a car waiting on the other side. Jamie Song looked taken aback, but West gave him a friendly slap on the back and guided him by the elbow to the waiting car. There was a bulletproof screen between them and the driver and the secret service agent in the front. They took off their hats and gloves and loosened their overcoats, enjoying the immediate warmth from inside the car.

'Mary look after you OK?' began West affably. 'I had meant Lizzie, my daughter, to be there to meet you as well, but she got tied up.'

Song folded his gloves together and patted them down. 'I appreciate it, Jim. And I appreciate you coming out here to meet me. The pilot said something about this being an emergency landing site.'

West didn't pick up on Song's conversation. As the car pulled out, the crew of Marine One battened the aircraft down to keep it there until the weather improved. He let the Chinese President look out of the window where there was nothing to see except snowflakes falling so fast that the windscreen wiper had trouble moving them.

'I wanted to get you alone, Jamie, to ask if Mehta has talked to you yet?'

'Yes, he has. He called me shortly before I left – that is, if you're referring to his suggestion that we secure Pakistan's nuclear arsenal.'

'That's the one,' said West lightly.

'Yes,' said Song pensively. 'I've thought a lot about it. It's not just a matter of sending some guys in to take out some nuclear detonators, as you know.'

West nodded. 'If you want to do it, Jamie, you have our support. That's all I wanted to say.'

Song glanced sharply over with an expression of surprise, as if he had anticipated opposition, when West hadn't even wanted discussion.

Song tucked his gloves into his fur hat and loosened his coat further against the warmth of the car. 'I can't see it working. Mehta wants a whole package: the neutralizing of the nuclear weapons *and* the rooting out of the terror networks. We can't even do that in Tibet. So he knows we won't succeed in Pakistan. Then, when the next terror attack strikes India, Mehta sends in his troops without fear of a nuclear reprisal.' Song shook his head and smiled. 'I'm not even sure if it's a clever suggestion.' He spoke not like a man who understood the knife-edge of military brinkmanship, but as a boardroom negotiator who believed that, whatever the outcome, he did not stand to lose everything.

'It'd be helpful if we could find a way through,' said West softly.

Song didn't look at him. His eyes were staring straight ahead. 'The way through is to restrain Mehta and let Pakistan destroy the cancer within it.'

'Musharraf promised that and it didn't work.' West

turned in his seat to face Song. 'Mehta's the one with his home blown up. Does he not have some right of retribution?'

'You don't get it, do you, Jim?' said Song, unwilling to hide his exasperation. 'If we go after the terror groups in Pakistan, they will target our western border area in Xinjiang. If that happens, we could throw away thirty years of economic growth to fight a damn civil war.' He slapped his hand on the door of the car, his eyes red from the jet lag and the cold. 'India, Pakistan and Kashmir are living examples of what we should *not* do. Now, I will help you if I can, but I will not jeopardize China's national interest in order to protect your own. If Mehta wants to start a war with Pakistan, then it's up to him. If you want to try and stop it, it's up to you—'

'Because it's in your interests that it *does* happen,' whispered West, barely able to conceal his anger. Song had his gaze focused out of the window, watching evergreens hanging thick with snow as the car slowly climbed a steep hill.

'I'll forget I heard that,' retorted Song brusquely.

The car slowed to take a sharp upward curve, the heavy armoured chassis handling it clumsily. The back wheels spun, slewing the car across the road, until the four-wheel drive locked in and the front wheels pulled it out of the ice patch.

Song turned back inside the car. 'Do they have a spare couple of presidents in Camp David in case we roll down the mountainside?' he quipped, as if their irate exchange had never taken place.

'A heap, Jamie,' said West tiredly. 'There's no one more easy to replace than a national leader.'

*

Mary Newman kicked off her shoes, opened a small bottle of Chardonnay from the minibar in her chalet, took a pad of Camp David notepaper from the desk, dropped down into the small sofa and picked up the phone. 'Lizzie, you want to come over now?'

Five minutes later, Lizzie West knocked, poked her head round the door, then held it open for Meenakshi to wheel herself inside as well, bringing a burst of weather behind her.

'Now, before we start, Meenakshi and I are pulling out of the dinner,' said Lizzie. She and Newman helped Meen-akshi out of the wheelchair, and steadied her while she took off her coat.

'Right by the fire, and I'll be fine,' said Meenakshi, pointing to a Native American woven rug which lay in front of the hearth. Newman put out a couple of cushions for her, and they lowered Meenakshi down. Lizzie hung their coats on the door. Both women were dressed in heavy natural-wool pullovers and jeans. Managing to kneel, Meenakshi stoked the fire and put on another log. The flames caught its edges and flared up.

'I love this place,' she said, staring into the glow. 'It reminds me of a holiday home we used to use in Darjee-ling, before my mother went chasing richer men.' She lay down, propping up her head on her elbow. 'There's something about mountain air – it does calm the troubled mind,' she said dreamily. 'Some day I'll write a medical paper about it.'

'How long are you in bandages for?'

'Don't tell anyone, but it's not as serious as it looks.' Meenakshi winked playfully. 'The key is to keep the weight off my legs. In a week or so, I should be fine.'

'Then you have no excuse to run away from our dinner,' said Newman, who had looked crestfallen at Lizzie's announcement. She had come back from walking the paths of Camp David, sorting out her thoughts, enjoying a few moments alone and away from her job. Meenakshi was right. The weather and the mountain air were having an effect and for some crazy reason she had been looking forward to an informal Camp David dinner hosted by Jim West. She had planned to be womanly again, and think of clothes, food and small talk instead of matters of state.

'I saw Dad after he got back with Jamie Song. He looked like thunder,' said Lizzie, sitting on the edge of the sofa. 'He told me a bit about what went on earlier. I wouldn't go near a meal like that if you paid me a million dollars.'

'Then I'll be the only woman there,' said Newman, tucking her feet under her on the sofa.

'Caroline Brock's still here.'

'Is she going?'

'Dad's expecting her.'

Caroline's presence at the dinner, without Lizzie or Meenakshi present, meant West planned to broach the topic of the smallpox. With Lizzie and Meenakshi there, Newman could have passed as another civilian family member, but the conversation would be bland, the occasion would be one of bonding, not substance.

'I'm sure it'll prove more useful for us to stay away,' said Meenakshi, with a suspicious lilt in her voice. She kept her eyes towards the fire, drawing shapes with the poker in cold ash fallen from the grate.

'Have you two got better offers?' asked Newman curiously.

'Depends how you look at it,' said Lizzie. 'When I told Dad Meenakshi and I wouldn't be joining him this evening, that cunning fox of a father of mine insisted on an alternative arrangement. He has set us up with Miss

Kiyoko Miyake, the stunning personal assistant to Prime Minister Sato.'

'Who speaks three European languages, Chinese and Hindi,' added Meenakshi admiringly.

'And a rather sullen character called Alexander Yushchuk who looks like a reincarnation of Dostoevsky,' said Lizzie. 'The Brit, Charles Colchester, who's far too old and stuffy for any of us. And the rather dashing and mysterious Lazaro Campbell, who seems to have a soft spot for our very own Meenakshi.'

Meenakshi turned away, instinctively lowering her eyes at Lizzie's teasing. But she quickly recovered. 'Quite rightly so,' she countered, tearing herself away from the grate to make her point 'But he'll have to do a lot more than save my life to win my affections.'

'And why so?' persisted Lizzie, watching a smile spread over Meenakshi's face with a glacial slowness.

'A touch too arrogant, for a start.'

'I rather like him,' said Newman, laughing.

'Doesn't mean I have to.' She turned her smile into a captivating grin, then dropped it immediately and returned to the fire.

'But it doesn't stop you from fancying him,' teased Lizzie.

'Now that's different,' replied Meenakshi, who at first seemed to be focused entirely on the flames, then was struck by another thought altogether. 'Mary, how come Jamie Song doesn't have anyone with him?'

Newman shrugged. 'Jamie probably knows America better than he does China. I suspect he feels more relaxed when he's not being watched by one of his own staff.' She tore a sheet off the pad and handed it to Lizzie. 'What do you think? Casual and rough enough for our distinguished guests?'

Lizzie quickly read through, glanced in surprise at Newman who raised her eyebrows and nodded. Both women burst out laughing.

'Dad asked you to do this?' gasped Lizzie.

'He did. But I'm not too familiar with his tastes.'

Lizzie read out loud. 'Pumpkin soup; pan-fried veal in red wine sauce; boiled new potatoes with asparagus tips, and soft Camembert cheese soufflé for dessert. Apart from the cheese soufflé that sounds like Jim West through and through.'

'Should I change it?' asked Newman tapping her pen against her chin.

Lizzie shook her head and handed the list back to Newman. 'No way. He asked you. You deliver. Mum was always at him to widen his culinary tastes. But she never dared go against him.'

Silently, Newman folded the notepaper. As she was contemplating her forthcoming role as presidential hostess, the telephone rang. Reluctantly, she picked it up.

'Secretary of State,' she said.

'Mary, it's Pete. Can I drop by?'

'Sure,' said Newman with breezy sarcasm. 'This is what down-time is all about.'

Not until the cheese soufflé had been finished, praised and cleared away, a coffee pot brought out with a cheeseboard, crackers, a bowl of fruit, and a trolley of liqueurs, brandy, vodka and whiskies offered around, did Jim West carefully turn the conversation by asking Vasant Mehta when Meenakshi would be out of her wheelchair.

It was an odd-looking dinner table, with West at one end and Newman at the other. The President had Caroline on his left and Andrei Kozlov on his right. Next to Kozlov was Stuart Nolan, then Peter Brock, with Toru Sato on

Newman's left. Jamie Song faced Stuart Nolan across the middle of the table with Caroline on his right and Vasant Mehta on his left.

Chris Pierce had intended to be there, but was working on intelligence coming in on Patton's bioterror sweep. So there was an extra place on Song's side. When West spoke, therefore, it was right down the table to Mehta, a question thrown out in such a way that the side conversations between Brock and Sato and Song and Caroline tailed to a halt.

'Thankfully, she'll make a full recovery,' said Mehta. 'They managed to put a tourniquet on the artery, and get out most of the shrapnel.' He didn't mention that it was Campbell who had applied the tourniquet as his daughter's blood turned the back lawn from green to red.

Mehta said no more, and West looked silently down the table, straight past Newman and through the window beyond, chewing cheese and a cracker. He was throwing open the floor to whoever wanted to take it. This is why they were all there, and a daughter's injury was as good a starting point as any.

'Perhaps, Mr President,' said Kozlov formally, 'I can contribute.' He shrugged and sipped his vodka. 'Let me say this: Russia is resting now. You, all of you,' he waved his hand around the table as if the host and guests were a family of adolescents, 'you have decisions to make that Russia has made over the past few centuries – and mainly got wrong – which is why we have chosen during this cycle of global change to take a break.'

He pushed back his chair so that it was apart from the others, clasped his hands together and stretched them cracking his knuckles. 'Each nation, as it develops, has choices. It is torn between the inner soul of its villages and the riches outside its borders. In eighteenth-century Russia, Peter the Great turned his back on the east and chose St

Petersburg as the capital to force our country out of its stagnation and embrace western culture. We became a nation where we only spoke Russian to our servants, and spoke French among ourselves. Not like you, Vasant,' he stressed, waving a finger at Mehta. 'You had a language imposed upon you by a colonizing power. No, we decided that our own language should be deemed socially inferior. So what happened? It created huge resistance flowing from the intellectuals and the artists down to the villages. No wonder Alexander Pushkin sought out the Russian village life. No wonder Ivan Shishkin ended up despising his foreign teachers in Europe, and only felt artistic freedom when he returned home to Russia. No wonder, on finishing with their universities, thousands of students abandoned St Petersburg and Moscow and headed deep into the countryside – and no wonder they were disappointed, as they discovered that despite their idealism, the reality of village life was a small-minded brutality, and that the poverty was endless.' Kozlov paused for a moment, allowing his thoughts to be absorbed. Then he lowered his voice and spoke more slowly. 'They discovered that finding Utopia is never easy, just as this evening we will find that politics are never tidy. Jim West has brought us together in midwinter in an idyllic mountain setting. Our minds may be clear, but the way through is not.'

Kozlov, the stubborn intellectual, had turned up unshaven for dinner, openly telling all that he had spent the afternoon drinking with his soulmate Alexander Yushchuk. He took centre stage now as the man who had endured years of condemnation by family and colleagues, a man who published his bank statement in the Russian press each month to avoid allegations of corruption, whose past gave him the credentials to hold the floor. He stood up, walked to the end of the table, stepped past Newman and poured himself another vodka from the trolley.

'Vladimir Putin took the same gamble as Peter the Great,' said Kozlov, walking back to his chair and sitting down heavily. 'There was resistance. My election has been the result. I happen to believe that Russia's future *does* lie in empowering the villagers, freeing the serfs if you like, and not in embracing NATO, the IMF, Hollywood and all your American values. If our love-in with America over the past twenty years had managed to seep wealth deep into the countryside, then perhaps I would not now be in office. But it didn't. Perhaps, after so much suffering, the Russian people are too impatient. Perhaps they know I will return a little bit of their own soul to them. They don't want tsarism. Nor do they want Marxism, but they want to feel they can create their own way and not copy that of another country. Of all of you here, I am the most neutral. Russia at this time is neither empire-building nor are we vulnerable and lashing out. We are here because of a series of terrible events. None of us planned them, I am sure. But each of us has chosen a career which means that we must decide how we will deal with them for the sake of humanity.'

Kozlov drained his vodka and stood up again, steadying himself on the back of his chair. He stepped round, putting both his hands on West's shoulders, then took them off, shaking his head. 'No,' he said, laughing to himself. 'I will leave you until last.'

Mehta looked up to see Kozlov heading towards him. But Kozlov ignored him. He gave Newman a wide berth, rested a hand on Caroline's shoulders, brushed passed Jamie Song, then stopped behind Sato, who remained rock steady, his face unreadable. Caroline glanced across the table at Newman, then back again to West, who was watching, fascinated at the Russian President's mix of drunkenness and insight. The Japanese Prime Minister flinched as Kozlov's clumsy hand rested on and squeezed his shoulder.

'Prime Minister Sato, you are an old warrior, indeed,' said Kozlov. 'In the evening of your political life, you find the younger generations restless. Uncle Sam defeated you and recreated you, but has never allowed you to forge your own path.' He pointed across the table to Jamie Song, who returned Kozlov's look quizzically with a thin, amused smile. 'Now, the Dragon awakes and threatens. If you leave things as they are, Japan will shrink in stature. How can it do anything else? So what do you do, Prime Minister?' he challenged, slapping Sato on the back. 'Preside over your nation's decline or fight for its future?'

Kozlov poured himself another vodka, drained the glass and left it in front of Sato, then walked round to Song, who turned round in his chair to face Kozlov. 'And what of the Dragon himself, who has so cleverly taken in McDonald's and American Express, but retained his authoritarian and Confucian way of life? You, Mr Dragon President,' he emphasized, jabbing his finger playfully at Song, 'are the envy of the developing world. The talk in the markets of Delhi and Moscow is "How can we do what China did? What is the formula? Will it work for us?" Your success is your own. Your vision is understood. Why should you stop? Would we if we were in your position?'

Again, Kozlov walked around to the other side of the table, stopping briefly behind Nolan, who paused in the packing of his pipe: 'And what about me, Andrei? Am I an old warhorse like Mr Sato?'

'Yes, both you, Stuart, and your nation,' said Kozlov. 'Britain is like Russia. We have fought, conquered and retreated. You now happily play under the umbrella of Uncle Sam. Having created America, there is no shame for you in its success. And those of us still out in the cold find your history comforting.'

'Bravo,' mumbled Nolan, looking back and squeezing the Russian's hand, as Kozlov walked unsteadily back round to settle on Mehta. He leant lightly on the table, between the Indian Prime Minister and Newman, looking at her as much as Mehta when he spoke. 'And you, Vasant, are bruised. Your nation is strong, yet it feels it is a victim. What has India done wrong? It has retained its democratic institutions. It allows its citizens to vote. It does not send people to labour camps. It gives us literature, films, music, software technology and chicken tikka masala. Of all of us, India is the most complete society. Yet also, perhaps, it is the most innocent. Who is to blame for what has happened to you? Your finger might point to Jim West for negligence; to Stuart Nolan for the sins of his colonial ancestors; to the uninvited Qureshi, dictator of a country whose regimes have kept you weak over the past half-century. But of those of us at the table, your finger points to Jamie Song for supporting your enemy and ensuring he survives. You could walk into Pakistan tomorrow. You could bomb it into oblivion, as Jim West's predecessors did to Toru Sato's predecessors. But the rising Dragon will do all it can to protect Pakistan and to ensure the failure of your mission.'

He stepped back, steadying himself with the back of Song's chair, and tapping a finger lightly on the Chinese President's shoulder. 'Yet we are here tonight to tell India to hold back. Do not attack. Become a victim again. All right, you say, I won't attack, but neutralize my enemy, once and for all. And on hearing that, we retreat, don't we, afraid of the monumental task you have set us?'

As he walked slowly back to his own seat, Kozlov's mottled face arranged itself into a bemused smile all of its own. Nolan lit his pipe. The smoke, pulled by a draught from the window, drifted across the table. Kozlov examined the glasses in front of him and chose the one with mineral water. 'And, Jim,' he said slowly, 'you are also a victim, having buried fifty-eight of your citizens from the tragedy at Yokata. Like Vasant, you would dearly like to march into North Korea. And who do you blame, apart from yourself? The Soviet Union, of course, but it is a generation since it was defeated. No, Jamie Song is where your finger also points, and it is Jamie who is telling you to be restrained and not attack, for it is China, and China only, which holds the power to do that. So what do you do to create the face of your great nation for the next generation? Do you take charge, yet again, or do you take note of the backlash against you from Iraq and the War on Terror, and hand the mantle to China – or, dare I mention, Japan – and do what Britain did last century?'

Kozlov leant forward on the table, his head lowered, tapping the tablecloth with a single finger. 'You, Jim,' he said softly. 'The shots are yours to call.'

West leant across and laid his hand on Kozlov's elbow. 'Brilliantly put, Andrei. Brilliantly put,' he said, his fingers toying with the base of a wine glass. The lighting around the table was dim enough to get a sense of the night outside, where snow had stopped falling and a small half-moon had risen into view, surrounded by ragged clouds.

'Vasant,' said West, looking over to Mehta. 'As Andrei said, you're the victim. Tell us what you want, and we'll see if we can do it.'

Mehta looked up with a sharp, sombre expression. His face was weathered and tired, and he spoke with his fingers entwined, resting on the table. 'I am tired with argument. I said what I had to say at the United Nations. Either of you, and I don't care which, must end Pakistan's terror. What you did with Musharraf was a joke,' he said accusingly to West before turning his eyes just as fiercely to Song. 'And you, Jamie, you gave them the bomb, and don't you dare deny it around this table. Now it's your responsibility to take it away from them. Or get Jim West to do it. Or I'm going to do it. Pakistan needs to be

dismembered as a nation and put back together again.
Nothing less will suffice.'

'Andrei,' said West. 'You're Vasant's main ally.'

'We support,' said Kozlov bluntly, 'no question, whatever India believes it needs to do.'

'Taru?'

Sato shrugged. 'You have the moral right, Vasant. But
if you go in, it will end in nuclear war. Therefore, we need
to look forward and get a guarantee from the other nuclear
powers that they will not intervene. If it is to happen, it
must be confined.'

'You're telling us to plan for nuclear war?' exclaimed
West.

'If we had planned for Hiroshima and Nagasaki, our
casualties would have been far less.' He took a quick look
towards West. His eyes, caught in the light of the room,
were at first angry, but became enveloped in a huge
sadness.

'If you two want to do it,' said Nolan, 'we'll commit,
and I'll bring some of Europe with me. Britain could
draft a resolution that Pakistan is a failed state, etcetera,
etcetera.'

'Jamie?' asked West.

'I'm not convinced I could bring the military with me,'
said Song, avoiding the direct explanation he had given
West earlier. He smiled, mocking himself. 'The president
of such a powerful nation is not always in charge. It would
take time to persuade them, and Vasant says he doesn't
have time.' He looked across to Nolan. His expression was
the most youthful and relaxed of anyone there. 'Stuart, if
you want to put forward a UN Security Council resolution,
for US or European intervention in Pakistan, China will
not veto it. Depending on the wording and depending on
my own political opposition we will either support it or
abstain. If the invasion is successful, then China will be

happy to provide engineers, technocrats, whatever is needed to rebuild the nation again.'

'Will Pakistan fight, Vasant?' asked Nolan, pouring himself a coffee.

'They'll fight,' said Mehta. 'And they'll go nuclear if they can.'

West's eyes shifted to Brock, and the table fell quiet as the atmosphere suddenly changed from discussion to decision-making. 'Draw up a plan, Peter,' West said in barely a whisper. 'And Mary, the usual on the diplomatic front. We need as many countries with us as we can get.' West reached across Kozlov to take the coffee pot from in front of Nolan. 'Vasant, can you bear with us while this works its way through?'

Mehta nodded, lightly putting his hand on Newman's as a gesture of reassurance. 'A few days, yes, but not much longer.'

A gust of wind caught the door, making it rattle, and swathes of misty drops blew against the glass. West glanced behind him at the thermometer which recorded the outside temperature. It had risen enough to replace snowfall with rainfall.

'There is another issue, about which something has cropped up only today,' said West. 'We believe that North Korea has procured a particularly lethal form of smallpox through a theft at a laboratory in Australia and from your labs, Andrei, at Pokrov. We believe that it is experimenting with the stuff on human beings and trying to set up a system through which it can be delivered.'

Kozlov gave West a sidelong, shrewd glance. 'From Pokrov. Yes, I can confirm that. Whether it went to North Korea or not, I can't say. But that it is missing, yes, that is true.'

'All our intelligence points to North Korea,' said West. 'Andrei and Jamie, can either or both of you handle it?'

'You make it sound so simple,' Kozlov said, his head down, concentrating on pushing the edge of the tablecloth with his fingernail. 'What do you mean, handle it?'

'Ensure that North Korea does not have this weapon,' said West.

Kozlov shook his head mournfully. 'I told you, our days of empire are over. I am sorry about Pokrov, but it was an American plan to seal our laboratories, and the plan—'

'The virus should have been destroyed long ago,' said West brusquely. 'Smallpox is banned – the 1972 Convention – and Moscow knows it. Within months of signing it you set up Biopreprat, hired thousands of scientists and violated that treaty.'

Kozlov threw up his hands in mock surrender. 'I apologize, Mr President. Russia apologizes on behalf of the late Soviet Union.'

'We can help on North Korea,' said Song quietly. 'But it will not be through force. And we will not do it under threat from the United States. If Park Ho has this smallpox virus, we will take it from him. We will also seal his missile silos. But it will not be known what we have done.'

'Not even by us?' asked Sato.

'Not even by you,' said Song, his face masked and unreadable as he answered. 'But let me tell you this. Andrei is right. One day far in the future China will want to be a superpower. Whether it is a hundred or two hundred years from now does not concern any of us. It is far from the crises that face us today. We have been working at modernizing our country for sixty years and still have twenty million people living in poverty and forty million illiterate and uneducated. Why should we be interested in expanding our borders and colonizing new territory? We believe we do have the right formula for dragging a nation out of poverty, and some might think us successful. But by no means are we there yet. So it is in our interests to stay on good terms with the United States, and to build our friendship with Russia and India. Our closest rival – if you want to use that word – is you, Sato. But we should not let history get in the way of what we can achieve together.'

For a moment, Song, whether deliberately or not, let his cover slip. He looked up at Sato, with a burning appeal in his eyes, then he settled on West. 'If you go it alone, Jim, you will unleash forces in China that I may not be able to control. If you hold back, Park Ho will be removed from power. The status quo will be restored. On that you have my word.'

West didn't speak. He was intent on what Jamie Song had said, unsure of whether to read it as a threat or an offer. Brock ended the silence with a question to his wife. 'How long, Caro, would Park Ho need with his tests, and how long to deliver it?'

'The worst-case scenario—' She tapped her cheek while thinking. 'A couple of weeks. But he's not going to deliver this by missile. The virus wouldn't survive that. He'd have to have some other system ready. The best of which would be another human being.'

'A couple of weeks,' muttered West, pushing back his chair and putting both hands on the table. 'We're with you for a couple of weeks, Jamie. Let's talk after that.'

One by one, Jim West delivered his guests into the hands of secret service agents who escorted them the short distance to their chalets. He turned back into the room, grateful to see Mary Newman and the Brocks helping themselves to a nightcap and settling down on the sofas away from the dining table. He hadn't looked forward to being left at Aspen with just the shuffling feet of the staff clearing the table. West stood by the dying fire, rubbing his hands, then turned and took the whisky Peter Brock had poured for him.

Newman was close enough for him to catch her perfume. For the first time he noticed how she had dressed for the dinner – a beige cashmere pullover and camel-colour pants with a pair of brown suede ankle boots. She had begun pulling the left boot off, but remembering where she was, and catching the disapproving eye of Brock, she stopped. West grinned and moving across to the huge window slid it open a bit to let the night air cool the room.

'Kick 'em off if you want, Mary,' said West. 'You guys were quiet, but great. So I want to know what you think.'

'On North Korea, Jim,' said Caroline Brock, 'my two-week scenario was very much worst case. You could have much longer. He's got to work out a way of getting IL-4 to react with smallpox and achieve the maximum infection. Given his technology, I'd say we're not in any immediate danger. But if it isn't fixed within six months to a year, start worrying.'

West stuck his hand out into the weather to check for rain and brought it back covered in glistening drops. The moon was consumed by dark clouds and the mountains forged harsh black rims across the skyline. 'Pete, you'll check things with Tom and Chris, before you turn in?'

'Sure will,' said Brock. He glanced at Caroline. 'We'd better get going anyway.'

Mary cupped her hands around her whisky glass. 'You know—' she began. Then seeing the Brocks get to their feet, she halted herself. West looked sharply in from near the window. Brock helped Caroline on with her coat. Two waiters began removing the glasses from the table. A gust of wind broke a branch from a tree and lifted it up to crack against the window glass.

'What are you cooking there, Mary? You got something on your mind, tell us.'

She smiled uncertainly, took another sip of whisky, put the glass down and got to her feet. 'It's a long, rambling academic analysis, best saved for the morning, I guess.'

Caroline buttoned up her coat. Brock wrapped a scarf around his neck. 'I'm seeing Caro home. Then I'll check the communications room, and drop back by in five or ten minutes,' he said, looking at Newman. 'Why don't you tell Jim what you're thinking, Mary? We can chew it over when I get back.'

As the Brocks closed the door behind them, the cold through breeze it had caused in the room stopped, and the warmth of the fading fire returned to the area around the sofa. West, still standing up, wasn't sure where to sit, until Newman patted the cushion next to her. 'Don't worry, Mr President,' she said, quietly so the waiters wouldn't hear. 'I'm not going to pounce.'

West smiled gratefully. 'Thanks, Mary. It's been one hell of a day.' For a moment, they each took refuge in their nightcaps, letting the sudden quiet of the Aspen living room seep through and change the atmosphere. West threw Newman a sideways glance. 'Do you miss David?' he asked, catching her eyes, then looking away. Newman didn't answer immediately, letting the question hang until West broke the silence: 'You don't mind me asking, do you?'

'Not at all.' Newman tilted her head towards him. 'It's not nice being betrayed. But do I miss having someone around? Sure, I do. It has to be someone who doesn't lie to you, which David did, so no way do I miss that.' She smiled. 'I won't ask about Valerie. It's written all over your face, every minute of the day.'

'That obvious?' sighed West.

'I'm afraid it is, Mr President.'

West laughed softly. 'Shall we make a new rule?' he

suggested. 'When we're out of the White House and it's just the two of us, or even Pete and Caro, Jim's fine. It doesn't have to be—' He took another sip of whisky, letting the sentence finish itself.

Newman gave him a quizzical look. 'Jim's fine, is it?' she said, running her finger down the arm of the sofa. 'Any other occasions?' she teased. 'Or just when it's like this?'

'Well, what I can do is draw up a list,' began West, rolling his eyes sarcastically. He was about to go on when Newman jumped to her feet. 'You guys,' she shouted at the waiters. 'Can you just leave it all there, and excuse us for a moment.'

The waiters slipped away, and Newman walked over and studied the glasses and crockery on the table, her hand cupped pensively under her chin. She took off her spectacles and adjusted her focus to what she was examining. 'Just what I was thinking,' she said, pointing to Kozlov's place.

'The wine in his glasses, both red and white, is hardly touched. He swayed in before dinner, asking for sparkling mineral water and claiming he had been drinking with Yushchuk. Only after the meal, when the trolley came round, did he ask for a vodka. While talking to us, he filled it three times, which for a Russian is the equivalent of a teaspoonful.' West was standing next to her. She put her hand on his elbow to emphasize her point. 'He needed to show the vodka to give his speech the aura of a soul-searching, vodka-soaked Russian intellectual. But Andrei Kozlov was stone-cold sober throughout.'

'That doesn't mean he was lying,' said West.

'No, it doesn't,' agreed Newman slowly. 'In fact, far from it. He was sending you a message when he talked of freeing the serfs by not embracing NATO, the IMF and American values. Then, take what Kozlov said with this strange fish,' she said, pointing at the place where Song had been sitting. 'He's the one who really worries me. Not an ounce of humour in him all evening, then threatening us with forces he might not be able to control.' She leant against the table. 'He said there were twenty million Chinese living in poverty, in a population of what—'

'A billion, just over,' said West.

'Do you know how many live in poverty in America?'

'More than thirty million according to the US Census Bureau,' said West. 'Just over 16 per cent of all Americans. Any American aged twenty has a 60 per cent chance of spending at least one year living in poverty at some point in the future. I've just been in Detroit delivering a speech on it.'

'Exactly.' Newman went back to the sofa and waited for West to join her. 'We have thirty million out of what – a total population of 300 million. Jamie Song has twenty million out of 1.1 billion. Who's doing better?'

'Different kind of poverty.'

'Sure, but he wasn't citing statistics just for the hell of it.'

'I'm not sure I'm with you, Mary.'

Newman leant back and stretched her arms behind her head. 'I said it was a rambling academic analysis, and to be honest I don't know where it leads us, but my gut instinct is that we have to read underneath what both those guys said. I wouldn't trust them to stay with us on this one inch.' She brought her right hand down in front of her face. 'Not even one inch. Not even a millimetre,' she said, moving her thumb and forefinger closer and closer together until they touched.

'You know what they were saying,' she said, not bothering to hide her tiredness. 'Song was saying: "We're better than you." Kozlov was saying: "If you make us choose, we're with China."'

'And what about Mehta, his great ally?'

Newman laughed coldly. 'Mehta's in a quagmire, isn't he? He's expendable. Let him be our great twenty-first-century nuclear weapons experiment. No one wants to touch him.'

The words of Jamie Song in the ride back from the helicopter returned to West, echoing from Song's unreadable oriental face in pure Bostonian English. *You don't get it, do you, Jim?* Song speaking as if he was addressing an American simpleton.

'Thank you for frankness, Mary, however unpalatable it might be,' said West, shooting a look towards the door as it opened, light spilling in from the hall. Brock stepped in, followed by Pierce and Patton, who was speaking on a mobile phone. 'Do we have thirty minutes? ... Good ... I'm with the President.' He closed the call, flipped shut the phone and said, 'I'm sorry, Mr President, but I need an instruction on this now.'

Patton pulled up a hard chair. His heavy chin jutted forward and his eyes flickered across a file he rested on his lap. The others found seats around the room. Newman fetched a fresh bottle of water from the kitchen and poured them all a glass.

'I want you to bear with me, Mr President,' said Patton. 'I'll tell it straight through. We have time. Then you can decide.'

'Very well,' said West. The room had been transformed. For a moment it had been a sanctuary, but now it had suddenly exploded back into reality. He would have much preferred to have listened to Newman's late-night theories. Instead, he had Tom Patton with a new and real threat to America.

'Two days ago, a Cuban fishing boat landed at Key West,' began Patton. 'The skipper was found tied up in the cabin. Straight away the coastguard recognized it as anything but a routine alien-smuggling run. It was a hijacking – something completely different. On the boat were three Cuban fisherman, four if you count the captain. Their fishing permits and licences were in order. There were also two defectors, a husband and wife. Until a couple of weeks ago, Ernesto Tomas Morera, aged forty-eight, ran Cuba's air traffic control service. The wife, Elena Blanco Morera, aged forty-two, was a fairly high-ranking officer in Cuba's intelligence agency, Dirección General de Inteligencia or DGI. Both of them check out with our records. Elena's job was China.'

West, suddenly alert, looked across at Patton. 'Go on.'

'Why did they want to defect?' asked Patton rhetorically. 'Because suddenly the government had asked them to do things they knew they couldn't. Ernesto was told he had to go head up a neighbourhood committee in some place called Campechueta right at the other end of the island. Elena walked into work one day to find her in-tray filled with visa applications from West Africa.'

He paused for some water and drained the glass. West refilled it for him.

'It was Elena who spotted what had happened. A completely coincidental oversight had linked her job with Ernesto's in an area so sensitive that the DGI decided they would have to be separated. Over the next week, Elena dutifully issued visas for Africans. Ernesto made a show of preparing to take up his new job. But they also tracked down a boat crew, paid them some money and arranged the boat to get out. The crew omitted to let on that they would have to overpower the skipper.' He shrugged. 'But that's by the by. At the weekend, they made their escape and I've just come from hearing and corroborating their story.

'Over the past two weeks, according to Ernesto, there've been two flights by Chinese transport aircraft into Havana, using the Russian-built Antonov 225 – the biggest mother of a transport aircraft – flying across the Atlantic from Dakar in Senegal. Elena's China desk had been handling a deal, struck about ten years ago, that gave Cuba medium-range Chinese missiles in exchange for electronic eaves-dropping facilities to listen in on the eastern American seaboard. If you remember, the Russians made a final pull-out from Cuba as part of their new relationship with us after Nine Eleven. The Chinese moved into the vacuum. The missile part of the deal has begun to be implemented now.'

Patton stopped for a moment to make sure that West and all in the room understood what he was saying. 'The missiles, according to Elena, include the DF-15, the DF-3 and the DF-21. Which ones are actually there now, she doesn't know.'

'You got any corroboration?' asked West. Patton took out of his briefcase a sheaf of photographs stamped with the circular logo of the National Imagery and Mapping Agency which handled satellite and surveillance imagery. 'As soon as we heard, we bought in the latest commercial satellite imagery over Cuba,' he said.

'We didn't have our own?' queried West.

'Most of it's tasked over Asia,' said Brock.

'The Ikonos satellite came up with this. It only has 0.75 metre resolution,' explained Patton, handing a photograph to West. Newman leant over to see. Brock and Pierce looked from over the back of the sofa. 'Our analysts reckon this is the Antonov 225 at Havana's main civilian airport. It's the only one that will take an aircraft so big. Now see this—' He pointed to a blurred oblong shape by the side of the aircraft. 'We believe this is a missile container. See its size against the aircraft. It's big. Very big.' Patton pulled out another image. 'We sent up the Global Hawk. It works with images like a computer search engine works with words. We told it what we were looking for, and a few hours later, after mapping the whole of Cuba, it came up with this. The main road between Havana and Pinar del Rio. See here. The road is closed for repairs. A convoy of three trucks: on the back of each is the same image picked up by the Global Hawk, matching the container seen by the Antonov 225.'

Even in a room of close friends, Jim West wanted to give nothing away about the thoughts running through his mind. The heated air in the room suddenly felt oppressive, and a sense of dread, like when his wife had bravely told him the diagnosis of her impending death, spread through his whole body, until it swept across his face and settled into a grey, controlled dullness emanating from his eyes.

'Someone fill me in on what these missiles do.'

Chris Pierce stood up and walked round to the window. Realizing that the President was looking at him against the backlight of the wall lamp, he moved further in and stood with his back to the fireplace. 'The DF-21 has a range of about 1,200 miles; the DF-15, 400 miles; and the DF-3, about 2,000 miles, which produces an arc to Tucson, Denver, Minneapolis/St Paul, Chicago and the eastern seaboard. The Chinese themselves can hit Los Angeles, Phoenix, Salt Lake City, so they've got us on both sides, covering the whole of the United States.'

West shook his head in disbelief. 'They're doing under our noses what we went to the brink of nuclear war to stop the Soviets doing in 1962? Did they believe we wouldn't find out?'

'According to our defectors, the deal was struck in January 2002,' said Patton. 'Elena Morera confirms that the first missiles only arrived two weeks ago. What we don't know is why has it taken so long to put it into action – and given the strengthening of our relationship with China, why now?'

'It's in blatant violation of every arms proliferation agreement,' said Newman.

'Pakistan, Korea, now China and Cuba,' said Pierce. 'I can give you military plans and scenarios, Mr President, but what's really needed is heavy diplomacy. We've just got too many fronts coming in on us.'

Patton cleared his throat. 'Except, right now, there's a Chinese transport plane on its way to Havana. It's halfway across the Atlantic, three hours from landing.'

'Bring it in,' said West without hesitation. 'Land the son of a bitch down into Guantanamo. Strip it out. I want to know every nut and bolt that it's carrying.'

Outside, away from the lit pathways between the chalets, Jamie Song and Andrei Kozlov trudged through rain which fell in fine drops, slicing into the snow. They meandered through shrubs and clusters of trees, their shapes softened by streaks of light refracted through rain splashing on to pathway lamps. Sometimes they disappeared altogether, absorbed into an empty, sooty darkness in the woods.

On the Camp David surveillance video, they were only filmed properly when they greeted each other on the cross-roads of two paths and Jamie Song said, 'When I talked of us meeting soon, I didn't expect it would be in the grounds of Camp David.' That was according to experts who later read his lips. They pulled up the collars of their coats, lifted the earflaps of their hats, and headed off, heads lowered, away into the grounds where no one could know what they were saying and only occasionally would their hunched, slow-walking figures be caught on camera.

Had the night been clear and cold with white falling snow, it might not have been unusual to walk off a good dinner. But this was a damp, windy and unpleasant night, where two men would only be out talking if they felt nowhere else was safe to do so.

In the morning, a Lincoln Town Car limousine pulled up outside Jamie Song's chalet. The Chinese President gave his hand luggage to the driver who put it in the boot. Lying on the back seat was a copy of the *Washington Post*, with a brief final-edition front-page story about a US air and naval military exercise in the Caribbean. As the limousine pulled out away from the trees around the chalet, Song had a long, clear view of the mountains. The wintry morning light had brought a drop in temperature, and fresh snow covered the dirt which had been brought in by the rain. Song's overcoat was still damp.

The limousine did not head out towards the main gate but swung round to Aspen where Jim West raised a friendly hand in greeting. When the car stopped, he opened the back door himself and got in. Secret service chase cars pulled out in front of and behind the Lincoln and motorcycle outriders flanked the convoy as it set off.

'Thought I'd ride with you,' said West, with a brief smile. Unlike Song who wore his coat, West was dressed only in a dark-blue denim shirt and jeans. 'Something's cropped up which I thought we could sort out.'

'I hope it's a pleasant surprise,' said Song, moving the newspaper to clear the seat for West.

'We'll see,' said West, looking at Song curiously. Here was a man who had been educated in America, had become rich through America, who spoke and maybe could think like an American, but who was turning against everything American. West couldn't bring himself to believe Jamie Song would authorize sending missiles to Cuba. What he needed to know was whether Song had the power to stop it.

'Last night, after you had left,' said West, 'Chris Pierce, my Defense Secretary, dropped by. We've been carrying out military training in the Caribbean over the past couple of days with live firing and all that. A Chinese transport plane flew right into the exercise area. Unfortunately, the pilot didn't answer our radio signals. He claims he doesn't speak English or French, if you can believe that, considering the plane had come from Senegal. So we sent up some fighters. It got a little dangerous for a while, but eventually we brought the plane down into Guantanamo Bay.'

Song glanced across sharply, but didn't say anything. West looked straight ahead at the bullet proof screen sealing the back seat from the driver and bodyguard in front.

'You guys did a similar thing some years back, I remember, with one of our EP-3 surveillance planes.'

'Before my time,' said Song dryly. His hands were on each knee and he kept his eyes on West.

'The crew is fine. Nobody's hurt. No equipment is damaged. But we did look inside the plane.' West stopped there. Song appeared completely secure in what he was hearing, his eyes fixed unfalteringly on West.

'And what was the plane carrying, Jim,' he asked softly, 'that has brought you into my car on this cold morning?'

'A missile that could strike the United States,' said West, his deadpan delivery matching Song's. He detected a flicker of reaction. It could have been shock, possibly anger, but it was suppressed immediately with a quick, thin smile and a slight shifting of the hands. From the top pocket of his shirt, West pulled out a sheet of folded paper, unfolded it and passed it to Song. The photograph had been taken inside the plane, showing a case prised open, its wrapping unfurled, and the fin of a rocket.

'I'm told it has a range of 400 miles,' said West, 'and that three other types are on order. The most powerful has a range of 2,000 miles.'

'This isn't the anti-Castro lobby playing games?' asked Song, offering the picture back.

'Keep it,' said West, shaking his head. 'We've got plenty more. And no, this is not Miami propaganda.'

'I see,' said Song, lowering his head and looking away from West for the first time since the accusation. 'So we have two issues to deal with. One is the confirmed hijacking of a Chinese aircraft by the United States and the kidnapping of the crew—'

'Jamie, don't go down this road,' said West, not hiding the exasperation in his voice.

'. . . The second is the allegation that we are supplying offensive missiles to Cuba.'

The limousine's engine whined as the driver changed from automatic to a low gear to handle the curves in the road to the helipad. West wound down his window, sending a beam of sunlight across Song's face, causing him to squint. Cold air rushed in. The snow had stopped and apart from the crunch of the tyres on the road and the low purr of the engine the huge silence of the mountains bore down on both of them.

'You've got to be straight with me, Jamie. I can't mess with the safety of the US. You know that. Just tell me what the hell is going on.'

Song, irritated by the sun, let his eyes flare. 'Don't push.'

'Then don't fuck around.' West snatched the picture from Song's hand and rattled it in front of his face. 'Did you know about this?'

'No.'

'Do you have an explanation?'

'I'm not in Beijing. How can I have?'

'I want your word. Then I'll tell you what I'm going to do.'

Song shook his head. 'You have my word, and I'll tell you what I'm going to do.'

West twisted in his seat so he was now face to face with Song. 'Any Chinese aircraft heading for Cuba will be shot down.'

Song shook his head. 'You can't—'

'I can, and I will. I was restrained over your buddies in North Korea. I've kept my patience with your buddies in Pakistan. But you screw us in Cuba—' West shook his head and swallowed hard. 'Goddamn it, Jamie. We're both old enough to have been alive in '62. Maybe I'm a sucker, but I don't think you know it's happening. So help me on this, or I won't be able to help you.'

As the limousine straightened out for the last mile to the heliport, Marine One passed overhead, casting a quick flickering shadow over them. Song buttoned up his coat and took his hat and gloves in his hand. 'You will return the plane and the crew within forty-eight hours,' he said. 'If there is a missile inside, you can keep it. If any of this leaks out into the public domain, by whatever means, I will be unable to do anything to help you. If these conditions are not met, I cannot help you either in Korea or Pakistan. If they are, I will try my utmost. On that you have my word.'

The car drew to a halt. The motorcycle outriders stopped further ahead, their blue lights flashing. The riders dismounted, took off their helmets and stood at attention on either side of the red carpet furled out for the Chinese President. A secret service agent opened Song's door. West let himself out on the other side. On his signal, just before

Song boarded, the White House photographer recorded
the scene of West and Song at the steps of Marine One,
one in an open-neck shirt, the other in the formality of a
woollen overcoat, the pair of them shaking hands, then
embracing each other, and West staying, unflinching in
the icy mountain crosswinds, both hands raised and waving, as the helicopter lifted up and vanished through the
winter clouds towards Washington.

By mid-morning it turned out to be a bright winter's day.
Jim West asked for coffee to be served on the patio. The
sun was bright, although Patton was working in an overcoat and Mary Newman and Caroline Brock were wrapped
in colourful Gore-tex jackets. They all wore shades to ease
the violent reflection from the snow. West, Brock and
Kozerski sat with their backs to the light, looking into
Aspen's reception area where staff were rebuilding the log
fire and polishing the table after the previous evening's
dinner.

'Chris, you need to get to New York tonight. I want
you face to face with the Cuban ambassador to the UN,
but not in the UN building. Go to the Waldorf or
something. Give him seven days for us to get full access to
those missiles.'

'You sure you want me for this?' asked Pierce, glancing
over at Newman.

'Sometimes I wonder if I gave you two the wrong jobs,'
said West, his face enveloped in a cloud of his own breath.
'This will not be a diplomatic meeting. So yes, Chris, I
want you because you're the man who's going to order the
strikes the second the Cubans go past that deadline. That's
why I'm giving him a week – because there's no negotiation. Your job is to get that message through their thick
Marxist skulls.'

Pierce nodded contritely. West cupped his hands round his mug of coffee for warmth. 'Tom, I want you to put everything into cracking any North Korean cells in this country. Anything it takes. And if there's a single case of any suspicious disease, I want to know about it.' He glanced across at Kozerski. 'John, if Tom's got something to tell me, make sure he can get me wherever.' The table was alive with sunlight and the dancing fog of coffee steam and human breath.

'Mary and Pete,' continued West, 'I want you both to go flyabout. Mary, follow up on the diplomatic side by calling in on Sato, Song and Kozlov – as soon as they're back. By the time you're with Song, Chris's deadline on Cuba should have four days to run. If Jamie can't sort it in that time, he won't be able to.'

'What about the media?' said Newman, pulling up her collar against a gust of wind cutting round the edge of the lodge.

'Tell the press, but don't take any of them with you. Only deal with heads of government. I don't want any mixed messages. Call me any time. But I want you to start in South Korea – with Pete.' He glanced across to his National Security Advisor, letting everyone guess that he and Brock had hatched the plan earlier that morning. 'You'll both be flying out separately. Hopefully, your trip, Mary, will attract the press coverage and Pete will get away quietly. You're to go to Panmunjom, stand with the binoculars, reaffirm US commitment. Pete's going to be tapping our security allies – Taiwan, South Korea, Singapore, the governments we can really trust – for a loan of intelligence agents.'

40

Chungchongnam-do, South Korea

From the window of what was called her *yogwan* or wayside inn, Mary Newman looked out at the battleship-grey mass of the Yellow Sea and the estuary of the Kum River running into it. Outside the compound, stretching down to the water, was flat land of endless rice paddies where patches of shallow water, broken up by the crops, reflected sunlight like fractured mirrors.

Her room was magnificent. She walked into a comfortable area of minimalist beige furniture decorated with Korean porcelain and calligraphic scrolls. Along the whole front was a balcony with gas heaters attached so that guests could sit outside on a sunny winter's morning. A dining table was set in an alcove. Two sharp brass candleholders sculpted in the shape of naked, but graceful women were the only objects on it. A short corridor led round first to a second room, which was kitted out with video link, satellite phone, computer, multichannel television and short-wave radio. A printed note gave a number to call for technical or secretarial assistance.

Further down was a set of double doors made up of small frosted glass panes. Through them lay the high-ceilinged master suite, with a low and hard king-sized bed and a view out on to the mountains. The bathroom was almost as big again, with a double-sized tub and a discreet card laid on the sink with a number to dial should a guest wish to be hand-rubbed by a blind Korean masseur.

Newman was exhausted after her visit to the Kunsan air-base. She was still wearing the souvenir combat flying jacket given to her when she had stood in an aircraft hangar, flanked by two F-16 fighter aircraft, and ringed by 1,500 service personnel listening to her brief address. She had reminded them of the history of the Eighth Fighter Wing, known as the Wolf Pack, and of their duty – as the mission statement read – to deliver lethal airpower, to defend the base and to take the fight north, if ordered to do so.

After reading from notes prepared for her, Newman had dropped her hand by her side, taken off her spectacles, and brushed back her fringe. 'Look, I don't know if I'm meant to say this, but I will,' she said, lowering her voice and bringing her mouth closer to the microphone. 'I've just flown down from Camp Bonifas and Camp Liberty Bell up by Panmunjom. Before that I was in Washington and Camp David. The last couple of weeks have been like I've never known before. All you guys are in the front line, and I mean that in the very real sense of the words. Some of your grandparents might have fought in the Korean War, and the reason you are here is because that war has never really ended. A lot of people died, but there was a stalemate and no glory, and things pretty much went back to what they would have been if it had never happened. The reason I am here is that we're closer to war on this peninsula now than we have ever been in the past half-century. The President is working his damnedest to make sure it doesn't happen. But if it does, I know you'll serve your country and that you'll win. God be with you.'

In her lavish suite, with those words reverberating around her jet-lagged mind, she hung the jacket in the wardrobe, slipped out of her clothes, ran the shower, smelling the hot springs sulphur in the stream of water and stepped under it.

Since David had walked out on her, Newman had learned to relish her time alone. She enjoyed the luxury of letting her mind wander without interruption, and as the water cascaded down her back, it took her back to the start of the long day. After flying into Seoul from Washington in the early morning, she was taken straight from the airport to the newly opened rail link to Panmunjom, along a line which, hopefully, one day would run uninterrupted between North and South Korea. She had laid a wreath at Panmunjom in the Military Armistice Commission hut where Lieutenant Lee Jong-hee, sleeper agent, had murdered an unknown compatriot and fled to the North. She had lunched just south of there at Camp Liberty Bell, making the same speech as she had at Kunsan. Her visit was so last-minute that only local stringers and wire agencies were able to shout questions at her – and she had answered none, promising a full statement at the end of her visit.

From Panmunjom, a helicopter had taken Mary Newman to the presidential palace in Seoul, a cavernous blue-roofed building known as the Blue House, where the diminutive and highly intelligent President Cho Hyon-tak stood at the massive open doors to greet her. Even Newman, who was only five foot five herself, stood an inch above Cho in the photo-call handshake. But what he lost in height he made up for in hyperactivity and blunt talking, with idiosyncrasies of accent and mannerisms picked up from his years at Columbia Business School and living as a student in the rougher areas on the West Side north of Central Park.

When Cho guided her into the meeting room, she found Peter Brock already there, and papers spread out on a conference table among a scattering of coffee cups. Also there were Cho's advisers, two young men and a woman, and also an older man whom Newman recognized as an intelligence chief from the Agency for National Security

Planning, one of the umbrella intelligence agencies. Clearly, they had been at it for some hours.

'Let's leave it, Peter, for a moment and see if Mary can knock some sense into us,' said Cho with a smile, clapping his hands for the coffee pot to be refilled. 'Coffee OK with you?' he asked, beaming at Mary, who hesitated just for a second, but it was enough. 'Bring some tea, ginseng and water, still and sparkling,' he added. Tentatively, he pushed open another door in the opposite wall and peered round to see if the room behind it was occupied. He glanced back at Mary conspiratorially. 'It's empty,' he said. 'Let's sneak off in here.' As his advisers lined up to join him, he held out a hand. 'Just the three of us,' he said, winking at Brock. 'Then I can speak my mind.'

On the surface, Cho acted like an overgrown kid, nervous and mischievous. But as soon as they had sat down, with a refreshments trolley in front of them, Newman saw at least one layer of the mask peel away. Cho became even more American, slipping into the role of a Bronx street fighter.

'I was telling Peter,' he said, breaking off to wave his hand at the trolley. 'Help yourselves. Let's be in the trenches for a bit.' Newman had expected the quip to be followed by a smile, but Cho's expression was sombre. 'I'm in a fucking dilemma, Mary, like I was telling Peter. Jim doesn't know about it. But then I didn't know the stakes until Peter got here this morning. The bottom line is this. We hate the fucking Japanese. All right? They came here in 1910 and they fucked us over and we haven't got through the counselling yet. Everyone in Asia hates the fucking Japanese – except the Taiwanese and that's because they hate the fucking Chinese. And maybe the Indians, because they live too far away. "So what?" you say.' He sipped his coffee, put the cup on the table next to his chair and stood up. He looked around for a window and, finding

there wasn't one, he paced the room, head lowered and
hands behind his back. 'If it comes to a fight with North
Korea, you're going to be using your bases here and in
Japan. That makes us allies with the Japanese while we
bomb the shit out of our brothers north of the border.'

He stopped, looked up at Mary and shook his head.
'No. No. No. No fucking no, if you get my message.' He
stabbed his finger in the air to make his point. 'I've got a
new fucking generation of troublemakers to deal with. The
last generation, they wanted democracy. They hated the
fucking dictators. And they won. This new lot, they love
their brothers across the border. You get it? If they love
their brothers, they hate you. I know it sounds crazy. Here
we are, a living example of how the developing world can
become the developed world, the fucking miracle which
has escaped most of the rest of the Third World, how
South Korea, battered and pummelled by war, used the
American security umbrella to pull itself up and succeed,
and the young kids don't appreciate it at all and want to
fuck it up.' He clasped his hands in front of him and
lowered his voice. 'You get my drift, both of you?'

'Cho, there's nothing I like more than a straight talker,'
Newman smiled. 'Even if your language leaves something
to be desired.'

'Good,' said Cho, putting his chubby hands on his small
hips and leaning forward before beginning his pacing
again. 'So, second point. What happens if that shit Park
Ho loses and North Korea collapses?' He stopped in front
of Brock and shook his finger. 'I'll tell you what will
fucking happen. For three months, you'll all be in there,
China, Russia, you guys, the damn Europeans with their
blonde aid workers and their strapping lovers, Australian
backpackers and their home-grown dope plants, the huge
goddamn white bandage of the UN, their Toyota Land
Cruisers, their 192 fucking languages. And you'll all fuck it

over, just like everywhere else. And you'll say to me: "No, Cho, it's too sensitive for South Korea to be seen in there right now. Give it time. Let the international community handle it."'

He swung round to Mary, eyes glaring, halfway between humour and fury. 'Just like you did in Kosovo, Afghanistan, Iraq and all those other post-Cold-War fuck-ups. Then what will happen? Colombia or Kazakhstan will blow up. And the Toyotas, the backpackers – the whole lot of you will be shipped off there and you'll leave us with the mess of what? Do you know what?'

He retrieved his coffee from the table, sat down and crossed his legs, his silence switching the question from rhetorical to real. Both Newman and Brock stayed quiet, hoping he would give the answer.

'What, Peter? Tell me what we will be left with.'

'We won't abandon you, Cho,' said Brock.

'You fucking would if there wasn't a North Korea any more,' he laughed. 'What are you going to do, move the ceasefire line up to the Chinese border?'

Brock shrugged. 'Tell us. Tell us what would happen.'

'Reunification,' he said in barely a whisper. 'Fucking reunification.' The flare of his eyes faded and his expression, overcome by daunting reality, lost its fire. 'Look what happened to West Germany when it absorbed the East. Calculate it for us and it makes it ten times worse. Ten times the cost.'

For a moment he seemed to retreat into that ultimate nightmare. Brock nudged him on. 'So what's it to be, Cho? What's the way through?'

'Keep it local. Jamie Song and I will handle Park Ho. We can strangle him.'

'And in his last throes of life, he launches a few missiles?' suggested Newman.

'I'll nuke him.'

Cho let those words settle in the room. He fixed Brock and then Newman with an unflinching expression of certainty. No wonder he didn't want his advisers with him. South Korea's dozen or so nuclear reactors would give it ample uranium or plutonium. Its scientists had the knowledge. The parts could be procured from here and there. For Newman, it was like hearing the mechanical clicks of a round being put in the chamber of a revolver. She had known the likelihood of South Korea, Taiwan, Israel and a few others having nuclear weapons. The declaration of it in a meeting like this had elevated it to another level.

'You'll nuke him?' said Newman sceptically, not reacting to Cho's declaration and keeping to Cho's Hollywood-style language. 'If he doesn't mind being nuked by us, why should he mind being nuked by you?'

'That's what you don't see,' said Cho. 'You know why Park Ho's such a shit? Because his mother was killed by a GI in front of his eyes when he was a kid. So you've got a mind there no one can deal with. If his country is pulverized by you guys, he'll fight you back and feel good about it. He'll be avenging his mother's death. He'll be proving that *juche* is not a piece of crap, that it can take on a superpower. But if he fights me, what the fuck does he get? Nothing. No point getting nuked by little old Cho. If he's going to get nuked it has to be by Uncle Sam, and if Uncle Sam's not going to do that, Park loses. That's how he's thinking. He's Korean, I know how he thinks. We're all a bit crazy.'

Cho stopped pacing, tapped his head and his face broke out into a huge smile. 'There you go,' he said, sitting down and patting Brock's knee. 'That's my rant. Nothing to read between the lines.'

In the shower, Mary Newman laughed as she recalled Cho's language. The steam and warmth soaked into her tight shoulder muscles, letting her think more clearly about the meeting. Newman turned the shower water to the highest pressure, then switched the temperature to cold, letting her body absorb the shock right down the spine. She let it stay there until the goose pimples had subsided. Just as suddenly, she turned the water off, reached for a towel, covered herself and stepped out on to the warm underfloor heating of her bathroom suite.

Darkness had fallen, and through the window she saw the wavering lanterns of farmers making their way home through the rice paddies. Somewhere high above was the high-pitched roar of fighter jets from the base taking off into the night. But it took her a few minutes to work out the other strange sound, which sent a tremble through the building, until she remembered the base commander telling her tonight was artillery practice, the pounding of the big guns which would be moved up to the front line of invading North Korean troops.

Newman draped a robe around herself, loosened the wet towel, hung it on a rail and walked along the short corridor to the living room. She mixed herself a gin and tonic and checked her watch. Peter Brock would be at least another half an hour, and if she greeted him in her bathrobe, what the hell!

Cho had refreshed her and frightened her. As he was ushering them out of the room, having dropped his nuclear bombshell, he had unashamedly homed in on Newman's personal life. 'You getting married again, Mary?' he had said, grinning at Brock.

'Too busy stopping nuclear proliferation,' answered Newman smartly, taking up his offer to step out of the door in front of him.

'You should be married,' Cho retorted loudly so that all in the vast adjoining room, advisers and tea staff included, could hear. He tapped his chest. 'Follow my example. I have one wife and two mistresses. If Cho does anything stupid, he has three women to tell him he's talking shit and is going to fuck things up. Everyone needs that, Mary, even someone as brainy as you. Everyone needs to be told they're talking shit.'

Before Mary could answer, Cho had beckoned over his intelligence chief. 'I've told Mr Brock he can have as many agents as we can spare,' he instructed. 'You two work it out between you. Remember two things. We have big problems at home with infiltration, and that the United States is our number-one ally and no argument.'

As the helicopter had lifted off from the grounds of the palace, Newman saw shimmering winter scenes of Seoul, smashed to rubble in the war and now recreated as a Confucian American dream city. She flew over the hills and parks of the northern side, across the Han River, the pilot taking the helicopter higher to clear the skyscrapers of the business and commercial districts, glistening with advertisements and lights. If only Seoul could have been replicated amid the Catholicism of Latin America and the tribalism of sub-Saharan Africa, if only Pakistan had taken a lead from South Korea, if only it had downplayed its nuclear weapon as a friendly instrument of diplomacy and not declared it as an Islamic bomb – as if Cho had made a fanfare on television of his Confucian bomb, and not casually mentioned it in a very private conversation to people who mattered; if only . . . Her train of thought had wandered with the throb and clatter of the aircraft which had delivered her to Kunsan where, after delivering her speech, she had insisted on being driven through the red-light district of nearby Silver Town. Through the darkened windows of her Mercedes, she watched Americans, barely out of their teens, draped around Korean prostitutes, drunk and wayward, stumbling from bar to bar. How many secrets would they give away to gentle, seductive prodding? A small network of North Korean agents would probably have maps of every aircraft hangar, mess room, set of traffic lights and bowling alley on the base.

Newman must have dozed off in the chair, because a buzzer woke her, with the familiar and slightly distorted face of Peter Brock staring into the security camera. She fumbled for the remote, pressed open the door, pulled her bathrobe around her and got up. Brock appeared, looking as worn out as she had felt about an hour earlier. 'Sorry, Mary, have I barged in?' he said, hesitating.

'No, Pete. Come in,' said Newman. 'I was catnapping.' She eyed her own half-drunk gin and tonic, where the ice had melted and the lemon had sunk to the bottom of the glass. 'How was he? I mean, is what we're doing working?'

'It's working,' said Brock confidently, putting his briefcase by the door and looking around admiringly. 'Wow,' he exclaimed. 'You've hit the jackpot, at least for tonight.'

'Great, isn't it?' said Newman. 'A huge bed, the biggest jacuzzi I've seen in my life, the first heated balcony in the world, and no one to share it with.' She picked up her glass, went into the cloakroom by the door and tipped the contents into the basin.

'You want a drink?' she asked, heading for the bar, and plugging in the kettle.

'Sure,' said Brock. 'But just water. I need something to wash away Cho's caffeine.'

Newman laughed. 'And I need another coffee. Hot and black.' She tore open a sachet and poured coffee powder into a cup. 'Where have they put you?'

'Over in another wing. But nothing like this,' said Brock, unscrewing the cap and drinking straight from the bottle.

'Did you dissuade him from his nuking venture?'

'I hope so,' said Brock. 'He had a point, though. Park

would dearly love us to strike from Japan or a carrier. If
the strike comes from South Korea it confines the conflict.'

'But then you have a bloody land war across the DMZ.'
The kettle clicked itself off. Newman filled her cup and sat
down again.

'After you left, though,' said Brock with a grin, 'he was
more interested in getting you married than knocking out
Park Ho.'

'Oh my God,' said Newman, feeling herself blushing.
She put down the coffee and cupped her chin with her
hand. 'That man's a menace.'

Briefly, they fell into a companionable silence. Unlike
her own, Brock's face was too expressive to hide much of
what he was thinking. His talent was analysis more than
negotiation where his eyes gave too much away. She sensed
that Brock would not have mentioned Cho's marriage line
unless he planned to move it on somewhere. 'Do you
think Jim will go for a second term?' she said, casually.

'He's just past the mid-terms,' said Brock thoughtfully.
'I guess he's thinking of it. Why? Do you want my job next
time round?'

Newman threw her head back and laughed. 'Not at all.
I'm thinking of quitting. Getting myself a life.'

Mockingly, Brock raised his eyebrows, and swept his
hand around the room. 'You mean all this is not a life?'

She eyed him bashfully. 'You know what I mean.'

'With Jim?'

'I think we've both been thinking about it,' she said,
lowering her head so Brock couldn't see her embarrass-
ment. 'Maybe we've been thinking about it too much.'

'Well, I'll be damned,' said Brock, crunching his hands
around the water bottle.

'Don't tell me, with all that stuff in the press, that
you're playing the innocent.'

Brock put his hands in the air as his face cracked up in

a smile. 'I leave Caro to get involved in these things. But if he runs again, what then?'

'If he agrees, I become the First Lady, or whatever.' She uncrossed her legs and sat up. 'I like Jim. I like him a lot. He's one of the most decent men I know. The way he handled Valerie's illness and death has been an example to us all. Maybe it's too soon. I don't know. The thing that worries me is if even now my feelings towards him – even his towards me – affect our judgement. As you know, Chris and I don't exactly see eye to eye.'

'If I had noticed it, Mary, I would have told him,' said Brock firmly. 'And I haven't.'

'So I can keep my job, then?' said Newman with a smile.

Brock whistled through his teeth. 'With South Korea going nuclear and you marrying the US President, this has been one hell of a day for me.' He slapped his knees and stood up. 'I told Cho we didn't need entertaining tonight – just a quiet meal to chew things over together. That OK with you? They're fixing it in a private room downstairs.'

Newman was on her feet as well. 'Sure. I'll slip on a tracksuit or something.'

'You got anywhere I can call Caro?' said Brock, picking up his briefcase from the floor.

'Follow me down the corridor and turn off to the left just before the glass door to my room,' said Newman. 'They've got better stuff there than we've got at State.' She began leading the way. 'There's a number to call if you don't know how it works. But I'm sure you'll be fine.'

Newman went through the frosted-glass doors to her suite and heard the automatic lock click into place. She washed her face in the bathroom and fiddled with her make-up. Half of her wanted to throw on a tracksuit, like she had said. The other half wanted to dress up because of the beautiful tranquillity of the place they were in. She examined her scant options hanging, suitcase-creased, in the wardrobe. Deep down, the adolescent in her wanted her to be attractive to Brock, so he could pass it on to Jim West. That was why she was dithering, because, here in this strange, unfamiliar place, she was making the personal stakes so high. But eventually she ended up with her white tracksuit, a new pair of trainers, but with light mascara and lipstick and the same perfume she had used for the dinner at Camp David.

Through the frosted glass, a light flickered as another artillery shell smashed into the ground miles away and shook the building. A light went off, making the corridor dimmer. She slid open the balcony door and stepped out into the ice-cold evening air. A click behind her made her jump. Above, the gas heater automatically flared up. She felt the warmth immediately, but a chill wind blew up from the rice paddies. She shivered and wrapped her arms round herself. She waited a few seconds in case she could see the flash of the artillery gun. Back inside, she heard another click, like a door opening, and a spit of rain hit her on the face. She stepped back and closed the door as the spit became a downpour, loudly assaulting the windows.

She checked herself in the long wardrobe mirror, rearranging strands of hair thrown out by the sudden change of weather. The glow of the heater on the balcony dimmed and quickly faded, leaving the place in darkness. She looked for the switch to an outside light, couldn't find one and gave up. Just as she was heading out, she had a craving to make a phone call, to a son, daughter, or husband, and say: 'Hi, I'm in this incredible place in the middle of nowhere in South Korea. You wouldn't believe it. You should be here with me—'

Dismissing these difficult thoughts, she unlocked the door with the remote and it slid open. Indeed, one lamp had gone, somewhere. The corridor was lit from the living room.

'Pete, you finished with Caro?'she asked gently, a few feet away from the door of the office suite. She couldn't hear him speaking. The door was open, but no sound came from the room.

'Pete,' she called out loudly. 'You there?'

There was no answer from the living room, either. A shadow passed a table lamp. Newman moved forward and looked into the office. Her hand went to her mouth. No scream, just an empty dryness thrown up before her brain could even take in what she saw.

Brock's body was slumped forward on the desk, blood streaming from the back of his neck, running down the curls of the telephone cord and dripping on to the floor.

She turned round, saw the shadow again, her hands fumbling for the remote to open the door and get back into her room. She heard a dull thud as a round from a silenced pistol splintered wood in the door frame above her head. The door was open, and Newman ran, hurling herself down, hitting the floor, pressing the remote again to get it closed, and crawling away as two more shots smashed into the room, one exploding into the television set, the second splattering out plaster above the bed.

In the tiny gap before the door closed she saw the killer, thin lips pursed in concentration, wearing a black poncho-style raincoat, exactly matching the darkness outside, water dripping on to the floor.

He fired again.

His shape, darkening the corridor, now appeared blurred coming closer and closer. He fired twice more. But each time the bulletproof glass blocked the shot. Keeping on the floor, she edged herself towards the telephone by

the bed. Another round. She glanced up towards the
balcony door. That would be bulletproofed as well. Newman's VIP survival training with the secret service told her
that if she stayed put, help would be with her within
seconds – well, minutes at least. She was the goddamn US
Secretary of State. Where were the two secret service guys
assigned to her? Where were the Korean bodyguards?
Where the hell was everybody? She picked up the phone.
The line was dead. She crawled to the wardrobe and found
her mobile in the briefcase. He was right up close to the
glass, his head against it, peering in. She heard the scraping
of metal on glass as he ran the end of the silencer down
the pane. He tested the door latch and his hand dropped
away.

Newman keyed in her mobile's pin number. It bleeped
and she saw the distorted shape of his head jerk up,
alerted. The battery was half gone. The signal only showed
two bands. She flipped down her phone book and pressed
the White House. She had a code, given to her by the
secret service. They had made her put the number in her
mobile.

He stepped back from the door. Without rushing, he
bent down and picked up another weapon. Newman
pressed 'call'. He unscrewed the silencer and switched it to
the new weapon. The phone did nothing, except emit a
whining tone of disconnection. His movements were confident and deliberate, as if he knew no one was coming
and that whatever he did, however long he took, he would
be safe.

He aimed the first shot at the pane of glass closest to
the latch. A crack appeared. A second followed, then a
third, each one of the more powerful rounds weakening
the bulletproofing. Newman turned her head left and right,
looking where to go. She had no choice. She opened the
balcony door with the remote. Above her head came the

whoosh of the gas heater lighting up. A squall of rain swept on to her. Below her was soft rain-dampened grass and rice paddies. She would jump and run, if she got through without a sprained ankle. Run and scream. That was her plan – as simple as they come.

The central half of the balcony was taken up with the sliding glass door. On either side was brick wall. Newman rolled behind this, stood up, went to clasp the rail to jump and stopped dead. A huge transparent perspex shield covered the open space of the balcony, with only tiny slats for ventilation. Like the heater, this new obstacle must have been automatic and weather-controlled. But it completely blocked her escape.

She banged on it, fury welling up in her throat. She slammed both fists into it, just as she heard the first pane of glass shatter in the bedroom door. The black-gloved hand of her attacker slid inside, turned the lock and opened it.

Against the walls on each side of her balcony prison was a row of four plants potted in earth. To her right was a heavy wrought-iron table with six chairs and under a dark-green protective cover was what looked like a barbecue with a plastic tube running to a gas cylinder on the floor. Another tube ran from a second cylinder to the heater. To the left were two sunloungers. Through the perspex, she could make out majestic angry clouds swirling under a bright moon. In the distance, near the base, was tracer from live-fire exercises. Rain smashed relentlessly against the perspex, glistening and running down and away.

He was inside the room, but still nonchalant, strangely not caring about her. He turned on a flashlight and shone it through on to the balcony. He let off three rounds in rapid succession, all on the same spot, and a fourth, which broke through, cut a tiny hole in the glass and sent a crack

splaying across it. Suddenly Newman found herself caught
in the harsh white beam of his flashlight. He turned it off
and looked straight at her. He was standing in the middle
of the bedroom. She stayed absolutely still. For a full five
seconds his eyes were on her, and behind him she could
see her own reflection in the wardrobe mirror, her face
twisted with fear and anger, the face of a terrified little girl.

He cocked his head to one side, as if he had heard
something. His were hard eyes. He squatted down, turned
on the flashlight again, crouched and looked under the
bed. His eyes were off her for a second, and Newman
slipped out of his line of sight. Straining through the dark,
she searched the remote for a button that would open the
perspex balcony wall, but found none. There must be a
switch. She felt along the wall, looking for one. Plants
brushed her face. She ran her hands along the rough brick.
Moonlight, refracted by the perspex and rain, played tricks,
making it black in one place and throwing tricky light on
another.

He fired. The door cracked even more. There was a
ledge between the glass wall and the brick of the balcony
wall. She clambered on to it and felt up the wall to a metal
trellis trailing plant leaves. She tested her weight on it. The
door shattered, collapsing into tiny squares like a car
windscreen. He stepped through, his feet crunching on
them.

For a flicker of a moment he was confused, as he tried
to work out where Newman was. The silence which had
been menacing was broken by another squall of rain
against the perspex. From a dark edge of the wall, Newman
climbed higher up the trellis and found a metal bar
stretched along the roof of the balcony. He was attracted
by something through the window. There was quiet again,
apart from the low whine, just a few feet from her, of
burning gas from the heater. With horror, she realized that

he was seeing her reflection, blurred and distorted, thrown out into shadows created by the flames.

Squeezed in the corner of the balcony ceiling, she had nowhere to go. He turned towards her, no confusion about him now. She gripped the metal bar. Her hands were numb, but she managed to swing herself out, lift her feet, then swing herself back, forcing her legs up and smashing her trainers into the gas heater.

Sparks flew out, but nothing else. He raised his weapon. Newman hurled herself backwards. He fired, tearing brickwork out of the wall next to her. She flung herself forward, drawing on every reserve, feeling the heater break as she crashed into it, fire shooting out, a roar, and then curling, running flames, and his face alert, thinking, as he stepped back. She fell, the world spinning around her. Fingers of flame leapt around the balcony. He was burning, his hands up against his face. She heard herself screaming, watching as the fire reached the gas tank near the barbecue. She dragged herself, half stumbling, half crawling towards it, only knowing that she had to destroy him, plunging her hand into the heat and wrenching the tube from the cylinder, knocking it over, rolling it towards him, then hurling herself back into the bedroom, just as the balcony was engulfed in a roaring inferno of exploding gas.

She breathed in, choking on the smoke. He was ablaze, but conscious, a killing machine in his last throes. On the wall just inside her room was the switch she had been looking for. She punched it. The perspex balcony cover slid away, creating a sudden tunnel of oxygen, which threw the fire into the room.

The air was sucked from his lungs. His hand let go of the weapon, his arms flailing as he threw it away from him. Newman picked it up, not caring about the heat, running backwards to get away, then turning, holding it with both hands, keeping her finger on the trigger, feeling round after round leave the gun for his body. Her hand was burned from the metal of the gun, her hair singed and her eyes streaked with soot.

She staggered backwards, out of the bedroom, balancing on the wall and came to the office, where she saw Brock's body, just as it had been only a few minutes ago. The air was cooler. She breathed in deeply and walked unsteadily towards him. The telephone receiver was on the hook. He must have just finished speaking to Caro. He had jotted down a number on a pad. She felt his neck. He was still warm. His eyes were open, and if it wasn't for that and for the pool of blood still gathering on the floor, Peter Brock, one of her oldest friends in the world, could have just fallen asleep at his desk.

From behind, she heard the click of a weapon. She turned to face a single man, uniformed, with gun drawn. 'Freeze. Hands on your head.'

She kept her hands by her side. 'Where were you?' she whispered.

'Hands on your head. Don't move,' came the command again.

She stepped forward, her eyes on fire with anger. 'You're meant to protect us, you piece of shit,' she said, knocking the weapon away. 'Why don't you ring Caroline Brock and explain where you've been? Her mobile number's on the pad on the desk there, right next to the body of her murdered husband.'

The Secretary of State sank to her knees, put her blackened, watery face into her burned hands, and burst into tears.

41

Delhi, India

The dining room of the Prime Minister's official residence in Delhi was a charred shell, giving off odours of disinfectant, tar and other building chemicals. A tarpaulin stretched over the roof had become loose. Its edges flapped in the wind, and men shouted at each other from ladders, trying to secure it. It was the first breeze Delhi had had for some days, and with no rain the city had been left under a dome of pollution which stuck in Meenakshi's throat, making her lungs feel tight. She leaned her walking stick against the wall in the hallway and, keeping clear of the walls, she managed to take a few steps, stopped to absorb the pain, then moved on again towards her father's study.

Mehta had insisted on staying at the residence once the ordnance had been cleared and checks had been carried out for biological and chemical weapon fallout. 'We shall not leave,' he had thundered as he pushed Meenakshi's wheelchair through the door to meet the gaping, jagged space of what had once been the dining room. 'And we will tell India we are not leaving this house. No terrorist will expel me from my home.'

The stale smell of destruction had even drifted along to his study which was in a different wing of the house. It was familiar to Meenakshi, who had treated patients in India's most severe areas of decay: rotting, murdered corpses, burnt-out houses and collapsed buildings. Hers was a country of riots, flood and earthquakes, each leaving its own specific stench which finally had reached the one place in the world she had wanted to see as sanctuary.

She leaned in the doorway, pushing her hair back from her face with her free hand. Her father was standing, hands on hips, his back to her, staring at the wall. Deepak Suri, his right arm bound tight in a sling, held a mobile phone to his ear in his left hand, and was speaking softly into a green telephone which was on open speaker, although the conversation was too quiet for anyone to hear. Her father's private secretary, Ashish Uddin, was at the long trestle-like desk pushed up against the wall, working on a laptop. A television, showing the BBC, was on in the corner.

'What are you plotting, Father?' said Meenakshi tenderly as she made her way into the room and sat down in an upright chair near Uddin. In normal times, she would never have ventured into such a meeting. But recently those barriers had been cast aside. Race Course Road had become a fortress. Meenakshi, Uddin and the staff had been shown down into the underground bunker there, and instructed on how to use the survival kits. Mehta himself had checked out the bunker beneath Raisana Hill, which stretched under North and South Block with tunnels to the Parliament complex. Preparations were also being made for him to operate from the new command and control centre in Bhopal in central India, where – if Delhi was destroyed – he would stay until there was 'resolution', as he called it.

'We're plotting peace, I hope,' answered Mehta, turning round, and giving Meenakshi a kiss on both cheeks. 'How was your day?'

'Bloody depressing,' she said. 'It's as if this damn country thinks that by going to war all the problems will be solved. But all they're looking for is someone else to blame.'

'Rommy called,' said Mehta, glancing towards Suri, who with half an ear was trying to pick up what was being said.

'She wanted to fly over, and I told her India was the last place she should be right now.'

Suri motioned to Mehta, covering the mouthpiece of the mobile with his finger. 'We should go to the Bhopal bunker tomorrow morning, and let the press know as soon as you are there.'

'What time?' asked Mehta.

'05.30.'

Mehta nodded. Suri spoke into the mobile. 'That's fine. Let us see the draft of the press release, soonest.' He cut the call, freeing up his good hand to pick up the receiver of the green telephone.

'So you're stuck with only one daughter,' said Meenakshi, shifting her weight on the chair to get comfortable.

'You should leave, too,' suggested Mehta, but not with great enthusiasm. 'Go to London. Go to New York.'

'I'm staying here,' said Meenakshi firmly. 'If we leave this place empty, someone might come and rob it.'

'I'm not allowed to travel to Bhopal either,' said Uddin, pushing his spectacles up his nose and turning round. 'We'll both miss out on the excitement.'

'We're working on it,' Suri said, still on the telephone. 'It's almost finished and we'll get back to you with the PM's initial proposals then.' He cut the call and looked over to Mehta. 'Ashish will send them this, when we've finished. What we suggest is that the Cabinet Committee on Security meets in Bhopal bunker. A South Block photographer will be there and we'll put out a couple of shots with the press release.'

Uddin pressed the display button on his laptop and a map was projected on the wall, showing a draft battle plan, drawn up by Mehta and Suri. Green arrows showed the movement of fighter planes and bombers to airbases near the border. Symbols of battle tanks were clustered around the area between Amritsar and Lahore, and further down in the desert of Rajasthan. Missiles were being made ready at launch sites closest to the border, with railway lines being cleared of civilian traffic to transport troops westward towards Pakistan.

It produced in Meenakshi an unexpected reaction. She loathed what she saw. She knew it came from the trauma of the mortar attack. Nausea swept over her. Her cheeks burnt with a hot flush. 'You're going to do it, aren't you?' she whispered.

'Let's hope not,' said Mehta.

'Not if Qureshi's got any brains,' said Uddin with uncharacteristic bluntness.

'Then what the hell are you doing?' retorted Meenakshi. 'You're pushing him into a corner.' Her voice was louder than she meant it to be, the voice inside her screaming out that there had to be another way, and then another voice of reprimand, asking why she was taking it out on her father.

Mehta walked to her side and touched her on the shoulder. 'I wouldn't do this if we didn't have to. You know that, don't you?'

'I want to know it,' she said impatiently. 'But why is it always more guns and more bombs?'

'If you have another way, tell me, Meenakshi, because I'm flat out of ideas.'

Meenakshi curled her hand around her father's arm, looked up at him and spoke softly, her emotions now in better control. 'I have a patient in Bihar who is diagnosed with a form of sporadic schizophrenia. When he suffers an attack it's pretty dreadful for everyone. He sees and hears a world which doesn't exist. He becomes paranoid and violent. When he's well he works like an ox. He's intelligent, too, full of ideas and is a community leader. I knew he was sick, but I wasn't sure how much to tell the family.

If I told the truth, they would either treat him as an outcast, or they would put their all into containing his condition or finding a cure. In short, it would have destroyed the family and village structure. I decided to say nothing. He suffered an attack a month or so ago. He badly beat up a little boy, and it took two days for him to get back to normal. The boy luckily survived. The village handled it and people there got on with their lives.' She let go of Mehta's arm and pushed back her chair to make her legs more comfortable. 'That, father, is a daughter's view.'

'What happened to your patient?'

'He's still working. The quality of life in the village is better with him working than if he were incarcerated, which would bring shame upon his family and divide the village.'

'My daughter's view is much appreciated,' said Mehta. 'And I mean that,' he added thoughtfully, looking again at Uddin's map. 'Do you remember that Jamie Song gave Qureshi an ultimatum to deliver the ringleaders of the terror groups to him in Beijing? Jamie sent us the list of those who arrived on the plane. Not one important figure among them. They were nothing but foot soldiers. The man's laughing at us, and he's made a fool of Jamie.'

'For one man's sickness, my village did not choose to annihilate itself. Why are you preparing to kill 120 million people for one man's arrogance?' And why was she taking on her father like this? God knows, he had tried to stop things getting worse, and he bore the wounds to show it.

'Annihilation's not the point,' argued Mehta. 'As soon as we give him the signal, Jim West will talk directly to Qureshi. After that Jamie will speak with him, and then Andrei Kozlov.' He squeezed his daughter's shoulder.

Meenakshi clasped his hand. 'So what happens, if – you know – if it comes to a nuclear war?'

'It won't,' said Mehta firmly. 'Because if it does, Pakistan will be struck with a hundred nuclear weapons of between 10 and 100 kilotons.'

'Hiroshima was 14 kilotons,' interjected Uddin.

'There would be nothing left at all,' said Mehta. 'Our policy is well known. To attack India would be suicide, and Qureshi would never contemplate it.'

Suddenly, Meenakshi gripped his hand and put her other hand to her mouth. 'Oh my God,' she exclaimed, looking up at the television. 'I hadn't seen what was on.'

The camera concentrated in turn on each of three figures standing on a rain-soaked runway outside a US military transport plane. A coffin, draped in the Stars and Stripes, was lowered on to the tarmac by hydraulic lift. A lone bugler, in the uniform of the United States Air Force, played the *Star Spangled Banner*, while Jim West, Caroline Brock and Mary Newman stepped forward with their heads lowered. Caroline unclasped her hands, reached out to Newman, who took her hand then stepped forward with her and rested it on the flag on the coffin. The lens focused on Newman's face, red with burn injuries and her hair even shorter than before, cut to cover up the singeing. It made her look young, alone and vulnerable.

Six Air Force pall-bearers lifted the coffin off the ramp and marched to the waiting hearse. The camera shifted to a wide shot, showing a desolate, rain-swept scene. With the door of the hearse shut, the bugler stepped back. A guard of honour raised their rifles and let off a twenty-one-gun salute, and as the coffin was driven away Jim West stepped forward to a single microphone rigged up in the middle of the tarmac.

'The man who murdered Peter Brock is dead,' he said slowly. A gust of wind caught his hair and a squall of rain hit him in the face. West didn't move. 'He was killed by your brave Secretary of State, Mary Newman.' Briefly the shot went to a close-up of Newman, whose eyes were still lowered. Rain glistened on her hair, and the camera dropped to her clasped hands and the bandages around the hand, burnt from firing the gun.

'The United States of America will destroy the regime responsible for the murder of the man who was my friend and National Security Advisor,' said West. 'It will destroy any regime that supports those people now in charge in North Korea.'

He raised his hand and pointed a finger directly at the camera. 'You know who you are, and we know who you are. Not long ago, South-East Asia was beset with evil. Our allies in Britain, Australia and New Zealand went into Brunei and took it back from those who wanted to turn that part of the world into a prison camp for all who lived there. There are other nations which have been taken over by evil men. When I leave this airfield, I will be talking to my friends in China, Europe, India, Japan, Russia and in South-East Asia. I will then be with Peter Brock's family, paying my last respects as we bury a great American who died trying to find a way to avoid war. After that I will concentrate everything on ridding the world of evil nations.'

42

Islamabad, Pakistan

A swirl of dust and smells of Pakistan swept up from the runway as Hassan Muda stepped off the short internal Pakistan Airways flight from Karachi. He no longer carried the passport under the name of the Briton, Jonathan Desai, or the Australian, Ben Dutta. Muda arrived as a Kuwaiti businessman, Mohhamad Al-Shammari, wearing an open-neck blue shirt, denim jeans, trainers and a white linen jacket, which hung far enough beneath his waistline to conceal the Beretta 9mm he had picked up in Karachi.

Muda had specifically asked for an M1911 .45, and if not that, then a gun from a list of alternative .45s, specifying that he must have the larger-calibre weapon. But in the rushed transit through Karachi, the airport worker had thrust into his hands a cotton bag stuffed with a change of clothes and the pistol, wrapped in green cloth, at the the bottom. Once airborne, Muda had gone to the toilet and seen that it was a Beretta with a silencer attached to the muzzle.

He checked the magazine, left the breech clear, and slipped it into the back of his jeans. The Beretta, once the standard sidearm issued to US ground troops, was delicate and unreliable. It frequently jammed, and the bullet was too light, meaning that he would need at least two shots for his target to fall, possibly three with the decelerating effect of the silencer.

He stopped at the bottom of the steps to wait for Ahmed Memed, who was carefully coming down from the plane, making sure his robe did not get caught on the metal, but also taking his time, breathing deeply to savour the cool winter air of Islamabad.

On the tarmac, he gripped Muda's arm. 'It's good to be back,' he said. 'Very good.'

It had been a long fight from Pyongyang. Soon they had left behind the boulevards of modern Islamabad and edged their way towards Rawalpindi, where the poverty was more acute and the smells became hostile and caught in the throat. Set back from the road was a factory of some kind, its row of chimneys belching smoke out into a clear blue sky. At a gritty road junction, they turned left and drove through a residential area, the houses bigger and the compound walls higher, protected by bored guards with old weapons. Muda recognized where they were. They were waved through into the Pakistan air-force base, driving far inside, across two runways, and pulling up outside a two-storey building, with a corrugated-iron roof and concrete walls.

He let Memed go in first, then followed him through two sets of doors into a dowdy mess room, with smells of stale tea and tobacco, then left past an open door, a glimpse of cracked tiles and the familiar smell of sour urine, into a hallway with notices pinned on to a board, some yellowed with age, others freshly put up, and finally left again, through another set of doors and down two flights of stairs.

When Memed entered, Qureshi embraced him, and kept holding his shoulder as he introduced the cleric to the three military commanders with him.

'Gentlemen,' he said enthusiastically. 'Here is our moral light. Without his authority, I doubt any of us would have chosen the courageous path we have.'

He turned to Memed himself. 'May I introduce you to my colleagues Brigadier Najeeb Hussain, General Zaid Musa, Admiral Javed Mohmand.'

Muda was not mentioned. He stepped back to the wall near the door. On the other side was the bodyguard who had been with them from the airport. He had noticed two other men outside. The windowless room carried a smell of fresh paint, and there was a dry chilliness from the air conditioning. To Muda's right was a blackboard and screen. A raised platform of dark timber stretched out from there for about six feet. The rest of the room was sparsely furnished: half a dozen armchairs, a coffee table, a table near the wall with a television and in the corner furthest from him a desk with a computer.

'Let's sit,' said Qureshi, amiable but in command. He guided Memed by the elbow to an armchair covered with a faded blue linen. For just a moment before Qureshi took the chair next to Memed, Muda spotted indecision on his face.

Mohmand approached Memed, with hands clasped in front of him. 'Welcome. Welcome,' he said. 'In this terrible situation, we need guidance from a man of wisdom.' The bodyguard near Muda shuffled his feet. His tunic was too loose for him to be wearing body armour, and the neck was open. Mohmand stepped past Memed to take Qureshi's hand, then shifted back again to take the seat on the other side of Memed. Hussain and Musa, remaining silent, were left with the chairs opposite, edging them round so that the five men formed a circle.

'President West has stopped short of declaring war on us,' said Qureshi. 'A short time ago, he contacted me directly.' Musa looked sharply across to Qureshi, but did not meet his eyes. Muda detected surprise, which rippled through his expression to anger and then a look of betrayal. Zaid Musa seemed to be a man who knew how to keep his distance. Hussain's head was lowered, happy to let Qureshi lead for the moment.

Only Mohmand reacted. 'Then your leadership is acknowledged,' he said enthusiastically. 'Congratulations.'

To Muda, Mohmand was a man who lacked discrimination and spoke without a thought of the results.

'But we talked before the murder of Peter Brock,' said Qureshi, the darkness in his look enough to sober Mohmand. 'I suspect that whatever leeway we had for negotiation with Jim West then might by now have narrowed considerably.'

'Negotiation,' whispered Hussain. 'I'm not sure that is what this is about.'

'Let me finish,' countered Qureshi. 'We need to absorb the facts.' He coughed, and glanced up at the air conditioning vent. 'According to West, we have three choices. We let the US in to take over our nuclear forces and be subject to inspections Iraq-style. We can let the Chinese do it – although the UN would still be involved with inspections. Or we can brace ourselves for an Indian invasion. Of course, none of these options is acceptable. But what is acceptable, gentlemen?'

'Could we strike a deal with the Chinese?' asked Hussain. 'You were the last to see Jamie Song.'

'We might,' said Qureshi slowly. 'It might stop the immediate threat of war. But it would be messy.'

Mohmand leaned forward, impatient to speak again. 'Aren't we missing the main point here? Our war is with India, surely. Not with America. The threat comes from Vasant Mehta's emotional response to something we had no control over.'

Muda eased himself away from the wall against which he was leaning, and slid out the Beretta. His eyes shifted right, and he saw that the bodyguard had noticed his movement. Muda took a tiny step forward, pretending to shift weight. The bodyguard smirked. Muda had received no instructions about the bodyguard.

'It was not us who attacked the parliament,' said Mohmand. 'Nor did we mortar his house. We have committed no act of war, and Jim West has to—'

Muda raised the pistol and fired twice. His shots hit the bodyguard in the centre of the forehead. Even before he had dropped, Muda took three steps into the centre of the room, and shot Mohmand three times – once in the forehead and twice in the area of the heart. Muda twisted his body, just a fraction, keeping the pistol raised and was about to fire on Qureshi when Memed, with the faintest wave of his hand, signalled him to stop.

There was nowhere Qureshi could have gone. To have fumbled at the leather cover of his pistol holster would have been a ridiculous act of bravado. Across the room, the bodyguard had died without a sound. A single trickle of blood drained from the back of his head. Mohmand was dead, but the bullet had missed his brain stem, so the body was moving and a gurgling sound came from his throat. The armchair's blue linen cover was soaked in blood.

Memed had not moved. Muda stood there, his gun trained on Qureshi. Memed tapped his fingers on the arm of the chair, his expression a mixture of nonchalance and impatience. Muda was cool and professional, his gaze riveted on Qureshi's holster. Qureshi wondered where he had received his training. Probably at some camp in Afghanistan or Indonesia, backed up by evenings of watching paramilitary videos.

'Hassan Muda designed the mortars fired on Race Course Road,' said Hussain. Zaid Musa stood up and, with Muda, lifted Mohmand's body to the corner of the room and laid it next to the computer table. They left the corpse of the bodyguard by the door. Musa plucked a handkerchief from his tunic pocket and soaked up arterial blood which had got on to his sleeve.

Qureshi said nothing. Witnessing the cold-blooded

murder of two human beings, no matter how far they themselves might have been removed from innocence, left nothing but a numbness in his mind, particularly as he himself had been within a second of receiving three bullets from Muda's silenced pistol into his skull and chest, he presumed, just as Mohmand had. He looked at Musa, who returned his stare with unflinching certainty. Qureshi remembered the false sycophancy with which Zaid Musa had greeted him on his return from China. By reading the faces around the room, he became certain of one thing. Mohmand's death had been planned well in advance. As for his own, Qureshi just couldn't tell. But the moment he ordered the assassination of President Khan, he had expected to meet a violent death as well.

'Tassudaq Qureshi is my friend,' said Memed. 'I have known him for many years. I have eaten with his family.'

His words left a silence in the room. On a flicker of the eye from Memed, Muda lowered his pistol.

'If you are not with us, you will have to go,' said Hussain, his voice casual, almost comforting. As he paused, he pursed his lips.

To read Hussain's meaning, Qureshi needed context. His mind had cleared, and, like the pilot he was, he meticulously channelled away extraneous information and concentrated on what was in front of him.

'This is not about India, as we all know,' he said. 'It is about Pakistan, Islam and our nuclear strength.' He looked not at Hussain, nor at Memed, but at Zaid Musa, whom he guessed had ordered the killings, including his own – and had been overruled in the final seconds by Memed. 'We did not work all these years to create our weapons only to give them away to another power.'

'Park Ho is ready,' said Memed. 'Our alliance with him is an experiment which worked, thanks to your guidance, Tassudaq.'

Hussain's face relaxed with a noticeable expression of relief. Musa eyed him suspiciously, making no secret of the fact that he believed Qureshi's statement to be hollow, or, more realistically, that Qureshi had to be removed in order for Musa to take the mantle of leader. Qureshi's mind was filled with different strands of thought, bursting through. Images of his love for Tasneem and for his tempestuous daughter Farah, the blood on Mohmand's uniform, the Fantan tactical 5-kiloton toss-bomb attachment, the news broadcasts of Khan's assassination, the simplistic threats of Jim West – Qureshi was amazed how he could process them all to create the balance and single-mindedness that emerged.

He had trodden an intricate and tarnished road, but as he watched Muda lift the flap of his linen jacket and return the pistol into the back of his trousers, Qureshi allowed himself the luxury of relief when a man knows he will never have to make another major decision in his life again.

Qureshi was offered an F-16B with a navigator, but he refused. The F-16 might have been the aircraft of choice, but it was too sophisticated for the job, he had argued. Yes, it was versatile enough for ground attack, but its primary role was air defence, and he had confounded them with details, challenging them to let him do it his way, with the system he had devised and with the aircraft he wanted.

When disobeying orders, it is best to act alone. The aircraft he chose was a single-seater and he knew it well.

Winter coal smoke drifted across the corner of the tarmac where the old Chinese-built A-5C Fantan was parked, red stoppers in its two WP6 turbojet engines, with four technicians working on sockets under the centre line of the fuselage. The Fantan was the first Pakistani aircraft to be successfully modified for the delivery of a battlefield nuclear weapon. It was the aircraft which Qureshi felt the most at ease in handling. He had stood firm, and even Zaid Musa had acknowledged that he should have his way.

Nor had he let them dictate the type of bomb he would deliver. Qureshi, an airman of a bygone age, preferred the lowest technology available so he had ordered the 'gun bomb' with 20 kilograms of highly enriched uranium-235 from the Kahuta nuclear weapons complex just thirty miles away. In the low night temperature of Islamabad, the metal casing felt chilled as Qureshi brushed his hand along the cylinder jacket – such a small weapon compared to the missiles and conventional bombs the aircraft was designed to carry. It was barely ten feet long from its flat snub nose to its stabilizing base fins – less than a fifth of the aircraft's overall length.

Qureshi had been a young pilot in the late 1970s when the Pakistan air force had learned of the project to build Kahuta and provide the nuclear deterrent that would enable Pakistan to survive as a nation. His commanders had been furious that they had not been consulted, pointing out that the site was only four minutes' flying time from India and impossible to defend.

But they had been overruled. Nuclear scientists, working on the weapons programme, commuted from Islamabad where their families were well housed and their children educated at the best schools. They were close to the seat of government where decisions could easily be sought, yet they worked in such a desolate and mountainous area that it was never included on the tourist route, and soon all foreigners were banned from the area. At the time, he was flying training sorties right up against the Indian border, including practice runs for defending Kahuta from enemy attack.

Qureshi searched for some kind of symbolism – resolution even – in what he was about to do, and tonight, on the tarmac, in his flying kit and with just the specialist technicians to load the weapon, he chose to think of the success of Kahuta and the ingenuity with which Pakistan's bomb had been created.

Inside the bomb itself was a bullet of U-235 which would plunge down against the U-235 target rings on detonation. As with his aircraft, Qureshi had chosen technology that in essence had not moved much further on since the Hiroshima bombing in 1945.

The bomb was hoisted below the fuselage and slid gently into place. The technicians' fingers spread across the outer casing to make sure it remained protected. Four adjustable rubber braces were brought in to secure it and the bracket clipped in under it. Apart from the 23mm cannon, Qureshi had ordered all other armaments to be taken off the aircraft. Without its air-to-air missiles and 500 kilograms of conventional bombs, the A-5 would be lighter, faster and easier to handle.

He climbed into the cockpit and checked the radar and fusing system which would determine exactly when detonation took place. He set the barometric-pressure fuse at 2,000 feet and made ready four radar fuses which were designed to bounce signals off the ground to set off the detonator once there was an agreed reading between two of the signals. Such safeguards ensured that the weapon would not explode prematurely. As an extra precaution the radar signals would not begin to be emitted until the bomb had been released, so that the signals did not confuse the fuselage of the aircraft with the ground.

Qureshi flipped the bomb-release switch, which was mechanical and not electronic. The bomb slumped down on to the braces, and the technicians lowered it on to the cradle of the trolley. Qureshi climbed out of the aircraft and walked alone across the tarmac, carrying his helmet under his arm and using the lights of an officers' mess hut to guide him to his destination.

In any other circumstances the room would have been welcoming and might even have induced a warm feeling of nostalgia. He could never remember it even having a fresh coat of paint. The wall carried yellowed photographs from action sorties going back to 1971, when East Pakistan had been lost and had become Bangladesh.

Only Najeeb Hussain was waiting for him, standing by the window, away from the stark light, and watching Qureshi approach. The others were in the command and control bunker under the base. Hussain was a friend, as much as any friendship could survive the pressures of leadership. As Qureshi came in, Hussain put his hand on his shoulder and indicated a pot of steaming coffee. Qureshi glanced up at the wall map.

'I've sent Tasneem to London,' he said softly.

Hussain nodded. 'I understand. What reason did you give?'

'She's looking for a job for Farrah.' Qureshi let out a small laugh. 'A couple of nights back, we talked about Farrah's future. I have to tell you, Najeeb, she is the most reckless girl, but she is my favourite. A father shouldn't say that, I know, but this is a night when such things can be said.' He walked over to the map and ran his finger down the border with India.

'Farrah's still in Lahore,' he said. 'She won't leave. What pressing reason can I give her?'

'Lahore will be fine. It is too close to the border. They won't touch it,' said Hussain confidently.

'Javed is in France,' said Qureshi, almost as if he was reassuring himself. 'Akbar, Zeenat and Bashir are at boarding school in Karachi. They won't touch Karachi, surely?'

'Just remember that in all our wars, we have never

targeted each other's cities,' said Hussain. 'The fighting has been kept to the battlefield.' Hussain joined Qureshi at the map. 'After you have done this, they won't touch anything,' he said. 'How can they?' He stabbed his finger. 'You take off. You fly down the border within Pakistani airspace, you nip across and drop here, right on the Pir Panjal Pass. Not a person around for miles. You have minimum yield. There'll be an avalanche and not much else.'

Qureshi shook his head. 'But are we underestimating Mehta's will?'

'If he bombs us back, it will be in a similarly remote part of Pakistan. Then we will have had our nuclear exchange and we can get down to business.'

'You think that is what Musa and Memed want?' Qureshi said sharply.

'This is not the time to argue,' insisted Hussain, forcing a smile. 'We have made our decisions.'

Qureshi couldn't work out where Hussain stood. In twenty years together discussing the future of Pakistan, he now realized he might never have known the man's beliefs at all.

'Would you have shot me?' he asked softly.

Hussain looked out of the window, where the moonlight was outshone by the artificial illumination outside and half hidden by clouds through which Qureshi would soon be flying. The reflection in the glass showed Hussain's face, desolate and turned away as he mustered an answer. What arrangements had they each made to get to this place and this situation?

'I told Memed you would see it through. Musa wanted you dead,' Hussain said in barely a whisper. 'From the day we overthrew Nawaz Sharif in favour of Musharraf we have all trodden the same path.'

For some time, Qureshi looked at Hussain. It wasn't a stare: more an attempt at understanding. Perhaps it was a realization that he had never accepted how it would have to end; even that he had never imagined it would get this far.

Hussain pulled a sheet of paper out of his pocket and unfolded it. 'This is today's propaganda picture for the Indian press,' he said, handing it to Qureshi. Vasant Mehta was shown with various military commanders at the strategic command centre in Bhopal. In the background was a battlefield map, pointing out the positions of artillery and tanks along the Rajasthan border.

'Believe me,' said Hussain. 'What you are going to do tonight *will* usher in peace. We can turn on the tap and turn it off. It was you, Tassudaq, who organized the assassination of Khan. Such a short time ago, but you seem to have forgotten. It was I who commissioned the attack on the Indian Parliament. Musa called in Muda's mortars to destroy Vasant Mehta's home. The major attacks have been commissioned by us, not by any fly-by-night separatist group. And it was you, Tassudaq, who transported the weapons across to Pyongyang, so that Park Ho would also have the same option of carrying out a limited tactical strike.'

'Is he ready to go?' asked Qureshi. He picked up his helmet from the table and filled a cup quarter full with coffee.

'Memed has spoken to him.'

'Good,' said Qureshi, draining his coffee. He turned, held out his arms and let Hussain embrace him. 'I will not let our country down,' he whispered, patting Hussain on the back. Without another word he walked out of the door and back to his aircraft.

He stood by the cradle as a technician removed the rear plate of the bomb, took out the tiny green plugs blocking the firing signal, inserted cordite which would spark the primary detonation and screwed the plate back on to the outer cylinder. The bomb was lifted back under the fuselage.

Qureshi climbed into the cockpit. This time he brought the cover down, raised the head-up cockpit display and started the engines. As he taxied round, he looked for Hussain in the mess hut. But the lights were off and the building had become a shape across the darkness of the tarmac.

The control tower had been briefed. There was no radio contact. Qureshi pulled down his goggles, carried out a cockpit check and then moved the engines to full thrust.

The light on the head-up cockpit display showed that the wheels were up and locked away and he eased the aircraft into a gentle climbing turn to the north, making sure he kept well within the Pakistani fly zone so close to the border.

At 5,000 feet he ran into choppy, moist cloud, then at 7,000 he hit turbulence in a mass of towering cumuli, more dense than he had judged by watching them swirl around the moon from the ground. Once through, he flew under a brilliant dome of stars, with a sense of suspension between land and sky, a smell of aircraft electronics in his mask, feeling that the bomb was already separated from him, checking that the wind was blowing from east to west, his thoughts back with Tasneem, wishing it was over, and understanding, perhaps finally, perhaps too late, that it would never be over because of the path he had chosen and there would never be a final resolution.

In the middle world in which he found himself, such contradictory thoughts did not seem out of place.

At the point where he was to cross the border, Qureshi took the aircraft in a tight turn and descended steeply. It was now that, if he was detected, the fighters would be scrambled to shoot him down.

The target was rushing towards him, nestled in the

mountains. He went lower and lower until the mountains seemed to brush at the plane's belly. He took the plane down until the threshold lights flashed, and then powered it, feeling the engines take the aircraft back up again, the mountains rearing around and releasing him back into the sky.

After he had passed through the cloud, Qureshi began to feel more relaxed. This was when the pilot of another aircraft would appear to kill him. But none did. Perhaps they thought he was performing a victory roll before crossing into India. They had no idea.

He reached the top of his shallow climb and checked his position. He put the plane into a leftward banking turn to gain another 5,000 feet. Then he gathered himself for the dive.

He began the descent lazily, then went steeper, then slowed again, and changed the angle of the incline so that the aircraft would not flip over on the sudden release of the bomb.

Gravity pushed his eyes back in their sockets. He began to sweat.

He broke through at 15,000 feet and kept heading down. The target was on the screen. Qureshi made three slight corrections. He was twenty miles from target. His ground speed was 420 knots. The G-force rushed through his body, sucking the skin of his face right against his cheekbones. The bomb sight locked on to the target. He waited eight more seconds, then released the bomb.

The aircraft jumped, suddenly much lighter, but he kept descending, pushing the aircraft until he had a visual sighting, then pulled the Fantan round in a loop to put as much distance as possible between himself and the nuclear weapon.

A bright light filled the plane from the fireball below, making the whole night sky shimmer. The aircraft juddered, then the second blast, the reflection from the forces hitting the ground, came seconds later and shook the Fantan still more. He kept climbing higher and higher. He could no longer see the ground, only a boiling cloud mushrooming, climbing like a hot-air balloon, drawing air inwards and upwards as it ascended, dragging behind it dirt and debris from the ground which clung together forming the stem of the cloud, getting taller and taller as if it were chasing him.

The plane bounced in turbulence. On the ground it looked as if smoke and fire were creeping up the side of the mountains. The bomb had exploded forty-five seconds after he had released it, 2,000 feet above the ground. On the edges of the mushroom cloud was a bubbling mass of purple-grey smoke. Inside was a burning core which made the ground burn like red coals.

Qureshi's hands and wrists ached from gripping the controls. He relaxed in his seat. They broke radio silence, at first the tower at Rawalpindi. Then Hussain's voice, a cry, dropping to a whisper, incredulous and confused. 'Kahuta,' he managed. 'He's betrayed us.' And Qureshi flicked the radio off.

The plane juddered as he levelled off at 16,000 feet, and he turned due east. He felt simultaneously sick and elated. He squeezed his eyes and opened them again.

A cannon shell from an attacking aircraft ripped through his wing. Smoke filled the cockpit, laced with the smell of cordite. Qureshi ejected and in the few seconds he had in the air, he had a brilliant view of his plane going down in a fiery spin towards the red and blue glow of the mushroom cloud.

Everywhere else looked tranquil and at peace.

43

Chunggang-up missile base, North Korea

'I can do it,' said Kee Tae Shin, standing at the base of the missile. 'But are you certain this is what you want?'

Park Ho would have taken the question from no one else. Park understood Kee better than any man in North Korea. Park was the man Kee had called upon when his wife was dragged away to a labour camp. Park was by his side when gunmen from the previous regime broke into his apartment and shot dead Kee's son and daughter in front of his eyes. It was Park who had tracked Kee's wife to Khechen prison, where he found her on the workhouse floor between rows of sewing machines, her spine broken from beatings, and sleeping in her own urine. It was Park who had knelt down, snapped her neck, then loaded her body into a helicopter and flown it back to Pyongyang, where he appeared, carrying the corpse in his arms, at Kee's door, his eyes wet with tears. And it was Park who had stayed up many nights with the distressed and lonely Kee, guiding him back to his science and skilfully steering his motivation towards support for the regime that had destroyed his family.

Without Kee, Park would never even have been able to make the choice over which delivery system he would use. Kee was one of Park's more brilliant creations and for that Park was prepared to be questioned, as long as they were alone.

He put his hand on Kee's shoulder. 'We have to create the threat of mutually assured destruction, a scenario which stipulates that if we are challenged there will be such terrible consequences that few people are likely to survive.'

Kee looked up sharply, his eyes following the contours of the missile and pointing towards the top of the rocket. 'They know we have this weapon, but they do not know how far it can fly. They know we have nuclear warheads, and they know what happens when one is exploded. But they do not know we have variola major, and they do not know we have a delivery system for it.'

Kee turned as the door behind them opened and Li Pak was ushered in. Unlike Park and Kee, Li had a wife and a son, and therefore everything yet to lose. There was a subtle difference in Li's expression. It was one of nervous enthusiasm, still motivated by the thought of creating something. Park and Kee, on the other hand, were men driven by revenge.

'Tell him,' ordered Park, as soon as the door closed behind Li. Li's presence made the space between the two missile fins and the reinforced concrete wall much smaller. The air was heavy with stale smells of oil and rocket fuel.

'We have successfully activated the interleukin-4 agent with the variola major virus,' said Li. 'Its effect on a human being is rapid and devastating. At the moment, we believe the strain we have created is resistant to the common smallpox vaccinia vaccine, and we are in the process of creating our own antidote to the new strain.'

Although the information was for Kee, Li looked only at Park as he spoke, unable to conceal his excitement.

'Can it withstand the impact stresses of delivery?' asked Kee softly.

'The liquid formulation when deep-frozen is stable in aerosol form,' said Li. 'If the technology explained to me by Comrade Park works, then, yes, the virus will survive a traumatic delivery impact. We have also put in an additive which lowers the freezing point. Your technology will allow the smallpox agent to travel in a refrigerated warhead with thermal shielding to allow it to survive re-entry into the atmosphere.'

Kee nodded. 'That is correct. We tested it over Yokata, and no one picked up what we were doing. It was a complete test of our guidance and delivery systems.'

Park shifted to the door and knocked on it twice. It opened from the other side. 'Come,' he said to Li. 'Dr Kee has something to show you.'

In the small room outside, two oblong-shaped metal casings lay on a table. Kee picked one up. 'You put the liquid formulation in here,' he said, tapping the inside. 'Right in the centre is a barometric pressure trigger. On re-entry, the warhead would release each of these capsules into the atmosphere. They would descend, stabilized by a fixed propeller which would cause the capsule to spin. Between 100 and 25 metres above the ground, the trigger would free the virus from the capsule, but would not destroy it, creating a cloud of infection which would float to the ground.'

Li nodded thoughtfully. 'A trigger, you say?' he muttered. 'Explosive or mechanical?'

'Mechanical. Just enough to prise open the capsule,' said Kee.

Li picked up the second half of the capsule from the table and examined it. 'It should work,' he said. 'We have tested the decay of our viral particles in varying conditions of heat, humidity and light. It would work with even a tiny explosion, if you don't trust the trigger.' He looked up at Park. 'Are we to test this system as facility for a fine-particles aerosol?'

Park laughed. 'Even a test will be seen as an act of war,' he said. 'Give Kee six capsules to put in his warhead.'

Li looked bemused. 'But that is nothing,' he said.

'How much do you have?' asked Park sharply.

'We haven't even begun to mass-manufacture yet—'

'Precisely,' snapped Park. 'And it will take you weeks to do so. You need 20 tonnes to infect 4,000 square kilometres of territory, and only then will we begin to destroy the apparatus of the United States. And by then, they will have developed a vaccine.' He took the capsule off Li and put it back on the table. 'No, Dr Li, you will prepare enough of the virus to show them that we have it and that we can deliver it. This is a weapon which complements the nuclear deterrent. Its purpose is to destroy those elements of society left functioning *after* a nuclear attack.'

'**We are treating** this as a first strike, Jim,' said Mehta, his voice on an open speaker in the strangely empty Oval Office. 'The very fact that Pakistan had an assembled bomb contravenes the spirit of every agreement we ever made about our nuclear arsenals.'

West had not even attempted to replace Brock. The bond between the two men had been so deep that he preferred to keep his own counsel rather than work with a stranger. He had asked Tom Patton to oversee temporarily both the National Security Council and Homeland Security, and Patton sat back alone on the sofa, his arms linked behind his head, listening to the stubborn defiance of the Indian Prime Minister. Mary Newman, fresh from the attack in South Korea, was back on a plane and headed for Beijing. Chris Pierce was in New York, locked in an office at the United Nations with the Cuban ambassador. John Kozerski had perched himself on the window sill and quietly drummed the glass as he listened.

'You are telling me that you will retaliate?' West asked Mehta. He was sitting behind the Oval Office desk, one hand around a glass of iced water and the other tapping the end of his pen against a pad.

'Yes,' said Mehta. 'That bomb was meant for India, Jim—'

'It exploded over Pakistan, less than thirty miles from the capital city.'

'Because the pilot was crazy, that's why. He lost it.'

'Lost it?' exclaimed West. 'He bombed his own nuclear-weapons-making facility. To me that is not the act of a madman.'

'Can you assure me, Jim, that Pakistan has no more aircraft and missiles with assembled nuclear weapons ready to launch?'

Out of the corner of his eye, he saw Kozerski point towards the television screen, where pictures were showing the roads heading out of Islamabad clogged with people fleeing. Instead of a national leader appealing for calm, it was being left to the news presenters. The army appeared to have melted away, back to barracks. Every road out of Islamabad, except for that heading for Kahuta, was blocked with humans fleeing on foot and in animal-drawn carts, ending the chance of any vehicle making faster progress. When violence broke out, there were no police or troops to intervene. The fighting subsided naturally, usually when one side or another had been killed.

'Have you seen the television pictures, Vasant?' said West. 'I'm looking at them now. This is a broken nation.'

'Cut it,' snapped Mehta. 'I have made my policy perfectly clear. Pakistan has made its intention known. It has assembled a bomb—'

'If you strike back—'

'You should have thought about that when you were propping up that dictatorship. Now listen to me, Jim, because I am going to tell you precisely what we are going to do.'

West beckoned Kozerski, who walked quickly over to the desk and pulled up a chair. West pushed over the pen and notepad and took a sip of water. 'OK, tell me,' he said.

'Until now, we have kept our nuclear weapon components in three different locations. Which is why all these years, Jim, there has never been a threat of mistaken nuclear exchange. Today, that is changing. Now the nuclear pit, the part which goes into the warhead, is at one place, mostly at the Babhu Atomic Research Centre near Mumbai. The warhead is somewhere else, and the delivery system – plane, missile or submarine – somewhere else again. We are bringing all those three together to assemble our weapons. We have 150 warheads, excluding the 2-kiloton type of tactical weapon used last night. In six hours time, our Mirage 2000 aircraft, the Jaguars and the Sukhoi 30s will be armed and ready to strike. Eight hours from now the Agni missiles will also be ready, including the long-range Agni 3 which we will declare to deter any interference from China. Twelve hours from now two Akula 2000 class nuclear-powered submarines will be at sea, each carrying a 20-kiloton warhead for missile launch.

'Should we detect any new threat from Pakistan – even an aircraft flying towards our border – we will carry out a full strike, meaning we will take out their major cities and military installations. The exceptions will be Islamabad and Rawalpindi because the prevailing winds would take the radioactive debris across into India. For the same reason, Lahore is also safe. Once our nuclear weapons are in place, our conventional forces will move into Pakistan across the Wagah border to Lahore, from Fazilka towards Multan, and from Jaisalmer across from Rajasthan to Sukkur. We will also put a naval blockade around Karachi. Once we are certain that Pakistan's nuclear weapons are under international control and the military is put under an interim UN command, we will withdraw our troops from Pakistan. If that does not happen, we will conquer that nation and reintegrate it back into India.'

'You will be fighting for a hundred years,' said West softly.

'We've been fighting for sixty already,' said Mehta.

'Have you found the pilot?' said West.

'Yes. It was Tassudaq Qureshi. We shot his plane down.

He ejected, landed safely and shot himself in the head before our rescue teams got to him.'

'Qureshi?' repeated West, looking over towards Patton and wishing that Brock was there to guide him. He wished he had not sent Newman and Pierce away. They might never have agreed with each other, but they showed a perfect path towards the middle ground.

'Exactly,' said Mehta. 'Qureshi led the coup against Khan. He was on a mission to carry out a nuclear attack on India, changed his mind and instead dropped the bomb on Kahuta – a target rich in symbolism. What that means, Jim, is that whoever has power in Pakistan now is more extreme than Qureshi and more than willing to use a nuclear weapon against us.'

A red light flashed silently on a telephone on West's desk. Kozerski stood and picked it up. West and Patton watched as Kozerski's face dropped into an expression of complete astonishment.

'What is it, John?' asked West. 'Sorry, Vasant, can you hold for just a moment?'

Kozerski cupped his hand over the receiver and looked first at Patton, then at West. 'North Korea has launched a missile. It's already flown over Japan and is heading out across the Pacific.'

Ahmed Memed sat in the corner of the room and heard the music, tinny and mournful, drifting up from the market below. He spread his hands, momentarily seeming unsure where to put them, before resting them on his knees. Muda sat next to him, his eyes cast down on the carpet. Across the room, also on the floor, but sitting more awkwardly, were Brigadier Najeeb Hussain and General Zaid Musa. They had the power of Pakistan's armed forces behind them, but they deferred to Memed because he was their legitimacy.

'I will tell you some truth,' said Memed. 'It should not have happened like this, but it has.'

For a few moments, he let a silence grow. His eyes were on Hussain, the man who last saw Qureshi alive and who should have read his mind. Muda, the assassin, was motionless. Hussain glanced towards Musa, but Musa's eyes were on Memed.

'War always contains bad things,' continued Memed, shifting his look to Muda, then down to his own hands. 'One way or another that is what happens. If we have resolve, we will win.'

Musa shifted to a more comfortable position. 'We will have your support?'

'They are not Pakistan's only weapons. They belong to the war. We must not lose the weapons we have. If we use them, it will show our resolve.'

Memed stood up. Muda was on his feet too, the bulge of his weapons showing through his loose, cotton shirt.

'You must work with our allies and you may have a problem with China,' said Memed, smoothing down his robe. 'I will help you.'

Musa and Hussain listened to the cleric and his assassin walk down the wooden stairs of the run-down tenement block in Rawalpindi. Hussain got to his feet and watched them emerge into the crowded, ragged streets where they would not be recognized. He felt Musa at his side, watching as well. Their figures in the window darkened the room.

Musa shook Hussain's hand. 'We've won,' he said, smiling. He slapped his hand against the window frame. 'We've bloody won.'

46

Washington, DC, USA

'It's come down north of Wake Island,' said Kozerski, his
ear still to the receiver, with Mehta listening on the line
which had remained open to India. Kozerski recited the
information as he was hearing it from the Pentagon,
'That's midway across the Pacific to Hawaii. The wind is
prevailing to the north-east. One freighter and one oil
tanker are in the vicinity. We're checking their registration
and the nationality of the crew.'

'Wake Island is a US airbase,' said Patton. 'The only
one around for miles.'

'Was that the target?' asked West, perching on the edge
of the desk and addressing the speaker phone to Mehta.
'Are you hearing this, Vasant?'

'Yes, Jim,' said Mehta. 'Keep the line open. We'll talk it
through when all the news is in.'

West pressed the button on his intercom. 'Jenny, can
you break the Defense Secretary out of his meeting in New
York? I need him in Washington now.'

'Yes, sir,' said Rinaldi with the same calmness as if West
had asked for a resupply of paper clips.

'And where is Mary?'

'In the air, sir. Three hours out of Tokyo.'

'Get her on the phone for me, please.'

'I want complete surveillance of all the Koreans on our
lists,' said Patton, talking into his mobile, and getting up
to find a clearer signal near the window. 'Cancel leave. The
four at the top of the list, move the SWAT teams in to hit
them at any time I say— No, I don't give a damn about

warrants. On my word, you move in. And I'm not going to ask if my orders are clear, because the President is right here with me and is witness to them.'

'F-16s with biodetector apparatus are three minutes from the target area,' said Kozerski. 'Mr President, do you want to hear this?'

'Patch it through,' said West, glancing at the speaker phone, and wondering if perhaps Mehta should not hear such highly classified primary intelligence. 'Vasant, who have you got with you there?'

'Deepak Suri and Ashish Uddin,' said Mehta. 'That's it and the line is secure.'

'OK. We'll keep you on.'

'Mr President, this is Squadron Leader John Tucker. We are about to enter the target area. I will relay directly—'

'Target location 29.15 North, 175.23 East,' said Kozerski. 'That's about three hundred miles north of Wake Island.'

'Nuclear radiation: negative,' said Tucker. 'Anthrax: negative. CX: negative. Sarin: negative. I'm through the target area, turning back and descending to one thousand feet.'

'What was the range of the launch?' asked West.

'Ball park, two thousand miles,' said Kozerski, studying a map draped over the coffee table in the middle of the room. 'Launch site is Chunggang-up, 41.46 North, 126.53 East. That puts it above the fortieth parallel.'

'If you're referring to Jamie Song's condition of no strikes above the fortieth,' said West, 'that's become immaterial.'

'The base was designed in 1990, specifically to target Okinawa,' continued Kozerski, relaying information from his earpiece. 'It was modified in 2005 to take the long-range Taepodong-2—'

'Variola major detected,' said Tucker.

'Smallpox,' whispered West.

'Liquid form, with stabilizing additive,' continued the pilot. 'There's an unidentified agent. We're bringing it into the aircraft and hope to hell it survives enough to find out what it is.'

'Smallpox,' repeated West to himself. God, how he missed Peter Brock.

'Mr President, I have the Secretary of State on the phone for you, sir.'

'Thanks, Jenny. Can you find Caroline Brock and ask her to come here right away?' His hand hovered over the speaker phone. 'Vasant, you still there?'

'Yes, Jim, I heard.'

'I'm cutting the line now. I beg you, don't do anything until we've talked again. We've got smallpox dropped in the middle of the Pacific and a home-goal nuclear strike on Pakistan. So far there aren't many casualties. Let's keep it that way.'

'Mary,' said West, cutting the line to Mehta. 'North Korea has launched a missile carrying the smallpox virus. Have you got enough fuel to go straight to Beijing?'

'I'll check.'

'The Secretary of Defense will be with you within the hour, Mr President,' said Rinaldi over the intercom.

'Get him on the line.'

'Anybody with any suspect disease, I want to know,' said Patton. A second mobile was ringing in his jacket pocket. He brought it out and flipped it open. 'Tom Patton,' he said. 'Tell the Surgeon General I want a report every six hours that we have no outbreak of any bioweapon-related disease. Six hours until I say it stops. Just hold a second.' He shifted his concentration to the incoming call. 'Sorry . . . he says he wants to defect . . . A MiG-29 . . . No. He does not come to the mainland. He wants to defect, he can fly into Guantanamo . . . fine, then he can ditch and we'll pick him out of the sea. No alien aircraft is coming near the US today.' Patton switched back to the second phone. 'No, every hospital. I don't care how small it is. Every goddamn hospital in this country.'

'Tucker, how long before you can identify that agent?' said West.

'I'll be back at Wake Island in five minutes, Mr President,' said Tucker. 'They should have something ten minutes after that. We've a plane standing by to fly the samples to Hawaii.'

'Do we have everything we need in Hawaii?'said West to no one in particular.

'John, can you get me Matt Lemont at Fort Detrick?' said Patton to Kozerski. Then he turned to West. 'I'll get you an answer to that in a couple of minutes, sir.'

'The Secretary of Defense, sir,' said Rinaldi.

'Chris,' said West, picking up the phone. 'North Korea has released the smallpox virus from a missile launch in the Pacific.'

'Dear God!' said Pierce. 'Where has it landed?'

'In the middle of nowhere. Three hundred miles north of Wake Island. A Taepodong-2 launched from a base near the Chinese border.'

'Mary was right.'

'And you're a gentleman to acknowledge it. Are we ready to strike?'

'We are, but—'

'I don't see any buts, Chris.'

'We're ready to attack, sir,' said Pierce. 'I'll put through the call.'

'When can you move?'

'Missile strikes could begin within the hour.'

'Put them on standby, then get yourself here. I need to

hear your objections face to face.' He was about to switch
lines with the button on the receiver, but stopped, with his
finger hovering. 'Chris, what did the Cubans say?'

'They deny it. I don't think the ambassador himself
knew.'

'You gave them the deadline?'

'I sure did.'

'Can we handle Cuba and Korea at the same time?'

'We can, sir. But not much more, particularly if handling Cuba means handling China.'

'Thanks. On second thoughts, Chris, hold there. I'm
bringing Mary in. I need both your views on where we go
next.' West switched lines to a conference call. 'Mary. You
there?'

'Yes, Mr President,' said Newman. 'We can get to
Beijing without refuelling.'

West saw Patton signalling from across the room. 'A
team from Fort Detrick is leaving now for Hawaii,' said
Patton. 'Roughly, twelve hours and we'll have all the
answers.'

'Any preliminaries from Wake Island?'

'Tucker's just landed. We should have something in a
few minutes.'

'Mary, Chris. Are you both across the line?'

'Yes, Mr President,' said Newman.

'I'm here,' said Pierce.

'In twelve hours, if the tests on the samples are conclu-
sive,' said West, 'I plan to strike every military installation
in North Korea. The strikes and bombing will go on until
Park Ho and his cronies surrender. Chris?'

'I would like to have China and Russia onside,' said
Pierce. 'I would like to have our troops away from the
ceasefire line. Right now, Mr President, we don't have new
casualties. I don't think any of us want to wake up

tomorrow morning to find the first body bags of 37,000 Americans being zipped up and loaded on to transport aircraft home.'

'Point taken,' said West, softly, realizing that Pierce's argument was exactly the one that he had put to Mehta. 'Mary?'

'First, and I hate saying this,' said Newman. For some reason, her line carried the roar of the aircraft, making some of her words difficult to distinguish. 'But better the casualties are among troops than among the civilian population in the US, which is what it would be if the smallpox virus was released there.'

'But it's not been released in the US,' broke in Pierce.

'Second,' said Newman, ignoring the interruption, 'I have a hunch Park *might* not attack across the border.'

'Was that a "might not"?' said West.

'Exactly, Mr President,' confirmed Newman. 'Park Ho might not attack across the border. And if our troops were withdrawn, I'm pretty certain he wouldn't.'

'Where the hell you get that from, Mary?' said West. Newman's deep intake of breath was audible over the line. West remembered the meeting, not that long ago, when he had snubbed her in favour of Pierce. If they had hit Park Ho then, perhaps he would be neutralized by now. Jamie Song would have taken it on the chin. Toru Sato would be satisfied for the time being, kicking his heels until another opportunity arose for him to fight the 'good war' he was seeking. Cuba would have been sorted out as a single issue, unconnected to wider events. Song, Kozlov and he could have found a way through with India and Pakistan, and most important of all, Peter Brock would still have been alive. The past was a slippery thing, and difficult to balance. What Mary had suggested then had been too dangerous. Just as right now what she was saying seemed to be completely off the wall. 'Go ahead, Mary,' said West gently. 'We're listening.'

'Cho's view is this,' she said. 'Park Ho wants to kick American butts. He wants to be hailed as the man who threw the US out of Asia and brought Japan to book. If he ends up fighting fellow Koreans in the south, he will have failed. If we launch air strikes on North Korea, he will retaliate against our bases in Japan, and he probably has a handful of missiles with a range to hit our western sea-board. But we have the defences to handle that. The only motive for him to attack the South is to defeat the US troops holding the front line. If they are removed, his motivation is removed as well.'

'Do you believe him?' said West, pensively, 'when he said he had developed a nuclear capability?'

'I do, Mr President,' said Newman. 'There is no point in declaring a nuclear weapon to an ally unless you propose to use it to help them. Cho's reading of Park's mind is better than any of us can have.'

'If we let Cho do that,' said Pierce, 'then Japan is bound to follow.'

'OK, thanks, Mary,' said West, in a manner that indicated the conversation was closing. 'I'll think about the balance between 37,000 dead Americans and two new nuclear states. Mary, if we go ahead with the strikes, I want you in Beijing, preferably standing right next to Jamie Song. Chris, see you here shortly. And I need to talk to you both again when you're not in airplanes. So Mary, get yourself to the embassy as soon as you arrive.'

West closed the call and spoke to Rinaldi. 'Jenny, get me Jamie Song, right away.'

Kozerski caught West's attention. 'Caroline Brock is on her way up.'

'Four hundred million doses are fine,' said Patton

bluntly into one of his mobile phones. 'But we need them disseminated ... No ... get them to distribution areas which are within two hours of any hospital in the US ... Yes, now, but no vaccinations without my ... OK, service personnel, I'm not talking about ... No, firemen, doctors, nurses ... OK, take your point, draw up a list of who has and who has not been vaccinated.'

As soon as he flipped shut the phone, Rinaldi's voice came through on the intercom. 'Secretary Patton, the US Coastguard needs to talk to you.'

Patton dropped his head, drew a breath, and Kozerski pointed to a red light flashing on a phone on the coffee table. Patton picked it up, while filling a glass with mineral water. 'He's ditched ... OK, fish him out, and get him to Guantanamo ... I want a bioreading from the area of splashdown.' He looked up, catching the eye of Kozerski and West and saying to neither in particular. 'Does anyone know if this virus survives in sea water?'

West and Kozerski looked at each other and shook their heads. 'We know damn all,' muttered West.

When the call was finished, Rinaldi came across the line. 'Jenny,' said Patton, 'can you get me General Bill Dayan, the commander at Guantanamo?'

'Sure,' said Rinaldi. 'And please tell the President that President Song of China is on the line. He wishes to speak in English.'

West put up a finger and switched the line to the speaker phone. 'Jamie, Jim West here,' he began. 'Thanks for coming on so swiftly. I assume you're aware of the North Korean launch.'

'We are,' said Song cautiously.

'Are you also aware that the missile was carrying the smallpox virus?'

'No,' said Song. 'I am not.'

'I've asked Mary to divert from Tokyo and come to you early.'

'I'm not sure if we're—'

'Jamie, she's touching down in a couple of hours. She's my personal envoy. I need her to tell me what the hell role China is playing in all this mess. And if you don't want her, I'll send her to take a couple of days off in Taiwan.'

'Point taken,' said Song smoothly.

As soon as the call was over, Jenny Rinaldi said: 'I've asked Mrs Brock to come through.'

Caroline Brock's appearance at the door of the Oval Office had an immediate calming effect. Her face was shadowed and disturbed, her eyes still tired and dried out of tears. She clasped her hands nervously in front of her and stepped in. She was fighting grief with concentration, and in the mixture of expressions that flitted across her face in those seconds was one of gratitude that Jim West had called her out of her loneliness to help avenge her husband's death.

West walked straight up to her, put his hand on her shoulder, guided her inside, bent over, touched the pot of tepid coffee on the table, poured some into a cup and handed it to her. 'Thanks for coming,' he said softly. 'We badly need you here, Caro. The North Koreans have—'

He was interrupted by Kozerski. 'The Wake Island tests are through. Variola major is confirmed. They need the equipment from Hawaii before they can make a final identification.'

'Smallpox?' whispered Caroline.

'Park Ho launched a warhead carrying it into the Pacific,' explained West.

Caroline sat down, sipped the lukewarm coffee and put the cup heavily back on the table. 'Do they know what strain?' she asked Kozerski.

'Do you have the strain?' repeated Kozerski into the phone. He looked at Caroline and shook his head. They need more tests.

'I need the DNA sequences from our library of smallpox strains,' said Caroline. 'Most specifically, Bangladesh-1975 and India-1967. If this does come from the Pokrov theft, it will be the India-1967 strain, which the Soviets preferred for weapons development. Even without IL-4, more than 30 per cent of infections were fatal, it retained stability during traumatic delivery and kept its virulence for long periods.' She paused and Patton repeated the question he had earlier asked West and Kozerski. 'Yes, Tom, it might well survive in sea water. Do we know exactly how it came down from the missile?'

Kozerski relayed the question. 'They're still studying the imagery,' he said. 'But right now, they believe a capsule broke off from the warhead, and then opened up like cluster bombs.'

Caroline nodded. 'A Soviet design,' she said. 'It was meant for the SS-18 long-range ballistic missile. They made it interchangeable between nuclear and biological war-heads. If Park Ho was using a full payload, the infected area could be more than a 100 square kilometres. I doubt, though, that he would do that. This is his way of declaring his potential, telling us he has the virus and can use it.'

'General Dayan,' said Patton, back on a mobile again. 'Tom Patton, Homeland Security, here … Yes … you have the Cuban pilot coming your way. I need you to do two things. I'm flying some specialists down for the interrogation. They should be with you in a couple of hours. If he starts talking before that, let him talk. If he gets beyond shitbagging the regime and on to substance, I want to know – particularly anything about China, Chinese weapons, anything like that. Secondly, I want every pore on his body checked for smallpox – or any other bioterror disease ... Vaccinating? ... Yes, of course ... I thought, they had been since 2001 ... Then if you have the doses, vaccinate them for Christ's sake—'

'Tom,' interrupted Caroline, shaking her head. 'No, don't do it.'

'General, hold back on that last instruction. I'll get back to you.' He cut the call, keeping his large hand wrapped around the tiny telephone.

'What do you mean?' said West.

'Mr President, if this is India-1967 and IL-4 or a sister agent—'

'Mr President,' said Rinaldi over the intercom. 'An urgent call from—'

'Jenny, give me a couple of minutes.'

'—IL-4 or a sister agent,' resumed Caroline. 'Then we do not have a vaccine against it. And we have no idea how IL-4 will react with the vaccine stocks we have.'

'You mean—' West let his question hang.

'I mean it could make it worse, much, much worse, if we use the vaccine.' She dropped her head. 'I told you at Camp David that you probably had six months before you needed to worry. I was wrong, Jim. I'm so, so sorry. It seems he had it up and running even as we discussed it.'

'What are you saying, Caro?' said Patton, flipping open his mobile and punching in the autodial number for Fort Detrick.

'I'm saying that if Park Ho has, say, 10 tons of this and can deliver it, he could infect maybe 4,000, maybe 10,000 square kilometres of territory. With the unknown factor of the IL-4, we just don't know. But he could destroy the United States as a functioning society.'

A silence enveloped the room. A telephone rang unanswered. West sat down heavily behind his desk. Kozerski remained absolutely stationary, still on the line, but not speaking, not relaying anything in. Patton stood, a telephone in each hand, one vibrating with a call, gazing through the window at the drizzle floating around a lamp outside. Caroline put her chin in her hands and said softly: 'There's a manual that was compiled by the Centre of Virology in Zagorsk. It has the recipes for culture conditions, nutrients and formulae for chemical additives to extend the life of the virus. There's an off chance the Soviets might have experimented with an agent like IL-4. We should check.'

But she knew it was a long shot, and no one answered, each wrapped in his own thoughts and responsibilities.

West only looked up when the door opened without a knock and Jenny Rinaldi stepped in. 'I didn't mean to barge in, Mr President, but something terrible has just happened.'

Jenny Rinaldi leant against the door frame and burst into tears.

47

Delhi, India

Lazaro Campbell felt the oxygen tank heavy on his back, and the bioterror suit was even more cumbersome because of the Kevlar flak jacket strapped around his chest. The cabin and cockpit of the Osprey V-22 were protected from nuclear radiation with a positive pressured filter system, but Campbell was kitted out because he intended to order the aircraft down and get out to see what was going on outside.

Although, seeing the wasteland, flash fires and smoky emptiness below, he wondered how anything or any living creature could have survived.

The Osprey approached central Delhi at a speed of 200 knots. No structures were left standing and Campbell was using GPS readings to get his position. Once he was above what had once been Connaught Circus, he asked the pilot to slow and switch the Osprey from being a twin-engine turboprop fixed-wing aircraft to a helicopter. While slowing, the two 400 turboshaft engines slid upwards to be at right angles to the wing and turn the long propellers into helicopter blades. The Osprey juddered briefly until settling into its new, more versatile role.

The pilot brought the aircraft down to 300 feet. Campbell closed off the cabin, turned on his breathing apparatus and gave himself a few seconds to acclimatize before checking his GPS again.

'Head south towards the US embassy in Chanakyapuri,' he ordered the pilot, relaying the coordinates. Campbell's orders had been simply to get into what was left of Delhi and identify any Americans who were still alive.

As the Osprey turned, he absorbed for the first time the scene below him, realizing that the black seared bundles, smoking in little balls, were human corpses which had vapourized within seconds, their internal organs boiled into nothing by the heat.

Some were in lines glued to the smoking ground. Some were clustered, flung together, then meshing. Some were individual and totally alone. The landscape around them bore the stark colours of grey and black, and of orange and yellow from burning fires.

The smoke hung in clusters, too. One moment the Osprey was flying through cloud whose debris clung to the windscreen so thickly that the pilot had to wiper it off with a high-pressure spray. Next, the air was so clear that Campbell could see a brilliant blue sky, wisped with clouds.

The same grey sea of debris covered the area that had once been the US embassy compound. He looked for remnants of something recognizable: the stubs of the arches of India Gate; the foundations of the government buildings of North Block and South Block; a statue toppled but intact; the contours of a road; the circular shape of Connaught Place.

But the 20-kiloton warhead, which had exploded 1,600 feet above Chelmsford Road, midway between Connaught Place and New Delhi railway station, had demolished everything. Temperatures at the blast areas would have reached 3,000 degrees Celsius. The heat had no discrimination. Nothing appeared to have survived. Campbell was looking down on the instant ruination of a city. Everything, as far as his eye could see, was a wilderness.

He had been sent in because there had been no contact from the embassy bunker. The Indian embassy in Washington, out of touch with its government, had given permission for the Osprey to go in. The readings of radiation, atmosphere particles, biological agents and much more were being computer-analysed on board and read simultaneously by scientists in the United States and India. A real-time satellite link had been set up between the Osprey and the Indian Bhabha Atomic Research Centre just outside Mumbai.

Since flying in, contact had been made with Vasant Mehta, just a few hundred feet from Campbell, but in a sealed bunker underneath Raisana Hill. The video camera on the Osprey's wings was relaying images directly to the Indian command and control centre there.

To the east, Campbell spotted movement through a clear patch of sky. He got the pilot to change course. It took some seconds to realize what he was seeing, and identify the path of the Yamuna River which ran north–south on the eastern edge of the centre of Delhi.

The smoke was thicker there, caused by a line of funeral pyres, the cremation of the dead by those who had survived. Here, Campbell had reached the half-world, where some had lived through the first blast but in such a state that he had to turn his eyes away. He coughed through his breathing apparatus. The air he breathed was clear, but his senses were with the stench outside.

Those on the ground did not react to the Osprey. They were not seeking help. Things had gone too far, and they knew that by the end of the day they would most likely be dead, too. Campbell got the pilot to descend to just fifty feet, where he saw that the river was not covered in debris as he had thought. It was filled with blackened corpses bumping each other like logs. Hundreds of thousands must have fled to the water to escape the fire and then drowned. More corpses lay strewn on the river banks, most of them with no faces. Their eyes and mouths had been burned, their ears melted and their hair singed to the skull.

On the other side of the river, further from the centre of the blast, a man and a child were propped up on a bicycle, leaning against a railing. Both were dead, with no sign, though, of how their bodies had survived as they did. The trees all around had been burnt by fireballs leaping across the water.

A line of people crouched at the river's edge, drinking the fetid, blood-stained water, and from the tattered remnant of a blouse, Campbell saw that they were high-school girls. Their skin was cracked, their heads bald and their faces were barely recognizable as human. On the other side, a figure, its skin blackened and hanging off like a rag, started to cross by crawling over the bodies like a bridge. Halfway, it sank, and did not come up again.

It was then that someone pointed, and the eyes of the living became distinguishable from those of the dead. They looked up at the Osprey at the figure of Campbell half out of the aircraft, their eyes now looking for someone to come and help. As they pointed, blackened skin hung from their fingertips and elbows. Dark liquid ran down their arms, and he saw how shrivelled or how swollen their bodies were. A woman turned and he saw the imprint of a child on her breast, where the two must have been scorched together, but left to live a few hours more. She opened her mouth to plead with him, and froth oozed from her lips. Then she fell backwards, but she remained conscious, and even as she was falling, she managed to hold Campbell's eyes in a stare that made his blood run cold.

'Take her up,' he ordered the pilot, and as they went higher the scene became worse because there was more of it. But at least Campbell could no longer see the eyes of the dying individuals.

'Back to Chanakyapuri,' he instructed. 'We'll take a last look round the embassy.'

After the scenes at the river, the ashen desolation of Delhi's diplomatic area came as a relief. There was no life at all. Campbell ordered the aircraft down to fifty feet again, just high enough to escape the debris flung up by the rotor blades, asking the pilot to criss-cross the area so that NIMA could map at least this part of post-nuclear Delhi.

Through the intercom, the co-pilot was calling the embassy on the high-frequency radio. If anyone was alive down there, they were locked in concrete with no contact at all.

'We'll map Raisana Hill and Rajpath as well,' said Campbell. The Osprey turned north-east and just as the pilot was about to take it up again Campbell spotted movement way in the distance.

'Stop,' he said. 'Hold your altitude. Do you see anything due east?'

'Heading over there,' said the pilot. He edged the aircraft towards the area. Campbell took a GPS reading. Down below, two figures were on their feet and walking. They heard the aircraft, turned towards it and waved. Then he saw a third figure, a child, being held by one of them.'

'Lower the winch rope,' said Campbell.

With the Osprey hovering, Campbell clipped himself on and slid down through clouds of dust thrown up by the rotor blades. He lowered himself into a haze, stumbling forward, getting his balance on the soft, crumbling moon-like surface. He drew his pistol.

'US government,' he shouted. His voice was relayed from a speaker on his helmet. 'Please identify yourself.' Then he remembered that even if they heard him, they might not be able to reply.

Inch by inch he trod forward, groping in the dust cloud, which was beginning to settle. He turned on the flashlight on his helmet, and through the particles of thick dust swirling in front of him a figure stood with its hands up straight ahead of him.

He wiped the glass of his helmet, peered forward, saw the face of Meenakshi and only then registered that her survival suit had an emblem of the Stars and Stripes sewn on to the sleeve.

Behind her, carrying a child, was a man he recognized as Vasant Mehta's private secretary. But as for the child he was carrying, they must have put the suit on it as a desperate act of madness and compassion. It was dead, its face a crumpled burnt shape, like those by the river: no eyes, no nose, no mouth, no human features, only an imprint of the holocaust.

Meenakshi lowered her arms, began a step forward, but her bad leg couldn't take it and Campbell caught her as she fell.

48

Washington, DC, USA

'We need Lazaro's pictures on the net right now, and out to every television station in the world,' said West. 'I have never seen anything so dreadful.' His expression was one of horror and anger. He stared at Kozerski. 'And uncensored. Let the kids see it, so that when they grow up they will despise this monster our ancestors created.'

Kozerski repeated the instructions down a telephone line. Chris Pierce sat with his feet up on the coffee table and a laptop balanced between his knees. The map was skewed and half on the floor. The cartons of takeaway Chinese and pizza were piled on a trolley with bottles of water and a coffee urn. In the corner of the Oval Office, Tom Patton was working at one end of a desk which Kozerski had procured and Caroline Brock was at the other. A permanent line on speaker phone was open to Fort Detrick, and both had their own laptop links.

The door to the office was kept open so that Jenny Rinaldi could be seen and could shout through instead of relying on the clogged-up intercom line. 'The Secretary of State is on the line from Beijing, sir,' she said.

'Mary, have you seen Jamie yet?'

'No, sir. I'm not pushing it, and he's promised me a meeting within three hours. The embassy report a heap of telephone traffic between Beijing and Moscow. Chris might be aware of that—'

'Chris,' shouted West across the room. 'Has the NSA got any increased traffic between Beijing and Moscow?'

'Not that's come to me. But I'll check.'

'Which indicates that Song and Kozlov have been talking, sorting things before Song wants to talk to us—'

'Jenny,' said West. 'Get me Kozlov in Moscow. Urgent.'

'Mr President,' said Kozerski. 'The first polls are saying that any strike against North Korea after what happened in Delhi would be deeply unpopular.'

'Yeah, well, we're not striking North Korea – at least not for an hour or so,' retorted West. He walked to the window and spotted for the first time daffodils in the garden outside, getting beaten down by the rain which hadn't let up for the past two days. His voice softened. 'Mary, what I want you to do more than anything is rest up and think. Stay fresh. I'm going to need a good brain in the next few hours.'

'Mr President,' said Patton, turning in his chair, his finger jabbing at the laptop screen. 'We picked up four suspects from Korean associations which we tracked back to Mason's original calls from Canberra. They were given blood tests. Two of the four showed antibodies to the smallpox vaccine. They were civilians. Not from the US or South Korean military.'

'So the only reason they would have been vaccinated is—' began West before trailing off.

'Because they were going to handle it,' finished Patton.

'Christ,' muttered West.

'We need to conduct further tests to see if there is an IL-4 component involved,' said Caroline Brock. 'If there isn't, find out from the suspects if they knew for sure that they'd be handling the IL-4 component of the variola major virus and that the standard vaccine would work.'

'They're not talking,' said Patton.

'*Make* them talk,' snapped West, slamming his hand down on the desk, then bringing it up to his forehead. He sat down and leant back in his chair.

'President Kozlov is not available, sir,' said Rinaldi.

'Good,' said West, getting sharply to his feet. 'I'm going for a jog. And every six hours, I want every one of you out of the office, for half an hour, to clear your heads. Do whatever exercise you have to, but do it.'

West stepped outside and two secret service officers fell in with him. Rain, caught in a gust of wind, hit him in the face. He wiped it away with the back of his hand. 'Stay well away,' he told the officers. 'I don't want to hear you. I don't want to see you.'

Water drained across the surface of the jogging track. The weather had been so hard that puddles were scattered across the manicured lawns, throwing them into a late winter disrepair.

West began jogging, but then stopped, because his mind was wandering. Valerie was the one who had kept telling him there was nothing like a brisk walk in cold weather for sharp, deep thinking. So he slowed to walking pace, not caring where he went or how he got there. He walked off the path, across the South Lawn, through the Children's Garden, avoiding the Rose Garden, where the press were huddled in a corner, working on shifts.

And it took him a full fifteen minutes, soaked through and with water dripping down his face, his hair matted on his forehead, before he had convinced himself that the destruction of Delhi was not just a nightmare; that the smallpox release over the Pacific had actually happened; and that if he was a general wishing to bring down an empire, he could not have planned it better.

West punched his fist through the air, anger welling up inside him, forcing it out of him, before he could settle down to think more clearly. He licked rainwater off his lips, spotted a bench at one end of the east side of the garden and sat on it, barely feeling the dampness seep through his tracksuit.

Could they have factored it in all those years ago when the Soviets went into Afghanistan, and the US bankrolled Islamic forces to throw them out? If Jimmy Carter had just handed Afghanistan to Moscow, what difference would that have made now? The Soviet Union would have collapsed anyway. It was economically unsustainable and Afghanistan would never have spawned Bin Laden and his clones. Should they have spotted it in the winter of 2002 when Islamic parties had done so well in the elections in Pakistan? And then what should they have done? Rigged the elections? What about when North Korea had fired its first long-range missile over Japan in 1998? Why didn't Clinton strike then? What about when it declared its nuclear weapons in 2002, threw out inspectors and reactivated its nuclear reactor? Why didn't Bush go in then? Because he was fighting another war in another arena; and had President James H. West been in the White House in 2002, he would have done exactly the same.

And where does the hatred come from? Under the American umbrella, Japan and the whole of the western Pacific Rim had been able to pull themselves from poverty to prosperity. Taiwan, South Korea, Singapore were all shining examples of how to transfer from third world to first world society. Even Vietnam, which had given America a bloody nose, was now an ally. China, the long-term strategic rival, sent tens of thousands of students to American universities every year.

And did the Islamic world have any legitimate grievances? In the last half-century, had the US ever taken offensive action against a Muslim community? West stopped, letting this thought seep through. He pulled up the sodden sleeve of his tracksuit top and began counting on his fingers: 1956, the US went against Britain, France and Israel in the Suez War, and kept Gamal Abdel Nasser in power – even though he was becoming an ally of Moscow; 1971, the USS *Enterprise* was in the Bay of Bengal supporting Muslim Pakistan against India; 1973, the US forced a ceasefire on Israel and rescued Egypt from humiliation and defeat; 1979, Jimmy Carter persuaded the Shah of Iran to go into exile, rather than face down Tehran's demonstrators with tanks and bullets; 1980, Washington poured millions into Afghanistan to undermine the Soviet invasion; 1982, it arranged safe passage for the Palestinian leader, Yasser Arafat, from Beirut to Tunisia. US troops protected Bosnian Muslims against Christian Serbia; they died in Muslim Somalia trying to defend ordinary people against bloodthirsty warlords; they acted as an honest broker between Muslim Turkey and Christian Greece.

'What a load of bullshit,' muttered West to himself, getting up from the bench with more certainty in his step. Pakistan and North Korea were both failed states, run by failed and embittered leaders. America was an enemy of convenience, because both countries had been unable to provide for their people. And he was damned if he was going to compromise. He walked back towards the White House, a solitary but determined figure. He saw Kozerski by the window in the Oval Office and waved, because he knew what he would get his Chief of Staff to do next. He crouched down and picked a dozen daffodils from a bed, and held them up to Kozerski, who waved back, a mobile phone in his hand. Valerie had always said the daffodil was her favourite flower, because it showed that the darkness of winter was about to end.

49

Beijing, China

From the windows of the American embassy's armour-plated Lincoln Town Car, Newman looked out at the lights on the edges of Tiananmen Square shining through the smog from cheap coal that engulfed the city. Soldiers, bored and stamping their feet against the cold, stood at intervals guarding this haunting symbol of Chinese communist power.

At this time of night, no one was around, and a furtive, eerie silence hung across Tiananmen's hundred acres and its buildings. Through the mist, Newman could make out the dark shape of the Great Hall of the People, further away the Mausoleum of Mao Tse-tung and lines of red flags flying in the strong wind.

There was no place so blatantly nationalistic anywhere else in the world. Tiananmen made Moscow's Red Square look like a suburban theme park. London's historic symbols were confined to chaotic traffic congestion on Hyde Park Corner and in Trafalgar Square. Washington had its monuments and icons, but none as arrogant as this. And India – she wished she hadn't followed this train of thought – India used to have the landscaped vistas of Rajpath and Raisana Hill. But like everyone else, Newman had seen the pictures. She shook her head at the thought, too grotesque and ghastly to contemplate.

Up ahead and just to the right was Tiananmen Gate, where in 1949 Mao Tse-tung had proclaimed his victory and had begun the upheavals and violence that created the robust one-party state China was now. His enduring portrait, its spotlight shrouded in smog, hung above it, looking down on Newman as her limousine slowed and turned right at the entrance of Zhongnanhai, just past the Forbidden City.

Slogans painted on the high red walls flanked the gate. On the west side, the Chinese characters translated as *Long live the great Communist Party*. On the east side, they paid a tribute – *Long live the unbeatable thoughts of Chairman Mao.*

The guards checked the Lincoln's number plate. A set of red metal double doors opened. The driver was waved inside and an anti-terror ramp slid down into the ground to let the vehicle pass.

Within the compound was a quietness which even at this early-morning hour did not seem possible in Tiananmen Square itself. The flapping of flags in the wind and the rumbling trucks from the provinces kept the square alive and in the real world. Zhongnanhai was a different place altogether, a tranquil place, where the snow was melting and the moonlight showed cracks in the ice on the lake.

As the car slowed, Newman saw Jamie Song, wearing no coat, just a scarf wrapped round his neck, walk out on to the steps. He was lit up by powerful lamps on the side of the building, both hands outstretched, although he would not have been able to see through Newman's tinted windows. In his expression, he managed to blend a smile of greeting with a deeper grief for what had happened in India. His was the face of a powerful man at a loss how to control events.

The driver pulled up and Song himself opened the door. His hand offered to take Newman's elbow to steady her in case of hidden ice. She let him take it, then turned and shook his hand. 'Jamie, these are terrible times and it's good to be here,' she began.

'I'm sorry for not being able to see you earlier,' he replied, guiding her up the steps and through a blast of heat being thrust down from the ceiling.

The meeting was a culmination of hours of frustration: Jamie Song's refusal to see her, and John Kozerski calling every half-hour from the White House, telling her that an impatient Jim West wanted to make an address to the nation – but Newman needed to see Song first. Finally, two hours earlier, West himself had called.

'I've done the sums, Mary,' he had told her. 'There's no turning back. There's no surrender. We're right and they're wrong. Their grievances are illegitimate, their methods abhorrent. If Song stands in our way either with Pakistan or North Korea, he is against us. I need you to make that clear. Once you have his response, I need to tell the American people what is happening. Cuba, Pakistan and North Korea – China is the key to them all. I can't let this situation hang, Mary. You've got to see the man. Give him three more hours, and if he doesn't show go back to Japan.'

Song took Newman's coat, hung it on a rack by the door and showed her into a small but comfortably decorated room.

'I've asked General Yan Xiaodong to join us,' said Song. Uncharacteristically for a Chinese official, Yan's jacket was off, his shirt sleeves rolled up, and he was bending down to stub out a cigarette as Newman came in. He jerked upright and met her with outstretched hand, his breath reeking of smoke. 'Secretary of State,' he said in heavily accented English. 'Welcome. Welcome.'

'Yan is my personal military adviser,' said Song. 'He lets me know what the generals are thinking, and we find ourselves in a situation where I'm sure many different generals are thinking many different things all over the world.'

He indicated that Newman should take a seat. She

chose an armchair away from the heating, which was drying up her throat. Song took a seat next to Newman's, and continued: 'Yan can explain some of the discrepancies that have become apparent in Chinese policy.'

'It is terrible, terrible what has happened,' said Yan. 'It must stop. Stop straight away.' He punched his fist into his hand to make his point.

Newman sat back and crossed her legs. Deliberately, she had brought no files, no notes, no photographic evidence of China's rogue alliances. The only administrative aid she had was a mobile phone in her skirt pocket next to her thigh, with a pre-programmed scrambler and a line directly to Kozerski at the White House.

'But we're meeting on your initiative, Mary,' said Song. 'So you go first.'

'I'll be blunt, Jamie,' said Newman, glancing at Yan and pausing for him to sit down. But he remained on his feet, in a corner of the room away from her and Song. The conversation was being recorded, of course, but with only three of them in the room, and knowing Jamie Song well, she spoke more frankly than she would have done otherwise.

'Almost simultaneously, North Korea released the smallpox virus against a target area in the Pacific and Pakistan destroyed Delhi,' she began. 'To both those governments, China is at best neutral, at worst an ally. On top of that, we have the issue of your missiles being secretly flown to Cuba.' She checked her watch. 'Very soon, the President will be addressing the nation. The focus, of course, will be the nuclear attack. But Jim wants to be able to say that China is with him.'

'What's he going to say?' said Song, leaning forward and putting his elbows on his knees. Suddenly, he seemed boyish, innocent, over-curious at what Newman had to tell him.

'Much of it depends on you,' answered Newman and stopped there, revealing nothing more.

Momentarily, Song glanced over at Yan, then sat upright in the chair, drummed one finger on the arm and, finally, clasped his hands together. For the first time, Newman sensed real unease in the usually urbane Chinese President. 'I am the President of China, Mary. But I am not the General Secretary of the Communist Party. Nor am I Chairman of the Military Commission. Most times, there is no problem with this arrangement. Right now, however, there is.'

He paused and fixed Newman with a stare. 'There is a debate going on now within the Chinese government, as you might have guessed. But this is an internal matter. Whatever arguments we have between ourselves, I remain the President of China. I will lead this country along the next path we choose to take. In your country, such debate takes place in the press and Congress, and you call it democracy. In China, we are more discreet, and you call it dictatorship. The depth of argument, however, is the same.'

Newman swallowed hard because of the dryness of the air, and she realized it might have made her look apprehensive. She looked quickly around the room for some bottled water. But there was none, and she didn't want to ask. 'Perhaps you could explain your options, Jamie,' she said flatly, but knowing that the options had already been discussed and a decision had been made.

'The missile shipments to Cuba – indeed the agreement signed in 2001 to move our signals intelligence to Havana – was carried out by the Military Commission. I knew nothing about it.' He shrugged. 'But the missiles are now there. So what do we do? The military relationship with Pakistan which began almost fifty years ago was handled by the Military Commission. The details, such as the transfer of the centrifuges to Pakistan to separate off weapons-grade uranium, were carried out without the Chinese President being made aware. The overarching strategic policy to prop up Pakistan in order to weaken India was reached many years ago, but the Military Commission handled the details.'

'And with North Korea?' asked Newman.

'We have discovered,' said Song, looking again at Yan, 'that some missile technology was illegally sold to North Korea. It was not government policy, but it has happened.'

'Unfortunate,' remarked Newman, her tone thick with irony. Briefly she closed her eyes and saw the Osprey's pictures of Delhi, the bodies in the river like an image from eternal hell, and she had to contain her anger as Jamie Song explained it away as administrative rivalry. She opened her eyes and found herself looking straight at Yan, who, remarkably, reacted by smiling at her and shaking his head. 'Terrible,' he said. 'Just terrible.' And he maintained the same expression throughout.

'The question is this, Mary,' said Song. 'What do we do now? What should I do, and what should Jim do?'

'This isn't the boardroom meeting of a multinational, Jamie,' whispered Newman. 'We're both looking into a goddamn abyss, if you don't sort your own house out.'

Song's eyes flared. She knew that she shouldn't have said it and admitted it. 'I'm sorry, Jamie,' she sighed. 'It's been a tough couple of days.'

'It's not a matter of sorting houses out, Mary,' said Song softly, his expression changing from irritation to sympathy. 'It's a matter of where we all go from here, and how much leeway we can give each other.'

'Leeway?' questioned Newman. But Song held up his hand. 'Please, let me finish.'

'I did not sanction Pakistan's nuclear strike. Nor did I provide or sanction Park Ho's missile programme and his biological weapons programme. I had no hand in the coup in which he took power. But, if I now set about undoing it all, letting you destroy the North Korean regime, letting you reprimand my government for getting it wrong, letting the US undermine the legitimacy of my nation as you did with the Soviet Union, letting you dictate policy on the post-nuclear-holocaust Indian subcontinent, letting you and Japan hatch the future security policy for the Asia–Pacific—' he gazed around the room, decorated formally with Chinese calligraphy and pictures of storks and mountains. 'I can't do it,' he said shaking his head. 'I have to take the situation as we have it now and use it. Yes, I know that is brutal, but that is how you wanted me to tell it. I have to use what we have now and move on. And so does Jim West.'

'How, Jamie?' asked Newman. 'How? Use what? What the hell are you saying?'

'Yan has talked to Park Ho,' said Song delicately. 'Park has promised to freeze his missile launches and put his smallpox virus back on ice, while we talk with him.'

'Talk with him,' said Newman incredulously. 'Jamie, this is not something about which anyone can negotiate. What the hell are you saying to him: "Put it on ice and if Jim West does something you don't like, bring it out again"?'

'No,' said Song firmly, his right hand gripping the side of the chair. 'No, Mary. That is not what I am saying.'

'Then what the hell are you saying? Because if Park's regime is not destroyed, and his missile and biological and nuclear weapons programme with it, he can use it any time he wants. And if you prop him up, you can turn that tap on any time you want.' Her voice was raised. She felt tiredness prickle in her eyes. She swallowed again, but kept looking at Song. She would be damned if she blinked first.

'All right,' said Song quietly. 'Let us agree to disagree

on that for the moment. I have managed to talk to Mehta. He is a broken man, trapped in the bunker, unable to leave. He is so horrified by what has happened that he told me he has no intention of retaliating and murdering innocent people – as long as I can guarantee that Pakistan does not attack again.'

There was the faintest ripple across his eyes, a shift of expression which showed that Jamie Song was claiming high ground and the first round which went with it. As far as Newman knew, West and Mehta had not yet talked. 'Andrei fixed it,' explained Song. 'The alliance between India and Russia is like your alliance with Great Britain. In times of crisis you turn to each other.'

Newman remembered Kozerski telling her that Kozlov had refused to take West's first couple of calls. They had spoken now, but their conversation had been brief and insubstantial.

'Have you given Vasant the guarantee over Pakistan?' asked Newman.

'Yes and no,' said Song. 'We don't know who is in control there at the moment. Nor do we know who authorized the strike on Delhi, although we suspect it was General Zaid Musa working with the cleric Ahmed Memed. He was the man who started the uprising in South-East Asia.'

'Stop,' said Newman, uncrossing her legs and sitting upright. 'Before Pakistan struck, Vasant asked you to guarantee a Pakistan no-strike policy, and you refused.'

'Exactly,' said Song, getting up from his chair. 'That was before the strike.' He glanced over at Yan, who checked his watch and nodded. 'Come, Mary, I have promised the BBC an interview. I would like you to listen in.'

Song held out his hand to help her up. He was running rings around her. She looked across to Yan, who remained loyally inexpressive on the other side of the room. He took a couple of steps to a door that connected with another room and opened it. A spotlight beam lit up his feet and Newman heard noises of radios crackling and furniture being moved.

For a second, Newman didn't move, held in her seat by confusion and anger.

'Come, Mary,' said Song again. 'All of us are trying to help. I have to balance my friendship and loyalty to you, my desire to stop all conflict, against the heaving movement and ambition of my people, most of whom are not as sophisticated in their dreams as you and I are. Unfortunately, the national will is less subtle than the personal will.'

As Newman stood up, the mobile phone vibrated silently against her thigh. She shot a glance at Song, then across to the open door. Yan stepped into the beam of the spotlight, throwing a huge, long shadow at their feet. It took a couple of seconds, while she was pulling the phone from her pocket, to recognize the silhouetted figure which crossed with Yan's as he went into the room. She pressed the answer button and heard Kozerski's voice. 'Mary, Russian and Chinese troops have gone into Pakistan. Are you with Song yet?'

'They've gone in?' she said in disbelief. 'Already?'

'The night skies over Islamabad and Karachi are white with parachutes,' said Kozerski with unusual eloquence.

Her expression must have told Song everything. His mask dropped. He simply nodded to confirm what Kozerski had said.

'I'll call you back,' said Newman. Suddenly detached, lost in a whirl of thoughts, she began following Song.

'Secretary of State,' exclaimed a cheerful voice. It was Song's son Yun. Jacket off and his tie loose, he moved easily, a relaxed man, used to power but without the responsibility of it. 'We came up for Dad's wedding anniversary but,' he paused, casting a long look at her, 'let's just say, it's been overtaken by events.' Yun gently touched Newman's elbow, and skilfully guided her away from the arc of lights coming from the studio. 'I'm only a spectator, but I am so, so glad you are here,' he said, dropping his voice. 'Dad needs your help to fix this. He's in a bind, but if he can't get out of it, no one can, and we're all sunk.'

The spotlight went off, prompting them both to look towards the door. Newman recognized the tall figure of Andrei Kozlov, with his head down to listen to words from his adviser, Alexander Yushchuk. Newman caught a glimpse of a television correspondent brushing the lapels of his jacket.

Newman stepped back, bumping into Yun, and leaving Kozlov's hand outstretched and grasping at air. There was no way she would go into that room and sit as an appendage while the leaders of two newly allied powers announced the invasion of another nation – however abhorrent the governing regime of that nation might be. If she spoke, she would be upstaging her own president. If she sat with them, she would be sanctioning their actions. If she remained silent in the room, she would be a symbol of America, the lame duck.

On a wall bracket behind her, she saw a television set. 'Jamie,' she said with a determined smile. 'Game's up. I'm not going in that room with you.' She pointed up to the television. 'Do me a favour and get your broadcast patched through here.'

Yun repeated Newman's request, while she brought the mobile phone back up to her ear. 'John, Kozlov's here. Both he and Song are about to go live on BBC World.'

50

'**We need a** short press release out right now,' said West, 'that Mary is in Beijing for talks with Kozlov and Song. Nothing more. Enough to give us a presence. Whatever is happening, the US is in the loop and we're talking to our allies.'

'That means we support the invasion?' said Pierce.

'Why not, Chris?' scoffed West. 'Do you want to go in and fight Russia and China to protect those rag-head generals?'

Kozerski repeated the President's instructions into his phone, while fumbling with the remote to get the right television channel.

'Where's Campbell?' asked West.

Green night-vision shots, bearing the logo of a Russian television station, flicked on to the screen. The camera was inside an aircraft. BBC World flashed up that the pictures were being carried live. A strap underneath said that the Russian and Chinese presidents would be giving a joint interview in a few minutes.

'Campbell's in Dubai, sir,' said Kozerski, turning up the volume to try to work out what was happening.

'I want him in Beijing with Mary,' said West. 'She needs someone with her whom she knows and trusts and who can protect her.'

'She has her own staff—' began Kozerski, although half his concentration was on the screen.

'What the President means, John,' said Caroline Brock, 'is that he doesn't want a repeat in Beijing of what happened in South Korea. And neither do I, dear God! Neither do I!' She got up, walked to West, held his hand for a moment, but looked away from him. She touched the top of her right cheek with a forefinger, and West saw how sad her eyes were.

Not so long ago, it was he who had been dropping by the Brocks' place in Georgetown to get away from the loneliness of a White House without Valerie. Now it was Caroline, newly widowed, who had found escape to an Oval Office crisis to stave off the prospect of a life without Peter.

The Oval Office had become a close-knit operations centre. West had rejected Pierce's suggestion that they move downstairs to the situation room. He insisted they remain above ground in the Oval Office with its windows and its views.

'Coming on,' said Kozerski.

The wide shot showed Song and Kozlov on upright chairs against a backdrop of Tiananmen Square. West offered Caroline his seat, which she took, and he leant against the side of his desk, reaching for a notepad and uncapping a ballpoint pen with his teeth.

The shot switched to the presenter Susannah Sampson in London, leaning forward towards the camera. 'You're seeing live pictures of Russian paratroopers jumping out of a military aircraft over Islamabad,' she said, glancing through the glass-top surface of her desk to her monitor. 'Announcements from Moscow and Beijing confirm that a joint Chinese–Russian force is moving into Pakistan with the specific aim of securing the nuclear arsenals to prevent further missile launches against India. Most of you will have seen the pictures from Delhi. They have appalled us all. The Indian High Commission in London has confirmed that India supports the Chinese–Russian action. It quotes the Indian Prime Minister, Vasant Mehta, as saying that if Pakistan is disarmed, India will not retaliate against the strike.' She cast her eyes down as if she was reading from a sheet of paper. 'Mr Mehta says – and I quote – "Having seen the horrible destruction of my own city, I cannot imagine any human being giving the command to inflict such dreadful suffering on any other human beings who are simply trying to go about their daily business."'

Sampson looked up and brushed a trail of hair from her eyes. 'And now we're going live to Beijing, where President Song and President Kozlov of Russia, who is in China to announce the operation, have agreed to speak to BBC World. As a point of explanation, they both want me to say that there are no ground rules for the interview and no questions have been agreed in advance. In a few minutes we will be opening our phone lines, and they'll be fielding questions—' She glanced up unexpectedly, then delivered a rueful smile. 'I'm sorry, I'm told we have a few moments before we can go to Beijing, due to interference on our satellite line. Many of you may realize that the nuclear strike on Delhi has produced a sea change in world opinion, not least from the Indian Prime Minister himself. It will be worth reminding you of his dramatic speech, not that long ago to the United Nations, in which he told the United States: "If you are to retain your position as the only world superpower, you will dismantle the authority of these men and everything they represent. If you do not act, India will go it alone."

'Well, the US did not dismantle the authority of the military leaders in Pakistan,' said Sampson, picking up the thread. 'But also India does not seem to be going it alone, despite Prime Minister Mehta stating his policy unequivocally in a magazine article, and I quote again, "Should the tragedy of a nuclear attack on India or Indian interests occur anywhere in the world," he stated, "then my government would obliterate the nation responsible, whether the attack came from the government itself or from rogue elements being nurtured by that government."'

Sampson paused for a few seconds, staring straight into the camera. 'It is astonishing that the reality of nuclear war has changed so many minds so quickly.' She shuffled papers on her desk. 'Now, I'm told that we can go to Beijing – also late breaking news is that Mary Newman, the American Secretary of State, is with the two presidents in Beijing. Until now we did not know she was there. She will not be appearing for the question time session, but at least we know that the leaders of the most powerful nations are talking to each other.'

West looked across at Kozerski and put his thumb up. In an instant America's public role in the night's events had changed dramatically.

'. . . to Jamie Song, who is going to make a statement.'

'Thank you, Susannah,' said Song. In his hand-tailored worsted suit, against the night-time backdrop of Tiananmen Square, there was a debonair look to Song. He was a man of the world, set apart from the more earthy and roughly hewn Andrei Kozlov.

'As you know, Russian and Chinese forces are moving into Pakistan. We have encountered some resistance in the military cantonment areas of Karachi, Multan, Lahore and Islamabad. We believe there is no longer any central government in Pakistan, indeed in the military itself, and that troops are taking their orders from their corps commanders. We hope, therefore, that the resistance is scattered and light; that it will soon end; and that our troops can finish their mission, which is to neutralize Pakistan's nuclear weapons. Our nuclear-warfare teams have arrived outside the hazard zone of the Kahuta facility, which was destroyed by a tactical nuclear weapon dropped by a defecting Pakistan air force officer. It is essential that leakage from this facility is plugged. Even from the brief résumé of events that I have just given, we can see that our action is long overdue. Indeed, President Kozlov, Prime Minister Mehta and I had discussed it. Unfortunately, all of us had misjudged the breakdown within Pakistan and the influence of extremist elements there. Now President Kozlov has a few words to say.'

The camera switched to Kozlov, catching him as he was straightening his tie. While Song's composure was urbane and his mood impenetrable, Kozlov's pockmarked and crinkled face appeared to bear all the twists and turns of his difficult life. His sunken eyes and the rubbing of his hands, skilfully picked up by the camera, made captivating viewing, for it was Kozlov who stated the unthinkable. From him it came across as being strangely acceptable. Perhaps Kozlov reflected his own nation more accurately than any of the other leaders.

'I spoke to Mehta,' he began bluntly. 'I said: "What do you want me to do?" He said: "Andrei, tell me what to do. I have led and lost. What authority do I have?"

'Russia and India are allies. In the Cold War the Soviet Union was Marxist and India was a democracy, and we were still allies. You can be friends with different systems. I told Vasant: "You can obliterate Pakistan, as you promised." Vasant said: "Andrei, how can I do that? Look at Delhi. Who but an animal would recreate that in Islamabad?"'

Kozlov paused and pressed his hand over his chin. His was a rugged face, but not from the weather and outdoors. It was hewn more by disappointment and hunger. 'Vasant said, "If you want to do something, tell me they are not going to fire another missile. Give me an excuse to tell the Indian people that I did not fight back because we knew they would never do it again, and that the men who did this are no more and that the nation is no longer a monster." That was when I asked Vasant to take Jamie's call.'

Kozlov looked over at Song. Briefly the shot went wide, showing them both at ease with each other, Kozlov not caring that he had come to Beijing, not caring about pride or face. His pause was uncomfortably long, but then he began again. 'What about Jim West? I asked Vasant, and you know what Vasant told me? He said, "It happened on Jim's watch, Andrei. It started on Truman's watch in 1945 with Hiroshima and Nagasaki, and it happened again on Jim West's watch with Delhi." Vasant told me he had asked Jim West to go in and stop Pakistan. That was after the attack on his house, and he was pretty clear during his speech at the United Nations. Vasant said: "Andrei, can you do it? Can you keep my hands free of the blood of nuclear war?" And I said: "Vasant, I can't do this by myself. But I can do it with Jamie Song. Why don't you talk to him? And the Indian Prime Minister said: "Andrei, go ahead. You have my blessing."'

'Son of a bitch,' muttered West. 'How far's he going to take this?'

'They will have decided that,' said Pierce quietly, tapping his finger on the ridge of his laptop.

51

Rokkasho-Mura, Japan

The Japanese Prime Minister's limousine, too low slung for the terrain, churned freezing slush underneath its chassis as it turned through the open gate of the high-wired security fence. Four-wheel-drive tyre tracks had hewn intricate patterns into the snow, hardened by weeks of cold. As the vehicle stopped, Sato lowered his window, and a red carpet was rolled out. The atmosphere in this cordoned-off, secret area was strangely unceremonial. Sato stepped on to the carpet and waited for his Defence Minister, Kenijiro Yamada, and Kiyoko to join him.

There could never have been any other way, thought Sato. If Japan was to break free of its Second World War defeat, it would have to embrace nuclear weapons. Being a victim of them was not an excuse not to possess them. At some stage, whether now or half a century on, Japan would no longer be protected by America, and she would have to stand up to China as an equal.

A delegation of scientists, their hands white-gloved, their breath creating a cloud around them, stood in a greeting line. Sato, Yamada and Kiyoko were led into a concrete bunker. Inside, they were confronted with a row of marker lights, dropping in a steep descent. The ceiling gradually became lower, but the corridor widened into a functional steel-walled passageway with hatch-like doors off the sides, as if on a warship. Gauges displayed the air pressure inside the rooms.

Yamada fell into step beside Sato. 'We are using 1.4 kilograms of plutonium,' he explained. 'It will yield a 14-

kiloton explosion, which is exactly the strength of the
bomb dropped on Hiroshima. The shock wave will be
contained within the Earth's crust.'

Sato nodded. He turned as he walked. Kiyoko quickened her pace and handed him two sheets of paper. One
contained the text of his short announcement, the other,
the agreed questions and answers for the NHK television
crew accredited to the event.

'Ken,' said Sato. 'As soon as we've done this, I will call
Jim West. And you must speak to Chris Pierce. Tell him
the Harushio-class submarines are deployed – one in the
Pacific and one in the Sea of Japan, and that they are
nuclear-armed.'

Yamada's face was impassive. Computer simulation was
now so sophisticated that nuclear testing was merely a
cosmetic act of muscle flexing.

'But what should we do about Oak Ridge?' continued
Sato.

Yamada stopped walking and turned to his Prime
Minister with a frown. 'Do you mean shall we reveal it?'
asked Yamada.

'I am thinking,' said Sato.

'Sir,' whispered Kiyoko, tilting her head at a line of
scientists behind them. Briefly Sato and Yamada edged
against the wall to let them through.

'When asked before, we have denied it,' said Yamada,
once they were out of earshot. 'Do we admit to lying?'

Sato shook his head. 'No, Yamada-san. In order to
obtain results, one can choose from many layers of reve-
lation. But the argument is compelling. In the 1980s, when
the Soviet Union was a major threat to the stability of the
Pacific, the United States exported its nuclear technology
and hardware to Japan. The United States understood that
– at some stage – America's monopoly on security in this
region would have to end, probably because of a challenge

from an unfriendly power with whom it did not want to fight. Whether we see that as North Korea or China, the truth is that moment has now arrived.'

'Cited in a memo from the National Security Council in Washington on 8 December 1983 to our Cabinet Research Office,' added Kiyoko.

'Thank you,' said Sato gently. 'Your detail is impressive, and the date significant. Congress banned the United States' own fast breeder reactor programme in 1983, while we were developing ours at Oarai and later at Monju. The Americans needed us to go ahead with it in order to keep up with their own research.'

'Hence the Oak Ridge decision,' said Yamada.

'Exactly,' agreed Sato.

'This collaboration will allow the United States to maintain a core of expertise—' cited Kiyoko. 'The Oak Ridge National Laboratory Review confidential email in August 1987.'

'The purpose was simply to allow Japan to acquire nuclear weapons before either India or Paksitan declared their own, or before China attempted to test its military resolve. So far, the plan has mostly worked perfectly, and the logic is solid.'

Sato breathed deeply, while Kiyoko brushed his lapels and straightened his tie. 'Do those sound like the words of an elder statesman,' she said with a smile.

Kiyoko moved back, her lips pursed in concentration. She stepped forward again, unbuttoned Sato's coat, slid it off his shoulders and held it up for collection while one of the staff hurried forward to take it. She straightened his jacket. 'Better. Much better,' she murmured, turning to Yamada. 'You, too, Yamada-san. You must both be impervious to the weather.'

'Let's see how Jim West reacts,' said Sato, moving forward again. 'If it gets nasty, we'll Oak Ridge him.' He chuckled at his westernized use of language. He slowed as he rounded the corridor. The flickering orange and red lights of the control room appeared in front of him. He glanced across at Kiyoko and saw that her eyes were apprehensive and excited like those of a child. The wind tunnel created by the pressurized ventilation blew a scrap of paper along the concrete floor. Yamada caught it with his foot, bent down to look at it, was uninterested and handed it to one of the staff. Sato detected something in his manner which while composed also indicated an unsolved problem. Both men knew that the television pictures of Yamada by Sato's side would be the sign that the younger man was being handed the mantle of leadership. Yet, as defence minister, he was about to preside over an action that could pit his nation against both Russia and China.

'Don't worry,' said Sato, reasserting his confidence. 'Jim West will act bruised but he will be relieved. Better to have a well-armed ally than a eunuch.' He handed his documents to Kiyoko and put his hand on Yamada's shoulder. A television camera spotlight hit their faces as they entered the control room together. Technicians, working in a horseshoe at their terminals, stood up, bowed briefly, then returned to their workstations. The television camera stayed focused on the faces of the politicians. Another covered the floor of the control centre. A third simply stayed on the countdown which began at 30 seconds.

On the stroke of zero, down a shaft deep in the ground on an uninhabited military-controlled island fifty miles away, the plutonium atom was split. Seismographs in Lop Nor in China, in Russia, in Australia and on Wake Island in the Pacific picked up the shock waves.

Sato unfolded his brief statement and turned to the television camera. 'Reluctantly and with much thought, Japan has just conducted a limited underground nuclear

test. We made the decision as a direct result of the recent
hostilities carried out by North Korea. These included a
missile attack on the the US airbase at Yokata, near Tokyo,
and the long-range missile launch into the Pacific, after
which the American navy detected a biological weapons
virus. Under such circumstances, I concluded that it would
be unreasonable for Japan – a wealthy and sophisticated
nation – to continue to rely on the United States for our
security.'

Up until now, Sato had been looking professionally into
the camera and reading off the autocue set up for him.
Briefly, he looked away and cast his eyes first at some
distant point beyond the camera, then down to the ground
and finally back into the lens, but with a completely
different expression. He had transformed himself from
detached politician into an old man, vulnerable, squinting
with myopic eyes and uncertain of himself.

'Japan is frightened,' he said. 'Yes, we have done bad
things in the past. But it was long ago. I was barely a child
then and now I am at the end of my years. We are sad and
frightened when we see what happened in Delhi. We are
frightened that missiles are fired over our country and we
can do nothing about it, because our ancestors were
butchers. But we are not butchers. We have shown how as
an American ally we can become a benevolent, economically successful Asian democracy.'

Then, as if by sleight of hand, the master politician
refitted his mask: not vulnerable at all, a national leader
who was determined that his words would be a legacy for
the history books.

'And to my friend President West, to Prime Minister
Nolan, to President Song and President Kozlov, to Prime
Minister Mehta and to all our allies around the world, I
have this to say. The events of recent times have amply
demonstrated what we have all known for some time. That

the days of America fighting wars to protect far-flung places are over. You have made your sacrifices, you have safeguarded this region while we have been able to grow strong and rich. But there comes a time when we have to bid our foster parents farewell and stand on our own. It is up to us to show our maturity.'

52

Washington, DC, USA

'Mr President, Toru Sato wants to speak to you urgently.'

'Sato. Japan,' said West to himself. 'Tell him to—' But he managed to stop himself in time, remembering how Kozlov didn't take his call, and he was now finding out what was happening along with the rest of the world by watching television.

Kozlov was still speaking. 'We have to rebuild Pakistan into a nation which works and which does not threaten. We have to neutralize the threat of North Korea, but also realize the aspirations of the people who live there—'

'I'll take the call,' said West.

'Stuart Nolan is on the other line from London,' said Kozerski.

'Give me Nolan first,' said West, picking up the phone. At least with the British, there was no standing on ceremony. 'Stuart?'

'I'll be quick,' said Nolan. 'First, we must not buckle on this. Their systems stink and their failure is all over the place. Does anyone believe this hogwash? I'll bring Europe into line, Jim. You have my word on this – even if it's my dying word. Second, we have specific human intelligence that the Pakistanis are holding out around the base at Chagai Hills in Baluchistan. This is one of their key nuclear sites. Damned difficult place to fight in. The Russians are bogged down, and they don't have the right kit to bust through. I'll get Charles Colchester to brief Chris Pierce directly. Third, on your agreement, I'm happy to hit Park Ho right now. We have HMS *Vengeance* in the South

China Sea. You might be under conditions from China, but that duplicitous little bastard Song never told *me* not to strike above the fortieth parallel.'

West found himself unexpectedly relieved. With Peter Brock gone, he should have talked to Nolan more often. 'Can you hold, Stuart? I've got to deal with Sato, then I'll be right back.'

He nodded at Kozerski, who put Sato on the line, but in the pause he couldn't help tuning back into the television, where Jamie Song was now talking: 'Look at the statistics of the World Bank which praises China and Cuba above all other countries in their work at poverty alleviation. Those countries living under the post-Cold-War American system of new democracies and IMF loans are simply becoming poorer and poorer – whole swathes of Latin America and Africa are worse off now than when we were fighting the Cold War. Why? Because this bogus system of so-called freedom is a breeding ground for tribalism, corruption and selfish interest groups. In China, we have found another way—'

'Turn it down,' said West to Kozerski, slowly waving his hand to make the point. 'Mr Prime Minister,' he said. 'Thanks for calling.' Out of the corner of his eyes he saw Kozerski signalling him, but it was only after Sato had begun speaking that he understood what his Chief of Staff had been trying to say.

'Mr President,' said Sato stiffly. 'This is a courtesy call. Given the new alliance between China and Russia, we have just conducted an underground nuclear test. Ken Yamada, my defence minister, will be briefing Chris Pierce fully.'

The blood drained out of West's face. 'Sato, for Christ's sake—'

'My nation demands it.' Sato paused awkwardly. 'I'm sorry, Jim. I wish it hadn't come to this. But it has.'

The line went dead. Kozerski, who had been listening

in, looked across and shook his head. 'We were getting seismographic analysis in from Hawaii,' said Kozerski, apologetically.

'Chris, Japan's tested,' said West.

The Defense Secretary, on the phone to the Pentagon, raised a finger in the air. 'Hold, please,' he said, then turned to the President. 'Atmospheric or underground?'

'Underground,' said Kozerski.

Pierce nodded. 'I'll get back to you,' he said, cutting his call and getting up.

Momentarily, West spoke to Nolan. 'Stuart, Japan's just gone nuclear. Can you hold for a couple more minutes?'

'He told us as much at Camp David,' grunted Nolan. 'I'll stay on the line.'

'Do we get Mary over there?' said Pierce. 'And if so, can she do anything?'

West, head lowered, listened to Nolan's acknowledgement, absorbed Pierce's question, and for some reason saw an image of himself with Valerie and Lizzie, walking hand in hand through tall grass one summer in France.

He brought Nolan back across the line. 'An underground test,' he said bluntly.

'Fourteen kilotons,' said Kozerski.

'Fourteen kilotons,' repeated West.

'What are you going to do?'

'I'm bringing Chris Pierce and John Kozerski in on this conversation, Stuart.' West allowed a few seconds for Kozerski to set up the conference call. 'All right, gentlemen, this is what I plan. Any objections or ideas, state them now. Mary stays in Beijing. Her aim is to nail down a new strategic alliance with China, Russia, Japan, India, the US and Europe. We'll send a team out to work with her.

'We describe Japan's tests as "unfortunate, but understandable". We underline the strength of the US–Japan security relationship. Stuart, I would like to take you up on your offer to strike North Korea above the fortieth parallel. Chris, we're going to go in between the fortieth and Pyongyang. Only the nuclear facilities and launch sites. Seal them off. And I want to strike the Chagai Hills in Pakistan, if we can stand up Stuart's human intelligence. Give Kozlov and Song enough warning to get their men out.'

53

London, UK

A screen slid up from the floor at the end of the Cabinet table in Downing Street. It concealed the whole wall behind it, and as it flickered on it divided itself into four squares, each settling into a different picture. Stuart Nolan's Foreign Secretary was on his way to Asia. The Defence Secretary was at the command headquarters in Northwood in a north London suburb. Nolan had just spoken to the prime ministers of Australia, New Zealand, Singapore and Malaysia, advising them of what he was doing.

'The screen on the top left is the camera inside HMS *Vengeance*,' explained Colchester. 'You will see the joint keys which the captain uses with the chief engineer to confirm your orders. On the bottom left is the image of the surface of the South China Sea through which the two missiles will break, courtesy of military satellites being relayed through NIMA in Washington. On the top right is one of the bases in North Korea. We'll switch it to black and white in order to get sharper resolution. On the bottom left is satellite imagery of the Chagai Hills. There is cloud moving in there, but a Global Hawk unmanned aircraft has been deployed, so the image might switch to that. If everything goes to plan, North Korea will be hit within one minute of the strike on the Chagai Hills.'

Nolan nodded. He was trying to find the right thoughts for this moment, but none came. He had not consulted Parliament. He had not notified the monarch. He had not called in the Cabinet. To have done any of those things would have been to delay and possibly postpone until it was too late.

'Let's do it,' he said. 'Send out the press release.' As Colchester took his seat beside Nolan, the Downing Street press statement was flashed on the screen as it was emailed to thousands of news outlets around the world. 'Following consultations with members, Britain and its allies in the Five Power Defence Agreement – which protects stability in South-East Asia – have declared war on the Democratic People's Republic of Korea.'

At exactly the same time, Nolan watched as the captain and chief engineer of HMS *Vengeance* each turned a key. Then the captain pressed the button for the launch. On the screen below, crystal-clear blue water swelled, creating a circle of white froth, which heaved upwards. Two ballistic missiles burst through, seemed to hover for a split second in indecision, then flared skywards towards North Korea.

The screen on the bottom left went blank. 'Cloud cover,' said Colchester quietly. Slowly it became grey. Then, just as more distinct contours of the Chagai Hills appeared, they vanished as quickly again.

'Thermobaric explosives,' continued Colchester. 'Pierce is carpet-bombing the place with them. It's about as close as you can get to a nuclear attack without actually going nuclear.'

Nolan walked closer to the screen, squinting to get a closer look. The picture jumped. The Global Hawk must have been buffeted in the turbulence. 'How high is it?' he asked.

Colchester glanced at a separate monitor displaying data by the telephone. 'Seventeen thousand feet, and holding it,' he said. He pointed to another section of the screen. 'Over there.'

The image over North Korea was more distant but

more stable. Colchester used the remote to split the screen into two again.

'Can't see a damn thing,' said Nolan.

'On the left is foliage,' said Colchester. 'On the right the side of a mountain. A lot of snow there.'

The smoke of two explosions slowly filled the screens like sprays of white salt, sending them into flickering whiteness, before revealing the black cloud that covered the satellite's view.

'Right,' said Colchester, unfolding a map and spreading it on the table. 'That was a confirmed hit on Chunggang-up, the base from which the smallpox missile was launched. And the second,' he paused, checking the data monitor, which was feeding information directly from the National Security Agency at Fort Meade to Menwith Hill in Yorkshire, then through a fibre-optic cable to London and Downing Street, 'yes, and the second confirmed hit is on Kanggamchan.'

'Still can't see a damn thing,' said Nolan. The success of the strikes and the varnished glare of the imagery left an empty feeling in him. He stared at the screen, trying to see victory, but instead found disappointment. He knew the phone was not about to ring with Park Ho's surrender.

'It takes a couple of minutes,' said Colchester, as ever fascinated by the technical. 'We'll be getting an integrated picture – that's a composite of images from satellites, unmanned vehicles and the fighters which have just been scrambled.'

'Park would be in Pyongyang, wouldn't he?' muttered Nolan to himself. 'That's where I'd be.'

'The Americans have launched on Kanggye now,' said Colchester. 'Thermobaric carpet-bombing. Twenty thousand work underground there. If they penetrate the mountain, they will have crippled his war machine.'

After the heated airlessness of underground bunkers the cold night air smelt good. Light snow fell and brought with it a silence. So different from rain. The night was frozen and black. He had wanted to see the stars, so he had ordered the street lights to be turned off.

Park Ho walked alone through a Pyongyang that would soon be engulfed in war. He headed for the river and pulled his collar up against the wind. The water was cold and black but flowed serenely, rippling with gusts of wind and reflecting the torch from the top of the Tower of Juche. It created a play of light and flame which captivated Park Ho, despite the chill of the night.

He was an intelligent man, but his life had always been at odds with his nation's place in the world. Koreans in the north starved. In the south, they were wealthy. But did that mean he should surrender his nation to the more successful system – the one that had killed his mother? When he had watched the pictures from Delhi, Park Ho accepted that Ahmed Memed had more courage than him. Memed had given him his resolve. His empathy for Delhi was blunted because his own country was under threat. Purposefully, as he walked around the monuments of Pyongyang that night, Park Ho reinforced himself with uncomplicated motives – a hunger for his own success and revenge for his mother's death.

A corner of the night sky changed colour, and soon dawn would come. Park Ho came to the monument of the Great Leader, where wreaths of flowers dampened by the night lay beneath bronze arms stretched out to protect all the people around him.

His expression was serene, showing no remorse, no expectation, nor was there any sign of moral purpose. By the time he opened the door at the foot of the statue, Park Ho had rid himself of all those issues.

He stepped inside and took the lift down three levels. They were expecting him, of course. For however alone he was, he was always watched.

'Get me President Song of China,' he commanded.

When Jamie Song came on the line, Park Ho recognized the voice of a defeated man.

In the morning, Park drove to the airport. It was a clear day, the clouds blown away by wind from the south, meaning that America's spy cameras would be watching from the sky. He stood by the aircraft as Ahmed Memed walked out of the terminal building. They embraced, Park in his uniform, Memed in his white robe. The cleric climbed the steps, looked back and waved. Park Ho stayed on the runway until the aircraft had taken off and set its course for China.

55

Kabul, Afghanistan

A white United Nations Russian-made helicopter landed
at Bagram airbase near Kabul in Afghanistan, staying on
the ground just long enough for a single passenger to
climb out and get into a waiting UN Land Cruiser. Dressed
in a light-green down jacket, the hood up, denim jeans
and leather walking boots, the passenger checked his
British passport that identified him as Robert Vines. His
accompanying papers were copies of his contract with the
United Nations Development Programme and a letter
stating that he was taking home leave.

The Land Cruiser dropped Vines at Kabul's international
terminal, where he was given a boarding pass in the premier
economy class cabin of a British Airways flight to London,
ensuring that air miles were credited to his account.

At Heathrow, he checked into the Hilton Hotel near
Terminal 4, under the name of Michel Juliet, travelling on
a French passport that had been issued in Lyon. He stayed
in the room for five hours, meeting the same man twice.
That afternoon, using Michel Juliet's passport with a matching green card, he travelled economy class on Virgin Atlantic to New York and took a cab to the Paramount Hotel
near Times Square where a suite was booked for him under
the name of William Thomas, an American from Los Angeles.

At each stage of the journey Hassan Muda destroyed
the documents of his previous identity.

Of all the hotels around Times Square, the Paramount
would be the most difficult in which to identify a face. He
had chosen it because the lobby was dark, lit only by dim

wall lights and candles. His suite was small and run down, but it did have two rooms in which he could work.

On the upper shelf of the wardrobe, underneath a spare blanket, Muda found a suitcase. Hanging the 'Do Not Disturb' sign on the handle, he double locked the door, closed the bedroom door, double locked that, lifted down the suitcase and opened it.

The contents were packed exactly as he had instructed.

He took out the NBC suit but put it to one side unopened, together with the respirator. He tested the bed, happy that it was firm enough, and laid the specially tailored Gore-tex waistcoat on it, opening up both sides. He took a strip of Semtex-H plastic explosive and slipped it into a polythene bag. Then he pressed a tiny electric detonator into the explosive, ran a wire outside the bag and attached it to a nine-volt battery which he slipped into a left inside pocket of the waistcoat. He cut open the lining of his own jacket and took out a wafer-thin plastic phial which he taped into a lower inside pocket of the waistcoat.

He repeated the whole process exactly for the right side of the waistcoat and finally cross-duplicated the detonators on to the batteries in case one failed. He folded the waistcoat, put it back into the suitcase and locked it. He checked the aerosol canisters at the bottom of the suitcase and left them sealed by his bedside.

Hassan Muda prayed.

Before going to sleep, he brought out another phial, opened a sealed packet containing a hypodermic needle and syringe, filled it and injected himself with the virus variola major.

When he woke in the morning, he had a slight fever, but not bad enough to stop him catching the train to Philadelphia, then Washington. By the time he was flying back to New York and going through at La Guardia, he had discarded his aerosol canisters.

56

Beijing, China

For Jamie Song, this was nothing less than a struggle for China's life. It was fierce and silent, being played out through satellite images, secure phone calls and in those shadows that had always lured his country towards its own destruction.

'Why?' he had asked Park Ho, when the unexpected call came through.

'Why not?' Park had responded. Historians would draw their own conclusions, but for the moment Song could think of no two words to describe more accurately what Park Ho was doing. He could, so he would.

'Because you will destroy us,' Song had said lamely.

'Only if you surrender.'

Park had ended the call. Now Song looked across the room to Yan, whose hand was on a telephone, about to pick it up. Two of Yan's guards stood at the entrance. Outside, the ice on the lake was gone, but the water was still thick with melting snow. The waiting cars were unfamiliar, the drivers and number plates from another military unit.

Yet there was tranquillity in the room. The murky shifts of allegiance among China's ruling elite were being played out somewhere on the end of Yan's telephone line.

'They won't accept it,' said Yan. 'I cannot persuade them otherwise. Neither can you.'

Song had no secrets. They knew what he stood for; had always stood for. The confusion lay with them. 'Why then did they give me the presidency?' he asked. 'They knew about Park Ho. They knew about Pakistan. What has changed?'

Yan did not answer. He was the conduit whom Song had hired, the loyal protector, fulfilling his role to the last before receiving accolades from the other side for a job well done.

'You will retain all your posts,' said Yan. 'Once these events have settled, your power will be restored.'

'To do what?'

'You are a peacetime leader,' said Yan. Without stating it, Yan was offering his sympathies.

'Do they want war?' Some did. But did they all? Surely not Yan? Surely not those who knew the missiles were not perfected; that the navy could not deploy and extend; that the pilots did not have enough training hours? So who wanted a war that would stall trade and growth?

'Give me one last shot,' said Song.

'To achieve what?' asked Yan, the negotiator.

'No territory has been seized. If anything, we have gained Pakistan.'

'You'll speak to West?'

'I'll speak to Newman. She is here. If it stops here, we will accept it. We stabilized Pakistan. They sought retribution in North Korea.'

'Above the fortieth parallel – against your express wishes.'

'We'll take it on the chin,' said Song. 'We're big enough.'

Yan began shaking his head, his brow furrowed in confusion. 'I will tell them,' he said. But as he picked up the receiver to make the call, another telephone rang, not from an office within Zhongnanhai but from China's central command and control centre in the Western Hills just outside Beijing.

Yan listened briefly. 'We may be too late,' he said, handing the receiver to Jamie Song.

Air conditioning hummed through the control room, bringing with it the stench of drainage. The space was smaller than anyone would have imagined, circular rooms with corridors appearing to lead nowhere, with ceilings impossibly low, the temperature, lights and ventilation as erratic as the generators which powered them. The food was becoming inedible and Vasant Mehta, a soldier trained in the Himalayas and the Rajasthan desert, was feeling helpless and depressed.

Since the Chinese–Russian attacks on Pakistan, then the American thermobaric bombing, he had been in limbo.

The commander-in-chief in him demanded that he be patient and stay in the bunker. The politician in him needed to be above ground amid the debris of his capital city. And should he be lynched by survivors, so be it. For he deserved it.

The father in him wanted to be in Washington, with his daughter Meenakshi, her life saved not by him but by the Americans. He couldn't even hope to speak to her in private, for every line in and out of the bunker was monitored. Military psychologists would have been having a field day analysing the mood swings of the first head of government since 1945 to have his nation struck by a nuclear weapon.

Meenakshi was in Washington, staying in the White House residence with Lizzie West, delivered safely there by Lazaro Campbell. Yet when Mehta asked to speak to him to thank him, Campbell was out of touch and somewhere else altogether. Romila had flown up from Argentina, and even Geeta had made an appearance, snatching the phone from Meenakshi, so that she could talk to her estranged husband. How proud she was of him; how she had always believed in him; how the three of them missed him so much. He let her talk, without responding or committing.

Mehta had even taken a conference call with Meenakshi, Lizzie, and West to find a line to destroy Jamie Song's argument which had so powerfully blamed democracy for causing poverty.

'Dad, if you're going to win this, you have to concede something,' Lizzie West had argued. 'Not on democracy, but on the international banking system and on commodity trading.'

'If I concede a damn thing – whether rightly or wrongly – I'm defeated,' said West. 'What I need is proof that he is full of bullshit.'

'Then talk about the human spirit, Mr President,' said Meenakshi.

'What about it?'

'Well,' and she drew a deep breath, 'I have worked both in Bihar in India and in Gansu in western China. Both are poverty-stricken. But in Gansu the government controls everything, even how many children are born. In Bihar, in the most appalling conditions, they still feel they have the right to speak out and make decisions.' Meenakshi's voice had become emotional. 'The thing is, Mr President, if you take away people's minds, they *do* lose everything. There is no happiness. You tell Jamie Song that we, in India, tried their methods in the 1970s and they failed. And if China ever becomes a shining beacon of the arts, of science, literature and music, with world-class highways, hospitals, schools and skyscrapers, then he can boast. But it is not now, and I believe it never will be, because at some stage the human spirit comes into conflict with the power that wants to control it. Our system – and your system, Mr President – allows for the growth of the human spirit. In China, it does not, and when there is conflict it will break the country in two.'

'You got that, Dad?' asked Lizzie bluntly. 'And if you need it, I'll get you the statistics to prove it.'

'Thanks, Meenakshi,' agreed West. 'Vasant, we'll hold on to your daughter for a while, if you don't mind. I think I've just appointed her presidential adviser.'

Mehta had found himself choking with pride, but laughing at the same time. The strangest thing was that no one mentioned Delhi. The conversation could have taken place before the nuclear strike had happened. Nor had they talked about the American bombing of Pakistan's missile sites in the Chagai Hills. Their own human spirit prevented them from lingering over even the recent past and propelled them forward towards a solution – until Deepak Suri cut harshly into the conversation.

Mehta turned. His Chief of Defence Staff, unshaven, his uniform stained and unwashed, stood up, signalled to his aide-de-camp at a computer terminal and raised a forefinger towards Mehta. 'They've launched,' he said. Mehta heard him both from his earpiece and from across the room.

'Vasant?' queries West.

'One second,' said Mehta abruptly.

'Eleven minutes to impact,' said Suri, his tone composed. 'Four, sorry, six missiles—'

'Warheads?'

'Don't know.'

The nod which Mehta gave to Suri was barely perceptible, and he gave it instead of a verbal command so that West would not hear. Suri turned fractionally and with the same forefinger gesture passed the command on to his aide-de-camp, who spoke into his mouthpiece, while repeating the instruction into the computer.

'Vasant? Vasant?' pressed West, the tension showing in his voice.

'Mumbai, Trombay, Pune, Bangalore, Chennai, Goa – first estimates,' said Suri.

But did it matter? Mehta asked himself. As a functioning society, India was finished. It would recreate itself, but for the immediate future it would be engulfed in tragedy.

'Vasant?'

'Yes, Jim,' said Mehta softly. 'Your intervention did not work. They launched and we have responded.'

'No.' It was almost a cry of anguish from the American President. 'No. Wait.'

'We did wait, Jim,' said Mehta. 'We waited after our Parliament was attacked, my house destroyed, my capital city destroyed. I think we waited too long.' His voice was distant as if he was talking to an unknown power somewhere far away, and that Jim West just happened to be the person closest.

'Karachi and Hyderabad are targeted by missile and submarine launches,' said Suri. 'Multan, Islamabad, Rawalpindi, Sarghoda and Peshawar. Islamabad and Rawalpindi will be the first hit. ETA eight minutes thirty.'

'Meenakshi, are you there?' said Mehta.

'Yes, Father.'

'We will not see each other again,' he said. 'You are now under the protection of Jim West. I love you more than anything, and on this terrible, terrible day, I can only see one ray of hope – that you are in America and not here.'

'I'm coming out. I'll be needed—'

'You are not,' said Mehta. 'It will not finish here.' No one, including him, could even imagine what would be left of India in half an hour's time. 'Jim, are you hearing this?'

'I'm here, Vasant.'

'My daughters are under your protection. Ensure they receive protection as if they were your own family.'

'ETA Mumbai four minutes twenty,' said Suri.

58

Moscow, Russia

'President Song is unavailable,' said Alexander Yushchuk, frowning when Kozlov simply tilted his head in response. The Russian President watched his daughter, whom he could see through the door, and whose cello music filled the small study. Satellite images of nuclear clouds over India and Pakistan were being relayed on a screen that Yushchuk had rigged up above his desk. Yushchuk was about to say something else, when BBC and CNN, showing on two separate sets, almost simultaneously, broke into their programmes and switched to the same pictures.

Kozlov had no idea what Ekatarina was playing. He had never been much good with music. Her boyfriend, his uniform neatly pressed and his boots polished, sat bewitched across the room, smoking. He was a confused young man from the army, an engineer whose bland practicality soothed Ekatarina. He had a military mind, yet tried to be an intellectual to impress her father, and Kozlov was not sure if he liked him; not sure if any father liked his daughter's first boyfriend. If Russia became like India, he would send them into the bunker together, so he could die knowing they would give him a grandchild.

He glanced at the screens, where there was so much destruction, all looking so much the same, that the thought of a kicking baby in Ekatarina's womb made him feel good.

'Get me Jim West, then,' he said softly.

Yushchuk pressed a button. 'Actually, *he*'s calling you right now.'

Kozlov stood up and kicked the door to close it. He caught Ekaterina's eye and noticed fleeting disappointment. A note faltered before she found sanctuary in the music sheet. Through the gap, as the door closed, Kozlov blew a kiss and smiled at her.

'Jim,' he said in English, giving the American President no time to initiate the conversation. 'The only useful thing you can do right now is make sure that Japan does nothing. If you have to make a statement, keep it bland. Do not respond; do not react; and do not threaten. I hope you understand perfectly what I am saying.'

'We need to talk properly—'

'No, Jim. We need to *think* properly. You chose to strike Pakistan. Nolan, with your blessing, struck North Korea. And this is what has happened. If Jamie Song has lost control in China, you are headed into a big war. And I have treaty obligations with China that would set Russia against the United States.'

59

Tokyo, Japan

'The only disaster we are equipped to deal with is an earthquake,' said Kiyoko, as Prime Minister Sato's disguised limousine edged through the Tokyo traffic. Sato rested his hand on her elbow but looked away, out of the tinted glass on to the teeming streets. After the tests, he had felt not exhilarated as he had expected but exceedingly tired, and he wanted to sleep for a very long time.

The later explosions over India and Pakistan had been picked up by satellites, even by passengers with video cameras on airliners not yet rerouted. Flaming red, encircled by grey and black and enveloped in the deep blue, stretched above the curve of the earth like a farewell banner.

'Start the broadcasts,' he said. He felt the shift of Kiyoko's arm as she concentrated on her telephone. He slid his window down a little. Bland music played from speakers in the streets. Then it stopped and a calm voice said: 'This is an emergency. Please go home. Close your businesses, go home and await further instructions.'

The pace on the street slowed. Heads tilted up to hear the message again. Confirmation was sought. The young found refuge in their mobile phones. The middle-aged, with families to protect, walked purposefully towards the nearest subway station. The elderly were reflective. A woman cried. A man dropped his walking stick and squatted on the cold pavement, his eyes looking far away. An old couple stopped, their faces worked over by the years, but their eyes as expressive as children's, while they heard the message for the third time. They embraced, clasped like statues, their age bringing a stillness to the street.

This was the generation that would have remembered Hiroshima and Nagasaki. They had lived through the firebombing of Tokyo. They were not the ones who had set Sato on the path to free Japan from its ties with America. Sato saw now, so clearly, that anyone who had lived through a nuclear attack would not care who ran their lives as long as they were safe. But they were not his constituents.

Kiyoko passed him the telephone. 'It is the White House,' she said gently.

Sato shook his head. 'Park Ho will launch on us,' he said. 'Jim West will tell me to do nothing. But I cannot do nothing, so we have nothing to discuss.'

They rode in silence. He looked up and saw they were at the corner of Hakumi-dori and Hibaya-dori, a junction dominated by the building from where General Douglas MacArthur ruled Japan after the Second World War. The driver turned north along Hibiya-dori into the Marunou-chi district, the home turf of corporate Japan. What had happened to the glory days of the 1980s, when the names of Mitsui, Mitsubishi and Sony were the national flags of Japan's success? Since the seventeenth century Tokyo's commercial capital had been in the east of the city, but after the firebombing it had been rebuilt in Marunouchi, with wide streets and square, squat buildings.

Where would they rebuild it after this, wondered Sato. Kiyoko touched him on the elbow. He turned to her. He loved her, yet she was a stranger to him. He had asked if she wanted to go to safety. She had refused, and although the mantle was with Yamada, she had chosen to be with him, and he was grateful. The telephone call was from Yamada, but Sato did not need to take it. Yamada had his orders: he was to see the war through until a Japanese victory – whatever the cost.

Sato took in the sharp smells from outside, tobacco smoke and petrol fumes, then slid the window up. If he was doubtful, Kiyoko's eyes were cool and directly on him. There was an unmovable calmness in them.

He touched her hand, and Kiyoko relayed the message back to Japan's Defence Minister.

By trying to play God and change the shape of Japan, had Sato brought about its destruction? But if it had remained as it was now, entrapped by America, it would have become a slowly dying nation, bereft of ideas and a future.

Kiyoko closed the telephone. She took his hand. 'Don't try to judge,' she said softly. 'It has happened.'

Across the road, Sato saw the line of cypress trees and the wall that marked the boundary of the Imperial Palace. The moat was serene and flat, and he watched in it the orange reflection of the sky lighting up with a flash and the ripples gently spreading out.

He had seen Delhi. He knew what would happen. Sato tasted something bitter in the back of his throat.

60

Zamyn-uud, southern Mongolia

Wind whipped up the sand into such a swirl that it was impossible to see across the runway. Even guarded from the worst gusts by huddling behind the undercarriage of the Osprey, Lazaro Campbell had difficulty hearing the instructions from Kozerski in the White House.

After the nuclear attack on Tokyo, China's airspace had been closed to foreign traffic. The temperature at the airstrip in the Mongolian border town of Zamyn-uud was fifteen below zero. Wind speeds fluctuated between nothing and sixty miles an hour, tearing the covers off the engine cowlings and forcing frozen sand into everything. Campbell's face carried a dozen tiny cuts and was now wrapped in a scarf, his eyes protected by goggles.

'Tokyo's gone,' he heard Kozerski say in his earpiece. 'No one's picking up the phone in Beijing. The British and Japanese embassies—' A gust sent a roar around the plane. The pilot and engineer were in the cockpit with the engines running to keep out the sand.

'John, hold. Just hold,' yelled Campbell. He ran against the wind. The sand hit him like driving rain. He reached a concrete hut, kicked open the door and fell inside to a sudden quiet. 'Right,' he said, catching his breath. 'Keep speaking. I got to the British and Japanese embassies.'

'Have been torched,' said Kozerski. 'In the case of the British, an APC turned up with a flame-thrower and cannon. They aimed to kill and they succeeded.'

Campbell squatted on the bare floor of the hut. He spotted a gas ring, a kettle, even an open sachet of instant coffee on a wooden table. Pierce had wanted him to go in from Seoul, but that was a 600-mile flight to Beijing, hitting Chinese airspace at Dalian. Campbell had vetoed the plan. Instead he had brought the Osprey into the Mongolian capital, Ulan Bator, in a C-130 transport plane, flying through Russian airspace. The Osprey then easily handled the 400 miles down to Zamyn-uud on the border. With extra fuel tanks, and a light load, with just Campbell, a navigator and a pilot, it could just make the round trip of 600 miles to Beijing.

'And we think they haven't gone for our embassy because the Secretary of State is in there. Most important goddamn hostage I can ever remember.'

'And my orders?' pressed Campbell, knowing the satellite line might cut out at any time.

'You get her out, Lazaro. If we cut a deal on your way down, fine. If we don't, go to the embassy and lift her.'

'Soon as we're airborne, the SU-27s will be scrambled and we'll be sliced into pieces.' The one thing Campbell hated was saying that a job would be dangerous or impossible. But unless he had missed something, that was exactly what would happen.

'The President's on the line to Kozlov to get you safe passage. Soon as that's done, we want you in the air.'

Campbell didn't ask why Kozlov was suddenly to be giving him protection over China. The satellite line was too fragile for irrelevant questions.

Five minutes later, Kozerski called again with clearance. The Osprey's twin engines roared, sending the sand into a cloud around it. Campbell pushed shut the door and locked it. The sand and dust obscured everything, forcing the pilot to switch to instruments. The Osprey took off as a fixed-wing aircraft and that was how the pilot would keep it until they reach Beijing. Campbell checked his weapons: a Browning 9mm pistol; a Heckler and Koch

MP5 semi-automatic; two shrapnel grenades, and two CS gas and two stun grenades.

The screen in front of him, illuminated by a forward-looking infrared display, revealed the bleak, brown desert countryside below as clearly as if it was a bright day with a cloudless sky. Satellite pictures showed military vehicles in central Beijing, the ruins of the Japanese and British embassies, and the main thoroughfares around Tiananmen Square clogged with people.

Up ahead, four Chinese air force SU-27 fighter aircraft fell into formation around the Osprey. They made no attempt at radio contact. Campbell heard the Osprey pilot notify the AWACs plane which acted as their control tower and was flying at 50,000 feet above the ground.

Campbell called Kozerski. 'We have an escort.'

'Hostile?'

'Not yet,' said Campbell. 'They'll let us in. But why should they let us out and lose the technology of the Osprey?'

'I don't have an answer to that,' said Kozerski. 'Like I don't have an answer to most things right now.'

They were flying at 283 knots. Arrival time over the US embassy in Beijing would be in seventy-three minutes' time, thirty minutes after nightfall.

61

Washington, DC, USA

'**Campbell will be** there in an hour,' said Kozerski, finishing the call.

'Have you got Sato yet?' asked West.

'Sato's dead. He stayed above ground in Tokyo,' said Pierce. 'Just hold a moment, Mr President—'

West turned to Kozerski. 'Is Kozlov still on the line?'

'The line's open. I can get him.'

'Is he in Beijing or Moscow?'

'Just back in Moscow, sir.'

'Japan's launched on North Korea,' said Pierce. 'A 20-kiloton nuclear warhead, airburst above Pyongyang at 2,000 feet.'

For a stunned moment, there was complete silence in the Oval Office.

'One launch?' asked West softly. An old saying came to mind. After the first time, the rest is easy. Amid the confusion and hard facts, a cold truth was coming out. How could he blame Sato? He would do the same, if one of his cities was hit. Only Mehta had shown self-control. And for that he had lost.

'President Cho from Seoul,' said Kozerski.

'Hold him for a couple of seconds,' said West. 'Chris, we have to go in across the DMZ. Now.'

'Our troops?' Pierce looked sharply at the President.

'They're fighting a war. They'll do fine. John, put Cho on.'

'Don't hit them, Mr President. Or they're going to hit us. Let it settle. We're emptying Seoul. I can't go nuclear

on the border because the fucking wind's blowing south.'
Cho sounded desparate.

'We're going in,' said West calmly. 'We have treaty
obligations with you and with Japan.'

'Fuck. No—'

'Cho, we've got to draw a line on this. It'll be fine.'

62

Beijing, China

In one earpiece, Campbell listened to commentary from the Pentagon; in the other, he was on the intercom to the pilot. As they came in over the northern suburbs of Beijing, the SU-27 escorts peeled away. The pilot of the lead aircraft gave a thumbs-up.

'Good luck, Osprey,' he said in English, breaking radio silence. 'Hope to see you on the way out.'

'Identification of armoured vehicles in the diplomatic quarter,' came the voice from the Pentagon. 'Units outside the British and Japanese embassies are loyal to the Second Artillery Regiment. Unit unknown. Units at the US embassy belong to the Zhongnanhai presidential security detail.'

The Osprey, flying at only 300 feet, slowed as it approached the centre of Beijing. Strangely, the neon signs flashing on the top of the buildings were symbols of American capitalism. Campbell took in Kenwood, Ford and Motorola, before becoming distracted by a glow in a side street like a bonfire suspended above the ground. He punched in the GPS coordinates so he could get a closer look from the satellite imagery. As the image settled, he checked it against what he saw outside and realized that two bodies had been strung from lampposts and set on fire.

Further along, columns of military vehicles moved towards Tiananmen Square.

'What's that in Tiananmen Square?' he asked the Pentagon.

'Still checking, sir. We believe they are tanks and APCs loyal to the Second Artillery Unit.'

'Shit!' said Campbell to himself. 'Take her up,' he instructed the pilot.

He pulled on his night-vision helmet. The landscape of central Beijing was transformed into a deep transparent green.

Two lines of military vehicles faced each other in Tiananmen Square itself. A single tank blockaded the entrances to Zhongnanhai. Four more were at the steps of the Great Hall of the People.

'Head for the embassy, and switch to horizontal rotors,' Campbell instructed the pilot.

The pilot brought up the Osprey's nose and in ten seconds transformed it into a twin-engined helicopter. 'Keep her steady,' said Campbell. With the aircraft hovering, he pulled open the door to get a better sense of what was going on.

The US embassy itself appeared untouched. But it was surrounded by a civilian crowd. They were bundled up against the night cold, warming themselves at flaming braziers and encircling the compound. Converging on the embassy from two directions were six – possibly eight – armoured personnel carriers. The sky itself was clear of aircraft, indicating that the power struggle was confined to a few units within the army. The air force would swing once a victor emerged.

'Stay back,' Campbell instructed the pilot. 'And take her up.'

'Lazaro, Kozerski here.' A voice in his other earpiece.

'Go ahead,' said Campbell. The Osprey kept climbing. So far, the crowd hadn't noticed it and Campbell wanted to keep it that way. When he went in, it would be sharp and fast.

'Just the Secretary of State,' he said. 'We're watching the pictures here.'

'It could go any way.'

'Correct. And the President wants the Secretary of State out of the embassy *before* the marines have to begin defending it.'

'You talking to anyone?'

'Negative. Kozlov arranged your air cover. But I don't reckon anyone has control of what's down on the ground there.'

'Wheeled armoured vehicles,' said Campbell, 'approaching the embassy from two sides. Six in all, maybe eight. You got anything on that?'

'Type 90s. Nine troops in each, plus crew,' said the voice from the Pentagon. 'You could be looking at fifty to a hundred men against you.'

The armoured personnel carriers, sealed down, no commander in sight, stopped at the edge of the crowd.

'As soon as you are overhead,' said Kozerski, 'the Secretary of State will come out of the embassy building into the garden at the back of the building. She will be moving in the middle of a six-man marine unit. We'll leave it up to you how you get her into the Osprey. Once on board, head north and you'll pick up your SU-27 escort.'

The Osprey pilot gave a thumbs-up. Campbell clipped himself on to the winch.

The aircraft's nose dipped, but the pilot maintained altitude, bringing the Osprey directly over the embassy. From the corner of the compound, there was a flash from one of the armoured vehicles.

'7.62mm machine gun,' said the Pentagon. 'If they get serious, they'll use the 25mm cannon.'

The crowd scattered. The armoured vehicles pushed through, crushing some as they went, and drew up outside the gate.

The pilot brought the aircraft down rapidly. The navigator primed the Osprey's weapons. Cannon from the armoured car smashed into the compound wall. A guard-house caught fire. A flare shot into the sky, lighting up the compound and the building.

The backs of the armoured vehicles opened. Commandos jumped out and fired scaling ropes at the walls.

'They're going in.' It wasn't Kozerski's voice, nor did it come from the Pentagon. Must have been another agency.

'Permission to defend the embassy?' The voice of the navigator, who could have cut down the Chinese troops.

'Denied.' Pierce's voice now, cutting across the line.

The Osprey was at fifty feet. The pilot slowed the descent. A searchlight beam swept across the compound, picked out Mary Newman, running across the garden, her marine escort surrounding her. It stayed on her. From somewhere from outside the wall came a sharp crack, and a marine fell. Campbell heard the shouting of orders and then the rhythmic thumping of a machine gun.

A marine sniper on the roof opened fire. The searchlight wobbled and went out. The pilot edged the Osprey down further. Even on rotor blades, the aircraft was never quite a helicopter. If the pilot descended too quickly without any forward speed the aircraft could roll and stall.

Campbell lowered himself down on the winch cable, unhooked himself from it and turned to fit it on to Newman. But she was being bundled back into the embassy building. A machine gun started up again in a series of five-round bursts that went on and on, breaking up the concrete in the courtyard and smashing ornaments in the garden.

Outside the wall was a scattering of single shots. From inside came flashes and sharper cracks from the marine guards.

Campbell could see Newman as a silhouetted shadow. He began to beckon her. But there was too much open ground. The beam of another searchlight cut across the lawn, wavering in the hand of a Chinese soldier on the wall, covered by withering fire directed towards the embassy building. An armoured vehicle broke through the gate. Campbell smelt the choking odour of tear gas. He watched Newman's silhouette shift slightly towards him, then a voice, louder even than the gunfire, called to her, and she disappeared into the darkness.

'I'm staying on the ground,' he told the pilot. 'Take her up. Take out the APCs. All six of them. Put a line of fire down on the wall. Then come back and get us.'

'Kozerski?' queried the pilot, referring to the White House orders.

'My authority overrules his,' snapped Campbell.

The roar of the Osprey engines created a cloud of dust from the massive 38-foot rotor blades, giving Campbell the cover he needed to run to the embassy building. The searchlight swept from side to side. Campbell pressed himself against the wall of the embassy, moving as far as possible into the building's shadow.

'Campbell?'

He turned. Mary Newman was sitting on the ground, ringed by marine guards. An armoured vehicle crawled towards them, knocking over the flagpole. The Stars and Stripes floated down, draping itself over the back. Just behind it, the embassy wall gave way and another armoured vehicle, covered in white concrete dust and other debris, appeared.

'Get back,' shouted Campbell.

The Osprey's weapons system opened up with a speed that surprised even Campbell. A ball of flame erupted against the lead armoured vehicle. Simultaneously, the vehicle which had broken through the wall was stopped. Four more air-to-surface missiles destroyed those outside the gates, while machine-gun fire cut down Chinese troops moving into the compound. As the Osprey turned, it dropped a flare to illuminate the terrain, then an air-burst canister of thick pink smoke, through which Campbell and Newman were to run.

Campbell grabbed hold of Newman's arm and pushed them both flat against the wall. She held his wrist so tightly that he felt her fingernails dig into his flesh. On the other side of the compound there was a mortar explosion. The Osprey was seventy-five feet off the ground and descending. Campbell ran, pulling Newman with him. He smelt burning. Another mortar. Then a third into the embassy itself.

It was too dangerous for the Osprey to land. It was as low as it could get. The back ramp was down. The winch cable swung back and forth, blown in the gale of the Osprey's intense rotor downwash. Campbell jumped and caught it. Newman stumbled towards him, and tripped. Campbell took her in his arms and lifted her into the harness.

Then a hand clasped him from behind, pulling him back. A Chinese soldier clung to Campbell's elbow with one hand and waved a pistol at him with the other. Campbell recognized the type. He was the man you sent out to kill, who did it well and enjoyed it, a good soldier, but slightly mad.

'Take her up,' said Campbell to the pilot. He let go of Newman, swinging in the harness. As the aircraft lifted, the soldier gained confidence. The orders must have been to take Campbell alive. He thrust the barrel of his gun into Campbell's chest.

Other soldiers were running towards him. Campbell took a hard look at his captor, then yelled out and knocked the soldier's gun up. Campbell fell to the ground, groped, plucked out the Browning, fired three shots into the soldier's head and neck and stumbled to his feet.

Machine-gun fire from the embassy building covered him from the pursuing Chinese soldiers. A smoke canister burst overhead and he heard the Osprey's rotor blades again. He jumped and caught the winch cable, clipping it on to his belt just as the pilot jerked him off the ground. Campbell crawled inside and suddenly, amid the judder of the fuselage and the noise of the engine, he felt warm and safe.

He lay back, feeling the surge of extra speed as the pilot tilted the rotors to fixed wing.

'You OK?' asked Newman, leaning over him. Due to the engine noise he could only read her lips.

'I'm fine,' he panted. He pushed himself up, unhooked two headsets and showed her how to fit one on.

'Pakistan launched again on India, and India has retaliated,' she said, looking not at Campbell but out of the window at the scenes below. 'Japan has hit Pyongyang with 20 kilotons,' she said. 'We're attacking across the DMZ into the north.'

Campbell, next to her, put his face to the window, too, and saw fires burning below. The higher they got, the more Chinese troops were in sight, converging on the centre of Beijing. The embassy was surrounded. How long did those inside have left to live?

The Osprey, built to carry twenty-four troops, appeared cruelly empty.

63

Washington, DC, USA

'**They're clear**,' announced Kozerski, pulling off his telephone headset and wiping perspiration from his brow.

'Thank God,' said West. To have lost Mary Newman to a Chinese mob would have been too much for him to bear. That he had sent her there in the first place had filled him with guilt. He should have guessed that China was cracking, that Jamie Song had lost his grip. West drained the cup of water in front of him and turned to the screen at the end of the table.

Pierce had persuaded West to move down to the situation room in the basement, where the imagery was clearer and communications more reliable. West had taken a seat next to Patton, who had joined them, along with Caroline Brock.

Kozerski stayed at the back of the room with the internal White House communications links. The directors of the CIA, FBI, NSA and other agencies remained in their offices. Half a dozen military and intelligence officers were around the table. The Vice-President was working from a secure location outside Washington. Marine One was on standby at the White House should evacuation be needed, with Air Force One fully crewed and fuelled ready for immediate take-off. National Guard fighter aircraft patrolled the skies over America's major cities.

Patton had ordered the arrest of twenty-eight Koreans suspected of sympathies with the North. Seven Korean associations were under surveillance and surrounded by police and National Guard. Smallpox vaccine had been sent to centres around the United States, with stockpiles distributed to mobile vaccination vehicles. The television and radio networks were running with the holocaust in India and Pakistan and the pending war with North Korea. There had been some incidents of panic buying at supermarkets and a brisk trade in gas masks. But Tom Patton had taken the decision to maintain normality as much as possible. Borders and airports remained open.

'Five minutes to target,' said Pierce, pointing to the images of B-1 and B-52 bombers which had flown in from Hawaii and US bases on the West Coast. He turned to a screen at the side of the table where a single image had been constructed with data from ground-penetrating radar, high-frequency seismic tests, magnetic mapping and thermal infrared imagery.

They showed the network of tunnels in the border area with clear outlines of the military hardware inside – long-range artillery, including the 170mm guns and 240mm rockets which could hit Seoul, and fighter aircraft positioned on underground runways for take-off. Under camouflaged cover were outdated military hovercraft, once designed to cross the DMZ without setting off landmines. But now their capability was questionable. Further underground thousands of men were in formation to pour into the South.

'Our aim is to defeat them in detail,' said Pierce. 'That means we kill or bury every soldier and every piece of equipment along the 151 miles of the DMZ. We're also deploying NBC detectors along the whole sector. They are self-propelling miniature unmanned vehicles which will stay airborne for twenty-four hours. Within five minutes of being activated they will detect any known nuclear, biological or chemical threat. Some are equipped with 360-degree cameras which will give added detail of the effect of the strikes. In other words, we should know within an hour under what conditions our troops will be crossing into North Korea.'

But as he glanced back at the radar images of the fleet of bombers flying at 630 miles an hour across the Sea of Japan, Pierce's expression turned into a look of horror. He put his finger to his headset. 'Repeat, for Christ's sake. Just say that again.'

All eyes were on Pierce as he reaffirmed what he had been told. 'Car bombs in Seoul,' he whispered. 'Wait—'

'Put it on the goddamn open speaker,' ordered West.

Kozerski flipped the switch. There was a crackle of static, then a crossed line, as Pierce locked on to the channel from the office of the chairman of the joint chiefs at the Pentagon.

'. . . at Itaewon, the US embassy, Chong-kak station. All car bombs. Gunman at Seoul International Airport, indiscriminate shooting in the departure lounge—'

'How the hell did they get the weapons in there?' muttered West.

'Mr President, explosions on two airliners on the ground. Please hold, Mr President—'

'Three minutes to target,' said another voice across the line.

'Holy shit,' whispered Kozerski. 'Look at that.'

On the side-screen, the blurred but recognizable images of heavy artillery turned and shifted position – but not enough for it to clear the cave. In another image, North Korean troops were pouring south through one of the tunnels. The hovercraft were breaking cover and being watched by the cameras of the Global Hawks.

'Is that artillery going to work?' asked West.

'Not where they are,' said Pierce.

'Maybe,' said Kozerski, his eyes on the new images from

a Global Hawk camera. A cloud of smoke from a soundless explosion appeared from the side of the mountain.

'They've cut a firing angle into the rock,' said Pierce.

'Artillery launch,' said the voice from the Pentagon.

'Surface-to-air missile on the airport perimeter,' said another voice, as Pierce listened across two channels.

'170mm. Second shell. No, third. Fourth. 170mm and 152mm. Seoul is in range.'

'Confirmed hit in civilian airliner . . . SAM—'

'What the hell's it flying for?'

'Seoul International Airport is a write-off. Pictures? Yes. The networks are showing them live, now.'

'North Korean troops are through the tunnels.'

'Thirty seconds to strike.'

Kozerski's voice broke through. 'Mr President, the Chinese ambassador is on the line. He has been instructed to tell us that his government will consider an attack on North Korea as an act of war against China.'

'He's too late,' said West bluntly.

At the end of the table Tom Patton put down his telephone receiver and grasped Caroline Brock's hand. She looked up at him. She was tired. Very tired. Her hair fell over her face. They had been working round the clock in the White House, and nothing needed to be said between them. Caroline pushed back her hair, stood up and put on her coat.

'Mr President,' said Patton. 'Suicide bombing in Times Square. Variola major is detected.'

64

New York, NY, USA

By the time Caroline Brock's helicopter was over Manhattan, the area of the bombing at 44th Street and Broadway had been cordoned off into a central area and an outer ring. Hazardous materials rescuers were working inside the cordon. Some of the critically injured were taken to a biohazard tent erected directly outside the entrance of the Helmsley Hotel on 42nd Street. There they were treated and tested. The hotel was being evacuated and turned into a quarantine hospital.

Those with minor injuries were led to the outer ring of the cordon where their wounds were examined. They had to discard their clothes. Stainless steel shower stalls were being set up for decontaminating hazard suits, equipment and people. Survivors and evacuees were showering and registering, then, after being vaccinated, they were allowed to leave.

Traffic between Fifth and Eighth avenues and between 39th and 46th streets was stopped and drivers were told to leave their vehicles so they could be decontaminated. They themselves had to line up to shower and leave their clothes to be incinerated.

Lines of Manhattan office workers, dressed uniformly in blue cotton pyjamas, wrapped in grey blankets and wearing green plastic sandals, filed out between the cars along pre-arranged routes, heading south and north along Broadway and east and west along 46th and 40th streets. On the way, they were vaccinated.

All health officials wore biohazard suits, their sleeves

marked with the yellow three-lobed flower indicating danger. Those inside the cordon worked wearing breathing apparatus. As the situation came more under control, firemen and police ensured that people got undressed, showered, and were vaccinated and their clothes collected for disposal before they left their buildings. Then, floor by floor, the great buildings of Times Square were closed down, each room checked, swept and sealed with red and white plastic tape.

From the air, the carnage around the area of the bombing looked like a trap, dangerous and eerily different from the rest of Manhattan. Yet that too was changing by the second. As news spread, so the mood transformed.

Caroline brought the respirator over her head, clipped it down and pulled on her gloves. A secret service agent sealed the cuffs with tape. The pilot kept the helicopter steady in the strong winds that whipped around the buildings, making any landing in high-rise Manhattan difficult.

He brought the aircraft down on the roof of the newly built Citic Towers Hotel, dropped off Caroline and her two secret service agents and took off again immediately. A figure in a red biohazard spacesuit was waiting for her.

'John Pincher, Dr Brock. Special adviser to FEMA, and reporting directly to Tom Patton.' He held out a gloved hand to her. Caroline wanted to shout back a reply above the noise of the helicopter engines, but Pincher's voice through his respirator was calm and slow.

'Thanks for meeting me,' she answered.

'The hotel has been evacuated. Nothing you're going to see will be a pleasant sight.'

Pincher led them down a flight of stairs to where firemen held the lift.

'Anything left of the bomber?' asked Caroline.

'The head is pretty much intact. We hope to have an

ID on him soon. Otherwise, bits of his jacket, a buckle –
and we've found a brass battery connection.'

'We need to get the blood sample from the head to Fort
Detrick right away. We might be dealing with a rogue
strain of the variola major.'

'You mean, the vaccine—' muttered Pincher.

'Might not work. Correct,' said Caroline, cutting him
off. 'Until we can find out exactly which strain we're
dealing with.'

The lift stopped and the door opened. Caroline gasped
and put one hand towards her mouth, forgetting that the
hand was gloved and that her face was sealed off by a
mask.

Laid out in the hotel lobby, row after row, stretching
from the reception desk to the grand piano and in towards
the bar, were the naked bodies of the wounded and of
those who had just died, all mixed together, with troops
armed with weapons watching over them. Hoses with
shower heads were being used to spray over them. Where
the hoses wouldn't reach, they were being drenched with
buckets of disinfected water.

'Formaldehyde,' said Pincher. He shook his head. 'It's
dreadful. It's humiliating. But it's necessary.'

They picked their way through towards the lobby door,
where heavy-duty plastic sheeting had been put up to
conceal what was happening inside.

'Are the ventilation ducts still operating?'

'They are,' said Pincher, lifting the sheeting to let
Caroline through.

'Shut them down in all the buildings,' she said, pausing
just for a moment at what she saw in front of her. 'We
don't want air going in or out.'

She turned to face Pincher, knowing that her brusque
instructions were a facade to cover her emotions. Her eyes
were watery, yet she couldn't wipe the moisture away.

'I know it means the heating. But turn it off. Find them blankets. Until we've got an all-clear.'

The site of the explosion was not as dreadful as the scene inside the hotel. It seemed uncannily less man-made – the act of just one individual, not of an institution. She was amazed at how swiftly America could mobilize. It was less than two hours since the attack, and here was a cordon with order inside it. The bodies of those killed instantly lay where they had fallen with yellow tags tied to their left ankles. If limbs had been severed, they were individually tagged, too. New York Police Department photographers moved easily around FBI forensic agents, firemen and others who were slowly clearing dangerous debris while being careful not to destroy evidence.

'Fifty-eight dead,' said Pincher. 'Two hundred and thirty injured. We reckon about another fifty won't make it.'

She could feel the edge in his voice. The bomb had not been that big. The lower windows of the buildings around Times Square itself were shattered. Firemen hosed down cars that had piled up, but they had not been flung in the air, as would have happened with a more powerful explosion. The electricity remained on, with the neon signs working as if the world was still a safe place. Coca-Cola, Budweiser, Panasonic, McDonald's had all survived. Even the red news electronic display ran unbothered by the death beneath it.

'US marines land in North Korea. Heavy fighting across DMZ. Seoul in flames. Bioterror scare.' Caroline stopped looking before it came round to the suicide attack in Times Square.

'I need to get the sample, take a look, then I need to be choppered to Fort Detrick. We need one sample to go there and another to go to the Center for Disease Control in Atlanta.'

While Pincher repeated her command into his radio, Caroline ran the implications through her mind. If a week went by before symptoms appeared, it would mean the IL-4/variola major strain might not be as lethal as she feared. But it was a big 'if'. Very big.

There was an uncanny discrepancy between the smallness of the explosion and the marshalled enthusiasm of the rescue teams going about their work. They were resolute, almost embracing the task, as if they were back at Ground Zero. There was a great American optimism about what they were doing, a belief that once it was cleared, however long it took, and once the grieving was over, life would go back to normal.

Caroline walked forward and stepped over a leg with a yellow plastic sandal still on the foot. A paperback novel lay pushed up against the edge of the pavement, squashed and burnt, but with the cover still somehow intact. Three cabs had concertinaed into each other, their yellow paint stripped off in the heat.

Where the bomber had stood was a small crater. The explosion had ripped through the paving slab and cracked a pipe where water was dribbling out, creating an oily black pool which oozed on to the pavement. A body lay there, a pedestrian close enough to die but far enough away for the body to stay intact. It was covered with a thin layer of dust and debris. A flashlight beam lit the corpse's face. She was young, her face purposeful and pretty, with no fear there at all.

'Excuse me, ma'am,' said a voice behind Caroline. She shifted to one side, as two firemen knelt down to try to look inside the crater and stem the water flow without disturbing the body.

'Get back. Everyone, just keep back.' Another voice, and Caroline glanced over and saw police linking arms as a crowd of onlookers stumbled in the crush to get a better view. How strange that everyone was so caught up in the experience. They were detached and curious, because the tragedy had not directly affected them. For a moment the rescuers and onlookers were liberated from dreary routine. Whether inside or outside the cordon they were confronted with the evidence of evil, which gave value to their own purpose. Here was the underbelly of war, the dark fascination that drew people to it time after time.

Caroline stepped over a complete corpse, the top of the beige raincoat it was wearing unscathed, but the collar lying in a pool of dark coagulating blood. The rest of the body was charred and shrivelled, reminding her of some of the photographs from Delhi.

But this was not Delhi. It was a single small suicide bomb – and initial traces of variola major. That was what nagged at Caroline more than anything. In the Wake Island missile the capsules had drifted down on a fixed propeller, limiting the trauma experienced by the virus and enabling it to survive. No explosives had been detected. So the Times Square bomb had not been a method of distribution, she concluded, just a signal of terror.

65

Washington, DC, USA

Mary Newman, her eyes sore and her hands bruised from the Osprey winch cable, flung her arms around Jim West, not caring who was watching. Lazaro Campbell held back, just inside the door, and edged round to where Kozerski was.

'What does Dr Brock say?' said Patton, speaking into one telephone and, while listening to the answer, giving instructions into another. 'Every piece of thermal imaging equipment, with SWAT teams, on every central square in every city. Anyone carrying a suicide vest, we want to see them and take them out. State capitals first—'

'It'll be a hundred dead in Times Square,' said Kozerski quietly to Campbell. 'But the casualties in South Korea are already over ten thousand – that includes 2,500 American troops.'

'Japanese air and seaborne invasion at Najin and Chongjin,' said Pierce to no one in particular. A colonel lit up the two cities on the eastern North Korean coast on the huge map now displayed on the situation room wall. 'OK, we're getting satellite imagery in from Yanji. Chinese troops are – Mr President – the Chinese are going into North Korea on the eastern seaboard.'

'We hold with the Japanese,' said West, his hand resting on Newman's shoulder. 'Tell Yamada that Sato might have messed up. He shouldn't have done what he did. But our security treaty must hold.'

Pierce stepped towards the satellite-imagery screen to get a closer look. 'That looks like Chinese mobilization at

Dandong as well. If they cross into Sinuiju they'll get the rail and road link down to Pyongyang.'

'Are we sharing this imagery with the Japanese?' said West.

'Yes, sir.'

'Good.'

'They don't have to fight each other,' said Newman. 'You can stop it, sir.' The 'sir' hung strangely after her affectionate entrance.

'Chris, how long have we got?'

'No Chinese planes are in the air yet. If they scramble, it'll be minutes. Otherwise, let's say an hour.'

West slipped his hand down to Mary's elbow and guided her towards the door. 'John, we're going to get some daylight for a few minutes. Campbell, you come and join us.'

'Sir,' said Patton. 'Dr Brock has confirmed interleukin-4 agent within the virus samples.'

West stopped and turned towards his Homeland Security Secretary. 'Do we know exactly what that means and how to deal with it?'

'Not yet, sir.'

'I don't want to know anything unless we know what it means.' West's anger filled the room. 'There are too many goddamn things happening for the President to be fed unprocessed data.'

West wasn't too sure where he was going. He needed a change of scenery. His short temper was a warning that either his thinking was becoming muddled or that there was too much for one man to decide on. And who was to say that his decisions were worth anything? Every step he had taken had led the world closer to its own destruction.

He walked on ahead, lost in his thoughts. As yet, none of the great powers had come into direct conflict with another. Could he keep it like that? If the trail went back to Zhongnanhai, would he want to keep it like that? Would it be a secret between him and Jamie Song which no one would know about until long after they were all dead.

He found himself heading for the residence. Maybe he was seeking a memory of Valerie's colours and something that would take him back to an era when he had a wife and the White House was an aspiration, a novelty, a prospect to be explored with pride. Today, Jim West would like to have been walking down a disused railroad in Oregon collecting firewood. He wouldn't listen to the radio or TV. If someone had told him about war, he would have muttered about 'those damn politicians' and kept walking, believing that the war would never reach him and his family. Whatever happened now, his aim must be to keep as much of the United States in that womb of self-assurance as was possible. Times Square had gone. The rest must hold.

'This OK for you two?' he queried humbly. Newman and Campbell, straight from the flight from Mongolia, simply nodded. They needed a shower and sleep. But first he needed their help. West opened the door to a stream of late-winter sunlight.

'Dad,' said Lizzie. She stood next to Meenakshi, the two of them facing West like warriors. 'Caroline's on the phone. She's been chasing you. And Tom Patton's been calling.'

'I'll take Caroline's call,' said West.

Lizzie handed him a cell phone. 'Caroline ... George Washington? ... when? ... OK. And where are you? ... and when will you be there? ... Fine.'

West cut the call. 'A thirty-five-year-old woman arrived at the emergency room of George Washington Hospital with a temperature of 103 degrees Farenheit, that's just under 40 degrees Celsius. She complained of severe muscle aches. The first blood tests showed a slightly lowered white blood cell count. That was thirty-six hours ago. She's now been diagnosed with smallpox, having been infected by contaminated airborne droplets. Her name is Juliet Mary Diamond. Dr Brock says other similar cases are being reported and that the A&E files at George Washington show that some people checked in but were sent home having been diagnosed with a presumed viral infection.'

No one spoke. The hospital was barely four blocks away. From the window, West could see across the White House gardens to the streets beyond. He couldn't tell that anything was amiss.

Lizzie stepped over and stood next to her father. 'Dad, take ten minutes off and do nothing,' she said gently, squeezing his hand. He nodded, turned, walked over to a soft, flowered sofa and sat down, patting the cushion next to him for Lizzie to sit as well.

'Mr President, Jim,' said Newman, glancing across to Lizzie, too. 'I'd like to get a line up to Beijing. We think we can contact Jamie Song, and we think he is still in charge.'

West's eyes changed from dull defeat to curiosity. 'Still in charge?'

'As we headed out from Beijing,' said Campbell, 'I was able to log the different units deployed towards the centre of the city. They are still under satellite surveillance and the embassy compound has still not been breached, meaning that someone is holding them back. In fact, the Chinese troops are further away now than when we were there. On the flight from Mongolia to here, I got the Pentagon China desk to run an analysis on the Chinese military units. The main move against President Song is coming from a place known as the Second Department of the People's Liberation Army. It's the leading force behind China's expansion of intelligence gathering, and has moved into Myanmar, the Paracel Islands and Laos. It built the listening station in Cuba and was responsible for the deal that ended up with missiles being shipped there. Their office is above ground in North Andeli Street, Beijing. That building, sir, is surrounded by troops and police loyal to President Song. There are more soldiers there than around our embassy. What we don't know is what is happening in the main command and control centre in the Western Hills. I imagine they are keeping their options open, and waiting to see which way the political wind blows.'

West listened hard, forcing himself to absorb what Campbell was saying. He was both in control of himself and on the point of exploding rage. While the smallpox virus might be floating in the air around them, Campbell was talking in a cold, unflinching and purposeful way, on a topic which was so removed from the immediate catastrophe that West saw how it might be a solution, albeit one that had come too late.

'The police and emergency services in Beijing remain loyal to Jamie Song. The Mayor of Beijing is not under arrest and is making radio broadcasts. The self-financing military units are with Jamie Song as well. They cannot afford the economic collapse of China. The problem is coming from the Second Artillery unit, which runs the missile programme, and military command areas in the north, closest to North Korea and Japan. There is also rebellion in Fujian across the straits from Taiwan.'

'Can you get me Jamie Song?'

'Yes, sir,' said Newman. 'The Mayor of Beijing is on standby. We'll call him. He'll patch us through to Song. I have already spoken to Andrei Kozlov. He'll come across too.'

'OK. Let's do it,' said West, standing up and glancing down at Lizzie. 'Meenakshi, do you think your father would do a worldwide broadcast for us?'

Meenakshi looked up, startled. Her mind had been

somewhere else. 'What do you mean?' she asked cautiously. 'I'm not sure Dad's in any state to talk to anyone.'

'As far as I can make out, Vasant Mehta is the only decent man among all of us. He took the risk for peace and lost. Why? Because we didn't do our jobs properly. In a few days, maybe a few hours, we're going to have a smallpox epidemic. There is no way we can cordon off Washington, New York or wherever else they've struck. That virus is going to spread. It's going to be down in Mexico, then through Latin America. It'll turn up in Europe, Africa and Asia. We cannot fight the virus and fight each other at the same time. We cannot afford to exact revenge. We have to contain the epidemic, eradicate it, and only then, if we really want to, should we pick up on the war.'

Newman was on her feet, taking off her glasses, with her hand to her chin. 'Mr President, you are not advocating a ceasefire on the Korean peninsula?'

'North Korea's the exception. Once Park Ho and his henchmen are neutralized, yes, I do propose a ceasefire. And if Jamie Song still has power, I think we can do it. If we fail, this world has only got one place to go, and that's on to the shit heap.' He put his hands affectionately on Newman's shoulders.

Forgetting where he was for a moment, and not caring who else he was with, 'Thank God you're back safely,' he said, kissing her on the forehead.

66

Fort Detrick, Maryland, USA

Only an expert scientist's eye would recognize what Caroline was looking at – a genetically engineered bioweapon supervirus. On a computer screen in a level-four biocontainment laboratory at Fort Detrick, she examined the image being sent to her from the Center for Disease Control in Atlanta. She identified the familiar contours and shades of variola major, its graceful near-figure-of-eight curves, wrapped in its usual host-cell membrane, giving off grey shades, with faded pink and blue on the edges like an aura. She was looking at the most complicated type of animal virus, yet against what she had in the other microscope it was horribly simple.

In her own microscope was the same virus, but with the interleukin-4 gene. It had created an extra layer across the top lateral body, minuscule to the untrained eye, but deadly in its simplicity. Caroline saw immediately how it would be resistant to standard vaccine.

It was not difficult to buy interleukin-4 and put it into a virus. Yet Park Ho had jumped a number of stages by taking the samples from the Australian laboratory, whose scientists had done much of his work for him.

Caroline lifted her head and wanted to rub her eyes, but the mask and biohazard spacesuit prevented her. She should have anticipated this. There should have been a warning years ago. Pox viruses were wide open for genetic engineering, and any rogue state would know how to do it. What did they care that millions could be wiped out? They had different minds. Different motives. The argument was dead that no nation would do anything as horrific as deliberately to introduce a killer disease with no antidote. There was no longer any logic of restraint. But the reality was that the United States, let alone the rest of the world, had no drug to stop this disease.

Caroline, alone in the laboratory, absorbed this stark truth. Up at Camp David, she had got it so, so wrong. Six months, she had told Jim West. Yet Park Ho had had it already prepared then. America's vaccine, though, was no closer to being ready. And the standard vaccine, for all she knew, would, far from curing them, make people more susceptible to the disease.

She picked up the phone and called Tom Patton. 'It's confirmed,' she said. 'We don't know what we're dealing with.'

'OK,' said Patton slowly. 'We have more cases now. One checked into a clinic near Reagan National and is now at GW Hospital. Two cases in New York, three cases in Pittsburgh, one in Colorado, two in California – Sacramento and San Francisco.'

'You mean confirmed cases?'

'No, sorry, Caroline. These are symptoms.'

'Right, Tom. Symptoms,' she repeated. 'But damn certain to be actual cases. All health workers have already been immunized with the vaccinia anti-smallpox vaccine. Let's leave them as they are—'

'Even if it doesn't work?'

'Hold on. Let me finish.' She was too brittle. It had been a long day. A long week. 'The vaccinia vaccine does not contain the variola virus. It's a calf-lymph derivative. We need to try some quick experiments with reformulated vaccines. We can now get a DNA sequence from the IL-4/variola major virus. We should get all strains of the vaccinia virus – Temple of Heaven, Copenhagen, NYC-BOH. We need the DNA sequences to all the variola major that we've mapped – India-1967, Yamata, Bangladesh-1975, Aralsk and whatever else they have done in Russia – to determine which, if any, we can draw from for the IL-4 element. Have we got anything in from Moscow yet? Remember I talked about it? The Soviets created a cloned library of variola DNA fragments. They have a complete analysis of the smallpox genome since it could be used as a biological weapon. We need all that data, right now. And we should start with Cidofovir as a new test vaccine. It's brilliant. It gets absorbed by the host cell and then converts into an agent which kills rogue cells. They've added a molecule of lipid or fat and it kills cowpox in mice. It's not so effective with monkeypox in macaques—'

'Stop,' shouted Patton. 'Caroline. Stop. You're losing me. I don't know what the hell you're talking about. And hold . . . I have another call coming in.'

Caroline drew a breath. Yes. He was right. She was gushing, trying to empty her mind all at once; trying to find some reason for optimism.

'Juliet Mary Diamond died with a seizure shortly after being vaccinated,' said Patton.

Caroline felt distant from the news, somehow disconnected – in the same way she had tried to make herself in the days following Peter's murder. 'She was our first patient? George Washington Hospital, right?'

'That's right,' said Patton tiredly. 'Juliet Mary Diamond. The first.'

'Then we have no antidote, Tom. In fact, it's worse,' she said slowly, hearing her own uneven breathing through the apparatus. She wished she could rip off the damn mask and take in air properly. 'She should have survived at least a week after admission. The vaccine strain killed her more quickly. We have no antidote, Tom.'

'I know.'

'So from now on, every patient who checks in will be

our guinea pig.' Caroline was thinking as she was speaking, spacing her words, so they weren't rushed, and both she and Patton knew exactly what she was saying. 'We will test on them every variation of every vaccine we can create until one works. It might kill them. It might save them. We don't tell anyone. We don't tell anyone about IL-4.'

'As soon as we announce smallpox, they'll be queuing up for vaccines.'

'We inoculate them, but give the healthy ones water,' said Caroline. 'Because if we use the vaccinia vaccine we'll be killing people who might otherwise survive.'

67

Dukchun Palace, Pyongyang, North Korea

The air was becoming contaminated with the stench from above ground. Smoke heavy with tiny particles of debris leaked through the outdated ventilation system and was being pumped into the laboratories beneath. The bombing had been so concentrated that Park Ho doubted the structure would withstand another wave. His only communication outside the country was through the fibre-optic link to the Chinese command and control centre at Shenyang across the northern border. They were choosing what to tell him and what to show him. They told him that North Korean forces had broken through South Korean and US defences; that Camp Bonifas had been overrun; that his agents were causing terror in Seoul, with car bombs, assassinations and drive-by shootings; that the airport was in flames; Tokyo was destroyed; Sato and his mistress Kiyoko were dead, and Yamada had fled to the US base in Okinawa; that Ahmed Memed was in Beijing under the protection of the new government; that Hassan Muda's bomb had devastated Times Square, and that West was expected to beg for peace within the hour; that Park Ho would be victorious.

Park Ho thanked Shenyang for the news. He wondered if Ahmed Memed had told them about the variola major experiments. In all the planning, Ho had never mentioned it, knowing that, even by Chinese standards, he might be seen as going too far. Qureshi had not known either. For Memed, an epidemic that could wipe out the human race would have a religious dimension. God would decide who lived and died; therefore God would recreate the world. Memed's belief was so strong that he expected the virus to distinguish between the chosen and the godless. And Park Ho had let him think that. After all, it was Memed's bombers who were waiting for the signal all over the United States and Europe.

But he had not told Memed about the vaccine. Only Li Pak and his team knew about that, and about how powerful a weapon a simple syringe and vaccine would become.

By now Park Ho was used to the different grades of biological warfare production. He stopped in a small chamber, totally quiet except for the hum of the pressurized air flow, and put on a biohazard suit. Behind the glass, he saw Li moving towards him through a complex network of rooms. Li was alone, and there was something hesitant about the way he moved.

The last time he had been here, Park had seen an array of animals – rodents, sheep, primates – each in its own cubicle into which was pumped air laced with the smallpox virus.

What Park Ho now saw made him stare at Li in complete anger. Not because the virologist was incompetent. He was far from that. But any talent, however great, could not be tolerated in the face of insubordination. Park Ho had expected to meet the recovered British ambassador, Bob Robertson. Instead, he was faced with fresh prisoners from the labour camps, both men and women, covered in oozing pustules, some of which were so close together that it was impossible to see the skin between.

Li's terrified eyes faced him through the mask. 'We need more time!'

'Robertson? Where is he?'

'Dead, comrade,' stammered Li, trying to find sanctuary in the old Marxist form of address.

'Jozsef Striker?'

'Dead.' He pressed his finger against a glass cubicle where a figure lay shivering on the floor. The pustules covered so much of the skin that he couldn't tell the sex of the victim. 'That is why I have to resort to using them again.' Li's head was lowered, his voice through radio communication quivering and pleading. 'We need more time, General. Science is not exact—'

Park Ho struck Li hard against his mask and tore out the air tube. Li flailed, trying to seal the suit again. Park drew a knife and slashed the sleeve, drawing blood from Li's arm. Li staggered, choking. Park Ho caught him, slipped the knife into his neck and dropped him on the floor. He quickly left the biocontainment area. Stripping off the suit and not bothering to shower, he put on his military uniform and walked into the underground atrium. Much of it had survived the first wave of bombing. A guard saluted him.

'Have you made an exit yet?' demanded Park Ho.

'We are still digging, comrade.'

A line of soldiers, in green hard hats, carrying pick-axes, drills, even a chainsaw, appeared at the end of the corridor. They were covered in dust from the chipped and broken concrete. Their heads hung low and they carried their tools listlessly. There was a staleness in the air, a pungent smell of burning that caught the back of the throat. Park Ho felt a tightness in his lungs. The guard dropped the salute, and he didn't care. He was ashamed that he had given in to his anger and killed Li Pak. The urge to kill was a strange instinct, and with humans it might have nothing to do with simply staying safe or eating. Often, it ended up being a necessary thing to get through the day.

'You,' he shouted to a soldier at the head of the work gang. The man looked up but did not even salute. He stayed where he was, not bothering to move towards Park.

Then his gaze fell on the epaulettes and medals on the uniform, and he realized who was addressing him.

The soldier shook his head. 'Every exit is sealed,' he said. 'They have used a hardened chemical formula. It is like a foam. By the time we get to it it is setting. Very quickly. Then it is tougher than concrete.' He turned and pointed at the soldier behind him, whose drill shaft had snapped in two.

'When can you get us out?' said Park, his voice less harsh. He had built loyalty by being one of the men. If he was to die with them, that was how it would be.

The soldier pointed ahead. 'We will try up here. But I think it will be impossible. Unless there are tunnels we don't know about.'

A line of dust fell from the roof above, then a chunk of plaster.

'There are not,' said Park Ho.

The soldier coughed and spat out black phlegm mixed with blood. 'The whole structure has been weakened,' he whispered, his throat still clogged with phlegm. He spat again. 'We are trying to prop up the roof before it collapses. Then we will find a place where the foam has not reached and try and drill through to find air.'

Park Ho went into the office. The room had once had a lift up into the hotel foyer. The computer screens were frozen, but the three soldiers there were watching a television on whose screen the picture was faded but still discernible. They turned. Two had handkerchiefs over their mouths. They saw Park, but their attention remained on the screen, where Vasant Mehta was speaking against a backdrop of still pictures of the nuclear aftermath in Islamabad, Delhi and Tokyo.

'Where is this from?' demanded Park impatiently.

'The fibre-optic line from Shenyang,' said one of his men, concentrating on the pictures and showing Park Ho no respect. Never before would they have seen uncensored television, and they looked as if a secret mould had been broken. A simultaneous translation in Chinese was being run over Mehta's voice, and the soldiers, who had worked up on the Chinese border, understood the gist of what the Indian Prime Minister was saying.

'. . . must stop,' said Mehta. 'India has lost millions and millions of its citizens. Over the next years many millions more will die. We can no longer function as a nation. We have no hospitals, no emergency services. Nothing. Pakistan is the same. For what? A piece of disputed land? A different God? Why? Why? Why?' Mehta swallowed hard, looked behind him, pointed, smiled and rubbed his right eye. 'I challenge you to tell me which city is Delhi, which is Islamabad and which is Tokyo. Because I don't know. What is the point of trying to preserve something if it ends up being like this, being exactly like your enemy's city?'

Mehta fell silent and buried his face in his hands. When he looked up again, his eyes were full of tears. He was unshaven. He noticed his shirt collar was skewed and brought it back into place. 'I am sorry,' he said. 'I cannot leave this place without a nuclear warfare suit on. I can no longer smell the smells of India. That has gone. I am told that the nuclear dust clouds from India and Pakistan have combined as one and it is drifting east. I hear that the winds from Tokyo are blowing west, so those two big clouds will join together as well. Where? Maybe over Thailand or Vietnam, where they'll poison people who have nothing to do with our squabbles at all, people who have just tried to live.'

The room shook, catching Park Ho off balance. He steadied himself with a hand on the wall. Another raid. But somewhere else. It was like a distant earth tremor. The screen flickered and then settled.

'. . . President West. Jim West is a friend of mine. My

daughters Meenakshi and Romila are under his care now. He is not an evil man, just as the United States is not an evil nation. Any more than India is, or Pakistan is, or Japan is. He asked me to make this address because he sees a holocaust coming, something unstoppable and totally destructive. There is smallpox in America. To us, in India, that might now seem nothing. But when the virus reaches us – and it will reach us – it will kill all those of us who are not already being killed by radiation. In America, there is vaccine. In India, we have nothing left to give.'

A crack appeared in the floor and more dust fell from the ceiling. But Park Ho ignored it. His mind was completely on what Mehta was saying. He had talked about a vaccine and made no mention of IL-4. He was lying. Or he hadn't been told. Jim West had set up the whole broadcast to lie to the world.

'. . . be peace, to stop the spread of this terrible disease—'

'Put me through to Shenyang,' snapped Park Ho. One of the soldiers looked round curiously, because to do that they would have to cut the broadcast. But his questioning lasted only a moment. Even now Park's presence brooked no dispute. The soldier diverted the link and pointed to a telephone.

'Can you put this line through to Washington? . . . No? . . . Why not? . . . I don't accept . . . then get this message to the Americans. I have the vaccine for the IL-4 strain of variola major with me here. If they destroy this place, they destroy the cure. These are our coordinates . . .'

Park Ho ended the call and did up the top button of his tunic. The tremors were getting more powerful. They were carpet bombing, using thermobaric explosive again, trying to seal off his ventilation, suck out the air and suffocate him. The lights flickered, then went out, and emergency lamps working off batteries came on. They had only been designed for evacuation. They would not last long.

'Put me through to Toksong-gun,' he said. 'Quickly, before the lines go.'

A huge shudder ran through the whole complex, breaking the glass wall in the office and throwing open the door. The structure had buckled, crushing the two sealed doors leading to the biocontainment area. There was no vaccine and the virus was out, circulating in the stale air that the trapped survivors were breathing.

'Have they struck you yet?' asked Park Ho when he got through.

'We're clear. Nothing,' said the missile engineer, Kee Tae Shin.

'Then you have your orders,' said Park. 'The *juche* ideal is now in your hands.'

68

Beijing, China

When the car stopped, Song recognized a mix of uncertainty and arrogance in the driver's eyes, watching him in the windscreen mirror. They showed the expression of a man not sure who was in power, and uncertain about whom to avoid and whom to respect.

A gush of cold air came into the car, bringing with it the acrid smoke from the fires burning around Tiananmen Square.

When he had called the meeting with his political opponents, Jamie Song had made three conditions. He could see his wife, Xiaomei, on to a plane for Hong Kong that would connect directly with a flight to Vancouver, Canada. The meeting would take place at a venue of his choice. And he could visit, alone and unimpeded, the place where he was now. Apart from that, the agenda would be open. Any topic could be discussed.

Jamie Song stepped out of the car, his feet crunching on ash and broken glass. Wooden placards lay strewn along the pavement. Banners had been blown against buildings, stark red Chinese characters against the now dirty white of the cotton. Firemen played a hose on a café across the road. Next door a supermarket window had been broken. A television set lay smashed in the gutter.

The soldiers had been told he was coming, and kept their distance, not even acknowledging who he was. Yan stayed in the car, but with the engine running and the back door open. He lit a cigarette.

Up ahead, wisps of smoke drifted up from a ruined

building, floodlit from a crane which swung round to move away burnt-out cars blocking the road. The flickering beams from soldiers' torches played over the rubble, damp and glistening from rain that had been falling in a fine drizzle.

Jamie Song walked on to see what he had come for. As soon as Yan had told him, Song had asked that everything be left untouched.

Throughout his political life, Jamie Song had known that the ghost of the Chinese Communist Party would always cast a shadow over him. Every two steps he moved forward, the party had hauled him back one. They wanted him, but not enough to give up their privileges. He could have made his future in America, as an exile, as a millionaire, as part of the Chinese diaspora. He had always known that when the time was right he would be spat out towards a foreign land, his usefulness over. After all, he was only the president, and the party was the party.

Another crane, at work somewhere else, swivelled. The glaring yellow beam of its searchlight sparkled on the glass of a damaged window. As it moved, it lit up a hanging shape, for less than a second, as if what it revealed wasn't meant to be. Song quickened his pace, tripping on a coffee table that had found its way on to the street and catching his balance against a wall, grimy from a leaking water pipe above. Smells intensified. He had never before thought of the number of different odours burnt material gives off.

Silence. It was some time before Song realized that the cranes had stopped working. There was no noise from the soldiers in the rubble. The quiet enveloped him. They were paying their respects. Perhaps. Or simply waiting to see what he did.

He trod on a piece of wood, torn away from somewhere, and half blackened by fire. He picked it up, felt a nail at the top and dropped it. He felt an urgent impatience to move forward. But he was wrapped in fear about his reaction, about how he could stop himself screaming out and crying, in front of men whose respect he needed.

Song moved ahead slowly, trying to imagine what it would have been like to be here during those moments of madness.

'He was in a café with friends,' Yan had told him. 'It was very sudden. They recognized him. I am very sorry.'

The shape lit up by the crane's searchlight had been a reflection in glass. Song turned the corner, and looking down the street he saw the chaos left by the riot. Beyond that was a stillness. Nothing there had been touched, as if a line of demarcation had been drawn, or they had been stopped in time. Street lamps showed up steady drops of rain so light that he could barely feel them.

Between the stillness and the mess was the lamp post, still working and illuminating the corpse of his son as if the body were a marionette. Yun had been hung by the neck, his head wrenched horribly back and his arms hanging limply by his sides. His feet were bare. Someone had torn his shoes off. Scorch marks showed on the left side of his body, reaching his waist. Then they must have stopped it. But by then Yun would have been dead.

There were other lamp posts, with empty cords hanging where Yun's friends must have been murdered, then cut down. A stepladder was by the lamp post, just as Song had asked, with a knife resting on its top rung. As he approached, two soldiers noiselessly stepped out from somewhere. Song climbed the ladder. His face was now next to Yun's face, which smelt of ash. He touched the face. It didn't move, of course. But what was wrong with hoping that your son had just overslept at the end of a hangman's rope, and that his eyes might open and he might speak? But the dry and protruding tongue was wedged between the teeth, and he knew it was true.

The death had been simple and brutal in line with Chinese culture. After you have done it once, it is not difficult to get used to killing.

Song cut the rope and the soldiers took the weight. They carried Yun back on a stretcher, and Song walked beside him. Tomorrow would be his wedding anniversary, and Xiaomei would be safe in Vancouver, albeit dying from grief. Perhaps he would tell her that Yun was still alive and recovering. Perhaps that would save her.

As Song approached with the body, Yan got out of the car and walked to a Jeep Cherokee behind. A captain opened up the back of the jeep, where the back seats had been pulled down and a board fitted to take the body.

On the way to the China World Trade complex, Yan briefed Song on who would be at the meeting. Song listened, pushing out the images of Yun's death to make way for what he needed to do to win.

The car drew up at the base of the high-rise building and stopped. 'You know what will happen if there is no agreement?' said Yan, as he opened the door to get out.

'Do you think I care?' retorted Song, not bothering to mask the anger in his eyes.

The owner of the building was not a politician, nor was he a member of the Communist Party. He was a Hong Kong entrepreneur who knew Jamie Song well, and was indebted to him for the help that Song had given him in expanding into Europe and the United States. He was a man respected by all the participants, which was why Song had chosen the venue and the others had agreed. He understood the forces lined up against Song.

A lean man, with a long, thin head, the building's owner was at the bottom of the lift to meet Song and Yan. The three of them rode up together, but with no conversation apart from an initial greeting. On the twenty-fifth floor, the owner stepped out first and punched a code into

a lock on the door in front of them. It clicked open. He
turned on the lights and opened up the conference room,
which had views over Beijing, where fires still burnt in side
streets.

'The others are next door,' the owner said softly. 'They
will be with you in a few minutes.'

Bottled water was beside each place on the table, with a
notepad and a sharpened pencil. Biscuits were on plates in
the middle and at the side was coffee ready to pour, and
hot water for tea. No servants were on duty. That was how
this gathering of three of the most powerful men in the
world had wanted it. The owner withdrew.

The first to come in was Chen Jianxiong, a corpulent,
short man with a large, angry face. He was dressed in ill-
fitting military fatigues. As Chairman of the Military Commission, Chen controlled the armed forces. He had
demonstrated his brutish power by ordering armoured
vehicles to attack the American embassy. He had revealed
his genius for subtlety and mixed messages by allowing the
Osprey in and out of Beijing under an air force escort.
Chen was a mechanic by trade, beginning his working life
in an army factory building jeeps. As a commander, he
had served in the north-east, handling the North Korean
border, and on the eastern seaboard, playing war games
with Taiwan. He was a no-nonsense officer, exuding power
and courage. He acknowledged Song with a nod, took off
his military greatcoat, flung it over the back of a chair,
ignored Yan, and went straight to get himself a cup of tea.

A couple of minutes later, the General Secretary of the
Communist Party, Fan Yucheng, appeared, punching the
code of the combination lock himself. He stepped inside,
saying nothing, taking off his overcoat and scarf. He pulled
up a chair, sat down and lit a cigarette. Fan was tall with a
bookish demeanor, a shock of grey hair and thick spectacles, which he removed and replaced with reading glasses.

He was a structural engineer, a creator of buildings, and his credentials were in provincial administration. During his long career, he had handled Tibet, Xinjiang and Hong Kong, and had served as the Mayor of Shanghai. He was also the man who had written the political doctrine under which Jamie Song worked – *Shiji Wenhua*, which clumsily translated into 'pragmatic civilization'.

It was this doctrine that was now being tested.

Song and Chen took their seats. Yan remained standing. Although middle-aged, he was the youngest there and he knew his place. He did not speak, nor did he show any expression as the three others spoke. He waited on them, with ashtrays, water, coffee and tea, treating them each equally, efficiently, but without servility.

Jamie Song had called the meeting, and was the first to speak. He began without reference to Yun or to the violence that they had all witnessed outside.

'Thank you for coming,' he said softly. 'It has been a difficult time. Tokyo, Delhi, Mumbai, Islamabad, Karachi – whole societies have been destroyed. How did it ever come to this? So far China is intact. It is up to us to keep it that way. That is the service we can do tonight for the motherland.'

Song paused, but neither of the two other men spoke. They had risen to high office by being good listeners and keeping their own counsel.

Song continued. 'I do not want China to think of itself again as a victim – as it has done for the past one hundred years. And I do not want our future to be determined by guns, threats and massacres again. All of us here have worked hard to ensure that does not happen. Our achievements have been good. Our government, our stability, our growth are the envy of the world. In the past weeks, forces have been working against each other. Pakistan is destroyed. North Korea is destroyed. India is critically wounded. Japan is wounded. Pakistan and North Korea – these have been friendly nations for many years. India and Japan? Yes, one day we might have had to challenge them for supremacy, but did any of us wish this upon them? Tonight, I hear that Pyongyang has been destroyed by a nuclear bomb from Japan, and we have not heard from Park Ho for several hours. He may be dead. Perhaps that is good for all of us. But did any of us actively hope that this would happen?'

Song's question was not rhetorical. He let it hang, his gaze down on the table, alert for a reaction. Fan stubbed out his cigarette, tipped another from the packet for himself and offered one to Chen. He knew that Chen had his own cigarettes. He also knew that Song did not smoke. Yan, noticing the gesture, stepped back to distance himself from the shift of alliances.

'I haven't come here to argue my own case,' continued Song. 'I have my views and you know them and that is why you appointed me to be president. Nor do I want to fight with you. Let us tell each other where we disagree. Let us close the gap in this room tonight. Let us send the soldiers back to their barracks and move forward. For what is happening outside is bad for China. Money will stop coming in, and we might not become as wealthy as we should. We are pragmatic men. We have enabled great change to happen in our country without forfeiting our culture and our system of government. We must be proud of that.'

Fan lit his cigarette, passed his lighter to Chen, pushed the ashtray into the middle of the table and glanced up at Yan. Yan stepped forward, removed the ashtray, emptied, wiped it and returned it to the middle of the table. He walked around, filling each glass with water. Jamie Song sipped his water, edged the notepad in front of him and rolled the pencil on the table under his fingers. 'Events have moved so quickly that historians will take generations to unravel them. But let me tell you frankly, I do not want to fight America, although if we don't stop now, that will be the next stage. I believe America has been good for China. It has invested money here. It has educated me and our younger generation.'

Abruptly, Song took his hand off the pencil. Inadvertently, he had reminded himself of his son, Yun, and the image of his body hanging in the darkened street flashed across his mind. He clasped his hands in front of his chin, looked down and recovered himself. 'It has allowed us to develop without intervention. One day, we may have to fight the US. But why not wait until we are stronger? Why not wait until our knowledge of technology is greater than theirs, our roads wider, our schools and hospitals better? I can see no reason to wage a war which may drag this country back into the dark ages. To stop war, there will have to be compromises, of course, just as there will be tonight between the three of us. But we can make that happen.'

Song stopped, glanced up towards Yan and pointed towards the pot of coffee. Yan poured a cup and kept it black, but stirred in a lump of brown sugar, which was how Song liked it at this time of night. He brought over the cup and topped up Song's water glass again as well.

Neither the ideologue, Fan, nor the military commander, Chen, wanted to show weakness by speaking first.

After a decent interval, Song helped. 'Comrade Yucheng, you are the architect of *Shiji Wenhua*. Tell me, please, how my own plans can fit into your vision. For indisputably it is this which has guided China so successfully through the past years.'

Fan cleared his throat, and looked at no one as he spoke. 'The party must ensure peaceful development within China. If the motherland is threatened by external

forces, that is a different matter. The party must represent
the fundamental interests of the overwhelming majority of
the Chinese people. We do not need elections to tell us
what these interests are. Our track record is proven. The
party must continue on its path of economic growth and
modernization. In our foreign alliances, frankly, I do not
trust the United States. I applaud, Comrade President, the
allegiance you have forged with Andrei Kozlov. I believe
we should forge a new alliance now with India and help
her recover.'

He shrugged, dropped his cigarette, still alight, into the
ashtray. 'You haven't told us which compromises would
be acceptable to us and which would not. Do we sacrifice
North Korea, and allow US troops on our border? Do we
give up Cuba, when the Americans can send an aircraft
carrier with missiles to threaten our cities at any time? Do
we give way to the constant pressure to change our
political system? Do we yield when they want us to hold
elections, borrow their money, watch their films, read their
magazines and believe in their gods? And why do they put
all these pressures on us, when we have done more for our
poor people than any other developing nation? With
Russia and perhaps India, and under the doctrine of *Shiji
Wenhua*, can China now become a beacon for all the poor
people of the world, ruined by debt, tribalism and corruption? Has our system not been proved right? Has their
system not failed time and time again? Why do we speak
of compromise? These are big questions, and on them I
only know one thing. When this problem began, we put
down just one condition, one small condition, so that we
could remain neutral and uninvolved. We asked them not
to strike above the fortieth parallel, and they ignored our
wishes. A British submarine fired a missile. Why? Because
they wanted to draw us towards war. Why? Because they
want to defeat us before we become too strong.'

Song thought Fan had more to say, but he stopped unexpectedly, throwing the room into an unexpected silence with the shadow of an American broken promise as backdrop. Fan had drawn the lines, and there was no going back. Song wondered if he had walked into a trap of his own making; whether, after the death of his son, his judgement had gone and he had set himself up for a fall.

'This is a good discussion,' said Chen, abruptly. He stubbed his cigarette out, stood up, leaned over the table and swept his large, stubby hand around it in a circle. 'I am not a draughtsman, so this picture is not good. But it will work. I fix cars. That is my trade. I know that the gas will not burn if sugar is in it. I know that the distributor will not fire if it is wet. I know the body will rust if it is not treated. I know these things and that is my job.' He drew the imaginary circle again. 'This is my engine. This is China. And I know she won't work if she's fucked with.'

With Chen's bluntness came raw power. He slapped his hand down on the table. 'Here is our north-eastern border. Within a month, with North Korea defeated, South Korean troops will be here. Their factories are already in Yanji and Tumen waiting to move in. The whole of this area, which we used to call Manchuria, will be colonized. In the west, Xinjiang – Americans will destabilize it and begin an uprising. Tibet, too. In the south they'll use money and bribery, and in the east Taiwan will interfere. If we show ourselves to be weak, all these things will happen. China will break up. There will be one superpower in the world and it will not be for the world's good. And you talk about Cuba. It is I who made this agreement with Castro in 2001. I negotiated it for us. This will stay. They have missiles in Taiwan. We have missiles in Cuba. They are one hundred miles off our coast. We are one hundred miles off theirs. That is as it should be. They have sent an aircraft carrier to the Taiwan Straits to threaten us. I say, fuck them. They do that to us. We do that to them.'

Chen sat down, withdrawing from the debate as rapidly as he had joined in. Yan hovered with tea, but Chen waved him away.

'I am a businessman by trade,' said Song. 'My job is to negotiate and win.' He wrote the figure 1 on the pad and put a bracket around it. 'OK. So we stay in Cuba,' he announced, keeping his gaze away from Chen. He wrote the figure 2 with a bracket. 'The thirty-eighth parallel as the divide between North and South Korea remains.'

'The regime stays in place,' said Chen, his contribution an indication that compromise was available.

'The old regime. Park Ho will have to go.'

'The old regime is acceptable,' said Fan. 'And its policies. No elections. No human rights lawyers.'

'Pakistan?' said Song.

'We keep it,' said Fan. Even in such closed company his acknowledgement of control there was surprising. 'What is left, we keep.'

'Russia? They fought with us in Pakistan,' said Song.

'Yes. Russia can work with us there, as it works with us in Central Asia,' said Chen.

'Taiwan?'

'Status quo. Nothing changes unless they change it,' said Fan. 'If they want us out of Cuba, we want them out of Taiwan.'

'Park Ho? If he is alive, the Americans will want him. The Japanese will want him.'

'He will not be alive,' said Chen.

'Memed? I understand Ahmed Memed has sought sanctuary here?'

'He stays here,' said Chen.

'If they connect him with the suicide bomb in Times Square?'

'He stays.'

The Chinese were skilful at pretending they did not have issues, and until that moment the three men could have been talking as if there was no substantive conflict between them. But now Chen was staring straight at Song, arms folded, unrelenting.

Fan waited for the new atmosphere to settle and then delivered the argument to support Chen's statement. 'If we give Memed sanctuary,' he said smoothly, 'he will deliver the loyalty of Iran and Saudi Arabia. He has influence in Central Asia and he can bring calm to Xinjiang.'

Song wondered if there were more issues that would now arise. But the other two fell into silence. They knew that only Song could deliver their message to Washington and argue on the television networks. And Song had now decided that however much ground he had lost, he would remain as president of China and lead the nation come what may. When his power was restored, he would move to eradicate those who disagreed with him.

'All right,' he said slowly. 'I anticipate the outstanding issues with the US will be Cuba and Memed. I cannot see them compromising on Cuba. On Memed, perhaps.'

'We stay in Cuba,' said Chen.

'Do we complete the missile shipment?' said Song, using the same bluntness. Perhaps here there was room for negotiation. Missile shipments stopped. US inspection of facilities. Warheads separated.

Chen closed his eyes and shifted in his seat. Song thought he had found a point of flexibility, but then Chen pushed back his chair and stood up. 'The Americans have smallpox. They have no strength left.'

Yan deftly had his coat ready and held it for Chen as he put his arms through the sleeves. Yan opened the door and called the lift. The owner of the building appeared, holding the lift while Chen stepped inside, then joined him for the journey down. Yan returned to the room, resuming his position as the silent adviser.

Fan was on his feet, too, dropping his pack of cigarettes into the top pocket of his shirt. 'You have a right to be angry,' he said with an edge of sympathy in his voice. 'You have lost your son. I am sorry. A father and a son have a sacred bond. You are a brave man to have called this meeting in your grief.'

Fan could have left the room then. But he was a more decent man than Chen. He had seen his own father killed in the Cultural Revolution and he understood that mob killing on the street was different from the slaughter of men on the battlefield.

'I do not agree with Chen's methods,' continued Fan. It was an unexpected admission. 'Whether he designed it like this, I do not know. The events that have brought us here are military. Yet we are men of politics and diplomacy. I do not like our allegiance to Park Ho. I do not approve of biological warfare. But I did approve of Memed's coming here because of his influence in the Islamic world. And I do agree with Chen's analysis. If we keep our nerve we will emerge from this stronger. Chen is right. It is not a time for compromise.'

'Thank you,' said Song. The reality he faced was ungraspable and he handled it by answering quickly and quietly. 'I will negotiate with Washington along the guidelines we have discussed.'

He took time underscoring the points he had noted down, while Fan put on his coat. Yan showed him out and pressed the lift button. Song got up and stood by the window, seeing his reflection in the glass, superimposed on a glimmer of dawn light in the sky. The owner of the building was not there. He watched Fan get into the lift. Yan shifted his weight. For a moment, Song thought that Yan would leave as well. But the lift doors closed, and Yan came back into the room, poured himself a coffee and sat down.

'I need to speak to Andrei Kozlov,' said Song.

'I'll arrange it.' said Yan. 'One hour from now?'

Song nodded. Yan pulled a phone from his pocket, but as he was about to dial a number, he noticed a warning light flashing and the phone vibrating.

'Yes,' he said sharply, glancing down to get a pencil and paper, then not bothering. 'We're on our way,' he said, ending the call and turning towards Song. 'That was Chen,' he said. 'North Korea has launched four Taepodong-2 missiles at the United States.'

69

Washington, DC, USA

'Confirmed, sir,' said Pierce, his voice barely a whisper but the sound carrying to everyone in the room.

'Warheads?'

'No way of telling.'

'Trajectory?'

'Not certain at present. The western seaboard,' said Pierce. 'Way beyond Hawaii.'

Jim West sat transfixed, staring at the screen in the White House situation room. His silence, lasting only a few seconds, was fathomless. Kozerski, Pierce, Newman, Campbell, Patton and others stood in a circle, but several feet behind him, giving him space to think. The screen flickered and picked up images of the missiles. It was unable to agree on data between radar and satellites, so the picture, jumping and blurred, was unsettled.

'Strike back,' ordered West.

'Launch,' said Pierce, shifting away, and issuing his instructions in a low voice. 'Malmstrom – five Minuteman 111s – yes. Toksong-gun, Dukchun, Kanggye, Mangyong-dae and Kanggamchan.'

The screen divided. The pictures tracking the missiles remained unsteady. The cameras on the silos at Malmstrom Air Force Base, Montana, relayed images in clear colour.

'One hundred and five seconds,' said Pierce. 'Moving out of the boost phase.' He turned to West. 'We will not be attempting a boost-phase intercept. We have nothing in the area.'

To hit a missile in the boost phase, the interceptor missile needed to be within 150 miles of the launch site. Toksong-gun, embedded deep in a mountain range, was sixty miles from the nearest coastline, and no American-equipped warship was close.

The launch site was also only fifty miles from the Chinese border.

After the boost phase, the missile would take twenty-five minutes to reach its target. Satellite data from tracking the trajectories of the missiles was being deciphered and coordinated with information from long-range radars working out of the United States, Greenland and the United Kingdom. Computers were calculating the best early point to take out the missiles. If the first attempt failed, a second wave of missiles would be launched as a back-up.

The missile-defence technology had been debated and tested for more than three decades. It was still embryonic and it had never been used for real. The four missiles, travelling as if in a convoy, changed colour as they broke out of the earth's atmosphere. From silos in Alaska, sixteen interceptor missiles were launched against them.

'Decoys?' said West.

'We don't think there are any,' replied Pierce. 'They've thrown everything they've got at us.'

'Evacuations?'

'Rescue and health personnel are on standby,' said Patton. 'But they don't know what for.'

'Good,' said West. 'To evacuate would be to surrender.'

His attention turned back to the other screen, where a flare of light wrapped in smoke pouring from the ground indicated that the first Minuteman 111 was being launched. For a second it seemed to falter, hanging in the air, the flames lighting up the bleak, brown landscape around it. Then it picked up, becoming a speck trailed by a graceful arc of smoke. Three more Minuteman 111s launched, one after the other, their outer shells almost fifty years old but their software, engineering, guidance and fuel systems constantly updated and modernized. Never before had they been used to strike an enemy country.

'Thirty-three minutes,' said Pierce. 'These are single-vehicle with 5-kiloton warheads. Low yield, and only military targets.'

'Low yield,' repeated West, wondering if he was being too cautious again. Caution and compromise had brought things to where they were now. Each time, he had thought there was a way through, but each time his delay had escalated the risk.

'Tell the Chinese,' said West. He turned in his chair. 'Chris, straight through to their command and control. And the Russians.'

'Sir,' said Patton.

'Yes, Tom?'

'Six simultaneous suicide bombings.'

'Oh shit.'

'Baltimore. San Francisco. Denver. Elizabethtown, that's in Pennsylvania, Southampton on Long Island. Dallas . . . hold on.' West watched the missiles from Alaska reposition themselves towards the Taepodong-2s. 'This from Downing Street, sir. They have bombings in Piccadilly Circus, London, and Birmingham.'

'Smallpox?' asked West, as if a suicide bombing without the variola major virus would be fine – just an everyday event.

'Don't know yet – ' he listened to the incoming call. 'OK. Stand by. Mr President, we have an ID on the Times Square bomber. His working name is Hassan Muda. He escaped the Philippines with Ahmed Memed . . . OK, go on. Give me all of it,' said Patton. 'Get those pictures over here soonest. Yes. And Muda. Yes. Incontrovertible . . .

Yes. No. It has to be something we can release to every government, every network, every . . . you got it. Good.'

Patton kept the line open, but concealed his voice from the caller. 'Ahmed Memed is in Beijing. He is under the protection of the Chairman of the Military Commission, Chen Jianxiong. He is inside Zhongnanhai. Muda is also the prime suspect in the mortar attacks on Mehta's house.'

'As soon as we've hit North Korea, I need to speak to Kozlov,' said West. 'What are the casualties, Tom?'

'Still coming in. Dallas, at least thirty dead. San Fransico, forty. Elizabethtown, three. Should know more in a couple of minutes.'

West's gaze fixated back on the screen, where the four North Korean missiles and the sixteen American ones were getting closer to each other.

'Kill vehicles primed,' said Pierce.

The image showed the small front end of the interceptor missiles breaking away from the rockets to seek out their targets. They would fly independently, guided by their own avionics, constantly updated by radar and satellite computer data. Their task was to identify the enemy warheads and destroy them.

'Three failures,' said Pierce. His tone was level, as if he did not expect the defence system to work perfectly. Three kill vehicles had failed to separate. The technology was still brand new, and at extreme temperatures, flying at five miles per second, this was one of the most common test problems.

'Thirteen left,' muttered West.

'What the—?' exclaimed Pierce, as four interceptor missiles veered off, away from the targets. He glanced down at West, but the President was absorbed in the screen. There was nothing he could do now. 'Back-up launched,' said Pierce.

'Strike one,' said Kozerski from the back of the room.

The closest person to him was Lazaro Campbell and he slapped him on the back, looking round to see who else was joining in the brief celebration. Newman smiled. West didn't move. Patton, while missiles were heading towards American soil, was only interested in suicide bombings. 'Variola major detected in Elizabethtown,' he said. Kozerski and Campbell listened as if a knife had sliced through their euphoria.

Another interceptor knocked out a Taepodong-2. 'Strike two,' whispered Kozerski.

'Caroline . . . Tom Patton . . . Elizabethtown . . . Yes . . . Can you get there? Good. Let me know soonest. We'll alert the Harrisburg hospital, and we should assume it's in the other target areas.'

On the screen, two Taepodong-2 missiles remained in flight. 'A couple of minutes should give us a clear,' said Pierce.

'Any more launches?' said West.

'Negative, sir,' said Pierce. 'Third stage.' The main missile sections fell away, leaving the smaller third-stage solid-fuel rockets and the warheads moments away from re-entry into the earth's atmosphere. 'It's going to be close,' said the Defense Secretary.

'Oh my God,' said Kozerski.

All but two of the interceptor missiles veered off towards the now defunct second stage of the Taipodong-2s. Each of the four back-up missiles followed, taking a trajectory that would let them gain ground not on the incoming enemy missiles but on the interceptors.

'What's going on?' asked West.

'God knows,' said Pierce. He pressed his headset button. 'Can you correct it? . . . I know it's a guidance malfunction,' he shouted, 'but can you fix it?'

'Shit,' muttered Kozerski, as the kill vehicle of an interceptor broke away and destroyed another interceptor.

'They said it could never happen,' said Pierce, shaking his head.

There was complete silence in the room, no longer from concentration, nor from hope that things could ever get back to normal. It lasted well past the break in the line of defence. Someone should have spoken, but no one wanted to. The satellites and radar were confused because they were not meant to follow the missile as far as this. The picture jumped and skewed. The target coordinates flipped over like stock prices, as computers tried to calculate where the warheads might land. Patriot missiles were fired. One hit its target. One North Korean missile remained in flight.

Everyone stood aghast, helpless, staring at the screen, its data becoming meaningless. They were numb to what was happening.

The closer the warhead came to earth, the clearer the picture became. It changed from a spongy blue-grey mass around the outer atmosphere to images of high-rise buildings, the coastline. Highways emerged as distinct shapes. The name of the city appeared at the bottom of the screen, the district, the ground zero strike area, compiled by data from a new computer at a battle management control centre. A box screen showed a street map: the buildings, the day-time and night-time populations, the hospitals, the bunkers, the agencies, their contact numbers and their lines of control.

A yellow flare tore across the screen. Briefly it went to black. It came back with flakes of light appearing like jagged shards of heat searing up from the ground. They could see it was blindingly hot, bright and destructive, with a grey-black spiral surrounded by licking flames.

Slowly, second by second, the camera lenses were blocked out by a cloud.

70

Elizabethtown, Pennsylvania

The helicopter turned into the wind and came gently down on a tarmac quadrangle behind the Elizabethtown fire station. Caroline Brock brought the mask over her head and sealed it. She had begun to feel feverish just after taking off from Washington. But she hadn't slept, it seemed, for weeks. She was running on adrenalin. She needed sleep, but she didn't want to go home. It was too lonely.

As she jumped down, her tongue found a lesion on the side of her mouth. Her legs didn't support her weight as they should. A muscle spasm shot through her thigh. She walked quickly out from under the rotor blades, just making out the voice in her headset. 'It's Oakland ... a single 10-kiloton warhead ... ground zero six kilometres east of Oakland Airport.'

A wave of nausea swept through her. She couldn't see through the mask. Maybe it was clouded up. She fumbled. She had to sleep. Another lesion. Her knees buckled. Where was her strength? She righted herself. Someone was holding her up. Ahead was the red of a fire engine. She could make out the colour, but not the markings.

'Caroline, it's Tom here. Are you in Elizabethtown?' A voice, distorted and ringing. Too much information. She had to get away.

'Tom—' she managed. Her throat was on fire. She coughed. A wave of heat began rising up inside her body, striking out her energy. 'Tom, I'm no good,' she whispered. 'I'm sick. I'm infected—'

She fell with the sentence unfinished. Caroline Brock remembered nothing else until she woke up in a hospital bed and saw the pustules on her hand.

71

London, UK

'We stay with them, Charles,' said Stuart Nolan. 'Every inch. Shoulder to shoulder. No surrender. Put it out now.'

Through the window, the Downing Street garden looked idyllic, daffodils shining in clear sunlight. Nolan stood by the French windows, his hand running back and forth down the cold glass.

There were 350 dead in London and Birmingham. Variola major had been detected in both cities. The pattern had been exactly the same as in Times Square – the aerosol dispersal of the virus first, followed by the suicide bomb. The detonations had been at the optimum time, just before dawn, in dry cold conditions, so that the virus could survive for several hours before latching on to a victim.

'Are you sure?' asked Colchester, handing Nolan a Cold War document file. Nolan opened it where he was standing. For the past hour, Colchester had been feeding him with documents analysing nuclear conflict. He quickly read this one.

'A nuclear attack would mean the loss of nearly one-third of the population,' said the report. 'Blast and heat would be the dominant hazard, accounting for more than 9 million fatal casualties, against fewer than 3 million from radiation. Four million of the 16 million casualties would be caused by a single bomb on London. The standard of living of the reduced population, although substantially lower than at present, would still be well above that of the greater part of the world. The country would be left with sufficient resources for a slow recovery.'

'They write as if it's something they can plan for,' said Nolan.

'In those days they did,' agreed Colchester. 'The key was how to prepare to strike first and not get found out.' He picked up another file to give to Nolan, but the Prime Minister shook his head. 'I've seen enough,' he said, closing the file in his hand and tossing it on to a coffee table. 'Thank God, it's Jim West's call,' said Nolan.

Britain had a harsher view than America, and it was this conversation that Nolan needed to have with West before he addressed Parliament.

'He's through,' said Colchester, switching the line through to Nolan's telephone.

'Whatever you want us to do, we will do, Jim,' said Nolan. 'I am placing our forces, conventional and nuclear, under your command.'

'Caro—' Nolan heard West say. 'Right. I'm going down there . . . George Washington . . . I don't give a damn . . . Sorry, Stuart. Oakland's been hit. Of course, you know. I heard that, and thank you. Chris Pierce knows – hold a moment, Stuart – Tom, yes . . . Thank God for that – Stuart, sorry, no Chuck's called in. He lives in Oakland. Runs a transport company there. But he's fine. Damn nuclear attack and all I think about is my son. Now, give me your advice.'

West spoke fast and staccato. Nolan needed to break through and get his attention, just for five seconds. He needed to state Britain's view, however unpalatable it might be, and he didn't bother with niceties. 'We must destroy China's nuclear capability,' he said. 'If it helps, we'll fire first. China has gone the same way as North Korea and Pakistan. Except it's more lethal.'

'Memed's in China,' said West.

'Exactly. The Cold War rule was that the first to strike would be the winner. They now know our missile defence is fallible. Strike China now and stop Russia in its tracks.'

'Have you talked to Kozlov?'

'No. Have you?'

'We can't get hold of him.'

'Biological weapons were specifically designed to destroy what radiation and the nuclear explosion does not. That is why they are being used now,' said Nolan. 'Whatever moves you make towards peace now, there will be another trigger, another disaster, which they will try to blame on rogue elements, but will in fact be being carried out on the instructions of the centre. It's war, Jim, but we can win. We can pull through.'

72

Washington, DC, USA

'Everything within a one-mile radius is destroyed,' said Patton. 'Everyone is dead. It was an airburst so there is early fallout. Wind speed is twenty miles an hour. The radiation zone will be ten to twenty miles, with the contamination of water and food supplies stretching further.'

Patton was speaking, leaning heavily on the conference table in the situation room, reading off a computer screen and typing instructions into another keyboard as he did so.

'The transport system within the target area is destroyed. We will airlift out what casualties we can. But it means going in with NBC protection.' He looked up. 'Mr President, a lot more people are going to die. We are probably looking at 100,000 killed in the target area and another 100,000 dead over the next few days. We just won't be able to get them out.' He glanced up and pointed. 'This is it. We're getting the first pictures.'

The wind had carved a shape out of the heavy haze, giving a clear view to the ground. West stared at what he saw. At first, he could barely distinguish them from the images of Delhi, Tokyo and Pyongyang. These were fresher, though. The cameras had moved faster. Everything was shattered amid huge flickering pillars of yellow flames. There were no visible traces of the neighbourhood where until a few hours ago people had gone about their daily lives. It had vanished utterly, leaving not even a remnant of what it had once been. No corpses. No twisted buildings. No advertising hoardings. No sign of society at all. Just sudden and thorough destruction in the most extreme form. Hospitals, schools, homes, offices, fire and police stations – everything which made up a community was gone. No other weapon created by man could reduce a place to nothing so completely.

And what about when the rescue services had managed to cut through and evacuate and airlift? What about when the nausea and vomiting started? The diarrhoea, fever, the bleeding from the skin, the ulceration of the mouth, loss of hair, the slow, agonizing and unstoppable regression to death.

West stopped pacing the room and headed for the door. 'Mary,' he said, 'can you join me for a moment?'

They stood in the corridor, the lights seeming brighter because of their exhaustion. West's expression was difficult to read. There was fatigue as if he had taken on another age and it was still settling. His hair fell awkwardly and needed a cut. One shirt sleeve was rolled up, just underneath the elbow. The other was down, with the cuff hanging open. The ink from a ballpoint pen had leaked on to his right hand. He looked behind him to check they were alone, except for a secret service agent far down at the corner of the corridor.

'I want to say this to you, before I say it to the nation,' he said. 'I'm sorry, Mary. I should have followed your advice.'

Newman breathed deeply. 'Mr President, this is not a path we want to go down right now.'

'If I had been your age, I would have struck first. I would have been rash. But I'm an old warhorse who doesn't want to fight. I see too many sides of the story, and I have the worst handicap of them all. I have doubt.'

'There are a few leaders out there who are about to lose big time.' She took both his hands and clasped them in hers. He looked at her, his eyes boring straight through her, and suddenly he did not feel tired at all.

'If I was ten years younger, I wouldn't say this, but we're going to give it one last shot. Try Kozlov and Song. Work your way down until you get someone. And try their ambassadors here as well.' Newman dropped his hands and nodded. 'And Mary, can you ask Chris Pierce to join me out here?'

West watched his Secretary of State turn back into the situation room. In the few seconds before Pierce came out, he found himself looking straight down the corridor at a secret service agent. 'They've nuked Oakland,' said West, his voice bouncing off the walls of the narrow passageway.

'So I heard, sir,' said the agent.

'What would you do?'

'I would never have run for your office, sir.'

'Good answer.' West rolled up his loose cuff. 'But if you had?'

'I guess I'd kick ass, sir.'

Pierce, hearing the conversation, paused as he came out, glancing up towards the agent and back down towards West. 'Maybe you should have run,' said West, walking away from the agent, and letting Pierce fall into step with him.

'I'm going to give Mary an hour to get something substantive from either Kozlov or Song – or both,' he said. 'Cuba's our bargaining chip. If we can start negotiation on Cuba, maybe we can hold off on everything else. But if we don't succeed, you have to be ready.'

'Against Cuba?'

'And China, Chris,' said West firmly. 'And China itself.'

Pierce nodded. 'Just heard from CINCPAC, sir. We've seen inside Park's bunker.'

West's eyes flickered with renewed interest. 'And?'

'We're still identifying his body. But we have confirmation that he was using human guinea pigs to test the virus. Some of the chambers were intact.'

'We need any evidence that traces it back to China. Anything. A scrap. Let me know.'

Without another word, West turned and walked back into the situation room. 'Tom, I'm going to head down to the smallpox ward at George Washington Hospital. How many cases do we have now?'

'More than three hundred confirmed here, plus sixty-five in Britain – and it's moving across Europe and down to Latin America.'

'Get me a suit,' said West. 'And when I'm there make sure I have time alone with Caroline. John, as soon as I get back, a live address to the nation, from the Oval Office. Then Air Force One to Oakland.'

'Mr President,' said Patton. 'Sorry, but we need to get you to a secure location.'

'I didn't hear that,' said West. 'I didn't hear it at all.'

'Jamie Song. Line three, Mr President,' said Kozerski.

West took the call. 'Jamie,' said West, trying to keep it friendly.

But instead of Song, he heard the voice of an interpreter, translating, then Jamie Song's voice speaking in Chinese, and then the translation. 'Yes, President West, how can I help you?'

West pressed on, trying to cut through the formality. 'Jamie, let's do a deal on Cuba, and unwind everything else from there.'

He waited for the tortuously slow translation process, drumming his fingers on the telephone receiver. 'Cuba is a sovereign nation and a close ally of the People's Republic of China,' came the reply.

'Jamie, if you're hearing this—' he glanced at Kozerski, who nodded, meaning that the voice signature matched that of Jamie Song. 'Jamie, you are hearing this. So I'll say again. You know that some elements of Cuba are non-negotiable. But if you want, we can talk about it. OK?'

West gripped the receiver and looked down at the floor. Far from being angry, he was sounding desperate. It wasn't as he had planned.

'President Song will speak to you shortly.' It was the voice of the interpreter. Song had delegated. West dropped the receiver into its cradle. 'OK,' he said slowly. 'I'm not sure this is going to work. I need to talk to Kozlov.'

Kozlov recognized what Ekatarina was practising as Haydn's Second Cello Concerto. He had asked and she had told him. At any another time, Andrei Kozlov would have put his daughter's name down for the Conservatoire in Paris. He would have liked her to have studied in New York, too, and known the nervous energy of that city. He had understood she would never be able to do that at the moment when he knew the threshold had been crossed. For a hesitating instant, Andrei Kozlov wondered why it had come to this. Six times already Yushchuk had opened the door of his study, walked over to where he was sitting in a hardback chair, twenty feet away from where his daughter was playing, and whispered in his ear that the White House, that President West, that Secretary of State Newman, that Chief of Staff Kozerski was on the line wanting to speak.

Each time, the only thought in his mind was the darkness moving across the world and forming itself into new borders, immigration posts, bleak metal structures, uniforms and armies. Ekatarina looked briefly up at him without missing a note. He tried to find a metaphor for her love of music and for what was swirling around in his head. But there was nothing at all, which was surely why no accomplished musician had ever become the leader of a nation. If you are lucky enough to be born with talent, you cherish it and find sanctuary there. You do not volunteer for a life of office.

A shaft of light came through from the study, casting

Yushchuk's flitting shadow across the room. Kozlov stood up quietly, put his fingers to his lips long enough for Ekatarina to see and walked to the study. Yushchuk handed him the telephone.

'Jim,' said Kozlov softly. 'At Camp David, I told you Russia was resting. I might have been wrong. I'm sorry.'

'We're giving China until the top of the hour to hand over Memed, and we're taking out their missile sites in Cuba. Out troops are on the outskirts of Pyongyang. We will stop there, if China wants to talk.'

Kozlov detected anger and hesitation. West was threatening, but with reluctance in his tone.

'Are you talking to Jamie?' asked Kozlov, keeping his voice measured and low. Through the closed door, he could still hear Ekatarina's cello.

'Yes, we've got through. If we can deal on Cuba, maybe the rest will fall into place.'

'Good. Good,' said Kozlov. 'Then perhaps Russia can rest.'

'Have you talked to him?'

Yes, Kozlov thought to himself. Many times, but he would not tell West. Three hours last night. An hour this morning.

'This is between you and him,' said Kozlov.

'And if we fail?'

'They will hand over Memed. But they will not do it immediately. They will allow you to take Pyongyang. But not immediately. They will pull out of Cuba. But not immediately. They will stake their position from a moral high ground, and you must listen. They will claim that instead of arguing, America threatens to murder them. You must not give them the opportunity to say that. They will say that China and America are the civilized world, and that China's views must be treated equally. They will argue that poverty has not been solved because America has stopped caring, that America has had it too good for too long, and that it has fallen to China to protect the poor from darkness and give them hope. Let them speak, Jim. Listen. Be patient. You Americans are always in such a rush.'

Kozlov had spoken with a brooding authority. West's own patience was on the edge.

'If your citizens were being bombed and dying from an incurable epidemic, wouldn't you be in a rush?'

'Jim, I was elected with a specific mandate to make Russia less reliant on the West. I have put in place substantive policies to honour that mandate. Included in that was a defence treaty with China. I cannot change all that just because it is becoming difficult. If the US and China cannot resolve their difference, then Russia will support China.'

'Come what may?'

'Yes.'

'It's madness, Andrei. Utter madness.'

'Some spark of purity might come from it,' answered Kozlov. 'But empires are never founded on sanity.'

Washington, DC, USA

Tom Patton had been shielding them from the worst. Or perhaps he hadn't known. Mary Newman helped Jim West adjust his NBC suit. She sealed his gloves around his wrists, checked his suit for punctures and adjusted his air mix. Lazaro Campbell did the same for hers and then the President and Secretary of State went together into the isolation ward.

Order had been maintained as much as possible, but too many patients were being admitted. Men, women and children were lying together, and mattresses were laid out in rows at the foot of the beds, leaving only a narrow strip of floor to walk on.

This whole level of the hospital was quarantined. Temporary biodecontamination showers had been set up outside the door of the ward, with a thick lead-lined curtain hanging between them and the stairwell. To begin with, blood samples from each patient had been flown to Fort Detrick for analysis. But now the numbers were so overwhelming that only basic care was being provided. The dead were taken out of the southern door, down to the basement and incinerated without any autopsy. The cause of death was only too clear.

Caroline Brock had been offered some privacy, but she had insisted against it. Now she must have been beyond caring. West could only recognize her bed by the picture taped to her headboard of her and Peter a couple of Christmases ago at the Georgetown house, her sitting on his lap in front of the tree. A couple and their child lay silent, weak and shivering on a mattress that West had to step over.

Caroline's pustules were clustered so densely that they ran together down her arms and across her chest. They were haemorrhaging and coating her body with a film of blood and pus. Her fever was so high that sweat ran down her face; none of the normal skin was visible, only the outlines of the mouth, the nose and the eyes whose lids were flickering, the force of life trying to open them but failing.

A feeding tube dangled useless above her, swinging and brushing her face. She must have ripped it out, because of the pain. Newman moved it to one side. She took a tissue to wipe Caroline's lips. Caroline screamed as the tissue touched her mouth. Her pustule-covered hand came up to push Newman away.

'Caro,' whispered Newman. 'It's me. Mary.'

Her head turned ever so slightly.

'It's Mary. And Jim.'

All Newman wanted to do was tear off the mask so that at least Caroline could see her. But to do so could be to sign her own death warrant. Caroline's eyes flickered open for a moment. Her mouth moved, but instead of speaking, a pustule broke and blood trickled between her lips. Caroline spat it out.

West turned to a nurse, hovering behind them. 'How long before she dies?' he asked.

'A day at the most,' said the nurse.

'Is she conscious?'

'Many patients remain conscious until their last breath.'

From across the ward, there was a wail. In the next bed, a groan, then a baby's cry, piercing and unrelenting, for there was no one to comfort it. Under the fluorescent light, West saw a buzzing fly which should never have got in. It flew down, circled and landed on a patient's shoulder. Then it hopped across to the forehead and ended up on the closed eyelid. It had picked up some pus on its wings and movement was more difficult. The patient lay there dull and not responding, even when the fly jumped again, landed in the inflamed mouth and became trapped.

One or two lifted their hands, begging for help. The nurse – there was only one – moved to them. She could do nothing. But at least she was there.

West returned to Caroline's bed. Newman was sponging her with cold water. Caroline's eyes were open and it seemed she knew who they were. West took a notepad by the bed and wrote simply, 'To Caro and Peter. My closest and dearest friends. Goodbye.'

He gave it to Newman, who read it and understood. Then West did one of the hardest things. He turned and walked out of the ward, leaving Caroline Brock to die.

'My fellow Americans, I am speaking to you from the Oval Office at the White House,' said West, keeping his eyes steady in the glare of the television lights for the practice read-through. He had changed into a dark suit, with a black tie hand-embroidered with the American flag. 'You know why I am making this address, and I do not intend to take up much of your time. I will begin by laying out the events which have led to this, and then tell you how we plan to move on.'

Without warning the lights cut off and West blinked. Kozerski stepped in front of the desk. 'Jamie Song from Beijing, sir. He wants to talk urgently. He's speaking in English.'

West could see Patton just outside the door talking to Campbell, Meenakshi and Lizzie. Jenny Rinaldi, looking back and forth to Patton, was on the phone. Newman walked past them, into the room and straight to West. 'Caro's gone,' she said quietly. Her hand, fresh from her

NBC suit, was warm when she laid it on his. West's gaze was cast down like a man trying to ignore the truth.

Newman lifted her hand and moved away, loosening her scarf. Now that she had delivered the news of Caroline Brock's death, she was unsure of where she should go.

'I don't know what the Secretary of State thinks,' said Kozerski, scanning through the words on the autocue underneath the camera, 'but looking at this draft, my hunch would be that we don't apologize for anything. Let that come later. Not now.'

Newman stepped back. Kozerski had broken the strange interlude she had found herself in. 'I second that, Mr President,' she said. 'The American people want to know about your strength, not your regrets.'

'Let's hope I don't have to say it,' said West. He lifted his head and didn't bother to hide the tears that had come naturally with the news of Caroline's death.

'Do we have a deal with Jamie?' asked West, bringing out a handkerchief. Skilfully the make-up attendant was with him, combing his hair and dabbing the skin-toner around his eyes.

'He wouldn't say,' said Kozerski. 'He wants to talk to you.'

'If you'll all excuse me,' said West, unclipping his microphone and walking over the lighting and sound cables towards his private office. He caught Newman's eyes, her look of hope and curiosity, but he had no equivalent to return to her.

Fighter planes, patrolling Washington, flew loud and low over the White House as he opened the door to his private office.

The red light was flashing on the desk telephone. West picked up the receiver. He didn't sit down or perch against the side of the desk.

'Jamie,' he said softly. But he heard nothing except the

sounds of an abandoned telephone line. He felt something
well up inside him, ridding him of doubt and clearing
away the brooding darkness that threatened to envelop
him. It was the most basic instinct, the one that keeps a
person alive, the one that rids him of hesitation and gives
him complete belief in his own existence.

'Jamie?' he said again, louder.

'The line's gone.' It was Kozerski's voice coming across.

West did not return the receiver to its cradle. Outside,
he watched the greyness of the lingering winter. It seemed
so long since the missile had hit Yokata, yet not long
enough for the seasons to change and the colours to
sharpen. He saw his own reflection in the glass looking
back at him like a stone-faced stranger.

Epilogue

My name is Lazaro Campbell. I am writing from a secure location where we have been for several months. I am not permitted to say where it is, exactly how we live, or who is with me. However, for the purpose of this report, some exceptions have been made, and I am permitted to give an outline of what happened after the war with China and Russia began.

Shortly before the President made his address to the nation, we launched against Cuba. We tried to talk to China again, but failed. In response, China launched against Taiwan and our military bases in Japan.

We targeted the key Chinese long-range missile facilities of the Second Artillery Regiment. For the record, they were: 80301 Unit in Shenyang, Liaoning province; 80302 Unit in Huangshan, Jiangxi province; 80303 Unit in Kunming, Yunnan province; 80304 Unit in Luoyang, Henan province; 80305 Unit in Huaihua, Hunan province; 80306 Unit in Xining, Qinghai province; and the Second Artillery headquarters at Qinghe in northern Beijing. These were air and missile strikes with conventional warheads.

After that, events moved with horrifying speed. Even now we are still piecing together the exact sequence.

Russia entered the war by striking the missile interceptor bases at Fylingdales in England, Thule in Greenland and Fort Greely in Alaska. Andrei Kozlov telephoned Jim West offering a ceasefire. His attack, he said, had been to take away our missile defence capability and level the odds with China.

But while those negotiations were going on, China struck Kobe and Kyoto with nuclear-armed missiles and invaded Taiwan.

The President ordered a second-wave assault against China, using nuclear weapons against their hardened and isolated command and control bunkers. We tried to reach Kozlov again, but failed. We took pre-emptive action against Russia's missile sites. We hit twenty-six of them including the Moscow Institute of Heat Engineering, which makes their Topol-M long-range missile and the test site at Plesetsk, just north of Moscow. Again, these were conventional strikes – which is why some of them did not work.

'Should we have done that?' Jim West keeps asking. 'Should we have done a pre-emptive on Russia?'

But Mary tells him to keep his thoughts on the future. 'You might as well ask why you didn't go nuclear earlier,' she scolds.

There was no single turning point. It was an inevitable slide that had no beginning. You could begin with the inadequate Treaty of Versailles that ended the First World War, or with the failure to stop Hitler, or our inability to grasp the new centres of power after the Cold War, or our failure to go into Baghdad after the first Gulf War. The origins of the Third World War go much further back than the beginning of my account.

I can only understand those initial strikes by examining the minute-by-minute chronology we are compiling. Each was a logical response. Never could I have imagined that man could act so brutally and so swiftly, all the time knowing the consequences.

Yet I was part of it, and I never thought of walking away.

Nuclear explosions destroy electronic communications, so all but the military facilities broke down. Some satellites continued to work for a while, as did our own command centres, but essentially we watched the world collapse city by city.

London, Paris, Berlin and Brussels were all destroyed on the same day, and about that time both Europe and the United States stopped functioning.

The strike on Manhattan added a new layer of realism. That was the moment that we shed our remaining optimism and accepted that the world as we knew it no longer existed.

We watched the attack from satellite imagery. There must have been sixteen separate warheads ranging from 20 to 100 kilotons. For the first few seconds, with the clouds of dust and rubble, I was reminded of Nine Eleven. But, of course, this was much more thorough. As they disintegrated, the buildings became hidden in smoke. The stems of clouds from different explosions seemed to drift together to create one vast mushroom that hung over the whole of Manhattan. It wasn't about the Empire State Building, the Statue of Liberty, the already trashed Times Square. It became an image of a cloud framed by the Hudson and East rivers that slowly spilled out and engulfed them all.

I got NIMA to bring the picture close to Kenmore and Mott streets, where my parents lived on the eighth floor of their apartment block. They would have been there for sure, but by the time the cloud had cleared my neighbourhood looked no different from the diplomatic quarter of Delhi after the strike on that city.

After getting back from Delhi, I had called my mother. My father had been out getting supplies, gas masks, NBC suits and things. My mother told me they had been watching the news. She told me to look after myself and come and see them when it was over. The conversation lasted perhaps a minute. She was more upset about what would happen to Cuba than anything else.

When the cloud cleared, we saw bodies in the East River, just like those in the Yamuna in Delhi – rows of smouldering, blackened balls that had once been human beings. When I realized that any of those could have been the bodies of my mother and father, I stopped looking. I refused to watch the destruction of any more cities. My inbuilt safety valve for human survival kicked in. I slept for twenty hours straight.

The nuclear war gave way to the smallpox epidemic. The health system collapsed and the virus spread unchecked. People headed south into Mexico and north into Canada to escape the war, but they took the virus with them. Boats and private aircraft left Britain for the neutral countries of Europe. Soon the epidemic was everywhere.

In Colombia, villages were firebombed to try and contain it. In Turkey, cities were cordoned off and the inhabitants shot by troops in NBC suits. There was no vaccine and no wherewithal to create one. Eventually the disease took over the world.

One by one, the networks went off the air, and eventually we lost contact with other centres. Chris Pierce and Tom Patton at the Pentagon went quiet after the strike on Washington. Stuart Nolan had managed to get to a bunker in Britain's west country. But we heard nothing from him after London was hit. John Kozerski had refused to come with us. He brought his family to the White House bunker, and we presume they died there. Yamada went silent after China's nuclear blitz. We thought we had raised Cho in South Korea, but it turned out to be a prankster from the Cook Islands in the Pacific, so far unaffected by either smallpox or the nuclear cloud.

I should mention how Jim West, myself and others

came to be where we are now. Jim refused to leave, but
Tom Patton instructed me to get him to a safe place. I
used a tranquillizing gun while he was on the telephone in
his private office. It turned out that he had been talking to
his son, Chuck, who was just outside the radiation belt
around Oakland. Jim was never able to raise him again.
The drug lasted until we were on board Air Force One. I
can't say where we headed.

We made sure that Jim kept his word to Vasant Mehta,
and Meenakshi is with us. We were unable to locate
Romila or Geeta. Lizzie is here, working on a fairer
economic plan for whatever world survives. Some members of Congress and other allocated officials came. But
the numbers are far less than the allocations and, even
allowing for the confined space in which we live, there is
plenty of room.

The place has been built with flair. We have ultraviolet
for the plants that provide natural oxygenation, electric
cars, a swimming pool, gym, running track, restaurants
and self-catering apartments with views outside our windows created by video montages. Cooks, cleaners, technicians and staff had been kept here on rotation, so it was
like checking into a massive out-of-this-world resort.

The aim is to create as much space between us and the
catastrophe above ground. In that way we would be able
to begin leading as normal a life as possible and plan for
the future. In a strange way, it's working.

After weeks of silence, our first contact was with Vasant
Mehta in Delhi. It was also our first experience of genuine
shared joy since the war began – when Vasant learnt that
Meenakshi was alive.

After absorbing the multiple strikes from Pakistan, India
was not attacked again. In nuclear terms, it had suffered
just a scratch, compared to the Mutually Assured Destruction taking place in the US, Europe, Russia and China.

Mehta explained how India was already rebuilding communities. Some areas had escaped both radiation and smallpox. Scientists had been taken in NBC-secured aircraft and vehicles to set up laboratories there. Mehta wanted them to exchange research data with the virologists at Fort Detrick who had been working on a new smallpox vaccine. But we had lost contact with Fort Detrick.

Indian meteorologists were also tracking the radiation cloud, which had gathered and joined with the clouds over China and eastern Russia. A huge mass of radiation had drifted across South-East Asia and was over the Pacific, moving towards Hawaii and the western coast of the United States. Similar clusters of lethal clouds had formed over Europe.

Kozlov and Song have also been in contact, but even encased in our bunkers none of us is giving ground. The war has not ended. It is in a lull. Every so often, either we, Russia or China launch a small warhead as a reminder that hostilities have not ended.

We are getting used to our new lives. For a while Mary and Jim were open about their relationship, even sleeping together in one apartment. Now, possibly because of the personal intensity – and the war – they have drifted apart again. In their work, however, they seem unchanged.

Meenakshi is pregnant. When Vasant heard, he joked that he thought any child with Cuban, Scottish and Indian blood would run a far better world than they had.

I often think back on the events and wonder if there could have been another way. The truth is that the attack on the Indian Parliament, the assassination of the Pakistani President, even the missile strike on Yokata, would never have been sufficient reason to set us at each other's throats.

The zealots who led the war, Park Ho and Ahmed Memed, were unknowns to us. I doubt even they had planned to fight. They simply wanted to enjoy the spoils of victory.

I remember one evening, in Washington, just after getting back from confronting Qureshi, and news had leaked out about the Camp David summit. I wandered into a bar and noticed renewed laughter and chatter. The waiters were whistling. My cab driver talked about Jim West: 'man clever enough to take them to the brink,' he said proudly, 'get what he needs, then pull back.'

Everyone was happy because we thought there would be no war.

How stupid we were. It had always been only a matter of time before the nuclear weapon stopped being a deterrent and became simply another weapon of war.

All most of us want to do is live our lives in peace, have our children, buy our houses, pay off our loans, play our sports, go on holiday. Few of us seek conflict. Who wants to see their cities bombed, their countries ravaged and their families killed? Surely it's a matter of common sense.

So why did we do it?

Author's note

My thanks to those who helped me with *The Third World War*, either in conversations, briefings and on-the-record interviews, or through their writings in books and journals. Among those are Richard Rhodes, *The Making of the Atomic Bomb* (Simon & Schuster, 1986); Jonathan B. Tucker, *Scourge, The Once and Future Threat of Smallpox* (Grove Press, 2001); Andrew J. Nathan and Bruce Gilley, 'China's New Rulers: What They Want' (*New York Review*, 2002), as well as dozens of others including Jon Cohen's brilliant account in *Atlantic Monthly* (July/August 2002) on mousepox and interleukin-4.

The concept for this novel – the third in the series of books which have become known as 'future histories' – straddled the attacks of September 11th 2001 and the Iraq War. As I wrote *The Third World War*, the simultaneous threats of Iraq and North Korea became more and more embedded in the public consciousness.

Weapons of mass destruction, biological and chemical warfare, pre-emptive strike are now part of our everyday language. This is the sharp end of a debate as to which political system delivers the most to its people. And it may be settled with bombs. It is as if the Cold War aftermath has finally shaken itself through and this is what is left – a sense that our communities are under threat, that our values are being questioned, and that our lives are no longer as safe as they were a few years ago.

My great thanks, however, to the many colleagues in

the BBC who have sent me to far-flung places and allowed me to observe.

From Aralsk in Kazakhstan to Cuidad del Este in Paraguay to Bouake in the Ivory Coast, I have been privileged to talk to people from all walks of life and political leanings and feed their views into this book. They are far too numerous to name, but their insights have been just as valuable as those of the politicians, academics and members of the classified world who have been so helpful with their time and knowledge.

My very special thanks to my publisher William Armstrong, who published the first best-selling *Third World War*, by General Sir John Hackett, in 1978 and has presided over *Dragon Strike*, *Dragon Fire* and *The Third World War*. Without his great intelligence and love for ideas, these books would never have been written; to my agent, David Grossman, who has been with me since the beginning; to Simon Lipskar in New York for his guidance; to Nick Austin, Cressida Downing, and Cait Murphy for their work on the text; and at Macmillan Nicholas Blake, and to Nicky Hursell, my editor who sorted out the manuscript for publication before an actual Third World War broke out.